ALSO BY ROBERT BRYNDZA

DETECTIVE ERIKA FOSTER CRIME THRILLER SERIES

The Girl in the Ice

The Night Stalker

Dark Water

Last Breath

Cold Blood

Deadly Secrets

Fatal Witness

KATE MARSHALL CRIME THRILLER SERIES

Nine Elms

Shadow Sands

Darkness Falls

COCO PINCHARD ROMANTIC COMEDY SERIES

The Not So Secret Emails Of Coco Pinchard

Coco Pinchard's Big Fat Tipsy Wedding

Coco Pinchard, The Consequences of Love and Sex

A Very Coco Christmas

Coco Pinchard's Must-Have Toy Story

STANDALONE ROMANTIC COMEDY

Miss Wrong and Mr Right

Raven Street Publishing

www.ravenstreetpublishing.com

Copyright © Raven Street Ltd 2022

Robert Bryndza has asserted his right to be identified as the author of this work.

Cover design by Henry Steadman

Ebook ISBN: 978-1-914547-0-58

Paperback ISBN: 978-1-914547-06-5

Hardback ISBN: 978-1-914547-07-2

ROBERT BRYNDZA

A **DETECTIVE ERIKA FOSTER** NOVEL

FATAL WITNESS

For my readers

PROLOGUE

The knock on the front door was soft, almost timid, so she didn't think to leave on the chain. When she opened the door, the man was standing very close and he looked filled with pent-up rage. Before she had time to react, he reached in through the gap with his gloved hands, and in one lightning-fast move, he gripped her head, clamping one hand over her mouth and the other on the back of her head. Lifting her off the ground, he propelled himself across the threshold and inside.

The gloves were black, and made of soft, supple leather, but his hands inside felt like iron. He tipped her head back as he dragged her across the room, and all she could see was the ceiling. His body jerked as he kicked the door shut. The hand on the back of her head held a clump of her hair, the other pushed her nose flat, covering her mouth. The shock made her limp, like a rag doll, and he threw her onto the small sofa bed.

She lay there, dazed, staring up at him. It had taken no more than three seconds.

'Scream and I'll kill you. Understand?' he said. She had no time to understand. He loomed above her, smelling of sweat and

1

bad aftershave, and then he punched her in the face. Her head snapped back, and the whole left side of her head felt numb, hot, and cold. The bed creaked in the silence and he climbed onto it, crawling up her body, the smell of him stronger... Overwhelming. His fist came towards her again, and this time everything burst into stars and bright black.

When she came around, she didn't know how much time had passed. She was lying on her front, and her hands were tied so tightly behind her back it felt that her shoulders were being pulled out of their sockets. There was thick tape over her mouth and one of her nostrils. Her mouth was filled with fabric which had been packed in deep, and it was resting right against the back of her throat. She gagged and tried to swallow.

The curtains were closed, and the living room was gloomy. The door leading off the living room to the bedroom was ajar, and she could see him through the gap in the door, loading a stack of notebooks into a backpack. He'd been wearing that small, blue sporty backpack when he opened the door. It looked odd, with the blue straps over his smart pin-striped suit jacket. She tried to swallow again, but the material in her mouth pressed against the back of her throat. It was going to make her throw up and she was going to choke. She shifted on the bed. She experienced a moment of euphoria when she found he hadn't tied her legs.

She shifted around on the bed and her eyes scanned around the living room and kitchen. *A knife.* She had to get a knife. She looked back at the gap in the door. He was trying to find something... pulling out books from the shelf, rifling through drawers. He found her USB keys and dropped them into the backpack. She was the one tied up, but he looked scared. She had to move fast while he was distracted.

As she moved her head, and the material packed into her mouth shifted, pressing against her tonsils, she gagged. The blood pounded through her body and made the bruise on her face burn. As she inched down the bed to the edge, the thin mattress of the sofa bed tipped forward and she lost balance, rolling off the bed and hitting the floor with a thud, landing on the swollen side of her head.

The sound echoed through the floorboards, but he didn't notice. He was possessed with something, by something, still concentrating on the computer on the desk, typing something.

It took a great effort to get up, and she scooted over to the wall, leant into it and managed to pull herself up to her knees, all the time trying to control the lurching urge to throw up as the gag filled her throat. It was hard to breathe, and twice she had to stop.

Finally, when she got to her feet and stood swaying in the centre of the room, it felt like a triumph. She hurried around the bed, unsteady on her feet. There was a box of Scrabble close to the edge of the low table against the wall with the television, and she felt her leg bump into it. The box teetered on the edge, but she couldn't reach down to push it back. It fell onto the floor with a clatter, scattering the Scrabble tiles over the carpet.

He was still there at the desk, typing something. The kitchen was just a few feet away. She saw the block of knives next to the oven.

There were eight knives, but the counter was set at a height above her waist, and with her hands tied tight behind her back, she couldn't reach.

To get the knife, she had to lean over and hook the knife block under her armpit, like a lasso. Twisting her body to the side, she leant up and over the counter. Her arms screamed out in pain as she lifted them behind her back. She had a small amount of movement in her bound arms; she shifted them to the left, and using the gap between her body on the left side and her arm, she tried to grab at the block of knives, but she couldn't get a grip on it.

She tried again, sweating with the effort, and a couple of times the pain got so bad that she saw stars. On the fourth attempt she managed to hook her arm over the knife block and it fell forward onto the edge of the counter with a loud crash.

The knives were now poking out horizontally and almost level with the countertop. With a surge of hope, she turned her back to them, and reached behind with one of her bound hands to grab one.

Her hand closed over the handle of the long carving knife...

'No, no, no,' said a voice. He was standing by the kitchen counter watching her. She took a step forward, still holding the knife, and heard the sleek slide as the blade came out of the block. Gripping the knife in her hand, she turned and backed towards him with the knife held out. She wasn't quick enough and he stepped out of the way. She tripped, fell backwards, and landed painfully on her bound hands and the knife handle.

'You're not going to leave me in peace, are you?' he said, coming back towards her. His voice was low and controlled. She cried out and kicked but he grabbed her legs, dragged her up off the floor, and threw her back on the sofa bed.

He picked up the knife and she saw him looking around, working out what to do. He gripped the bottom of the folding frame and tipped it up, raising her legs. Her body was bent in half and then she felt his weight on top as he folded her into the mattress, the metal frame crushing her. He folded the mattress again using all his weight on top. She felt a roar of pain as her shoulders popped out of their sockets, and her knees were up around her head. The gag in her mouth moved down her throat, crushing her windpipe.

And then the knife sank into her back, and then sliced open the side of her cheek, it plunged into her hip and then the meaty padding of her calf muscle. He was stabbing the knife through the mattress.

She couldn't breathe, and the frenzied stabbing continued, the knife plunging into her body as she was crushed under the weight of the folded-over mattress.

She wanted death to come quickly, but the three long minutes before her wish was granted was an eternity.

1

Detective Chief Inspector Erika Foster was standing in the empty front room of a crumbling Victorian terraced house. Outside the front window, a gloomy grey October evening was pressing against the glass. The floorboards were rotting in places, and above her head a yellow damp spot bloomed across the ceiling, met the wall, and carried on down, blistering the faded flowery wallpaper. A bare bulb cast a dingy forty-watt glow over the room. Her phone rang in the folds of her winter coat and she pulled it out. It was her sister, Lenka.

'Erika. I just tried to FaceTime you,' said Lenka, speaking in their native Slovak.

'I haven't set it up on my new phone,' said Erika, which was true. She switched the phone to her other ear and pulled up her collar against the cold.

'So, how are things in the new house?'

'Good. The movers delivered all my boxes, and...' Erika's voice trailed off as she looked around, trying to imagine how she was going to make it like home. A high-pitched rattle sounded through the walls.

Erika stepped out of the living room into the hallway, her shoes echoing on the bare floorboards. She'd turned up the thermostat to thirty degrees half an hour ago, and the central heating seemed to be in agony, but unable to warm things up. There was silence, and then the clattering of pipes started again, echoing down from the dark landing above.

'What's that noise? Can you call me on Skype?'

Erika looked at the hallway piled high with boxes. Her warrant card and police radio were balanced on the end box. Why did she think she could rough it? She had no bed, very little furniture. She knew she should have asked her landlord for another month at her rented flat, and done a bit of work on making the house habitable. This was the main reason she didn't want her sister to see the state of the place.

'Lenka, I haven't got Skype, either. And my computer is buried in a box somewhere.'

'I thought we agreed you would show me your new house? You paid so much for it... I don't know how people live in London with the way things cost. And now Brexit is happening. Is it really the best time to buy your first house?' There was a final screeching clank and then the boiler fell silent. 'I keep seeing in the news that they're going to start chucking Eastern Europeans out.'

'I'm not going to be chucked out. I'm a police officer, and I have dual citizenship,' said Erika. Lenka made a noise, somewhere between a grunt and a snort.

'Can you at least text me your new address, so I can send you a housewarming present?'

'Yes. I could quite literally use a heater in here.'

Erika knew that a housewarming present was the last thing on Lenka's mind. She wanted the address so she could look it up online.

'What's the area called?'

'Blackheath.' Erika went back to the front room and put her hand on the ancient radiator under the bay window. She felt a slight warmth through the cold metal. There were no curtains, and she saw her reflection in the glass. Erika was six feet tall and had always been thin, but she noted how particularly scrawny and drawn she looked. Her short blonde hair stood up in messy tufts. She moved to the wall, flicked off the light, and could now see out of the window to the dark expanse of the heath opposite. A row of streetlights lit up the road running through the middle, casting pools of orange across the scrubby grass.

'Does Blackheath mean anything?' asked Lenka.

Erika sighed.

'Yes, a heath is a patch of semi-wild ground, and...' She hesitated. 'And it's *Black* heath, because, apparently, it was used as a plague pit after the Black Death.'

'Dead bodies *are buried* there?'

'Apparently.'

'Don't you deal with enough dead bodies at work on the murder squad?'

'It's not like that. It's in a lovely area. With independent shops, and bars.'

'And a plague pit outside your front door!' Lenka snorted.

'They'll never build on it, so I'll always have uninterrupted views,' said Erika, repeating what the fresh-faced young estate agent had told her, with a straight face. 'It's close to work, and my colleague, my friend, Isaac lives round the corner. You remember Isaac?'

'The gay undertaker?'

'He's not an undertaker. He's a Forensic Pathologist.'

'Erika, how will you ever find a boyfriend if you surround yourself with dead people and gay men?'

'Lenka, I don't want a boyfriend, and I don't surround myself with gay men. He is one friend. Anyway. This is a fresh start for me. I sold the house in Manchester and after far too long renting here in London, I've bought my own place. I finally feel like I'm moving on since...' Her voice tailed off. She was going to say, *since Mark died.* Erika's husband, Mark, had also been a police officer. He'd died on the job over four years ago, during a botched drug raid. A few months after his death, Erika had moved down from Manchester to take up a post in London. It had been a rough four years, personally and professionally, but buying this house, for all its faults, truly felt like she was making a fresh start.

'Are you happy?' asked Lenka, her voice softening.

Erika had to think about that for a moment.

'Not quite, but it's the closest I've felt to happiness for a long time. Listen, I'll get my new phone set up so we can video call. But there's a lot of work to do on the house, and the garden is a mess.'

'I won't judge you. I'm just interested to see it.'

'I'll hold you to that. Give my love to the kids, and Marek.'

When Erika got off the phone, she found a woolly hat in the pocket of her coat and pulled it on. A bare bulb hung at the bottom of the stairs, but the light didn't reach to the landing above. She carried on along the hall, past the boxes and the door to a small downstairs toilet, which she kept closed. When Isaac had accompanied her to the second viewing of the house, he'd commented that the toilet reminded him of the movie *Trainspotting*, and he'd half expected to see a young Ewan McGregor crawl up out of the bowl.

It looked as if the kitchen was last decorated sometime in the 1970s. There was a small wooden work surface with a Butler's sink under the window, and Erika's new fridge freezer hummed in the corner, looking out of place against the yellowing walls. All Erika had unpacked so far was a kettle, the microwave, and a couple of coffee mugs. The thought of rummaging through boxes for plates and utensils and then heating something up in the grimy kitchen was too much. There was a chip shop two streets back, and it was getting late, so she decided to go and get something to eat.

When she left the house, the streets were empty and a mist was hanging in the air. Erika put her head down and her collar up as she walked to the chip shop. A delicious warmth and the smell of fried fish enveloped her as she stepped through the door. It was an old-fashioned British chippie with a huge silver fryer. The long, green Formica counter was dotted with grains of salt and vinegar spills, and next to the till were two huge jars of pickled eggs and bottles of vinegar and ketchup. Erika ordered a large cod and chips with a can of Dandelion and Burdock, and ate the fish and chips out of the paper sitting at one of the booths in the window. The road outside was quiet, and the mist seemed to be thickening. The other customers had taken their food home, so she was alone inside.

Erika looked down at the can of Dandelion and Burdock. It was a fizzy drink unlike any other. It had been Mark who had introduced her to it, when she first moved to the UK, along with fish and chips. She stared at the can. Four years on from his death, everything still seemed to lead back to him. Another memory came back to her from that fateful day, of Mark lying beside her, bleeding out from his gunshot wound. Erika closed her eyes. They'd never caught who pulled the trigger. It wasn't just Mark who'd died that day. Five of her colleagues were killed in total. Her team. She put her hand up to her neck and felt the scar where she'd been shot. Lenka's question came back to her.

Are you happy?

Erika looked down at the delicious fried fish and chips, and thought of the crumbling house that was hers. She felt content. Maybe she could put happiness on the back-burner for the time being and settle for just being content.

It was just after eight when Erika left the chip shop and came back out onto the pavement. The fog was now freezing, covering the surface of the tarmac in a dusting of white. On her way back to the house, still new to the area, she took a wrong turn, and found herself in a narrow road of terraced houses where a couple of streetlights were out. As she walked down, she saw how smart the houses looked, and stared ruefully at their sand-blasted brick-work and double-glazed sash windows.

Halfway down the road, there was a gap in the row of houses, and a modern concrete block of flats sat back from the road with a small neatly kept garden out front. The lights in all the windows were dark, but as she passed, a light flicked on in the ground floor window. A loud, blood-curdling scream made Erika stop in her tracks.

2

The scream came from behind the left-hand window of the ground floor flat. It seemed to echo in Erika's ears, and then it came again, longer, making the hairs stand up on the back of her neck. Erika hurried down the short path to the main entrance, which was a double-height glass door looking into a dingy hallway with a parquet floor. She tried the door handle. It was locked, and she could see a small red light glowing next to a card key entry pad. Erika ran back down the path and onto the grass on the left-hand side of the building. She reached up and knocked on the glass. There was now a sobbing coming from inside.

'Hello?' shouted Erika. 'I'm a police officer!'

She rummaged around in her pocket and found her warrant card, just as the curtain parted and a small woman with black hair cut into a short bob and a severe fringe appeared in the gap. Erika couldn't see inside the room. She held up her ID against the glass. The woman looked to be in severe shock. Her face was deathly white. 'I'm Detective Chief Inspector Erika Foster with the Met police. Do you need help?' The woman swayed a little and nodded. 'Can you let me in through the front door?' She seemed to be working on a delay. She hesitated and then nodded again, vanishing back behind the curtain. Erika walked back to the main entrance. The lights came on, and Erika watched as the woman, who looked to be in her late forties, emerged from a door to the left, and moved unsteadily towards the glass. She was wearing a baggy pair of denim dungarees with a wine-coloured fleece jacket over the top. On her feet were a pair of green Crocs, and she had on pink fluffy socks. She was hyperventilating, her white face was clammy with sweat, and it took her a moment to find the button to unlock the door. There was a beep and a click and Erika pulled the door open.

'Is there someone else inside the flat?' asked Erika. The woman nodded. 'Are they armed? Do they have a weapon?'

'No. It's my sister. She's dead,' said the woman. 'Oh my god... She's *dead!* It's... There's... Everywhere!'

Erika looked around the hallway. There were three doors in the corridor, and a lift and stairs at the end. The woman had come through the first door on the left.

'What's your name?'

'Tess. Tess Clarke.'

'Are you hurt, Tess?'

There was another pause as she looked down at herself. Erika noticed that the fleece she wore was grubby, and there were a couple of cigarette burns on one of the sleeves. Tess shook her head.

'Okay. Good. Now, Tess. What's your sister's name?'

Tess was staring straight ahead. She was shaking, her teeth were chattering and her eyes were dilated wide like two large pools of black ink. Erika wondered if her dilating eyes indicated drug use, but it was also a symptom of severe shock. She looked around and saw that the entrance area had a rather sickly-looking yucca plant in the corner by the glass doors, and next to it was a tan leather sofa. She took Tess by the hand and led her to it. 'Here. Sit down. Now, what's your sister's name?'

Tess perched on the edge of the chair and put a shaking hand to her mouth.

'Vicky.'

'And you're sure there's no one else inside the flat, apart from Vicky?'

Tess frowned.

'I don't think so... I only went into the living room. The bedroom is in the back,' she said.

'Okay. Can you wait here? I promise I'll come back, I just need to look inside.'

Tess nodded. Erika always kept latex gloves in her pocket, a habit from entering crime scenes, and she pulled on a pair and went to the door to the flat.

The metallic smell of blood hit her nose when she stepped inside. The front door opened out into a tiny, narrow hallway with a low ceiling. There was a clean, modern-looking white tiled bathroom directly to the right. It was empty.

The living room and kitchen were combined as one. On a small sofa bed, which was opened out, lay the body of a young woman, face down in a large patch of blood. Her arms were bound behind her back. As Erika moved around she saw that the woman's head was facing the door. She reached out and placed her fingers on her neck. Her skin was firm and cold, like putty, and there was no pulse. The sheer amount of blood on the sheets, and the fact her body lay at a strange angle, made it obvious this had been a violent attack.

Erika put her arm over her mouth, as the smell was overpowering, and skirted around the living room and the kitchen units, trying to avoid blood spots on the pale carpet. In the back corner was a closed door. She listened but couldn't hear anything. She knew she should wait for backup, but Erika, being Erika, was impatient. She saw a wooden rolling pin sitting next to a block of knives lying on its side, and grabbed it.

Bracing herself, she opened the door, expecting to see a small bedroom with a bed, but the tiny room was completely dark inside. There was a loud crash from inside the darkness.

'What's happening?' shouted Tess from the hall outside, her voice rising with panic.

Erika hesitated. Silence. She reached inside and found the light switch, and lifted the rolling pin. Fluorescent lights flickered on, illuminating a small room which looked like a recording studio. There was an empty desk with just an expensive iMac computer, and two office chairs on wheels. On the wall behind the desk was a large laminated map of Greater London, and it was covered with coloured drawing pins. There were also newspaper articles stuck up around the map. Next to the door a tall metal microphone stand lay on its side. She must have knocked it over when she opened the door.

There was a window in the corner, but it was blocked off with a giant square of polystyrene. At the opposite end of the room the walls were lined with what looked like hundreds of opened-out egg boxes. In this part of the room there was a small two-seater sofa and another microphone stand, with a professional-looking microphone. A thick black curtain was pulled back, and looked like it could be pulled across, to partition off this small recording booth.

'Hello? What's happening?' came Tess's voice.

'It's okay. I knocked something over. There's no one here,' shouted Erika.

She didn't have much time to think why the bedroom had been turned into a recording studio, only acknowledge that the room was empty. The flat was small, and the woman's furniture outside the recording studio all looked very cheap.

She turned back to the living room and moved closer to the

body lying on the sofa bed. It was difficult to tell the victim's age. The woman had long dark hair, but it hung over her shoulders and the side of her face, and large patches were matted with dried congealed blood. Half of her face was badly battered and her left eye was swollen shut. Her neck hung at an odd angle, it looked like it could be broken.

Erika slowly moved around the body. The curtains in the room were closed, and there was no sign that anyone had broken down the door, but a chair was turned over and there were magazines and a few items strewn across the floor; a candle in a glass holder, a pot of pens, and, bizarrely, a Scrabble box which had been knocked open, discharging the tiled letters across the carpet.

There'd been a brutal struggle, but no sign of a break-in. Did she know her attacker?

3

Erika checked to make sure she hadn't disturbed anything in the crime scene, and she came back to the front door. Tess was standing outside.

'What was the noise?' she asked. The terror of what she'd seen still clung to her face.

'I knocked something over. Please, you need to sit down.' Erika led her back to the sofa and then called into Lewisham Row police station for police backup and forensics to attend the scene.

When she came off the phone the hallway was eerily quiet. The other two doors in the hallway remained closed.

'Does your sister live in the flat?' asked Erika, thinking of the recording studio set up in the bedroom.

Tess nodded.

'Is it her flat?'

'No. It's mine. My husband's. Ours. Vicky rents it from him... Us.'

'Do you live locally?'

'Round the corner. I own a restaurant, Goose, with my husband in the village.'

It took Erika a moment to work out what she meant. Some of the more well-heeled locals called Blackheath 'the village'.

Erika asked her how old Vicky was. Twenty-seven, Tess told her. And Tess explained that Vicky hadn't turned up to work her shift at the restaurant; that's why she came to the flat.

'And is your pub just around the corner?' She was trying to keep Tess talking until the ambulance arrived, she didn't want her to go into shock and collapse.

'It's not a pub,' said Tess. 'Goose is a quality restaurant.'

Only in England, thought Erika, *would a person still think to add on that detail, moments after witnessing the brutal slaying of a sibling.* She wondered how close they were. She looked back at Tess, sitting with her back straight and her ankles crossed in a finishing-school pose, which seemed to contradict her scruffy clothes and the Crocs.

There was a knock on the glass and Erika looked up to see Detective Inspector James Peterson standing outside. He was a tall, lean black man in his late thirties, but he looked much younger. His hair was shaved close to his scalp at the back and sides, and he had short dreadlocks on top. His perfect posture always made Erika think of a toy soldier, standing so upright. He wore jeans, trainers, and a thick purple fleece jacket. She got up and opened the glass door, stepping outside and pulling it shut behind her.

'Hey, I was just leaving the cinema in Greenwich when I got the call from control...'

'Yes. Jesus. It's a young woman's body. Looks bad. Her sister found her,' said Erika, indicating Tess sitting inside. He went to say something when an annoyed voice shouted, 'James, you've got Winky Bear!'

He turned and Erika saw there was a car parked at the kerb.

The interior light was on, and Fran, an attractive blonde-haired woman with very pale skin, was searching the back seat next to a young mixed-race boy strapped into his car seat.

Peterson put his hands into his jeans, and Erika spied a little white piece of material poking out from the pockets of his fleece.

'Is this what she's looking for?' she said, reaching over and pulling out a tiny white teddy bear with a cute face, and winking one eye.

'Yes. He's Kyle's favourite, thank you,' he said, and went rushing back to the car. Up until Fran appeared on Peterson's doorstep last year with his son, Kyle, Erika and Peterson had had an on-off love affair. Erika had tried to put Peterson out of her mind, and for the most part she'd succeeded, but it was difficult when they worked together. She'd hoped that one day they would be 'on' full-time and make a go of it. She shook the thought away.

An unmarked police car pulled up in front of Fran's with the blue lights flashing, and Detective Inspector Moss got out. She raised a hand to Peterson, and walked up the path towards Erika. She was a short stocky woman with shoulder-length red hair, and her face was a mass of freckles.

'All right, boss? I was just on the way home when I got the call,' she said. 'Is Peterson on duty or off?' she added, looking back at him clipping Kyle into his car seat.

'On. They couldn't find Kyle's teddy bear.'

Moss raised an eyebrow.

'I spent all afternoon trying to find a crack whore called Doris, and when we arrested her, we discovered she likes to throw her own shit,' she said, pulling a face.

'That's disgusting.'

'I know, and I'd just bought this new from Evans.' She indicated her smart grey trouser suit. 'I was lucky her aim wasn't great, but one of the poor Specials got it right in the face...'

Erika glanced back inside to check on Tess, and saw that she was now talking to an older man holding a full black bin bag. He looked like he was trying to extricate himself from the conversation.

Fran drove off, and Peterson hurried up the path, joining them as they walked back through the front entrance into the hallway.

'I really have to get this bag in the bin,' the old man was saying. He was completely bald, with a fleshy, jowly face. He didn't have any eyelashes or eyebrows and his skin was very shiny. His voice tailed off when he saw Erika, Moss and Peterson.

There was a beat of silence, a brief look of panic moved over his face, and then he regained his composure.

'Good evening. I live at flat number two,' he said, pointing to the door at the end of the corridor.

'What's your name?' asked Erika.

'Charles, Charles Wakefield.'

'That's leaking,' said Moss, pointing down at the bag, where drops of brown fluid were running out onto the tiled floor.

'Yes, if you'll excuse me, I'll just take this outside.'

'Let me,' said Peterson, going to grab the bag.

'No, it's okay. I can do it myself,' said Charles, pulling the bag away from him.

'I'll take it, so you can answer my colleague's questions,' said Peterson, going to grab the bag again.

'I'd rather you didn't,' said Charles, taking a step back. He went to put the bag behind him and then thought better of it.

'Is there something in there you don't want us to see?'

'Of course not.'

Peterson looked back at Erika. She studied Charles for a moment.

'Mr Wakefield. The flat there is a crime scene, and the way

you're acting is giving me probable cause to want to see what you've got inside that bag.'

'A crime scene!' he asked, his small piggy eyes opening wide. 'What's happened?'

'My sister,' said Tess, breaking down again in tears.

'Good lord, no? She's dead?' he said.

'Yes!'

'Please, Mr Wakefield. This is a crime scene. Show us what's in the bag,' said Erika.

'It's just my rubbish! Wh... wh...' Erika could see Charles was becoming agitated. He was trying to say something but his voice choked with a stutter. 'I... I ju... jus, wwwant to take out my rrrr... rubbish!' His face was now red.

'You need to give me the bag,' said Erika, losing patience with him and holding out her hand.

'No. No!'

Charles marched back up the corridor to his front door, leaving a trail of brown liquid. Tess was staring at him with her mouth open.

'Jesus. This is all we need,' said Erika wearily to Moss and Peterson.

'You can't come into my flat, not without a warrant!' he said, fumbling at the door with his keys. He got the door open and went inside, slamming it shut.

'Can you get that bag?' Erika said to Peterson. 'Try not to break down the bloody door, only if you need to... Actually, Moss, can you go round the back, in case he tries to jump out of the window? Do you know what's behind the building?' she said, addressing the last part of the question to Tess.

'An alley. It backs onto a row of terraces in the street next door,' she said. Peterson went to Charles's front door, and Moss went back to the main entrance.

'Forensics are here,' she said.

Erika saw a large white van pulling up, and a police support van arrived seconds after it. She went back to Tess, who was now shaking.

'She's dead. Who would do that to her?' she said.

'Let me get you out of here. Come to the police support van. Tess, we're going to take care of your sister. And find out who did this.'

4

Erika went back out to the road, where the forensics team were unloading. They were headed up by the Forensic Pathologist, Isaac Strong. He was a tall, thin man with close-cropped dark hair which was starting to show grey. His thin arched eyebrows always gave him the impression of insouciance, but he had warm brown eyes, and he'd become a good friend to Erika, as well as a trusted colleague.

'I thought today was moving day?' he said.

'It was. I stumbled on this crime scene on the way back from the chip shop. I've got a pretty strong stomach but this one is a lot to take in. The young woman has multiple stab wounds. I've been in, but I only touched the door handles.'

'Okay. I'll get to it.'

'It's the ground floor flat, number one,' said Erika. Isaac went over to his team of crime scene technicians, who were unloading silver steel boxes, lights on stands, and a stack of overalls in plastic. Another police car arrived containing two young policemen, pulling up behind an ambulance and a long line of vehicles now gathering outside the block of flats. Erika went over to the police car, and the driver rolled down his window.

'Evening, ma'am,' he said. They were both so young, she thought, as she peered inside.

'Can you lads cordon off the road, and once forensics have finished in the entrance of the building, go and find out how many neighbours are home, and if anyone saw anything?'

They nodded and got out of their squad car. It was suddenly very busy on the narrow road, and amongst the sound of talking and car engines, Erika heard shouting coming from the side of the building. Peterson and Moss were half carrying Charles, who was staggering, with a nasty gash on top of his bald head which was pouring blood.

'I'm a British citizen! I own my own home! I have liberties!' he was shouting, as rivulets of blood dripped off the edge of his chin.

'What happened?' asked Erika, moving over to intercept them in the front garden.

'She! She broke into my flat! Shouldered the door!' he shouted.

'I caught him trying to jump out of his back window with the bin bag. His foot caught on the sill and he landed in the concrete alley,' said Moss. She wore latex gloves. One hand was gripping his arm, and the other held the black plastic bin bag.

'And that's where I found him, lying in the alleyway,' said Peterson. 'Sir, you need to keep *still!*' he added, as Charles struggled and tried to twist his way out of their grip, elbowing him in the chest.

'Hey! Calm down,' said Erika, pulling on a fresh pair of latex gloves and taking the bin bag from Moss.

'Wh... what are you arr... arresting me for?' he stuttered. Blood was now running into his mouth and mingling with spit to give his teeth a pink sheen.

'Sir. You are not under arrest, but you need medical attention,' said Erika. There was a paramedic outside on the road with two policemen, and Erika beckoned them over.

'Can you please see to Mr Wakefield? He's had a nasty fall.'

'Nasty fall? More like police brutality!' shouted Charles.

'Oh dear,' said the paramedic, a small kind-looking woman in her fifties with twinkly brown eyes. 'Let's get you cleaned up, Mr Wakefield.' She seemed to placate Charles for a moment, and he allowed her and the two policemen to lead him to the ambulance. When they reached the doors, he looked back at Moss, who was still holding the black bin liner.

'They've got my bag!'

'Come on, sir, let's get you inside and sat down,' said the paramedic. They helped Charles into the ambulance, and the back doors closed.

'I bet that cut'll need stitches,' said Moss.

'Have you looked inside the bin bag?' asked Erika.

'No. But he was willing to jump out of a window to hide it,' said Peterson.

Erika took the bag from Moss, placed it on the road and untied the neck. A nasty smell hit her; a sweet synthetic perfume mixed with decay. She had a strong stomach, but she felt the recently consumed fish and chips stirring for the second time that evening. She took a step back and a few breaths of fresh air, and then activated the torch on her phone, held her breath and shone it inside the bag. They all peered inside.

She could see four or five plastic solid-gel air fresheners, but the white plastic was smeared with blood and what looked like mud. There was something with fur amongst the rubbish, and when she angled the torch inside, she saw the end of a cat's leg.

'Oh no,' she said, looking up at Moss and Peterson. They heard a muffled shout from Charles inside the ambulance. 'Can you please get me a plastic sheet from forensics and some evidence bags?'

Moss went off, and returned with a thick square of sheeting. They moved over to the small front garden of the apartment building, and opened out the sheet on the grass. Peterson pulled on a pair of gloves, and Erika carefully tipped the contents of the bin bag out.

The smell of sweet decay was overpowering, even outside in the blustery weather. There were old tea bags, three empty cans of Newcastle Brown Ale, a milk carton and some other soiled pieces of tissue paper, and ten solid-gel air fresheners. Amongst this were the matted bodies and heads of two decaying cats. They'd both been decapitated. Erika reached out to gently touch them.

'That's weird. Their bodies are frozen inside. Feel that.'

Moss and Peterson both gently felt the bodies with their gloved hands.

'Why would they be frozen?' asked Peterson.

'There haven't been freezing temperatures in London yet, it's still too early,' said Moss.

'Jeepers,' said Peterson, sitting back and putting the crook of his arm over his nose. 'Smells like they've been dead awhile. Neither of them have collars.'

'A collar isn't going to stay on a headless cat,' said Moss, giving him a look.

'I meant, there are no collars in the bag,' replied Peterson, rolling his eyes.

'He's put in *ten* air fresheners,' said Erika, counting through them. 'The gel in all of them is full. They've just been opened.'

Another muffled shout came from inside the ambulance. It rocked violently, and then the back doors burst open and Charles Wakefield ran out with a piece of large white bandage flapping on the side of his head.

'No. No! I don't want that. I don't like needles!' he shouted. He was followed by one of the policemen, who grabbed him and restrained him over the bonnet of a nearby police car.

Erika, Moss and Peterson got up off the grass and hurried over to the van just as the police officer was handcuffing Charles. Erika looked back and saw inside the ambulance there was a mess of discarded, bloody, bandages. The other policeman was bleeding from his nose, and blotting it with a wad of tissue.

'The bugger punched me,' he said, his voice thick and wet with the nosebleed.

'I should be allowed bodily autonomy!' cried Charles, still bent over the car bonnet with his hands cuffed behind his back. 'I told her, I don't want an injection!' His eyes were wild with fury, and the blood streaking down his face made him look like a madman.

'I was trying to give him a tetanus booster. He has rust in the wound,' said the paramedic, taking the blood-soaked tissue from the policeman and swapping it for a fresh wad.

'You bastards! I didn't do anything, I didn't!' Charles screamed with a childlike intensity.

'You shut up!' said the other policeman, pushing him down onto the bonnet.

Erika looked across the street, and she could see the neighbours opposite gathering on the doorsteps. A young girl had her mobile phone out, filming the spectacle. This crime scene was complex enough without Charles kicking off.

'Okay, enough!' said Erika, directing this at Charles and the policeman who'd slammed him down on the bonnet. 'Take him to the station, clean him up and book him for assaulting a police officer. He can spend a night in the cells.'

At this, Charles started to scream and shout.

'You can't do this to me! I'm just trying to live my life. Please, no! Please don't do this!'

'Wow. And I thought my five-year-old had bad tantrums,' said Moss as they watched Charles fight and try to wriggle free of the young policeman. He was taller, but Charles was heavy and stocky in comparison. The policeman was dragged to and fro, like a rag-doll, before Peterson stepped in and helped him to gain control.

'Please, sir, mind your head,' said Peterson, and they placed him into the back seat of the car. As they drove away, Charles was still at the window, raging and baring his teeth, his breath forming a circle of condensation, and reminding Erika of a rabid dog.

5

An hour later, Isaac gave them the all-clear to enter the crime scene. Erika, Moss and Peterson were wearing white Tyvek suits. Their hoods were up and they also wore face shields and shoe covers. When they went back into the flat, the living room was now a blaze of light. Two strong lights on tripods had been set up in opposite corners. There was a light underneath the open-out sofa where Vicky lay, and Erika could see where the blood had dripped through the thin mattress and onto the carpet. The room was small, and the sofa was next to the front window. She always thought that the lighting of a crime scene added a strange theatricality. The crime scene photographer was taking close-up shots of the body, and two SOCOs – scene of crime officers – were taking blood spatter samples from the wall and the carpet. The metallic smell of the congealing blood seemed stronger under the heat of the lamps.

'Okay,' said Isaac, crouching down next to the sofa bed. 'Vicky's neck is broken, and both of her shoulders have been dislocated. You can see where her hands are tied behind her back.'

'Yes.'

'Extreme pressure was placed on both arms, folding them back and dislocating her shoulders. She's also been struck in the face. Her front tooth is chipped.'

Erika looked down at the young woman, who looked so small. So vulnerable.

'There was a gag in her mouth, a rolled up pair of socks, and it had been taped over with masking tape. She's been stabbed in what seem like random places. Her lower back, neck, cheek, left hip. The knife also penetrated her scalp in several places.'

'There's so much blood on the mattress.'

'Yes, which brings me back to these stab wounds,' said Isaac. 'This is a roll-up sofa bed, a rather cheap one, and there are several punctures to the thin mattress... I think whoever did this, rolled her up inside the sofa bed and went mad stabbing her through the mattress... I think her assailant hit the subclavian artery during the attack. It's a major artery running directly from the heart and carries blood to the arms and neck. It would have led to this amount of blood loss. I'll know for sure after the post-mortem.'

'Hang on, you say you think she was rolled up inside the mattress when the stab wounds were inflicted?'

'Yes.'

'When the body was found, the sofa bed was open. So whoever did this opened out the bed after she'd died, to check she was dead?'

'That's for you to find out. I just give you the facts of what I see.'

Erika looked at Moss and Peterson, and she could see the shock in their faces. They'd seen some horrific crime scenes, but never anything like this.

'Do you have any idea of time of death?' asked Erika.

'Not yet.'

'Off-the-record, if you were pushed to estimate?'

'Off the record?'

'Of course,' said Erika with a weak smile.

'Based on what I can see... Between 3pm and 7pm.'

'That's a big window of time,' said Erika.

'That's the best off-the-record estimate I can give you. I'll know more after the post-mortem.'

Erika stared down at Vicky's body. She leant forward and gently lifted Vicky's hair. The young woman's face was blood-spattered and bruised. Her lips were drawn back in a grimace of fear, exposing her teeth. Her eyes were open wide and glassy. A death stare.

'She wouldn't have been able to scream, with the gag in her mouth,' said Erika.

'No. I doubt she could even breathe properly,' said Isaac. 'I'm surprised she didn't suffocate.'

Erika looked at the curtains, closed over the window. It was close to the small garden looking onto the road outside. *If I heard Tess scream when I was walking past, did anyone hear this poor woman fighting for her life?* she thought. She was reminded how close she lived, and thought back to the agent who had sold her the new house. How he'd rhapsodised about Blackheath being such a safe place, with a tight-knit village community. As far as she knew, no one had been brutally slaughtered in her old post code.

They all took a step back as two of the SOCOs moved to Vicky's body and lifted her right hand and then her left, taking swabs from underneath her fingernails. Her nails were cut short, Erika noted. Isaac was ready with a plastic bag and they dropped the swabs inside.

She took in the rest of the room. There was a long low unit with a flatscreen TV, and shelves on either side which contained four glass candle holders in different colours, and a lava lamp. Erika imagined that with good lighting the flat was cosy, but the harsh forensic lights seemed to expose its shabbiness. The wall-paper sagged with damp in patches, and the pale carpet was dotted with the ghosts of stains. There were scuffs and chips on a coffee table, which had presumably been pushed under the window when she opened out the sofa bed, and beside the window was a set of bookshelves which were chipped in places, revealing chipboard under the faux-wood finish. The bedroom door with the makeshift recording studio was open, and Erika could see through to where two SOCOs were working with fine brushes, dusting for prints on the black desk and the doorframe. The fine, grey fingerprint powder glittered under the bright lights.

'It would be worth finding out why Vicky was in bed so early,' said Peterson. 'Did she have company?'

'She's still dressed,' said Moss, indicating Vicky's blue jeans, white socks and the blood-soaked sweater. Erika turned her attention back to the living room and nodded.

'What about a murder weapon?' she asked.

'It's too early to be specific,' said Isaac. 'A long sharp blade. The stab wounds are random but neat and precise.'

Erika looked over to the kitchenette in the second half of the room. It was neat and clean, but the lights illuminated the torn, grubby linoleum and cobwebs on the ceiling above. She could see a knife block lying on its side on the counter.

'There's a knife missing from that block,' she said.

'We haven't found a weapon yet,' said Isaac.

Erika, Moss, and Peterson took a step back as a metal stretcher on wheels with a black body bag was pushed into the small living room. Three of the SOCOs moved into position and carefully lifted Vicky's body clear of the bed and onto the shiny black of the open body bag. They turned her gently over onto her back, and Erika watched as her body shifted limply and her hair fell away from her face. Vicky was petite, with a porcelain doll-like face, but the effects of rigor mortis were developing fast and her death grimace was more pronounced; lips peeled back and eyes open wide.

'I'll do the post-mortem tonight,' Isaac said. 'I'll let you know more as soon as possible.'

'Thank you.'

Erika took one last look around the flat at the blood-soaked mattress. There was a crackling of plastic as the body bag was closed and zipped up, entombing Vicky's remains in its shiny blackness. It struck Erika, how fragile life was. She wondered how Vicky had felt the last time she walked through her front door. Was she happy? Sad? Scared? Whatever she felt, she probably had no idea she would be leaving in a black body bag.

6

Erika, Moss and Peterson followed the stretcher with the body bag as it bumped its way down the short driveway to the black mortuary van parked out on the road next to the white police support van.

They stopped in the front garden and pulled off their crime scene coveralls, depositing them into plastic forensic bags.

'Can you sort out a search for the murder weapon?' Erika asked Peterson.

'Yeah. I'll get a team together to check out the surrounding gardens,' he said, moving off to the support van.

'Can you come with me to talk to Tess?' Erika said to Moss, adding, 'If you could go over to the support van and make sure she stays inside, with *that* on its way to the morgue van.'

'On it,' said Moss. The two young police officers who Erika had asked to interview the neighbours came out of the building towards her.

'Ma'am, there seems to be only one other neighbour in tonight,' said the taller of the two.

'Okay. What are your names?' she asked.

'I'm Constable Robbie Grant,' said the taller, who was very pale with a smooth flawless, complexion.

'Constable Amer Abidi,' said the second. He was equally handsome and fresh-faced, and as he nodded and smiled, the top edge of a tattoo on his dark skin peeked above his shirt collar. 'There are three floors in the block of flats,' he said, pointing back at the building entrance. 'And three flats on each floor. Vicky Clarke is at flat one, Charles Wakefield lives in number two, and at three, there are two sisters, Sophia and Maria Ivanova, both trainee doctors, but there's no one in.'

'Ivanova?' asked Erika.

'It's Bulgarian. Upstairs on the second floor is an elderly lady, a Mrs Wentworth. She lives alone at number four, directly above Vicky's flat. She says she didn't see or hear anything tonight. She was in bed by eight.'

'She's very hard of hearing, and a bit doddery. We really had to hammer on her door before she heard us,' added Robbie.

'She told us that flat five, the one above Charles Wakefield, is vacant, and in number six, opposite her, lives a businessman called Ray Fontaine. He's away most of the year working in China,' said Amer.

'Okay. What about the top floor?' asked Erika.

'The whole of the top floor is a penthouse flat, owned by a Henrietta Boulderstone, who also owns the building. There was no answer at her door.'

Erika watched as the SOCOs carefully loaded the stretcher containing Vicky's body into the back of the mortuary van, ready to take it to the morgue. Moss and Peterson were standing at the steps of the police support vehicle with Tess, who was watching her sister's body, her eyes wide. She had a blanket around her shoulders.

'Good work, guys,' said Erika, turning back to Amir and Robbie. 'If you can cross-check all that info is correct, that would be great.'

It was coming up to eleven pm but the road was busy with police cars and support vehicles, and every light in the surrounding houses was on.

It was quiet and warm inside the police support van. In one corner there was a small seating area with a table, and Moss slid into the booth beside Erika. They were both facing Tess, who sat opposite, cradling a plastic cup filled with tea.

'Thank you for your patience,' said Erika. 'Would you like some more tea?'

'This is my *third* cup of tea. What are doing about my...' At this point her voice broke and she pressed her eyes shut. Tears rolled down her cheeks. 'My sister,' she finished with a hoarse whisper.

'I have an excellent forensics team working inside the flat. We have officers talking to the neighbours and searching the area. And we'll shortly take this all back to the station and set up a full incident room,' said Erika. 'Are you happy to have an informal chat? I know it's late, but we find that people often forget things after the crucial first few hours.'

Moss picked up a box of tissues and offered it to Tess. She took one and wiped her eyes. She nodded.

'Earlier this evening, when I was passing the block of flats, I heard you scream from inside. How long had you been in your sister's flat before you found her?' asked Erika.

'I'd just literally arrived. Key in the lock, opened the door, switched on the lights and...' She swallowed. Eyes wide. 'I saw her lying there, and I screamed. I haven't screamed like that for... I don't know if ever.'

Erika nodded sympathetically.

'I checked my watch when I heard you scream. It was just after eight fifteen.'

'Yes. I left the house just after eight. I only live around the corner.'

'Did you see any neighbours, or anyone on the street when you arrived?'

'No.'

'Had the front door been forced open?'

'No. I used my key to open the door.'

'Did Vicky share any fears with you about her safety in the lead-up to tonight?'

'What? No... No.' Tess shook her head insistently.

'How well does she know her neighbours in the building?'

'They're all old. She's closest to the girls who live opposite. The Bulgarian sisters. They're not great friends or anything, but they're the only ones who are close to her age, twenty-seven.'

'That's Maria and Sophia Ivanova?'

'Yes. They both work long shifts at the hospital and Vicky's at home a lot, so she'll often take in parcels for them. Their mother sends them stuff from home, Bulgaria. That's how she got to know them.'

'What can you tell us about Charles Wakefield who lives next door?' asked Erika.

She looked up at them. There was a pause, and in the silence, Erika wondered if Tess has heard the commotion outside when they arrested him.

'He's a strange man. Vicky told me a few times that she's caught him listening outside her door.'

'Did Vicky ever talk about him specifically doing anything that she felt was threatening?' said Erika, taking care not to lead with her questioning. Tess looked down at her hands, thinking.

'No...' she said, finally. 'No. She just said he was a bit odd. Creepy.'

'What do you know about him?'

'Not much. He lives alone...' She narrowed her eyes. 'You don't think he did this to Vicky?'

'At this stage everything is a question,' said Erika. 'Did Vicky have a boyfriend?'

The use of the past tense seemed to hit Tess, and it looked like she needed a moment to recover.

'Yes. Shawn. Shawn Macavity. They've been on and off since they graduated from college six years ago. He lives in Forest Hill.'

Erika hesitated; she didn't know how far she could probe so soon after seeing the brutality of the crime scene.

'Tess. There was a knife missing, a large paring knife in the kitchen.'

'She never used those knives,' said Tess, instantly.

'Did you know a knife was missing from the set?'

'No. No. Why would I know that?'

The mention of a knife seemed to take her back to what she'd seen. Erika watched Tess as she pulled the grubby wine-coloured fleece closed, and seemed to shrink in the seat. Had she intended to leave the house today? On closer scrutiny, she was very well-spoken, the co-owner of what she insisted was an upmarket restaurant, and yet she was dressed so scruffily.

'Was tonight a planned visit? Was Vicky expecting you?'

'As I told you, she was due to work the lunchtime shift today. I left messages on her mobile, but she hadn't got back to me. That's why I came over tonight... I was...'

'Was?'

'Was ready to shout at her... It's not the first time she's been a no-show.' Tess dissolved into tears.

'What's been the reason before for her no-show?'

'Any number of things. She's hungover, she has an audition, although that one happens less frequently these days. And then sometimes she just can't be bothered. She knows I'll never fire her.'

'Why wouldn't you fire her?' asked Erika.

'I'm all she has, *had*... I can't believe I have to use the past tense now when I talk about her. My husband always tells me we should keep work and family separate. And now... Vicky.' She broke down again. Erika made some notes.

'You're doing very well, we're almost done,' said Moss, reaching out to touch Tess's hand, but she pulled it away.

'Where did Vicky sleep? Her bedroom seems to be an office or recording studio?'

'On the sofa bed...' Tess sighed, as if it embarrassed her. 'Vicky's an actress, and work is always, let's say, sparse. She recently converted her bedroom into a recording studio so she could make money narrating audiobooks, but that never quite worked out. She'd been doing a podcast, and, working for us to make ends meet.'

'What kind of podcast?' asked Moss.

'I can't remember,' said Tess. Erika could see she was starting to withdraw again, which was understandable.

'You've kept your maiden name? You gave us your name as Tess Clarke?' said Erika. Tess sat back and sighed.

'*Maiden*. That's such a quaint word... It's a long time since I felt like a maiden...' Her face crumpled and she looked exhausted and broken. She sighed and wiped her eyes. 'My husband's surname is also Clark, but without an "e". It's caused a lot of hassle, getting that "e" removed,' she said ruefully. Erika wondered who the hassle came from, the authorities or her husband.

'What's your husband's name?'

'Jasper Clark... No "e".'

'Do you have other siblings?'

'No. Our parents are in a nursing home on the south coast. Oh, God. How am I going to tell them? They both have dementia... I can't believe what's happened. I can't believe she's dead.'

Tess broke down completely, sobbing into her hands.

7

Erika and Moss watched from the steps of the van as Tess was driven home with her newly-assigned police Family Liaison Officer. Despite her scruffy clothes and unkempt hair, there was a certain nobility to how she held herself, staring straight ahead in the back of the car. Erika looked back to Moss, who was rubbing her shoulder.

'You okay?'

'I had to go hard on Charles Wakefield's door when I broke it down,' she said.

'He gave us probable cause to enter...' Erika mulled things over for a moment. Would it stand up in court, if a judge asked her to justify a search? She looked back at the busy crime scene, and thought of the brutality of the murder. 'Come on, while we have the chance, let's take a look inside his flat.'

They went back into the building, and pulled on fresh Tyvek suits. The bright forensic lamps shone out of Vicky's front door as they passed, and Erika noted that lights had the same effect on the lobby, illuminating the grease spots on the fading parquet floor tiles and the chipped paintwork.

The front door to Charles's flat was at the end of a short corridor leading off the lobby, next to a lift and staircase. Erika pulled on a fresh pair of latex gloves and pushed the door open with her elbow. She found a light switch and flicked it on. The entrance had a small hallway carpeted in a faded orange and yellow diamond pattern. When Moss pulled the door closed, a heavy silence seemed to descend. A clock ticked.

The flat had that fusty smell of other people. Erika could never quite put her finger on exactly what that was... It was never entirely unpleasant, like the smell of earwax, mixed with skin, slightly unwashed hair, and an unfamiliar cleaning product that doesn't quite win the battle for cleanliness.

The overhead light had a heavy shade, leaving the corners of the hallway in gloom. A rotary dial phone sat on top of the phone book and the *Yellow Pages* on a small shelf under a tall thin mirror.

'Jeez. That made me jump,' said Erika, feeling a surge of panic. She indicated a coat stand behind the door, which held a long black trench coat with a black trilby hat on the hook above.

'It looks like a person, standing with their back to us,' said Moss. Erika moved to the coat stand and gently lifted off the black trilby. The hat felt weighty and posh, and the label inside said JUNIPER & BROWN HATTERS ST JAMES STREET, LONDON.

'Avocado alert!' said Moss. Erika carefully put the hat back on the coat stand, and turned and followed her into the small musty-smelling bathroom. There was a brown carpet with an avocado toilet, sink and bath. A row of crispy dry orange flannels hung on a small wooden stand by the bath.

Erika moved to the sink and opened a small square mirrored cabinet above. There were three bars of Imperial Leather soap stacked on the bottom shelf, a crusty bottle of Old Spice aftershave, denture tablets, a bag of plastic disposable razors, and an array of prescription medications. There were eight bottles in total and the labels had all been torn off, leaving the paper residue. Erika took a photo of them with her phone.

'Pity he took off the labels. We could have seen what's wrong with him, and there's something very wrong with him,' said Moss, coming to join her at the sink. 'Look. I haven't seen a magnetic soap holder in years. My nan had one,' she added, indicating the bar of soap attached to an arm on the wall, with a small magnetic disc pressed into it.

Erika was troubled by the anonymous medication. She picked up a few of the bottles and peered at the pills inside and then closed the cabinet. She looked around. The bath mat hung over the shower curtain pole, with its octopus-like suckers facing out. The fibres of the grey pedestal mat around the toilet were compacted in two footprints. It smelt damp and fusty. The carpet was dry.

'If Charles stabbed Vicky Clarke, and it was a frenzied attack, he would have had to clean himself up in a hurry. It doesn't look or smell like he did it in here,' said Erika.

They came out of the bathroom, through the hallway into the living room. Moss flicked on the light, and again, there was a single overhead light with a heavy flowery shade, which gave the room a cave-like gloom.

'Where's his telly?' asked Moss. The room looked like something out of the 1950s, with a brown three-piece suite with lace covers on the back. A heavy wooden record player was in one corner, under a fringed standard lamp. There was a loud ticking, and Erika saw a tiny cuckoo clock high on the wall next to the door. A small gas fire sat on the floor in front of the armchair. Next to it was a round lace-covered occasional table where a tin of Newcastle Brown Ale sat next to a half-full pint glass of the brown liquid. Erika touched the can with her gloved hand. It still felt cool. Down the side of the armchair was stuffed a well-thumbed lingerie catalogue.

Erika picked it up. The women in the catalogue all wore large, transparent, fussy lace bras, and high-top lace knickers with suspenders. There was a big box of tissues balanced on the arm of the chair.

'This is an old catalogue,' said Erika, recoiling slightly at the crinkly pages.

'Looks like he's jerking off, 1970s style,' said Moss. Erika put it back where she'd found it.

A series of framed photos on a sideboard showed a lady with two boys. The photos must have been taken over a period of twenty years, but even in the early photos when the boys were tiny, the woman seemed severe and older than her years, with a short, greying bob of hair parted at one side and fixed with a hair grip. In the first photo she was pictured paddling in a rock pool with the two tiny boys, who barely reached up to her knees. In subsequent photos, the boys grew older, through teenage years to adulthood, and the pictures were of picnics and days out on the beach. In the last photo, the woman sat in a hospital bed next to a window where sunlight poured, glinting off her grey hair. She looked thin and frail and the two boys now looked to be in their early twenties. In all of the photos, Erika recognised Charles and even as a small boy, he had the same sheepish-yet-sinister smile. The other boy was handsome in comparison, with a broad confident smile.

A large bookshelf was filled with rows and rows of wine-coloured, leather-bound *Reader's Digest* novels, and the whole bottom shelf was devoted to books about Hitler and the two world wars.

They moved past a small, neat kitchen with ancient-looking grey Formica cabinets. At the back of the flat was the bedroom, sparsely furnished, with a single bed and a wardrobe.

'There's the telly,' said Erika, pointing to an old TV with a built-in video machine sitting in a corner unplugged, with the cable and plug neatly looped up and fixed with tape. The blank screen was covered in a thick layer of dust. 'I don't know anyone who hasn't got a telly.'

'I heard Madonna doesn't own a telly,' said Moss. 'Does that help?'

Erika rolled her eyes.

'Yeah. Hugely,' she said.

'And this is the window he tried to jump out of,' said Moss. There was a set of heavy red drapes, and a net curtain hung over the glass. Erika slid the net curtain to one side, and opened the large, single-pane window. There was a drop of just a few feet onto a small patch of grass outside, and an alleyway running behind the houses.

'That's where he hit his head,' said Moss, pointing up at the rusting edge of the window frame.

Erika noted a muddy footprint on the windowsill, and some mud stains on the carpet.

'Why did he have mud on his shoes? We saw him talking to Tess in the lobby with the bin bag. Did he go outside and find the dead cats? No, they were part-frozen.'

'That's where he was half out of the window, and then tried to climb back in,' said Moss.

She closed the window and they went to the kitchen. It had the same fustiness as the bathroom. There was no microwave, just an old-fashioned gas oven with the grill pan on a shelf above the hob. The fridge hummed in one corner. There was a stale smell of frying food, but the cracked Formica surfaces were clean and tidy. Erika pressed her foot to the pedal bin. It was empty, with a clean bag. The metal sink was empty too, with water stains. Moss crouched down and opened the freezer drawers.

'Nothing but potato waffles, and beef mince... Oh, and a bag of kippers. No dead cats.'

They came out of the kitchen into the hall. There was a tall cupboard door with a key in the lock. Erika opened it. It was lined with shelves up to the ceiling, and they contained household supplies, cleaning products, bin liners, light bulbs, toilet paper and scores more bars of the Imperial Leather soap from the bathroom.

'No TV, computer, or radio, and he's a bit of a hoarder,' said Moss, looking up at the stash.

'Yes, but that's not illegal,' said Erika.

'There's no sign of him doing a big clean-up, unless he wore protective overalls and rubber gloves, but the bin bag we caught him throwing away had none of that inside.'

'We need to check through the communal rubbish bins,' said Erika.

'Great, nothing I'd love to do more,' said Moss. There was a twanging sound, and the cuckoo clock in the living room began to signal the hour. Erika shuddered. Time seemed to stand still in this strange, creepy little flat.

8

An extensive search through the communal rubbish bins brought up no evidence of bloodied clothing or tissues. At 3am the forensics team finished inside Vicky's flat, and things started to wind down at the crime scene. Erika told her team they would reconvene at Lewisham Row station at 10am the next morning.

'Do you want a lift home, boss?' asked Moss. The forensics van had left the scene, and the police support van was pulling away. It was now very windy and bleak on the narrow road, and the taut crime scene tape gave off a low humming as it vibrated in the breeze.

'It's okay. My new place is two streets over.'

'It's late. Let me run you back and make sure you get home safe...' They got into Moss's car and she started the engine and fired up the heater. Erika put her freezing hands between her thighs and hunched down, waiting to warm up. Moss offered her a bag which contained sherbet flying saucers.

'Here. Take the taste of that dumpster dive out of your mouth,' she said.

'Thanks,' said Erika, taking one and dropping it on her

tongue. She felt the rice paper dissolve and then a delicious fizz of sweet-sharp sugar hit her system, banishing the memory of trawling through bags of fetid trash and rotting food.

'What do you now think about Charles Wakefield?' asked Moss.

'Leave him in a cell overnight, and then we'll put him in an interview room tomorrow.'

'Do you think he killed Vicky?'

'That would be nice and easy, but I'd have trouble linking him to the murder at this stage. Unless we find DNA.'

'Nice and easy never happens,' said Moss.

Erika nodded and rolled her eyes. 'Give me another one of those flying saucers.'

'I bought them for the kids, but they never quite made it into the house,' said Moss, shaking the bag and holding it out. 'Sugar is my favourite food group.'

'They're so good,' said Erika, sitting back for a moment and closing her eyes. 'Jesus. I've been up since five this morning for the house movers.'

They pulled away from the block of flats, where a lone officer was stationed for the night.

'It looks... erm. It's a fixer-upper,' said Moss, peering up through her window when they parked outside Erika's new house.

'I did that thing people keep saying, buy the crappiest house on the nicest street.'

'Well. You've achieved that.'

Erika laughed.

'Thanks for the lift. I'll see you tomorrow morning.'

'Night, boss. Get some sleep!'

Moss waited until she got in through the front door before

she drove away. It was freezing cold inside, and there was a breeze coming down the hallway. When Erika flicked on the light, she saw a line of neat muddy paw prints running along the wooden floorboards in the hall, coming from the kitchen. Erika followed them, and saw that the old cat flap in the back door was wedged open at an angle.

A loud miaow echoed through the house and made her jump, and then it came again. Erika followed the paw prints back out of the kitchen and down the hall, where they turned abruptly and carried on up the stairs. A pane of glass above the front door had the number 27 etched in fading paint. Where the streetlight was shining in, Erika saw two yellow eyes at the top of the stairs, glinting in the darkness.

'Are you my late-night intruder?' she asked. The cat gave a bright little miaow and came padding down to her, emerging into the light. Erika had been expecting some shaggy moggy, but this cat was a beautiful black with four perfect white feet, like little boots. It looked quite young, and was lean but not under-fed. It had the most beautiful green eyes.

The cat came to a stop at the bottom of the steps and sat staring at her confidently, unblinking. Its front feet splayed outwards, and the posture reminded Erika of Mary Poppins's posture with her feet turned out, when she took flight with her umbrella.

She crouched down and put out her hand. The cat got up and wound its way around her arm as she stroked it.

'My goodness, you have the softest fur,' said Erika as she moved her hand up, scratching behind the cat's ears. It let out a soft low purr that immediately relaxed Erika. 'Are you a boy or a girl?' she added, and peered down between the cat's legs. 'Ah, yes. Cock and balls. That means you're a boy.'

Erika got up and went to the kitchen to see if the cat would follow. He did, and he sat by the humming fridge. Erika had inherited a scrubbed wooden kitchen table and one chair. Boxes were piled high on and around the table. Erika opened a box which had 'TINS' written on the side, and found a can of Májka pâté.

She looked at the cat and he licked his lips.

'You have a talent, breaking into houses and working your charm. You've been here five minutes and I'm contemplating opening my last tin of my favourite Slovak pâté for you...' The cat stared up at her hopefully and blinked. 'And just like that, I've become the old cat lady,' said Erika. She found a tea cup and saucer, spooned half of the pâté out onto the saucer, and filled the teacup with water from the tap. She put them both on the floor by the fridge and watched as the cat tucked in, lapping at the glistening meat with a small pink tongue.

Erika thought back to the mystery of why Charles Wakefield had two frozen cat corpses in a bin liner. She felt another pang of sadness, seeing those beautiful creatures dead. She ate a spoonful of the pâté out of the can, and then gave the cat more.

It was almost four o'clock in the morning, but Erika was suddenly wide awake. There was a clinking as the plate flapped up and down on the floorboards as he licked it clean. There was still a draught coming from the open cat flap. Erika closed it, and checked that it was still working. She'd have to get some oil and fix its sticking. She expected the cat to leave after its food, but instead it followed her back up the hall.

Her feet echoed as she climbed into the darkness, and when she saw the cat padding along behind her, Erika was glad of the company. She felt around on the walls, her fingers brushing the air bubbles under the damp and peeling wallpaper, and flicked on the switch. There were four doors leading off the landing. The first door led to a tiny box room which looked out into the back garden. Next to it was an equally tiny bathroom, the third door along the hall led to another small bedroom, and the largest bedroom was at the front of the house, and it had a huge bay window.

Erika peered into the box room, saw her single blow-up mattress on the floor, and was pleased to see it was still inflated with her duvet and pillows on top. The house had a fireplace in every room, but this was the only room where the fireplace wasn't boarded up.

The cat followed her inside, hopped up onto the end of the mattress, and curled up contentedly. Erika had never had a pet. This cat was a stray, but a cute one, and there was something about him being here on her first night in the house that comforted her.

She changed out of her work clothes, kept on her socks and underwear, and pulled on a thick pair of tartan pyjamas. She'd bought some wood and firelighters from the petrol station, and she spent a few minutes building and lighting a fire in the tiny grate. She sat on the end of the mattress, feeding in larger pieces of wood as the tiny petal of fire grew to a blaze, and she rubbed her hands in the comforting glow.

She still had an old blue sweater belonging to Peterson that he'd forgotten to collect when their relationship ended. She liked to sleep in it, and it was on the mattress where the cat was half lying on it. She could see the label poking out from the collar: 'George at ASDA'.

'Hmm. George is a good name, what do you think?'

The cat stared up at her, blinking, and then got up and went padding out of the room. Erika followed him to the door as she heard him patter down the stairs, into the hall, and then there was a soft thwap of the cat flap in the kitchen.

'Okay. Bye, George,' said Erika, and she was surprised how sad she was that the cat had gone.

When she came back into the bedroom, the fire was now roaring and crackling in the grate. The wood she had bought from the petrol station sizzled and spat, and she watched as a bright red spark flew out and hit the inflatable mattress.

'No!' she cried, realising what was about to happen. There was a hiss as it landed and burned through the thin plastic, leaving a large hole. The mattress began to deflate rapidly, the duvet and pillows sinking down to the level of the old floorboards. 'Shit.'

Her room was suddenly less cosy. Erika climbed on top of the mattress, which was now flat as a pancake, and tried to get comfortable under the duvet. She was warm, but she could feel every inch of the hard floorboards under her back. After half an hour of tossing and turning, she gave up on trying to sleep and pulled out her phone.

Erika never used the podcast app on her iPhone, but she clicked on it, found the search bar, and tapped in the name 'Vicky Clarke podcast'.

The podcast graphic came up first in the search results. There was a photo of Vicky standing against a brick wall, wearing a boxy black leather jacket with her arms folded. She was looking into the camera with a grim-set seriousness and above, written in bold red type, was the title: V.A. CLARKE TRUE CRIME DETECTIVE.

It's a true crime podcast? thought Erika. *Why didn't Tess think to mention this?*

There were fifteen episodes uploaded, and each one dealt with a seemingly unsolved crime or series of crimes: arson, vandalism, catfishing. However, one episode caught Erika's eye and she froze, her mind going back to Charles Wakefield. It read:

THE MYSTERY OF THE CROYDON CAT KILLER.

9

Erika was new to technology – she'd only recently, and reluctantly, bought a smartphone – and it took a moment to work out how to play the podcast. She set the volume, placed her phone on the bedcover, and started to listen.

It began with an eerie echoing tune played on a piano, and as the dying light of the fire played over the ceiling in the small box room, Erika forgot the hard floorboards under her back. Tess had been rather scornful of her sister's acting abilities during their interview, but Vicky's spoken introduction surprised her. She commanded the microphone with a strong, engaging broadcast voice.

'The Croydon Cat Killer is the name given to a mythical figure alleged to have killed, dismembered, and decapitated more than four hundred cats in the United Kingdom. The killing spree began four years ago in Croydon, and has caused fear and terror for the residents of Greater London.

'In 2014, reports of cats found mutilated in residential areas started to spread out across and around Greater London, and as far north as Manchester. The police immediately launched an

*investigation, which carried on for several years. Officially, the Met police have stated that the mutilations had **not** been carried out by a human, and were likely caused by wildlife predation, or scavenging on cats killed in vehicle collisions.*

'However, the killings have continued, and in three cases, a shadowy figure has been caught on CCTV. Many locals, including vets and police officers (who have declined to go publicly on the record), are still convinced that a sick individual is responsible for these killings. And some worry that this individual might soon transfer their attention to people...'

The sound then cut to an interview with a woman who lived in Shirley, in South London. A spoon rattled in a mug, and a train clacked past on the tracks outside. The audio conjured up the image of a kitchen in small terraced house, the windows looking out over the back garden, perhaps steamed up by the kettle.

'I'm normally a heavy sleeper,' said the woman in a broad Kentish accent. 'But I sat bolt upright when I heard this sound.'

'What sound did you hear?' asked Vicky.

'That awful noise of cats fighting... A terrible curdling yowling. You hear it quite a bit round here... but it stopped, like the sound being cut off. And tha's what made me think something was wrong... I woke up Des, that's me 'usband, and I sent him to go and check downstairs. When he opened the door, he found the body of a decapitated cat on the back doorstep. Fresh, it was. He checked the garden with a torch and found fresh muddy footprints, male, sized ten, leading across the lawn to the fence...'

Erika shifted on the mattress, the hard floor bringing her back to the room again. She thought of Charles Wakefield's bedroom, in his dingy flat. The muddy footprint on his windowsill...

The podcast episode moved on to an interview with a man with a CCTV camera, who found the body of a cat hacked to pieces on his back step. He had a blurred image of a thick-set stocky figure in his back garden. Exhaustion, and the warmth of the fire in the small box room, caused Erika's mind to drift and as she dozed off, she saw Charles as the stocky figure on the back porch. His sleeves rolled up, gripping something limp and furry, his eyes wide as specks of blood clung to his smooth hairless face.

Erika woke with a start. She was freezing cold, and a gruel-like grey light was filtering through the thin curtains. She shifted, and felt the hard floor pressing into her hip bones. When she sat up, her breath was coming out in a stream of vapour. It was 7am.

Erika arrived at Lewisham Row station just before nine. It was a bright grey day, with a wintery chill in the air. Two cups of coffee later, she was still shivering from her first shower in the new bathroom. A frigid plunge under a freezing trickle of water. It hadn't helped that her car had iced up overnight. And the can of anti-freeze she kept in the car was empty. As she pulled into the car park, Peterson drove up beside her and parked in the next spot.

She also had a crick in her neck from where she'd slept badly on the deflated mattress. When she got out of the car, she tried to straighten up and winced.

'Morning. You all right?' asked Peterson. 'How's the new gaff?'

Erika was about to tell him the new house was fabulous and spacious and everything she'd ever dreamed of, but then thought, *why do I have to lie?* 'My airbed popped, so I ended up on the bare floorboards. And I have no hot water.' Peterson smiled as he took out his backpack and locked his car.

'I slept on the sofa, so I feel your pain.'

'That sofa is uncomfortable, but I would have given anything to sleep on something softer than floorboards.'

'I didn't get chucked out. It's Kyle. He has night terrors... That's why I was on the sofa,' added Peterson quickly.

'My mother used to have night terrors, she used to be half awake, half asleep, screaming like she was possessed by something.'

'I know! Kyle screams and thrashes around. His eyes wide open. Scary stuff, and it takes ages to get him awake and calm him down,' said Peterson, holding the door open for her. 'The only way he can calm down is if he sleeps in our bed with Fran. And our bed is so small...' They stepped through into the warmth of the reception area. It was small and run-down, and always seemed to stink of a mixture of sick and pine disinfectant. 'There's a big offer on at Bed World and it's just over the road, next to the DLR.'

'Okay. Thanks for the tip...'As they reached the front desk, Erika's thoughts moved to Charles Wakefield. 'I'll see you at the briefing. I'm just going to check on Mr Wakefield, and see how he enjoyed his night in the cells.' Peterson nodded and put his card key on the sensor next to the door. It buzzed and clicked open, letting him into the main station. 'Morning. Can I have a look at the last night's log, please?' she added to the Duty Officer on the desk. He handed her a printout.

Erika scanned down the list. It detailed all the arrests and incidents that had happened during the night, and she froze when she saw the last log entry.

'What the...' she said under her breath. 'Is this correct?' she asked, pointing to the entry at the bottom.

'Yeah. He went off first thing,' said the Duty Officer. 'Turns out that Charles Wakefield's brother is Julian Wakefield, the Assistant Commissioner of Police!'

10

Erika went to the door and buzzed herself into the station. She hurried down a long, low corridor which led past the central staircase and lifts towards the custody suite. Phones rang, and officers in uniform and support staff streamed by in the opposite direction, their weary faces tense and urgent.

Erika's mind was whirring. *Jesus. Why didn't Charles say that his brother was third in command of the whole bloody Met police?* She thought back to the photos in his living room, of the two brothers. She thought that the brother looked familiar.

She bumped into Moss coming out of the staff canteen with a coffee.

'Morning, boss. The Super wants to see you urgently in her office,' she said, swallowing a gulp of coffee.

'I thought she might,' said Erika. She turned on her heel and went back to the stairs, feeling a mixture of anger and anxiety growing in her chest.

Superintendent Melanie Hudson's office was on the top floor, at the end of the corridor. Erika knocked and waited.

'Come in,' came Melanie's muffled voice. When Erika

opened the door, she was sitting at her desk. She was a petite woman with fine blonde hair. Next to her was Commander Paul Marsh. He was sitting bolt upright in his chair wearing his dress uniform, which was immaculate. He had a deep tan, and his short sandy hair was still thick, despite being in his mid-forties.

'Morning, Erika,' he said.

'Morning,' said Erika cautiously, stepping into the office. Behind the desk was a view out over London, and in the far distance, amongst the haze, Erika could just make out the Houses of Parliament.

'Please, have a seat,' said Melanie, indicating the chair in front of the desk.

Erika had a good working relationship with Melanie, but her relationship with Marsh was complex. They'd trained together as police officers in Manchester, he'd been Mark's best friend, and for a few years they'd all been close – but a great deal had changed since then. In Erika's opinion, Marsh had put aside being a good police officer so he could rapidly rise through the ranks.

There was an awkward pause.

'It's good to be back in my old office. It looks a bit different to when I was here,' said Marsh.

'Yes. It's a lot cleaner,' said Erika. 'It used to look like a teenage boy's bedroom. Old coffee cups, and workout clothes everywhere...' Melanie didn't smile. Marsh looked annoyed. 'I presume you're here to tell me why a suspect I arrested last night has been released without my approval?'

'Erika, Commander Marsh has found time in his busy schedule to come and explain directly last night's developments,' said Melanie.

'Does nepotism need an explanation?' replied Erika. 'I just found out that Charles's brother is high up in the Met. I presume Julian Wakefield pulled some strings to let him off assaulting a police officer.'

Melanie shook her head, and snapped, 'For God sake's, Erika, be quiet and listen.'

She wasn't used to hearing Melanie snap at her, and it brought her up short.

'I'm sorry, but I had no idea of who his brother was when I arrested him. And despite that, I should have been notified that he was being moved from custody,' said Erika, feeling her cheeks blushing at the rebuke. Marsh drummed his fingers on the table.

'This is a delicate matter, Erika. A very sensitive time for the Met. As you know, public confidence in the police has been eroded by the press. This needed to be dealt with properly, but swiftly, to avoid this being dragged into the press...' Erika went to speak but he put his hand up. 'I can assure you that Charles Wakefield hasn't been let off with a slapped wrist. He was taken to Lewisham Magistrates' Court at 8am this morning. His case was first up, and he was found guilty of a Section 89, assaulting a police officer. It was his first offence – he's never had so much as a parking ticket – so he was given a three-month suspended sentence and has to pay a one thousand pound fine.'

Erika was surprised that he'd been convicted, but she felt cheated that she hadn't had the chance to grill him in an interview room.

'Where is he now?' she said, after a pause. 'Hiding out with the Assistant Commissioner?'

'No. It seems Charles is the black sheep of the family. I know Julian quite well, and had no idea until today that he had a brother,' said Marsh.

'My problem is that this wasn't just a simple case of him assaulting a police officer,' said Erika. 'I wanted to question Charles Wakefield in relation to the brutal murder of a young woman. He's the woman's next-door neighbour, and I don't know if he has an alibi for the time of her murder. In the weeks leading up to her death she had commented on odd behaviour from Mr Wakefield, stating that she felt uncomfortable and threatened by his presence. When we arrived last night on the scene, he was behaving very strangely.' Erika started to explain the rest of the events from the previous evening, and she also described the dead cats he was trying to conceal, and Vicky Clarke's podcast. Marsh put up his hand.

'You think he's a brutal murderer and the guy who's been killing cats for the past four years?'

'It's a disturbing coincidence.'

'Charles Wakefield, of course, should be treated like a regular citizen—'

'He's a regular citizen, is he?' interrupted Erika. 'I've never *ever* heard of someone being arrested at 11pm for assaulting a police officer and by 9am the next morning they've been tried and convicted!'

'You'll need a bloody good reason to bring him in for questioning,' said Marsh. 'And questioning him in relation to that bloody cat killer case.'

'The official name of the investigation is Operation Figtree,' said Erika. Marsh shook his head, now red in the face.

'The results of Operation Figtree ruled that foxes were killing those cats. Foxes, of which there are thousands in London. Do you know how much bloody money and police manpower that cost? Millions!'

'Yes, but—'

Marsh leant over the table and stabbed his finger in the air.

'If I hear you've arrested the Assistant Commissioner's brother in relation to—'

'Operation Figtree,' finished Erika, feeling a spark of enjoyment at Marsh's almost Hitler-esque rant.

'If I hear that you've arrested him as a fucking cat killer, your career will be over, Erika. I mean it!'

'I do think he could be involved with this murder.'

'Every development in this case pertaining to Charles Wake-field, however small, will have to go through me and Melanie. Do you hear?'

Erika sat back and crossed her arms.

'Erika,' said Melanie. 'Do you understand?'

There was silence. Marsh stared at her across the desk. A vein pulsed in his forehead, and for a moment she took a small thrill from riling him. *Top brass must really be panicking that I'm heading up this case*, she thought.

'Yes. Understood.'

Marsh picked up his hat and stood up from his chair.

'Melanie. Thank you for the coffee.'

'Yes, thank you. We appreciate you taking the time to meet with us,' said Melanie, getting up. Erika hauled herself out of her seat. She realised that she had to play the game.

'Paul. I'm not stupid. I'm sorry if I got... if things got heated. I'll let you know everything that happens.'

Marsh stopped at the door.

'Thank you,' he said curtly. 'How is your new place? Are you settling in?' he asked, doing an about-face and changing the subject.

'Yes. It needs some work, though,' she said.

'It's a lovely area, Blackheath... Do you remember that flat we shared in Manchester, our first year in the force? No carpets or central heating. Camp beds.' He smiled at the memory. 'It was fun though, wasn't it?'

Erika felt a sudden pang of remorse, and loss. Not only had she lost Mark, but she'd lost the old Paul Marsh. The good friend he used to be, before he was seized by his thirst for power and promotion. He was now three ranks above her, and she didn't know how to talk to him anymore, and when she did, it was a disaster.

'It was fun,' she said with a genuine smile.

'I miss Mark. I think of him often.'

'I do too. All the time.'

There was a brief moment when she saw the old Paul smiling back at her.

'Please be careful with this case, Erika. Okay?' he asked.

'Okay.'

He nodded, and then his smile fell away, and he was gone. After he'd left, there was a silence as Melanie walked back round her desk.

'I'm sorry,' said Erika. 'My relationship with him is always going to be weird.'

Melanie nodded.

'Just remember that I am also your senior officer. You may have a shorthand with Commander Marsh when you speak to each other, but it's not a good look to talk to him like that in front of me.'

'Yes, of course. So, what's really happening now? I have authority here as the leading officer, but we both know that there are ways that top brass can lean on me from above. Is Charles Wakefield now off-limits?'

'Unlike Marsh, I read the details of the case last night. This was a brutal, violent murder. At this stage I would be looking at Charles Wakefield as a potential suspect. But one word of advice, Erika. Be smart. Play the game. Don't go in like a wrecking ball on this, when the family member of a very senior officer is involved.'

Erika rubbed her face.

'Okay. Thank you.'

'And remember, when Charles Wakefield was processed last night in the custody suite, they will have taken his DNA. He's also on probation for three months. You can achieve a lot of leverage with all that. Just try to tread lightly, don't stomp all over this case like a mad elephant wearing army boots.'

11

Erika went back to the incident room, and she was pleased to see amongst the admin workers, her regular trusted team of officers: Moss and Peterson, along with Detective John McGorry, a fresh-faced man in his twenties with short dark hair, and Detective Crane, a shorter sandy-haired officer just a few years younger than Erika.

She quickly outlined the events of the previous evening, and the rapid conviction and release of Charles Wakefield. She moved along to where there was a photo of Vicky she hadn't seen before. It was a black-and-white 10 x 8 headshot. Vicky stared right at the camera with a Mona Lisa-esque smile.

'Who found this?'

'I just pulled that off a website called *Spotlight*, a registry for actors,' said Crane. 'She's done a bit of theatre and minor TV work, but nothing in the last two years.'

'I don't like the coincidence that Charles Wakefield had these two dead cats, tried to hide them from us, and Vicky Clarke had recently recorded an investigative podcast episode about the

Croydon Cat Killer. I'll put up a link to the podcast. It's worth a listen.'

'Do you think Charles Wakefield is the Croydon Cat Killer?' asked McGorry.

'That's not our focus right now.'

'Is he completely off-limits?' asked Crane, who was sitting with his arms folded and frowning at the crime scene photos pinned up on the large whiteboards running across the back wall of the incident room.

'No. We just have to be very careful how we approach him,' said Erika. She moved along the whiteboard to the crime scene pictures, of Vicky's body lying on the sofa bed. 'I think she knew the person who did this,' she said, tapping the photo. 'There was no sign of forced entry into her flat. The main entrance to the building has a card key entry system on the front door, and her front door has a Yale lock and a deadbolt. It's a small flat with only a front and back window. The front window was closed, and the back room which she used as a recording studio is blocked up with polystyrene.'

Erika moved to the crime scene photos taken from the makeshift recording studio. The black desk was covered with deposits of silver fingerprint power, which glinted in the light from the camera flash.

'I need you to push our colleagues in forensics. We need the results from the post-mortem, fingerprints, DNA, blood analysis. The cyber team has Vicky's hard drive. I need to know what was on it ASAP. I want her phone records, and her bank details. We need to look at her immediate family and friends. As with all cases, we need to build a picture of her life and we need to build it fast... Pull in any favours you're owed. Who has the results of the door-to-door?'

'That's me,' said Moss, standing up. 'We're a bit like the police station that had all its toilets stolen.'

'I don't follow?'

'We have nothing to go on,' said Moss. Despite herself, Erika smiled. 'The neighbours opposite didn't see anything, nor did people from the surrounding houses. Only three neighbours in Honeycomb Court were home at the time of Vicky's death: Charles Wakefield, an elderly lady upstairs called Mrs Wentworth, and the owner of the building, Henrietta Boulderstone.'

'I'm planning to go back after this briefing to talk to her,' said Erika.

McGorry put up his hand.

'I know that the whole cat killer thing is a bit controversial,' he said. 'But a mate of mine has been working on Operation Figtree for the past two years. I can have a quiet word and see if there is any link, however small, to the area. I could skirt around the whole issue of Charles Wakefield, just mention the building name.'

Erika hesitated.

'If you can fish around without dropping any names, then please, go ahead. But I can't emphasise enough that my arse is on the line, and if I go near Charles Wakefield I have to have a very good reason.'

'Absolutely,' said McGorry. Erika went back to the acting headshot of Vicky.

'We should also look into her career as an actress. Did she go for auditions? Does she have an agent? How much of her acting life bled into her private life? Her sister mentioned a boyfriend, Shawn, but actors live different, unpredictable lives. It would be useful to get as much background on her acting life as possible. Let's meet again tomorrow morning at 9am.'

With that, the officers went to work and the room filled with the busy chatter of activity.

12

Erika thought Honeycomb Court looked softer in the grey light of day. Its concrete structure appeared less brutalistic amongst the rows of red brick Victorian terraced houses.

She parked her car on the road outside and got out along with Moss and Peterson.

Charles Wakefield was outside on the small front lawn, holding a black bin liner with a tiny, wizened woman beside him. They were staring at the ruined grass, where it had been churned up the previous evening by the police cars and vans. Erika hadn't taken much notice of the front garden, which was next to the concrete pathway up to the front door. There was a wide, curved border of pampas grass and some dead flowers and an apple tree heavy with fruit. Quite a few apples lay around the tree, squashed into two deep tyre tracks.

'This is *dreadful*,' said the tiny woman, leaning down to pick up a crushed apple. Her voice had a high quavering register like the tootle of a clarinet. Charles held out the black bin liner and she dropped it in. He was dressed in pale golfing slacks with a high waist buckled over his paunch, and a diamond-patterned pullover. The old lady tilted her head upwards and noticed Erika, Moss and Peterson approaching. She had large cloudy eyes, prominent lips crowded with wrinkles, and a prodigious nose. Her forehead was very small, resulting in a low hairline, which almost collided with her bushy pale eyebrows.

'Yes, can we help you?' she said, imperiously.

Charles put his head down and busied himself picking up the fallen fruit. Erika introduced them all, and they flashed their warrant cards.

'Ah. So you are responsible for pranging my Knobbed Russet?'

Moss raised an eyebrow, and Peterson peered down at her.

'I beg your pardon?' said Erika. The woman pointed to the apple tree with her walking stick. The tree was bent at an angle.

'*Thus*. One of your police vehicles hit my Knobbed Russet... This apple tree is very rare...' She bent down and picked up one of the apples, and Erika saw it was ugly and deformed, with a puckered tumour-like growth on one side. 'Don't be fooled by their ugliness. They have the most beautiful flavour. Lovely in a pie or with a piece of cheese. You're lucky we have a good crop this year,' she added, pointing her stick at the tree still groaning with fruit, 'I just hope you haven't damaged the root structure.'

'What's your name, ma'am?'

'Mrs Henrietta Boulderstone. And I'd prefer *Mrs* Boulderstone, if you please... This is Mr Charles Wakefield.' There was something in her accent and manner which indicated she was posh, of old money.

'We've met. I hope your night in the police cells wasn't too uncomfortable?' asked Erika. Henrietta tilted her head up to fix Charles with a poached-egg Midas stare. He did something Erika didn't expect. He blushed, and a ruddy glow spread across his smooth shiny face. There was an awkward pause and he kept his head down. 'We're here to investigate the murder of Vicky Clarke.'

'Terrible business. *Terrible*,' said Henrietta, after a long pause. She kept staring at Charles. *Was she waiting for him to explain?* thought Erika. There was something childish and petulant about the way he was ignoring them, as he dug an apple from the muddy tyre tracks.

'How well did you know Vicky?' asked Moss.

'We exchanged pleasantries. We come from very different generations.'

'Were you at home last night? One of our police officers rang your bell.'

'Yes. I was in, but I retire very early, by eight o'clock. I'm lucky to be a very heavy sleeper, and my bell doesn't work. I only saw *this*,' she said waving her stick over the churned-up grass, 'when I woke early this morning. I own both flats on the top floor. I use one as my studio.'

'Are you an artist?'

'Yes. My medium is predominantly photography,' she said imperiously.

Charles had moved away from them towards the building to collect the last of the deformed-looking apples from the muddy tyre tracks.

'Did you see anyone unusual coming or going yesterday afternoon? We're looking at the hours between 3pm and 7pm,' asked Peterson. Henrietta moved her attention to Peterson and looked up at him approvingly.

'That depends on your definition of unusual,' she said.

'A stranger? Anyone acting suspiciously.'

'Define suspicious?' she asked, putting her hand to the heavy bronze necklace she wore. Her eyes had a girlish glee about questioning Peterson.

'Please, answer the question,' said Erika. Henrietta rolled her tongue around her mouth.

'No. I didn't see anyone suspicious. In fact, I didn't see anyone all day until Charles called by at 6pm, and we took the air up on my terrace, didn't we?' she added, turning her body to face him.

'Er, yes,' he said, looking up furtively, still trying to extract an apple from the dirt.

'Stop messing about with that and come over here,' she snapped. He pulled the plastic bin liner with him and came to join them. He seemed childlike and shy in the presence of Henrietta. 'You arrived at my front door, just as the six o'clock news was starting, and we went right out on the terrace.'

'Yes,' he said. 'I stayed for less than an hour, forty-five minutes.'

'And during that time on the terrace did you see anyone arrive or leave downstairs?' asked Erika.

'No.'

'And you went back to your flat?'

'Yes.'

'Did you see or hear anything unusual coming from Vicky's flat next door?'

He shook his head.

'No.'

'I enjoy visitors during the cocktail hour, but equally, I like it when people go back home,' boomed Henrietta, in contrast to Charles's one-word answers. 'I make no bones of that. I'm a good loyal friend, in short sharp bursts.'

'And Charles, what were you doing earlier in the day, between 3pm, and up until you called on Mrs Boulderstone?' asked Erika.

'I had lunch and then took a train into the city for a walk around Regent's Park,' he said.

'What time?'

'I left just before 2pm, and I was back home around 5:20pm. I had something to eat, and then went up to see Henrietta... I have a train ticket.'

Erika had pulled out her notebook and there was silence as she finished writing it down.

'Was Vicky sociable? Did she have many visitors?' she asked.

'Her sister, and her boyfriend, mainly visited, when I saw them that is,' said Charles. Henrietta nodded in agreement.

'What's his name?'

'Shawn Macavity. He lived here for a time with Victoria.'

'*Illegally*, I might add,' said Henrietta.

'How did he live here illegally?' said Erika.

'All of the tenancy agreements state that only the person or persons listed on the agreement can reside on the property. A tenancy agreement is a legal document, no?' said Henrietta. A bright yellow van pulled up in front of the garden with Derren Bryant Locksmith written in big letters on its side.

'If you'll excuse me, I have to deal with this,' said Charles, hurrying to meet the man getting out of the van.

'Charles is a good man. Misunderstood. He's not had an easy life. I've certainly benefitted from his loyal friendship,' said Henrietta in a low voice as they watched Charles usher the locksmith inside. 'He works as my caretaker for the building, but in a very loose sense. He provides light maintenance for the communal areas, organises the gardeners, and if anything needs fixing. He's trustworthy and honest.'

'Does he have a key to all the flats?' asked Moss.

'Good lord, no. As I said, it's a very loose arrangement. The flats are all private residences.'

'What about the other residents? There are only a few other neighbours?' asked Erika.

'Beryl Wentworth upstairs keeps herself to herself. Ray is

away most of the year, he works in China, something to do with computers. The Bulgarian girls are *lovely*. Sophia and Maria. So clever and polite. Trainee doctors. It's so nice to see foreigners here earning their keep.'

'Are they at home today?' asked Erika, ignoring the barb.

'No, we just knocked on their door. I know they work enormously long hours... night shifts.' She looked around at the churned-up garden. 'It's rather cold, will you help me upstairs? I can show you my studio,' she added, looking up at Peterson and offering her arm.

13

The lobby looked different in the daylight. The walls were a bright, cerulean blue, and the light pouring in through the windows seemed to dance across the paintwork.

Henrietta glanced at the closed door to Vicky's flat where crime scene tape was pasted across, sealing it shut.

'How bad is it in there?' she asked Peterson. He opened his mouth, and hesitated. 'Ah, as bad as that,' she added. Her face was ashen.

Charles's front door was closed and they could hear the rattle of the locksmith working on the other side of the door. Henrietta moved steadily but slowly to the lift at the back of the lobby, gripping onto Peterson's arm. Erika and Moss followed. They used the lift to travel up the three floors, and when they emerged onto the top, the ceiling was a few feet higher than it was on the other floors, and the landing had a long row of skylights which added to the feeling of lightness and space. There was a door on each side of the hallway.

'My studio is here,' said Henrietta. She took a set of keys from her pocket, and unlocked the door. 'Do come inside.'

Erika wondered why she'd brought them here – was it to show off her work? The studio was one huge open-plan room with a glass wall at one end and spectacular views out over London and Blackheath. The sun glimmered behind the clouds and it looked like a storm was brewing on the horizon. The back wall had a tall wooden shelf containing bottles of chemicals, and art supplies. There was a chest freezer and an old Red Bull branded fridge with a clear glass door filled with boxes of camera film.

'That's my darkroom,' said Henrietta, indicating a door beside the chest freezer.

The remaining walls were crowded with beautiful photos depicting textures and bold colours, and incredibly intricate shapes. In one photo Erika saw the uniformed ridges of the sand on a crystal-clear seabed, and in another it looked like an extreme close-up of ice crystals.

'What's this?' asked Moss, who was equally puzzled, along with Peterson, by a photo of a roughly textured silver disc.

'That is a coin, minted in the Norman era. It's an extreme magnification of the coin's edge,' said Henrietta, coming to join them and peering up at the photo. 'I have another one here of a snooker ball,' she said, pointing at a photo which looked like the rocky surface of a cliff face. 'When magnified to the extreme, there are peaks and troughs which wouldn't look out of place in a mountain range.'

'And what's this?' asked Peterson, pointing to a photo of a reddish mass which contained various bubbles and feathery fronds.

'The digestive tract of a horse. I didn't have the whole horse here in the studio, just the intestine. I've been doing a series of photos on the flesh and anatomy of wild animals. Hence, the freezer,' she said, pointing her stick at the chest freezer humming at the back of the room. A look passed between Erika, Moss and

Peterson. Henrietta caught it, and fixed her poached-egg Midas stare on Erika.

'What is it, officers?'

'Did any of your photography projects involve cats?' asked Erika.

'Yes.'

'And did you ask Charles to dispose of these cats?'

'Yes. Yesterday, after we had drinks, I asked him to deposit the bodies of two dead cats, which I had in this freezer, into the communal refuse bins.'

'Where did you find the dead cats?' asked Erika, feeling triumph but also a sense of alarm that her instincts about Charles had been wrong.

Henrietta hobbled over to a cluttered desk by the window, and leafed through a pile of papers.

'Ah, here,' she said, holding out a piece of paper. Erika moved to the desk and took it. 'I have to keep official records for the Arts Council, they fund a portion of my work. That's an invoice, of sorts, from Fogle and Harris Vets in Dulwich. The bodies of two cats, who sadly had to be put to sleep, were donated to me for photographic use.'

Erika scanned the invoice.

'How long do you keep the animals before you dispose of them?'

'I freeze them, and then thaw to photograph. I do have to be careful about decay, I only have an hour before things get nasty. I dispose of the smaller remains the night before bin day, so they're not hanging around and stinking up the communal rubbish bins. It's all legal.'

'Why didn't Charles tell us?' said Erika. 'He could have saved us a lot of time.'

'I've asked him not to tell people about this particular project. People can be very sensitive about these things.'

'But it went so far. We arrested him,' said Moss.

'Charles is very loyal. A very good friend, to his own detriment,' said Henrietta.

'Did Vicky ever talk to you about the arrangement you had with this local vet?' asked Erika. Henrietta looked up at her and her thick eyebrows knitted together in confusion.

'Why in heaven's name would she?'

Erika briefly detailed Vicky's podcast, and the episode she recorded about the Croydon Cat Killer.

Henrietta shook her head.

'No, no. I have no knowledge of this, what do you call it?'

'Podcast.'

'What is a podcast?'

'It's like a radio programme,' said Moss.

'Well, she never spoke to me about that. And as I say, I keep my own work very private. This is a very quiet street. A quiet building. I'm taken aback that this awful thing has happened here.'

'Why didn't Charles just tell us the reason he had the dead cats in the bag?' said Erika when they came back out to the car. She looked down at the invoice from the vet. 'He was legitimately disposing of them.'

'He did hit a police officer,' said Moss.

'But that's nothing to do with Vicky Clarke's murder... Isaac has estimated Vicky's death between 3pm and 7pm. Charles would have had to murder her between five and six, and clean himself up to go up to Henrietta's for drinks,' said Erika. Peterson arrived back at the car from the flats.

'Charles just gave me his train ticket and receipt from Monday,' he said, holding them up. 'He bought his ticket at

Blackheath train station just up the road at 1:55pm. And he took the 2:03pm train to London Bridge.'

Erika took them both from him and saw the timestamp on the receipt.

'He paid cash,' she said. 'But we can request the station CCTV. Did he tell you what time train he took back here?'

'Yes. He said he took the 5pm train back from London Bridge. It takes around twelve minutes, add on a few minutes' walk back from the station and it has him back here at Honeycomb Court by 5:20pm,' said Peterson.

'Has Isaac made that time of death official?' asked Moss.

'Not yet,' said Erika. 'We just have his estimate that Vicky Clarke was killed between 3pm and 7pm.'

'He could have done it, he had half an hour,' said Moss.

'You saw his flat, where would he have cleaned up afterwards? And disposed of the murder weapon? Bloody clothes? It's very tight.'

'What about Vicky's bathroom? The killer could have cleaned up there,' said Moss.

'Yes. Again, we're waiting on the DNA evidence from the crime scene,' said Erika. They sat in silence for a moment.

'I want to talk to those sisters, the Bulgarians, who live opposite. We still don't know if they were in on Monday,' said Erika. 'But first I want to pay Vicky's boyfriend a visit.'

14

Erika studied the buttons on the doorbell. There were six 'units' in the building where Shawn Macavity lived. Three of them looked to be businesses: 'BUZZY BEE CREATIVE' was below 'TIPPY TAPPY TOES LTD' and 'YOGA PET'. The name 'SHAWN M' was scribbled in biro on a little piece of paper above 'MR AEGEDFIST' and 'PERRY GORDON'.

Moss leant over to ring the bell just as the door opened and a young woman with long curly dark hair and a trench coat came hurrying out clutching her Oyster card and her handbag over her shoulder. She didn't give them a second look as she ran up towards the passage with her high heels clacking.

'Late for the train, that's London life for you,' said Peterson, turning, along with Moss, to watch the woman as she ran. Erika was pleased they didn't have to ring the bell. The element of surprise worked quite well.

At the end of the corridor a set of stairs led up to three closed doors. Shawn's flat was at the end. The whole building seemed to be badly constructed, with thin rattling walls, and their feet echoed as they walked.

Erika knocked on the door and a moment passed. She knocked again, and finally a skinny young man opened the door. He was only wearing a pair of baggy wine-coloured briefs, and he had a shock of long dark hair down to his shoulders. His eyes had a haunted look.

'Hello?' he said. They could see past him into a modern bedsit with a tiny kitchen and an open sofa bed.

'Shawn Macavity?' asked Erika.

'Yes,' he said, narrowing his eyes in confusion. He had a warm northern accent.

'I'm Detective Chief Inspector Erika Foster, and this is Detective Inspector Moss and Detective Inspector Peterson,' said Erika as they all flashed their warrant cards. 'We need to talk to you about your girlfriend.'

'Who?' he said. He folded his arms. The wind from the draughty corridor gave him goose pimples on his pale flesh.

'Vicky Clarke,' said Peterson.

'Vicky?' he said. 'We're not boyfriend and girlfriend. Not for a while. We're more like friends now...' He was tapping his bare foot on the floor, Erika noted, and seemed jittery. 'What's Vicky done?'

'Could we come inside?'

He hesitated, and moved to let them in, and closed the door behind them.

'What makes you think she's done something?' asked Peterson.

'You guys look the business, plain clothes. I just assumed...'

'I'm very sorry to tell you that Vicky was found dead last night,' said Erika. She watched closely as his face seemed to sag.

'Vicky?' he said.

'Yes.'

'Vicky's dead?' he repeated, incredulously.

'I'm afraid so.'

He sank down onto the sofa bed, with a melodramatic thud of the mattress springs, and put his head in his hands.

'I don't understand. Where?' he said, looking up at Erika.

'Her sister found her body at her flat in Honeycomb Court.'

'Vicky?' he said again. He was silent for a moment, and then he seemed to recover himself. 'Was there a break-in at her flat? I told her to be careful about locking her door. That area has really gone downhill.'

'We're still investigating,' said Erika. She looked around the bedsit. It was a mess of clothes and papers. Filthy dishes were piled up in the sink, and in the corner, a guitar sat on a stand next to an electric keyboard.

'Can we ask where you were yesterday between 3pm and 7pm?' asked Peterson.

'You think *I* did it?' he said, his voice rising in panic.

'We're asking everyone who was close to Vicky the same question,' said Erika.

'In the evening I was at work... Just here, at the Golden Lamb,' he said, pointing towards the window.

'What time did you start work?'

'Six until close, about eleven thirty, but I got there a bit earlier, maybe quarter to... It would take me about an hour to get here from Blackheath on public transport, so there's no way I could have been there at that time,' he said, clutching dramatically at his long straggly hair.

'And where were you between 3pm and five forty-five?'

'I was here all day, chilling, having a nap, until five twenty. I had a shower, ate a sandwich and I left to go to work at five forty-five. It's only up the road.'

'Can anyone corroborate this, that you were here all day?' asked Peterson.

'Well, no, but I was here.'

'When did you last see Vicky?' asked Erika.

'A week or so ago. We, er, she records her podcast on a Thursday and I've been writing and performing the incidental music sometimes... Wait, it wasn't last Thursday but the Thursday before. It was the eleventh I last saw her, at her flat.'

'And how did Vicky seem?'

'Fine. Vicky's dead? Really?'

'Yes.'

'I can't believe it. I thought Tess, her sister, would have phoned me. Does she know?'

'Yes. She found Vicky.'

'Yeah. Of course. Shit.'

'Do you have a good relationship with Tess?'

'I know her, sort of. She and Vicky don't get on all the time.'

'Why?'

'She's never approved of Vicky being an actor. I'm an actor too. We trained together. Her podcast... She was starting to do really well, with the podcast about true crime... She was trying to get sponsorship – right now she's only making a few quid from affiliate links.' Shawn still seemed distracted and in shock.

'Was there anything she was mixed up in that could have put her in danger?' asked Erika, wishing she had more information about the podcast episodes.

He seemed to zone out for a moment, and then came back.

'No. I think she's talked mainly to the victims of crimes. She hasn't been talking to anyone dangerous, not that I know.'

'Did she mention anything about anyone odd hanging around the flats?' asked Moss.

'It's London. You've got to take the rough with the smooth when it comes to odd people.'

'What do you mean?' asked Erika.

'No she hadn't mentioned anyone odd. I'm from Burnley and everyone is much nicer, friendly. It was a shock when I first came to London. There are a couple of girls who live on her floor, student nurses – they're nice.' He was gabbling now, unable to focus on one thing.

'Do you mean Vicky's neighbours across the hall? They're student doctors,' said Erika.

'Yeah. I've only met them once or twice. The woman who owns the building is a bit of an old cow, or can be, and she's got this weird guy pal. Charles. He's a bit nosy.'

'How?'

'Every time someone arrives or leaves, he's there, like a spy. He caused a hoo-ha when I stayed there, saying we were violating the terms of the lease. Tess sorted it out with Henrietta. I was paying rent, and Tess owns the flat. I just can't believe Tess didn't tell me, and she found the... she found Vicky's body?'

'Yes,' said Erika.

'I can't believe it,' he said, melodramatically. 'Can't believe she's dead.'

***

'What do you think?' asked Erika when she and Moss came back to the car parked on Forest Hill high street.

'He seems highly strung,' said Moss.

'We did just tell him about Vicky.'

'I know, but does it strike you as weird how many times he asked us to confirm it? He kept saying "Vicky? Really?" Over and over.'

'Yes, but there isn't a textbook reaction.'

'Come on. We've been doing this a long time. Something was off, wasn't it?'

'Yeah,' agreed Erika. Moss was right, there was something off that she couldn't put her finger on. 'He's an actor. Do you think he was acting?'

'If he was, he needs to get his money back from that drama school. He wasn't very convincing,' said Moss.

Peterson emerged from the Golden Lamb pub, waited for a gap in the traffic and sprinted back across the road to the car.

'Okay. His alibi checks out. The manager said Shawn arrived at ten to six for his shift. He stayed until closing.'

Erika thought for a moment.

'He could have killed her and made it back in time. He had ample time. He doesn't have a car. If he did kill her, he'd have to do it and then travel back to Forest Hill for work. Let's pull CCTV from public transport in the area.'

15

On the drive back from Forest Hill to Lewisham Row, Moss was next to Erika in the passenger seat. Peterson was sitting in the back seat, talking on his phone to Crane back in the incident room, asking him to find CCTV footage from Blackheath train station so they could check out Charles Wakefield's alibi.

'If Shawn was at Vicky's flat around the time she was killed, there's a good chance he passed that bus stop,' said Moss. 'He doesn't own a car. He would either have to go on foot, bike, or public transport.'

'Or Uber,' said Erika. 'Ask Crane to look at Uber journeys and taxis,' she added to Peterson in the back. He nodded.

'Nothing from Isaac,' said Erika, glancing at her phone.

'It's early days,' said Moss.

'He'd told me he was going to conduct the post-mortem last night, as soon as he got back to the morgue.'

'It's only just past lunchtime,' said Moss. Erika nodded, trying not to feel her impatience turn to annoyance. Isaac was a brilliant pathologist, and he was also a good friend. She knew that barring something unforeseen, he would come back with at least preliminary results. At a set of traffic lights, she dialled his number. It went straight to voicemail and she left him a message asking if he was okay, and to call her.

The incident room was busy when they got back.

'Boss, I've got Fiona Watson on the line,' said Crane, holding out the phone to Erika with his hand over the receiver.

'Who?'

'She's the Family Liaison Officer for Tess Clarke.'

Erika nodded and took the phone.

'Do we have any news on when you'd like Tess to formally identify her sister's body?' asked Fiona. She had a slightly camp, dry delivery.

'Our forensic pathologist is usually very fast, but I'm waiting to hear back from him,' said Erika, pulling her phone out of her pocket to check for a missed call or message from Isaac.

'Tess wants to know if she can leave.'

'Of course. Where does she want to go?'

'Work…' Fiona lowered her voice. 'Jasper, that's the husband, he's been ringing her all morning, saying that he can't manage at the restaurant on his own.'

'They've opened their restaurant today?'

'Yes. Apparently, they've got a lot of lunch bookings,' she said, with a tinge of disdain. 'It's just around the corner from where they live.'

'Have you spoken to the husband, Jasper?' asked Erika.

'Yes. I saw him at breakfast. He made us all a big fry-up. Black pudding, the works.'

Erika looked back at the crime scene photos on the wall. The violence of Vicky's stab wounds, her face and hair covered in dried blood.

'Even if I hear back, we won't be able to arrange an identification until later this afternoon,' said Erika.

'Okay,' said Fiona. 'I'll go with them to the restaurant, in case you need to get hold of them quickly. Keep me posted.'

'Everything okay?' asked Crane when Erika came off the phone. He was sitting at his desk with a computer screen filled with video files. Erika ran her fingers through her hair.

'If your sister died hideously, would you take the next day off work?'

'Depends what I did. If I was a brain surgeon and I had an important operation, I'd probably go in,' he said. 'If it was my mother-in-law, I'd be popping open the champagne.' Erika laughed.

'No. It's Vicky's sister and her husband. They run a restaurant in Blackheath. And it's a Tuesday lunchtime. I just thought they might close, out of respect.'

Crane nodded.

'That's reasonable to expect,' he said.

Erika went on, 'The launderette where I used to live in Forest Hill was always closing if one of the old ladies who worked there died.'

'Maybe it's the older generation who have more respect and value for life. Or maybe they can't close the restaurant, cos they need the money?'

Erika nodded and frowned.

'Fiona, the Family Liaison, just said that the brother-in-law made them a big cooked breakfast this morning, the works, blood pudding. Is that weird?'

'The blood pudding?'

'The sister was stabbed to death the night before. Tess finds her body. Then the next morning, they're up as usual, tucking into a big greasy cooked breakfast. It's weird. Isn't it?'

'People are weird, boss. Don't forget that. And being weird doesn't necessarily mean criminal,' said Crane.

'Okay, you're right,' said Erika. 'Sorry to bug you.'

'Any time,' he said. He turned back to his computer and clicked on a video file showing a view of the concourse and ticket office at Blackheath train station. Erika turned back to her computer and stared at the screen before googling *'Do restaurants close for family bereavement?'* She then deleted it, feeling stupid.

The rest of the afternoon crawled by. There was so much information coming into the incident room, and it all had to be checked and followed up on. Erika left two more messages for Isaac. By 8pm, everyone had gone home, and Erika decided to call it a day.

When she reached the exit to the car park, she was about to pull out of the junction, when she remembered what Peterson had said about the bed sale nearby. The last thing she wanted to do was visit a bed shop, but the thought of sleeping on bare floorboards spurred her on.

When she pulled up outside Bed World, the car park was busy, despite the late hour. Scrawled on the window in huge black and red bubble writing was: DOUBLE QUEEN AND KING DISCOUNT MADNESS!

Erika got out of her car and went inside, determined to buy the first decent bed she saw, and then skedaddle. There were a few other people milling around, and as Erika went to look at a queen bed with a nice modern-looking headboard, she saw Peterson and Fran two beds over. He was lying on the mattress and she was sitting on the end, testing the 'give'.

Erika was about to turn round and leave when they both looked up and saw her. Peterson froze, and then sat up. An odd look crossed his face, as if he'd been caught in bed with the wrong person. Fran got up and smoothed down her skirt.

'Shopping for beds?' she asked. Erika paused and looked around.

'I could use you on my team, with those powers of deduction,' she said. She meant it to come out jokingly, but she heard her voice and it sounded catty.

'Erika was telling me she didn't have a bed in her new house, and I told her this place was doing a discount,' said Peterson, who was now sitting up and adjusting his tie.

'Yes, sleeping on an airbed isn't much fun,' said Erika. *You could have told me you were thinking of coming here tonight*, she thought. There was an awkward pause.

'Well, nice to see you. We'll let you get on,' said Fran. And she turned her back on Erika, and started to talk about the width of the bed and if it would fit into their bedroom.

Peterson gave Erika an apologetic nod and turned away. Erika moved off to the other end of the store. Her heart was beating fast and she felt embarrassed. Glancing around wildly, she saw she'd stumbled into the children's section, which was full of beds shaped like racing cars, and dinosaurs, and there was even one which looked like a giant glow-worm. A little girl was bouncing up and down on the racing car bed, gripping the steering wheel.

Erika crossed to the other side of the store, and saw it was all couples, and couples with children, and she suddenly felt exposed for her single childlessness. A tall teenage boy, in a black suit like Lurch from *The Addams Family*, appeared at her elbow.

'May I help you, madam?' he intoned. He had a tape measure around his neck, and he reminded Erika more of an undertaker than a bed salesman.

'Yes. I want to buy that bed. Now,' she said, pointing.

'Lovely, madam. This is a *very* good choice. This particular bed has a patented four level internal spring system, impregnated with anti-bacterial, organically sourced cotton. And I can see, if you don't mind me saying, that you are a taller lady...'

'Yes, I'll buy it,' said Erika, cutting off his patter. Fran and Peterson were now lying side by side on an exotic-looking four-poster bed with a chiffon canopy. Fran was holding his hand and laughing loudly.

'Of course, madam.'

'I am in a hurry.'

'Yes, but can I interest you in our range of counterpanes impregnated with real silver? Providing 100% protection against bacteria and MRSA,' said Lurch.

'I just want to buy that fucking bed,' said Erika, losing her temper. His eyebrows shot into his hairline.

'*Madam*. Here at Bed World, we don't tolerate abusive behaviour...' he started to say. Erika's phone rang in her bag, and when she pulled it out, she was relieved to see it was Isaac. She moved away from Lurch and answered the call.

'Hi. I've been trying to call you, is everything okay?' asked Erika.

'I'm sorry, there have been some confusing developments, and I needed to be sure before I called you,' he said, sounding weary on the end of the phone.

'What is it?'

'It's the body of that young woman you found last night. It isn't Victoria Clarke.'

16

The entrance to the morgue was next to the tall chimney of the hospital incinerator, and when Erika parked and got out of her car, there was a nasty sweet smell of burning in the cold air. She pulled the neck of her sweater up and over her nose, and hurried to the door where Isaac was waiting for her, sitting in the darkness of the reception area where the only light came from a computer screen at the front desk.

'Hello,' he said wearily. 'Should I have waited until tomorrow to call you?'

'No. I need to know,' said Erika. She checked her watch; it was almost 10pm.

'I just needed a few minutes in the darkness,' he said, getting up. 'I've been working under bright lights for sixteen hours. Shall we go down?'

'Yes,' said Erika. 'I just don't understand. The sister found the body. We all took our cues from her.'

They moved down a long, sloping corridor with a low ceiling, their footsteps echoing off the concrete walls.

'I pulled Victoria Clarke's medical records just before I did the post-mortem,' said Isaac. 'It showed she was a healthy young woman. She'd never been to hospital. Never had an operation or any broken bones, not even a filling, which is impressive at twenty-seven.'

They reached a tall metal door, and Isaac opened it with his card key. A puff of cold air hit Erika, and they moved into the dimly-lit morgue. A long row of tall fridges hummed, and at the end of a row of stainless-steel post-mortem tables lay the small form of the young woman.

Erika walked towards the body, passing through the pools of shade to where it lay under a bright light. She tried to think back to the previous evening, when she'd seen her lying on the bed. The young woman on the table looked completely different. She was all beige. Her long dark hair was brushed back off her head, and had been washed clean of blood. Her face sagged with an open mouth, the jaw dropping down to elongate the face. The cheeks were hollow and the bloodlessness of her face made it hard to differentiate between the skin of her lips, cheeks and eyelids. A huge bruise stood up on her forehead, altering the symmetry of her face. Erika saw there was a small coin-sized clump of hair missing at the hairline on the left side of her head.

On a practical level, corpses were stripped of the adornments that indicate their lifestyle, their personalities – clothes, jewellery, and make-up. Death made the skin shrivel, and the face collapse and contract. Sometimes, a dead body would look as if the person was merely asleep. More often than not, they looked completely different to how they appeared in life.

'This young woman has had all of her wisdom teeth removed,' said Isaac, breaking the silence. 'I also found a faint hairline scar along her spine, and when I excised the area... cut it open, I found that she had spinal fusion surgery as a child. There was a small titanium rod in her back connecting three vertebrae.

This is an operation used to correct problems with the spine in adolescence.'

Erika stared at the body with the stitched-up y-shaped incision in the chest.

'Let me take you through the results of my post-mortem,' said Isaac.

Erika nodded.

'I can officially put the time of death between 5pm and 7pm, narrowing the window down. You found her body at eight fifteen?'

'Almost on the dot... That's when I went past the flats and heard the sister, Tess, scream. Well, she's not her sister. Did she really not realise this wasn't Vicky?'

'They have a similar build, and the same hair and eye colour. There are even similarities in the shape of their faces. And she was badly beaten and bloodied. Her left cheekbone is fractured, caused by a severe blow to the head. This is the same side as the bruising on her face, and this alters the shape of the face. And her top left incisor is chipped.'

Isaac handed her an evidence bag with a length of wire in a messy tangle.

'Her wrists were bound with wire. Copper electrical wire,' he said.

'Wire. Jesus,' said Erika, taking the bag.

'You can see where the wire cut into her skin,' said Isaac, gently lifting her left arm and then right and showing the deep lacerations on the skin around her wrists. He placed her arms back, and then carefully folded back the sheet covering her body.

'She was stabbed twenty-six times, and as you can see, all of these cover her body. She has some minor bruising to her upper arms, her right ribcage. Hair pulled from her left temple. No signs of sexual assault. And there were no drugs or alcohol in her bloodstream.'

'A crazed, random attack,' said Erika, feeling revulsion at the number of stab wounds covering her arms and legs, torso, breasts and her neck.

'Two of these stab wounds punctured her left lung, another hit the subclavian artery, as I suspected, which is a major blood vessel located in the thorax.' Isaac indicated the chest area. 'This major artery carries oxygen-rich blood from the heart to parts of the upper body, including the arms, head and neck. The subclavian arteries are on both sides of the body,' said Isaac, indicating on both sides of his neck down into his chest. 'There were two further stab wounds on the right side of the chest, and one of these punctured the superior vena cava which is a major artery connected to the heart. This, along with the stab to the subclavian artery, resulted in the catastrophic blood loss.'

'How long did it take her to die?'

'Her attacker hit two major arteries, but her heart would have remained pumping blood. If she was fighting to get away and out of the room, the rate of blood loss would have increased with her heart rate. It would still have taken several minutes.'

Erika looked back at the young woman. The minutes must have felt like hours for her, scared and bleeding to death.

'You said you thought she was rolled up into the mattress of the sofa bed?'

'Yes. Both of her shoulders were dislocated, and her neck is broken. I think her attacker bound her wrists when she was on the bed, and then he rolled her up in the mattress with the bed frame, and he used his weight to trap her inside. I think he was crouching on top as he stabbed at her through the mattress. His weight bearing down on her body rolled up inside would have caused her shoulders to dislocate and her neck to break.'

Erika had to take a deep breath and focus. This poor woman's death had been horrific.

She took her phone from her pocket and scrolled through to

find the photo of Vicky from the acting website. Isaac came around the table to join her, and Erika put her phone screen with the photo of Vicky next to the woman's face on the post-mortem table.

'The nose is similar. So is her hairline, but her lips are thinner and the eyes have a more almond-like shape, almost cat-like,' he said.

'Do you have any idea who she is?' asked Erika.

'No.'

Erika let out a long exhale. 'I now have an unidentified body, and a missing person.'

17

'Would you like to come and get some coffee?' asked Isaac, when they were outside in the morgue car park.

'That would be perfect right now, but I have to tell Tess Clarke that this body isn't her sister. I don't want to wait until morning.'

'I understand,' said Isaac. Erika took out her phone and the camera activated to unlock the screen with facial recognition.

'Oh my God, that's not pretty,' said Erika, seeing how old she looked, illuminated by the orange-tinged floodlights in the car park.

'You don't look old. It's just bad lighting,' said Isaac.

'I know you're lying, but thanks.'

'I've disabled the facial recognition on my phone.'

'Are you worried about the security aspect?'

'No. I just don't like seeing myself up that close!'

Despite the bleakness of her visit to the morgue, Erika laughed.

'Listen. I'll take you up on that coffee. Come over one night this week and see the new house, you're only around the corner,' said Erika. Isaac smiled and gave her a hug.

'Okay. I will. Don't work too hard. I'll see you soon.'

After Erika said goodnight to Isaac in the morgue car park, she sat in her car, and stared into the middle distance for a long moment, thinking of the young woman and the horrific violence she'd endured, and shed a quiet tear. A loud whip-crack made her jump, and then another, as two large raindrops hit the windscreen. There was a moment of pause and then the sky opened and the car was pummelled with rain. She looked through the rippling windscreen at the giant chimney belching out black smoke against the orange sky.

Ashes to ashes, dust to dust.

Erika tried to arrange the thoughts in her tired brain. She had to tell Tess Clark, that was a priority. And then they would have to identify this poor young woman, and find out what she was doing in Vicky Clarke's bed. Vicky was now a missing person, and whoever killed this unidentified woman now had a greater head start. And, of course, now Isaac had narrowed down the window for the time of death, it meant that Charles Wakefield or Shawn Macavity would have had a much smaller window of time to commit the murder. But who exactly were they now in the frame for killing? This case was now a mess, and Erika hated messy.

Erika drove over to Blackheath, and with a heavy heart, knocked on Tess Clarke's front door. They lived in a squat terraced house in a road which looked down over the heath.

There was a rattle of keys and Fiona, the Family Liaison Officer, opened the door. She wore a grey towelling dressing gown over a pair of royal blue pyjamas.

'What are you doin' here so late?' she said. Fiona's mouth was always grim-set with a jowly dissatisfaction, as if she'd been forced to consume a diet entirely of lemon juice.

'Are Tess and her husband home?'

'Yes. It would be helpful to know what's going on?'

'Please can you get them to come downstairs,' said Erika. She stepped inside, past Fiona, and closed the front door.

'I think they're asleep,' said Fiona, rolling her tongue around her mouth. The downstairs room was a kitchen and living room combined, and the low ceiling gave the room a poky feel, despite its size. Fiona had a sleeping bag on the sofa, there was a steaming cup of cocoa on the coffee table, and an episode of *NCIS: Los Angeles* was just beginning on the TV with the sound down low.

'I need you to go and wake them up, please.'

Fiona nodded and went off up the stairs. Erika heard the creak of floorboards above, and she moved across to the kitchen. It was what she would term a 'posh' kitchen, with an Aga, lots of rustic wooden furniture, and copper pans hanging from the ceiling. The window looked out onto a small paved yard with an ancient-looking tree, its bare branches moving in the wind. Erika noticed above the Aga there was a long magnetic strip with a row of lethal-looking knives.

A tall, lean man came down the stairs, followed by Tess and Fiona. The man wore a thin blue T-shirt and football shorts, which emphasised his muscular physique, and he had black hair cropped very short. One of his arms was awash with a sleeve of coloured swirled tattoos, and his wrists and fingers were heavy with silver bracelets and rings. Tess's short black hair was on end, and she wore a dressing gown similar to Fiona's.

'Hello, sorry to call on you so late. Are you Jasper?' Erika asked.

'Yeah,' he said, rubbing at his bloodshot eyes. Tess held the collar of her dressing gown tight to her neck.

'Is everything all right?' she asked. 'Are you here to ask that I formally identify Vicky?'

'No,' said Erika. There was an awkward pause. Tess turned to Fiona.

'I don't know what's going on,' Fiona said, folding her arms.

'Please, can you both sit down…' Erika said.

'Just tell me now, I don't like this,' said Tess, as she and Jasper went to the sofa and sat on top of the sleeping bag. Fiona eyed them for a moment, and then went to perch on the edge of an armchair.

'I'm very sorry to tell you that the body that you found in the flat at Honeycomb Court is not Vicky,' said Erika.

'What? What do you mean?' asked Tess. 'That was Vicky.'

'I'm afraid it wasn't.'

'But, I saw her, lying there.'

Jasper stared, with his mouth slightly open. Erika explained what Isaac had discovered during the post-mortem.

'This is a fucking joke,' said Jasper. 'Isn't it your job, as the bloody police, not to make these mistakes?' he cried.

'I'm very sorry. Your wife identified—'

'No, no, no,' he said, standing up and waggling his finger at Erika. 'Don't you blame my wife. This is typical of the bloody authorities…'

Erika looked at him and wondered exactly how this was typical. *Did Tess have another sibling who'd been wrongly identified as a murder victim?* She bit her lip.

'I can only apologise. In our defence, the woman shares similar features with Vicky,' she said. There was a long silence.

'If that wasn't Vicky… then who was it? That poor woman?' asked Tess, putting her hands to her face, reliving what she'd seen.

'I can't comment on that yet,' said Erika after a pause. 'I've come to you straight from the results of the post-mortem.'

She could see the incredulous looks on their faces.

'Vicky's not dead? She's alive?' said Tess.

'We're now classing Vicky as a missing person.'

'Missing. Have you tried tracking her phone? What about her credit cards?' asked Tess, standing up. She moved to the kitchen and grabbed her phone, which was charging on the counter, and dialled a number. There was a moment of silence as they all watched her make the call. 'It's gone straight to voicemail... Vicky, it's Tess. Where are you? Please can you call me as soon as you get this message!' She ended the call and didn't seem to know what to do next. She replaced the phone on its charger. 'What are you doing about this? You're just standing there looking at me!'

'We're reacting to this as fast as we can—' started Erika.

'Oh, well, *that's* good to hear,' said Jasper, his voice dripping with sarcasm.

'Sir. Vicky is now a missing person, and we'll be opening a missing persons case.'

'And when are you planning to do that?'

'That's happening as we speak,' said Erika. He shook his head and then saw Tess had started to cry. He got up and went to put his arm around her, but she swerved out from under it and crossed back to the kitchen, where she tore off a piece of kitchen towel and wiped her eyes.

'It would really help us if you could make a list of people who Vicky knew – *knows*,' said Erika. 'Friends, work colleagues, anyone else you can think of. Was she close to anyone who worked at your restaurant?'

'No. Vicky isn't popular at work, due to her habit of not showing up for shifts,' said Jasper.

'Don't...' started Tess, fixing him with a hard stare.

'Don't. Don't what? Speak ill of the dead? She's not dead now, is she?' Jasper seemed to realise that they weren't alone, and took a deep breath. 'I've always tried to help Vicky with the life she's chosen as a sometime actress.'

'*Actor*,' corrected Tess. He shot her another stare, rolled his eyes.

'Has Vicky gone away without telling you before?' asked Erika.

'Where would she go? She never has any money,' said Jasper. 'Tess has become this support group for her, supporting her, feeding her, lending her money. We often don't do things because Vicky is coming too and she doesn't have any money so we all have to go without!' He stopped himself.

'A day has gone by, and she's out there, missing,' said Tess, turning to Erika with a pleading look on her face. 'Please do everything you can to find her... I thought I'd lost her once, I couldn't bear to lose her again.'

18

Vicky Clarke crouched on the mattress hugging her knees to her chest. The storm raging outside had woken her, and she was scared and disorientated. It had taken a moment to remember where she was. The wind whistled and groaned and seemed to rock the house. A crash of thunder was followed by a bright flicker of lightning. The room was small, and there were no curtains. Lightning strobed again, illuminating the clouds behind the thick bars on the window. *Bars on the window*, she thought with a shudder. A heavy wooden wardrobe was at the base of the bed, and in the mirror, Vicky caught sight of her reflection. She looked like a scared animal, crouching on the mattress with her knees drawn up to her chest.

The ceiling creaked and something outside the door rattled. She shivered and pulled the long folds of the nightgown around her cold legs.

With another strobe of lightning, Vicky was seized with dread when she saw the high-backed chair next to the bed was empty. A cold sweat broke out between her shoulder blades. She'd gone to sleep with her backpack on the chair. Where was her backpack? Then she saw with relief that it had fallen off the arm, and now lay between the chair and the wall. There was another, long rumble, and a crash of lightning. She got up and retrieved the backpack, fumbling with the straps to get it open. She felt around inside, amongst the change of clothes she'd grabbed at the last minute, the wallet with her passport and money, her toiletry bag, and there, tucked at the bottom, was the small computer hard drive, the size of a glasses case. It was cold in her hand, and just seeing it filled her with an overwhelming fear.

There was a knock at the door, and she jumped. She pushed the hard drive back to the bottom of the backpack, and fastened the straps.

'Victoria?' came a woman's voice, raised above the storm. The knock came again. 'Darling, are you okay?' Another crash of thunder made the glass in the windows judder.

'Yes,' she replied, her voice croaky. She cleared her throat. 'Yes. I'm okay.' She moved across the room, feeling the cold stone floor under her feet, and she unlocked and opened the door.

Her friend and ex-teacher, Cilla Stone, was standing in the corridor. She was in her early sixties and dressed flamboyantly in a long mink fur coat, and a black character turban. She held up an old-fashioned oil lamp, which cast a warm orange glow around her and made the fur coat shine.

'I can't sleep in this *beastly* storm. Can you?' said Cilla. Her voice rang out in the corridor with a soft Scottish brogue that Vicky had always found so calming.

'No,' said Vicky, smiling weakly.

'Come on, sweetheart, I'll get the fire going in the living room, and we'll have a nip of something. Ride out the storm together!'

Cilla smiled dramatically, and Vicky noted that even though it was the middle of the night, she had applied fresh scarlet lipstick. Vicky followed Cilla and the light of the glowing oil lamp down a corridor lined with bookshelves. Thunder seemed to tear and rip at the house above, and Vicky's teeth started to chatter loudly. Cilla turned at the sound, and stopped at a large heavy wooden wardrobe. She opened the door. The lamp light shimmered across a line of fur coats hanging inside.

'You're frozen! Go on, grab yourself a wee fur coat... They've already kicked the bucket, you know. Help them fulfil their destinies, and let them warm ye up!'

Vicky was an uninvited guest, having shown up unannounced on Cilla's doorstep early on Tuesday morning, and she didn't feel like she could protest. Cilla grabbed a long brown mink coat off a hanger. 'Go on. Put it on. You'll catch your death.'

Holding her breath slightly at the smell of animal pelt, Vicky pulled the long heavy fur around her shoulders, and was suddenly glad of the warmth. She followed Cilla through into the living room, which was an Aladdin's cave of opulent furniture and antiques. A fire glowed in the grate.

'You feed the fire, and I'll make us some cocoa.'

Cilla went padding away with the lamp, leaving Vicky in darkness. The curtains were open on the two large bay windows, and the storm crashed and flickered, lighting up a vast empty beach where the waves pounded the shore. Vicky felt comforted by the fur coat and the strong heat from the embers of the fire pressing against her face. She knelt in front of the wood basket, found two pieces of kindling, and leant into the heat, pushing them into the embers. A moment later the room was lit up by the flickering flames, and she placed a bigger log on top.

She sat on the floor with her back leaning against a large squashy sofa. Cilla's house was kooky, not a word Vicky often used. It felt like a cosy haunted mansion. She huddled down in the fur coat, and was glad that she had this moment, far away from London, to draw breath and work out what to do next.

The violence of the storm seemed to be abating, and in between soft rumbles, she heard the sound of the rain falling against the windows and drumming on the roof. The warmth of the fire seemed to reach out and envelop her, and she tipped her head back, feeling the strong pull of sleep. She was jolted awake by the violent image of the young woman, lying dead on her bed in a seeping lake of blood.

Cilla came back into the room with steaming mugs on a tray, and a bottle of Glenlivet whisky.

Vicky sat up and moved her legs so Cilla could pass and put the tray on the huge coffee table by the sofa. There was silence as she poured a dash of whisky into each mug, and Vicky watched Cilla's face. She was a beautiful woman, with a smooth complexion, bright red hair and the most vibrant blue eyes which reflected the light from the fire. *Curious eyes*, Cilla called them, and she was adamant that her curious eyes, and her curiosity, had kept her young. Cilla, who was now retired, had been Vicky's teacher at drama school, and they'd formed a close friendship in the six years since she'd graduated.

She handed one of the mugs to Vicky, and those curious blue eyes searched her face, concerned and interested to know why an old student had pitched up at her door before breakfast. Vicky looked away, concentrating back on the fire where the log was now burning brightly.

'Thank you,' she said. She took a sip, and felt the warmth of the whisky, which was winning the battle for supremacy over the sweet cocoa. She hadn't eaten much – feeling unable to keep anything down – but she took a piece of the shortbread off the plate Cilla offered to her and bit into it. It was dry and crumbly, with a sweetness that exploded in the mouth when it dissolved.

'I'm sorry I had to put you down here, in the room with the bars on the window... Colin and Ray are coming to stay tomorrow morning,' said Cilla. Colin and Ray were two teachers from Goldsmith's Drama Academy. Vicky didn't know them as well as she knew Cilla, but she'd enjoyed both of their classes.

'I'm sorry. I didn't think that I'd be ruining your plans,' said Vicky.

'No! Dear God, you can stay for as long as you like. I'm just explaining why I gave you the worst room in the house.'

'I'm very grateful. Thank you for letting me stay.'

Vicky looked out of the window as the lightning flashed, lighting up the sand dunes where the long marram grass was blown flat by the gale. Cilla lived on a windswept corner on the west coast of Scotland, but it wouldn't be long until someone tracked her down. Caught up with her. Cilla took a sip of her cocoa.

'Vicky, dear. I don't want to pry, but this seems serious. You only have a wee bag with your things... Where's your phone? You're usually glued to the damn thing. Did something happen? Are you in trouble?'

Vicky wiped a tear from her cheek. She took a deep breath. 'I found...' She put her hand over her mouth, feeling sick at the memory of what she'd found.

Cilla looked concerned.

'Are you in danger?'

'Here? No. Here I feel safe. I just need to sleep,' said Vicky, silent tears running down her face.

'Okay. Don't cry. That's enough for me right now. You need sleep, you look ragged. Drink that up. The whisky will do you good.'

Vicky clutched her mug in her hands. Despite the warm coat, the fire and the heat of the whisky in her throat, she started to shiver. She felt the terror of what she had seen would never leave her.

19

Just before six the next morning, back in London, Maria Ivanova was walking from the train station back home to Honeycomb Court. She'd just finished two long sixteen-hour shifts at the hospital, and slept at the nurses' station the night before, grabbing a few hours' sleep, so she hadn't been home properly in two days.

Morrison Road was dark and empty and eerily silent. A heavy frost had coated the parked cars and they seemed to shift and glimmer under the streetlights as she moved.

Maria was so tired and focused on her bed, that she didn't notice the churned-up ground in the front garden of Honeycomb Court at first, or the crime scene tape across Vicky's flat as she crossed the lobby to her front door. It was only when she dropped her card key and looked up that she saw the tape. She froze for a moment, looking around at the empty lobby, and opened her front door.

It was very cold inside her flat, and when she flicked on the light, she saw that the living room was empty. Maria crossed to the bedroom at the back, and was surprised to see that the bedroom was empty too. She was expecting to see her sister, Sophia. Maria rummaged in her bag, and switched on her mobile phone for the first time in twelve hours.

There was no reply to the message she'd sent to Sophia almost thirteen hours ago. She scrolled through, starting to feel real panic as she saw there was a message from their mother, asking if Sophia was okay. She hadn't heard from Sophia either, which was very unusual. Both girls were in constant contact with their mother back in Bulgaria. They were a very close family.

Maria tried to call Sophia, but the phone rang out and then went to voicemail. The sisters were a year apart in age, and both in their fourth year of medical studies. In the past few months they'd been working alternate twelve-hour hour shifts in different hospitals. Sophia had lucked out with her placement at St John's Hospital in Lewisham, which was much closer to Blackheath. Maria's placement was in Hammersmith, so on top of working long shifts, she had a ninety-minute commute each way across London, which could stretch to two hours if the trains were busy. They had been working their placements for the past three weeks, and both found the pace, working in trauma medicine, thrilling and exhausting.

It hadn't been unusual for them to be like ships passing in the night in the flat they shared, but on most occasions the ships at least got to meet in the kitchen and share a few words and a cup of tea.

Perhaps she's been called in for another shift, thought Maria as she went to the fridge to see if her sister had left a note, but there was nothing. Had she gone out shopping? No, it was six o'clock in the morning. Had she met a guy? No, she would have left a message.

Maria shivered and sat on the sofa. She opened the 'find my phone' app on her phone, and logged in as Sophia. It showed that Sophia's phone was switched on. She felt a deep unease as the app loaded, and the compass graphic swung from side to side. When the map popped up, Maria was expecting to see the familiar roads around Lewisham Hospital, or a street around Blackheath, but a different map view came up and for a moment she didn't recognise the location. All she could see was a wide area of yellow, and her sister's phone looked to be in the middle of nowhere. She pinched the screen and zoomed out and then back in on the map, her heart starting to beat in her chest with panic.

The green dot representing the location of her sister's phone was in something called the Excel Waste Management Centre. As she zoomed out, she saw this was far out of London, past Dartford, near a place called Tilbury. She switched the map to satellite view, which gave more detail of the area, and there was a vast swathe of yellow sand and gravel and a huge industrial building.

Horrible images started to rush through her mind, and with shaking hands Maria dialled the emergency services. Why was Sophia's phone miles outside London, showing up on a landfill site?

20

Erika slept through her alarm, and woke at 9am, stiff and frozen on the hard wooden floor of her box room. The bright white light pouring through the gap in the thin curtains seemed to slice into her eyes, and when she sat up, her breath was coming out in vapour and she could see there was a layer of ice on the inside of the glass.

She was furious with herself. She'd called a briefing at 8am and she was an hour late. She *never* slept in. As she rushed around the house, pulling on her clothes and trying to find her car keys in the mess, she knew she had to get herself sorted with a proper bed, and heating, and hot water.

There was a thick layer of frost covering her car, and of course, she'd also run out of de-icer. She was scrubbing at the windscreen with her Tesco Club card when her phone rang. It was Moss.

'Is everything okay, boss?' Erika could hear the air of caution and discomfort in Moss's voice.

'Yes. Yes. Sorry. I'm on my way in,' she said. Her fingers were now numb, and she'd only cleared a small square of the iced-up windscreen.

'How close are you?'

'I'm still at home.'

'Maria Ivanova, one of the two sisters who live in the flat opposite Vicky Clarke's flat in Honeycomb Court, made an emergency call just after six this morning. She hasn't heard from her sister, Sophia, in over twenty-four hours, and says her sister's phone is showing up on a tracking app at a recycling centre in East London.' Erika's heart sank, and she forgot her freezing hands for a moment. 'I don't want to jump to conclusions, but I've read the log from last night. If the body we found isn't Vicky Clarke...'

'Shit. Okay. I'm just around the corner from Honeycomb Court. Can I meet you there?' said Erika. 'And can we send a uniform team out to that recycling centre, just in case?'

'Yes. Already on their way, and I'll be there ASAP,' said Moss.

When she came off the phone, Erika walked around to Morrison Road. The road was empty, and it looked strangely quiet in the grey frosty morning light.

Erika peered in through the huge glass doors of Honeycomb Court. The lobby inside was gloomy and empty. She rang the bell marked 'IVANOVA'.

'Yes?' said a quavering voice with a slight accent. Erika announced who she was, and a moment later a small, thin woman emerged from the door opposite Vicky's flat. Erika guessed that Maria Ivanova must be in her mid-twenties, but she looked very young, no more than sixteen years old. She was thin, with a muscular dancer's build, and wore tight jeans and a loose-fitting wine-coloured T-shirt. A small silver crucifix hung around her neck. Her ash-blonde hair was pulled back into a short pony-tail. When she came close to the glass door, Erika was ready with her warrant card. Up close, Maria's skin was like putty, smooth but bloodless. She was plain-faced and bird-like, with a small pointy nose and large round eyes.

'Why don't you have a uniform?' she asked sharply, looking Erika up and down. Erika realised that she must look a little dishevelled.

'I'm a plain-clothes detective. I've been working on another case, which might be connected with your sister's disappearance,' said Erika. 'Could I please come inside?'

Maria nodded and opened the door.

'Please, come through. Do you know what happened at number one?' she asked, indicating Vicky's flat as they crossed the lobby.

Jeez, she doesn't know, thought Erika.

'Let's sit down and talk,' said Erika as they went inside Maria's flat. She was trying to work out how to play this. She didn't know if the body found in Vicky's flat belonged to Sophia, but there were a few questions she could ask that could confirm this.

The flat had the same layout as Vicky's, with a combined kitchen living area and one small bedroom, but everything was the other way around.

'Please, sit down,' Maria said. Erika sat on the small sofa. Beside it, in the well of the bay window, was a folded-up duvet and pillows, and a small rail stuffed with clothes. Maria remained standing, leaning against the kitchen counter. Erika noticed a crucifix affixed to the wall above the bedroom door. There was a small flatscreen television on a long low table, and next to it were a pile of Bulgarian gossip magazines, some books, and DVDs. A table in one corner was stacked high with medical textbooks.

'When did you last see your sister?' asked Erika.

'Monday morning. I worked two long shifts and slept at the hospital.'

'Is it unusual for you not to be in contact?'

'We've been working long shifts in different hospitals. I work across London in Hammersmith and the commute is long.'

Erika went to get her notebook out of her jacket, and then realised she'd left it at home. She caught Maria watching her like a hawk. 'Can I ask you a couple of questions about Sophia's health?'

'Her health?'

'Did she have surgery on her back to insert a titanium rod?'

Maria narrowed her eyes.

'Yes... when she was a teenager. She had problems with her spine... between the thoracic vertebrae. Why do you know this?'

Erika felt her heart sink.

'Maria, please sit down.'

'No, no, no. Just tell me. What?'

Erika took a deep breath. 'On Tuesday evening, the body of a young woman was found in the flat opposite yours. Vicky's sister, Tess, made the discovery just after 8pm, and she wrongly identified the body as Vicky. It was when we did the post-mortem that the error was discovered.'

'I still don't understand,' said Maria, frowning and moving closer to Erika, looking at her intently.

'The post-mortem identified the young woman we found had a titanium rod in her back, and she'd also had her wisdom teeth removed. Vicky Clarke has never had surgery and she has her wisdom teeth. Both your sister and Vicky look similar.'

'But you're still guessing it's my sister? Yes?' she said, looking up at Erika, her face contorted in pain.

'We'll need you to confirm it's Sophia, but the medical...'

'How did she die?' interrupted Maria.

'She was stabbed,' said Erika, not knowing how much detail she should go into.

'And where was she in the flat?'

'She was found lying on the sofa bed in the living room.'

'No. It's not her. She wouldn't be there, in that flat, lying in the bed! I'm the only one who can confirm that it's her and until I do, it's not her!' she shouted.

Erika paused for a moment, wishing that Moss was here with her. Moss always knew how to speak to people, and tread that fine line between detective work and empathy.

'Can I ask if Sophia knew Vicky?'

Maria looked up.

'Hold on. If you thought it was Vicky Clarke lying there and now it's my sister, where is Vicky?'

'We don't know.'

Maria sank down onto the tiny sofa. Erika got up and filled a glass with water from the tap. She returned and handed it to Maria, who took a long drink. She put the glass down on the table.

'We know Vicky, as neighbours, not well enough to socialise. When our mother came to stay, she was kind and loaned us an air mattress and some nice bedding. She knew that we worked shifts, and she would often take in parcels for us and leave notes to say that she had them in her flat. Our mother often sends us Bulgarian sweets from home and our favourite magazines,' she said, indicating the pile by the television.

'Was Sophia perhaps closer to Vicky, without you realising?'

'We don't know it's Sophia...' Erika didn't say anything and watched as Maria pulled a tissue out of her pocket and wiped her eyes. 'I have to speak to my mother and father.'

Erika's phone beeped with a text message, and she saw it was Moss, saying she was outside the building. Maria was now on the phone, speaking in Bulgarian, so she slipped out of the flat. Moss was waiting on the other side of the glass, wearing a long thick winter coat.

Erika went to let Moss in at the main entrance.

'Hi. Have you read Isaac's post-mortem report?' she asked.

'Yes. I took the briefing this morning for you,' said Moss. Erika quickly explained that Maria had confirmed Sophia had the titanium rod in her back.

'We'll need Maria to make a formal identification,' said Erika. 'She's just on the phone to her parents. Can you take her to the morgue?'

'Of course,' said Moss. They came back into the flat, where they found Maria leaning over the kitchen counter letting out a low keening, crying sound like an animal in distress. Moss went over and quietly introduced herself, and put her arm around Maria's shoulders. Erika watched how Maria warmed to Moss instantly.

'Can I make you a cup of tea? Do you drink tea?' asked Moss. Maria nodded. Erika moved through to look at the back bedroom. There was a neatly made bed with a patchwork quilt and a pile of teddy bears leaning up against the pillows. Another rail was stuffed with clothes, and there was a line of shoes underneath, and as in the living room there was another crucifix above the doorway.

The window had a net curtain and big thick black curtains. Erika moved closer to the window and lifted the net. She could see a strip of grass behind the block of flats. Concrete fence posts ran along the back of the building, strung with three lengths of wire, which barely came up to waist height. Beyond this was the alleyway which ran between the back gardens of the houses opposite.

'What are you doing?' asked Maria. Erika turned and saw her in the doorway with Moss.

'Sorry. I was just looking. Is this your room?' she asked.

'Me and Sophia alternate having this room every month, and the other sleeps on the sofa bed. This is my month,' she said.

'Maria would like to change, before I take her to the hospital,' said Moss.

'Of course,' said Erika. Maria changed into a long black dress and black coat, and they helped her to her car outside.

'I'm going to stay here and take another look at Vicky's flat,' said Erika to Moss when Maria was safely in the back of the car. 'I'll see you back at the station.'

'Okay. And I'll call you, as soon as I know for sure about the identification,' said Moss.

She got into the car and Erika watched them drive away. Maria's pale face seemed to float in the back of the police car as she looked out through the window, and it pained Erika that she still seemed to have hope in her eyes, that the body in the morgue wasn't Sophia.

21

Erika went back to Vicky's flat, and opened the door using her key from forensics, breaking the tape seal put in place by the police. When she switched on the light, the blood-soaked mattress in the living room seemed to blaze back at her. She heard Isaac's words from the morgue: *'If she was fighting to get away, the rate of blood loss would have increased with her heart rate.'*

Erika leant down next to the partial hand print on the wall beside the sofa. It was the fleshy part at the base of the thumb and the forefinger, and the crease of the skin between the forefinger and the thumb was imprinted on the wall. Erika put her right hand up against the wall, and then her left. The print was of a left hand. The long curved crease in the skin was what psychics called the 'lifeline'. Erika compared the edge of her hand with the bloodied print on the wall. The hand was a similar size to hers, but Erika's hands were quite large for a woman.

'Whose hand is that?' she said to herself. She felt for her notebook and then remembered she'd left it at home. The sheets and the mattress on the sofa bed were with forensics, and she could now see the bed frame and through to where the blood dripped to the carpet underneath. Erika tested the frame, and then climbed onto it and lay face-up. She tried reaching up with her hand to the door from the lying down position. The door was to the right of the sofa bed. When she reached up with her left hand, it fitted the print on the wall.

'Was there a struggle, and she tried to get to the door before she was rolled up inside? Is that her hand? Or someone else's?' There could have been a struggle – the candle holders and a Scrabble game had been knocked off the bookshelf onto the floor. Erika lay on the bed frame for a moment, and tried to imagine the terror and the pain. What had she been doing before? Was she lying here when the intruder came through the front door? Did they have a key? Or did she get up and open the door?

'Why would she be lying in Vicky's bed?' said Erika, sitting up and hearing the springs creak in the old bed frame.

She got back up off the bed and looked around the room. There were grey deposits of the ash-fine fingerprinting dust over every surface; the door frame and handle, the front window, and the coffee table. Erika moved past this and looked at the kitchen. The block of knives had been removed and there was a small plastic number marking where they had been. Had the killer grabbed the knife, or did Sophia try to defend herself? Erika went into the bedroom at the back that was Vicky's studio and switched on the light.

The desk and chair were black, and there was more of the fine fingerprint dust, prominent and silvery across the surface. Vicky's computer had been taken away by the forensics team, and Erika made a mental note to prod them for details of the data on the hard drive. The sound was odd in the room, strangely muffled. Erika looked at the 'studio' section of the room where the egg boxes lined the walls, and then back at the window. She moved over to the uneven blocks of polystyrene, which were packed in, filling the window space. One of the bricks had been pulled out by the forensics team. Erika picked it up and slid it back into place. As far as she knew, the killer hadn't left through the bedroom window. How would someone leave and then pull the huge piece of polystyrene back into place? The killer would have had to leave through the lobby and then the main glass doors, but there was no residue or blood spatter on those doors. Forensics had checked with a Luminol lamp, hadn't they? Again, she cursed that she didn't have her bloody notebook.

Erika went back to look at the books lining the shelves. There was a large selection of true crime titles, and she ran her finger along the spines. There were books about the Black Dahlia killer, the Manson murders, the Yorkshire Ripper, the Moors murderers Myra Hindley and Ian Brady, and three books about Fred and Rose West and the Cromwell Street murders. There were books by FBI profilers, including *Mindhunter* and *Whoever Hunts Monsters*, *The Gates of Janus*, written by the Moors murderer Ian Brady, and *No Son of Mine*, written by the mother of the Nine Elms Cannibal. Seeing it all here made her shudder – so much evidence of evil deeds in one place.

She looked down and saw the carpet by the microphone stand was marked with two indentations, and there were two more under the desk. This must be where, presumably, her bed used to be. *She must have been committed to this crime podcast, if she was willing to convert her one bedroom*, thought Erika. She looked around at the studio; there were deposits of fingerprint dust on the walls and the microphone stand. How many people worked with Vicky on her podcast recordings? Shawn mentioned he played music. Did Vicky have an editor?

It felt warm inside the room, the polystyrene and the egg boxes providing an extra layer of insulation. She thought back to when she first saw the room. There had been a microphone stand, but no microphone. Why?

She looked up Vicky's podcast on her phone. As she scrolled through, she saw Vicky had uploaded episodes regularly every week, on a Thursday, since starting the podcast in June. The last episode was dated Thursday 11th October, so she'd missed uploading an episode on the eighteenth.

Where is that podcast episode?

Erika left Honeycomb Court and walked up Morrison Road towards the tiny co-op supermarket at Blackheath train station. Towards the top of the road, a few hundred yards from Honeycomb Court, there was a bus stop with a modern glass bus shelter. An older man and a young teenage girl were sitting on the plastic bench inside, and as Erika passed, she saw the man glance up at the real-time departures board. The orange digital display changed, showing that the next bus was delayed by ten minutes. Erika stopped under the display, and looked up and down the road. The bus stop was on the same side of the pavement as Honeycomb Court. She peered up at the digital clock under the departure board, and saw the tiny plastic dome covering the CCTV camera. Feeling a surge of excitement, she pulled out her phone and called Crane.

'Hi, it's me, I know you're knee deep in CCTV footage from Blackheath train station, but there's a bus stop on Morrison Road with a CCTV camera. Can you request footage from Monday, and see if it captured any of the action around Honeycomb Court?'

When she came off the phone, she bought a cheese sandwich and a bottle of coke, and then circled back to her car parked outside the house. It was still very cold outside, but she was relieved to see the sun was shining, and the thick layer of frost on the windscreen had melted.

She sat in the car with the heating on high, and wolfed down her sandwich, balancing her notebook on the steering wheel, and trying to remember everything she needed to write down. With the car heater directed on her feet and face, and the sandwich in her belly, she finally felt warm. Glancing back up at her new home, Erika saw that the windows on the top floor were still in shadow and the frost on the glass hadn't melted. The thought of another night shivering on the hard floorboards was depressing, and so was the thought of running the gauntlet at Bed World again. She remembered that she had an online Argos account. Erika took out her phone and logged in. She was about to search for another inflatable mattress, but instead decided to look for a bed. In just a few swipes and clicks, she found a decent-priced double bed, pillows, sheets, and a duvet, and feeling rakish and a little indulgent, she also bought a washer dryer. Better still, they were all available for same-day delivery. Erika reserved the latest slot, 8pm, and paid with her credit card. The whole exercise had only taken ten minutes. *Maybe smartphones aren't that bad after all*, she thought.

Feeling slightly better about her living situation, Erika turned her thoughts back to the case, started the engine, and set off back towards Lewisham Row station.

22

Vicky woke up in a soft warm bed, and when she opened her eyes, she experienced a delicious moment of amnesia. She saw the soft pastel colours of the thick bedspread and the view through the window of the sun-dappled bay, spreading out below the house. And then the memories all came crashing back to her. Sophia's misshapen face. Her blood-spattered body. Vicky felt a cold sweat break out on her back. Panic lurched through her, and her empty stomach stirred. She heard footsteps and the sound of Nutmeg, Cilla's Labrador, in the passage outside the door.

'Victoria?' said Cilla, knocking softly. 'Are you awake? Come for a walk, darling. It's beautiful outside.'

The vastness of the bay was breathtaking for Vicky. Cilla's house sat perched on a rocky cliff high above the beach, and they took a set of ancient stone steps down to the beach, where this morning the air was crisp, the tide was far out, and the sun was glinting off the ridges in the wet sand like thousands of mirrors.

When they reached the sand, Nutmeg went gambolling ahead, running towards a flock of seagulls on the sand. As he reached them, they took flight in the air, cawing.

The sea air and having the sun on her face seemed to cut through Vicky's fear a little.

They walked past a rock pool where bubbles floated up from the smooth sand in the depths and ribbon-like fronds of seaweed twirled lazily in the still water. Vicky wished that she was a sea creature, able to hide in the depths of a rock pool, and then escape out to the vast ocean. Her eyes began to run, partly from the cold air slicing across the beach, but she didn't want to cry, so she bit her lip. Hard.

Every time Vicky closed her eyes, she saw Sophia's body, lying on the bed... It had been left there as a warning. That's what it was. It terrified her how much he'd risked to butcher her innocent neighbour and... She'd confided in Sophia, and somehow, *he knew*. How?

It was insane that she thought she could run. Even now, two days later, the police must know her location. Britain was a small place... Vicky was now in a very quiet corner of the country, but her journey must have been caught on camera. She should have stayed in London, faced her fear, and spoken up... No, shouted loudly from the rooftops.

But Vicky knew how these things went. Who listens to a woman shouting? He'd threatened her, and he'd already proven that he could get away with it all. In her old life, the time before she stumbled upon all the horror, Vicky had seen the world in simplistic terms; bad people pay for their mistakes, and the good people win the day. If you remained honest and did the right thing, then all would be well. She used to judge the women who kept quiet about sexual assault. She was ashamed to admit that a part of her looked down on the ones who were too scared to report a man for assault, and then *he* came along. It frightened her. To speak up would be perilous. She would have to put her head up over the parapet and risk her life, and she was ashamed to acknowledge that she didn't have it in her. And this fear was rolled in with anger. Why was it her job to speak up and risk everything? *He* was the evil one. She hadn't done anything, but it was up to her to make it right? No. No. No. Let me live my life, leave me alone, she thought. He had the confidence to kill Sophia in her bed... *beautiful Sophia*... knowing she would be the one to find her. What reaction was he hoping for? She ran. She couldn't keep her food down. Terror was a constant companion. What else was he capable of?

Vicky stopped walking, and leant over. The smell of the salty air, and the sunlight glistening off the slimy fronds of seaweed on a rock, activated a powerful nausea. She heaved and retched, her stomach contracting painfully. Two long strands of hot bile hung from her mouth, and the wind caught them. There was nothing left in her stomach to purge.

'Oh, Victoria, *darling!*' said Cilla, turning back when she heard her retching. She rushed over, pulling out a packet of tissues from her pocket. 'Did you eat something dicey?' She pulled one out and Vicky took it, wiping her mouth. She managed to catch her breath and straighten up. Tears were running from her eyes. 'What do you want me to do?' asked Cilla, looking up at her with concern. Vicky retched again, and she kept the tissue clamped over her mouth. Did Cilla really think this was to do with dodgy food? To be fair, she hadn't told Cilla anything, yet. But she must have an idea... She was still in touch with lots of people back in London. Surely Sophia's death would be part of the local gossip?

'I just want to keep walking,' she said.

'This is the perfect place to do that,' said Cilla with a smile. 'Look. Beach for miles. Sometimes I just walk and walk, and I think that if I keep going I'll fall off the end of the earth.' She checked her watch. 'I have to go back soon, though. Colin and Ray will be here soon.'

Vicky took a deep breath and swallowed, still feeling a flutter in her diaphragm that might suddenly lurch back into retching again.

'I'll carry on walking, if that's okay?'

Cilla hesitated and the wind changed direction, blowing her hair across her face.

'They know their way around the house, and where I keep the spare key.'

'No. Please, go and see to your guests. The fresh air will do me good.'

'Are you sure?'

'Yes,' said Vicky. The thought that guests would be arriving made the situation seem all the more crazy. Colin and Ray lived in London, and they still worked at Goldsmith's Drama Academy. It would be highly likely that they'd heard something. How was she going to deal with it? She would have to come clean with Cilla, and then where could she run to?

'Take Nutmeg with you,' said Cilla, leaning down to ruffle Nutmeg's big wet head. 'He'd love to have a longer walk, wouldn't you?' She looked up at Vicky with the dog's baleful eyes in silent agreement.

Vicky carried on walking, with Nutmeg loping along ahead, sniffing at the sand dunes at the edge of the beach, and breaking into a trot to chase after the groups of seagulls basking in the sun. She glanced back a couple of times as Cilla grew smaller, walking towards the house, which was now a dot on top of the misty cliff.

Why doesn't Cilla question me more? thought Vicky. *If someone turned up at my door, unannounced, I'd be more curious... Or does she know already?* She tried to push the thought down deep to the back of her mind.

The straps of her backpack were rubbing at her shoulders through her thin coat. Vicky walked to the edge of the water and watched the waves for a moment. The sea was growing rougher, and a cluster of gunmetal grey clouds were starting to form at the horizon. She looked back and couldn't see Cilla. Nutmeg came loping up and stood patiently beside her as she stared out over the water. She sloughed off the backpack and opened the straps. He nuzzled closer and tried to push his head inside the bag.

'No. Sorry, no dog biscuits in here,' she said, gently pushing his head away. She reached down into the bag, under the clothes, and her hand closed over the metal hard drive. *The salt water would work quickly to destroy the data.* Vicky did the backpack up and put it back on. She looked up and down the vast expanse of the beach. The tide would soon be coming in. Cilla's house was the only building for miles. Trying not to think about it anymore, Vicky pitched back on her heels and then put everything into an overarm throw. The hard drive soared high in an arc, and landed with a soft splash in the choppy waters.

23

McGorry was standing by the row of printers when Erika arrived back to the incident room.

'Did you find the CCTV of Charles Wakefield at Blackheath station?' asked Erika.

'Yes, and no,' he said, pulling a face.

'What does that mean? Either he's on the CCTV or not,' said Erika.

'He's wearing a bloody hat,' said Crane, who was sitting at his computer screen surrounded by coffee cups and empty crisp packets. Erika went over to him. 'We've got him on the CCTV camera at Blackheath Station, buying his ticket at 1.55pm last Monday, the 22nd, and he took the 2pm train to London Bridge. I've also got him coming back into Blackheath station on the 5.12pm train from London Bridge. The only problem is that he's wearing a wide-brimmed black trilby hat in all the images, and with his stoop the brim covers his face.'

He handed her a series of print-outs. They all showed a portly figure wearing a long black trench coat and a black trilby, buying a ticket at the ticket office, and then walking across the concourse to board a train. There was a flash of his double chin, but the wide-brimmed hat obscured the top half of his face. Crane also twisted his computer screen around and showed her a CCTV video clip of Charles walking towards the train with bowed shoulders and hunched-over gait. She remembered seeing the long black trench coat and black trilby hanging on the coat stand in Charles's flat.

'Shit. Can you get anything from a camera on the train?' she asked.

'I've requested it,' said Crane. Erika watched the footage as it played again.

'When me and Moss looked around his flat, I saw his long black trench coat and a black trilby... But we can't see his face!'

'I'm going to keep looking, there's CCTV requested from London Bridge station, too,' said Crane.

'That's not the only CCTV footage we've found!' said McGorry, coming back from the printer and handing her a sheet of paper. It was a series of three CCTV images taken from the roof-mounted camera of a bus stop awning. The first image showed Vicky standing on the other side of the glass of the awning running parallel with the pavement.

'Where's this?' Erika asked, her heart leaping in her chest.

'It's the bus stop footage you asked me to pull at the north end of Morrison Road, about two hundred yards from Honeycomb Court,' said McGorry. Erika looked back at the images. The first was very clear. Vicky was looking up at the camera, wearing a baseball cap. The next two images had been taken moments later; in the second, Vicky was looking down, her face now obscured by the peak of the baseball cap. The white Adidas logo was clear on the front. In the third image, Vicky had her head down and was moving away to the right. She had on a pair of blue jeans, a thin blue coat, and was carrying a black backpack.

'When were these taken?' asked Erika, peering at the time

stamp and the very small writing on top of each image. 'My eyesight is crap.'

'The camera on that bus stop takes an image every two seconds,' said McGorry. 'The time stamp is 4.06pm. Monday. The same day you found Sophia's body in her flat.'

'How did you manage to get this so fast?' said Erika.

'I've got a contact at the TfL CCTV control room, and McGorry flirted with her on the phone,' said Crane. 'And it helped having a specific time frame and date.'

'Good work!' Erika looked back at the images of Vicky. 'Why would she be looking up at the camera? I presume with the base-ball cap, she's trying to hide?'

'On the newer bus stops in London, people don't often see that there's a CCTV camera next to the real-time departures board,' said McGorry.

'Okay. She could have been looking at bus times,' said Erika. 'So, what do we think, she found the body in her flat, ran, and didn't have a plan... She was working out if she could take a bus somewhere?'

'Unless *she* killed Sophia,' said McGorry.

'Really?' said Erika, looking up at him.

McGorry opened his mouth and closed it again.

'We shouldn't rule it out.'

There was a silence as they mulled that over for a moment, coupled with the inconclusive CCTV images of Charles Wakefield.

'I wonder if Vicky realised that there was a CCTV camera on the bus stop awning,' said Erika, studying the photos. 'Have you been able to find anything else?'

'She didn't take the bus, or at least a bus from that stop,' said Crane. 'We're working on the basis that she wanted to travel to a larger transport hub, so we've just put in another request for CCTV footage in the same time frame from Blackheath train station. As we know from Charles's *potential* journey, it's only a five-minute walk from that bus stop. Trains from there go south towards Gravesend and Kent and into Central London.'

'Yes,' said Erika. 'And her being on Morrison Road just after four puts her in the time of death range for Sophia.'

'McGorry found something else, too,' said Crane.

'There's more?' asked Erika.

'Oh yeah,' said McGorry. 'We also found an image of Shawn Macavity, taken at the same bus stop.'

'When?'

McGorry handed her another CCTV image printout, this time of Shawn. He was standing in the same place as Vicky and looking up at the camera.

'He looks like he's seen a ghost,' said Erika, peering in at the haunted look on his grey face. His long hair hung limply around his shoulders and he was wearing denim jeans and a thin denim jacket. 'What time was this taken?'

'The time stamp is 4.25pm,' said McGorry. Erika looked back at the other printouts.

'That's half an hour after Vicky was in the same spot,' she said. 'If they were both heading towards the station, they must have met. Does he get on the bus?'

'No, but hopefully the train station CCTV, when it arrives, will tell us more,' said Crane.

'Where do trains from Blackheath station go? Apart from London Bridge?'

'All over the place: Beckenham, Crystal Palace, Bexley Heath, Stratford, Trafalgar Square, Erith in Kent.'

'And presumably if she travelled down to Kent, then Vicky could have accessed the Channel Tunnel trains. Have we checked her passport data?' asked Erika.

'Yes, she hasn't left the country using her passport,' said McGorry.

'If we don't see her or Shawn at Blackheath train station, I'll need to request more eyes on a wider pool of CCTV footage,' said Crane.

Erika nodded. 'Of course. And guys, this is really good work. Bloody fast work. Well done.'

'Erika, I've just got the deets back on Vicky's hard drive from cyber crime,' said Peterson, who was working in the far corner of the incident room. She moved through the busy desks to where Peterson was sitting at the back. She realised that she'd left Bed World last night without updating him on why she was leaving so abruptly. In other times she had always kept her close team members up to date. She shook the thought away.

'What did they find?' she asked.

'Nothing. She'd wiped it.'

'Nothing at all?'

Peterson shook his head.

'I thought that even if you did wipe a hard drive something could be recovered?' said Erika, her heart sinking.

'Vicky had an iMac computer, and, apparently, it's possible to do a deep erase of an iOS operating system computer.'

'What does that mean in luddite language?' asked Erika.

'When you erase something from a regular computer hard drive, you aren't really erasing it, you're just making it invisible, and it can be recovered. What Vicky did was erase the data and overwrite it repeatedly with random letters and numbers.'

'And can anyone do that?'

'With an iMac or MacBook, yes.'

'Did they find anything else? Did she have anything in the cloud?'

'There was nothing else in her office or flat, no USB keys or data drives. They're working on her cloud account, but they don't have a password, and that's the problem.'

'Shit. How easy will it be to get into her stuff stored in the cloud...? I can see by your face that the answer is not very easy,' she said.

'We'd need to get a court order. It can be a long process and then there is always some pushback. This isn't an international or domestic terrorism case.'

Erika stared at the email from the cyber unit on Peterson's screen.

'What data would she have that she didn't want us to see? I presume that she had her bank details, photos, she also used the computer to produce her podcasts. Why would she delete all of that?'

'What do you want to do next?' asked Peterson.

'Shawn Macavity lied to us about being near Vicky's flat on Monday afternoon. He said he was at home all day before he went to work. Let's bring him in for a little chat.'

24

Shawn Macavity agreed to attend an informal chat with Erika and Peterson at the station, and he came in just before lunchtime. He looked surprised when they took him to one of the small interview rooms.

'Am I under arrest?' he asked. He looked a little like Erika felt – exhausted, with huge bags under his eyes. His long hair hung in greasy hanks around his face.

'You are free to go at any time,' said Peterson. 'But it would be advantageous to you if you tell us the truth.'

'Yeah, of course,' said Shawn. He seemed a little wired. His pupils were dilated, and he was drumming his fingers on the table. He saw Erika notice this, and sat back.

'Let's take things back to last Monday,' she said. 'You told us that you were at home in Forest Hill all afternoon, and you went to work at the Golden Lamb pub at 6pm?'

'Yeah. Did my boss confirm that?'

'He confirmed that you arrived at work around ten to six.'

'Good, good,' he said, blowing out his cheeks. 'Yep, that's what happened.'

'And you were at home all day? In your flat, in Forest Hill.'

'Yeah.'

'How much did your acting course cost you?' asked Erika.

'I beg your pardon?' he said, looking over at Peterson, who remained impassive.

'I just think you should ask for your money back.' Erika pulled out the CCTV image of Shawn at the bus stop. She slid it across the desk. 'This is you, at four twenty-five pm on Monday 22nd at the bus stop on Morrison Road. Two hundred yards from Vicky's flat. Quite a long way from Forest Hill.'

He closed his eyes. His head flopped down on his chest and his hair tumbled over his face.

'No, no, no, no,' he said. Erika took out the second CCTV image and slid it across the table.

'Can you look at this, please, Shawn? This is Vicky, twenty minutes earlier. In the same place.'

He looked at the photo and shook his head.

'I swear I had no idea,' he said.

'You had no idea about what?'

'I had no idea that Vicky came back to her flat, I don't know who killed Sophia. I didn't do it, though. I swear.'

'Did you go to Vicky's flat on Monday?' asked Erika.

He frowned and bit his lip.

'Yeah. But I just went there. I swear to God.'

'What time did you arrive?'

'Around half three.'

Erika and Peterson exchanged glances.

'Why did you go there?'

He sighed.

'For... for sex.'

'With Vicky or Sophia?' asked Peterson.

'Sophia,' he said in a small voice.

'Did Vicky know?'

He shrugged.

'I don't know, maybe, I told you before. We weren't together anymore, we were just friends, me and Vicky.'

'How did you know Sophia?' asked Erika.

'Through Vicky. They were friends, sometimes...' He sighed and closed his eyes.

'Sometimes, what?'

'Sometimes a bit more than friends,' he said, looking down at the table.

Peterson leant forward.

'Clarify that, please,' he said. Shawn looked up, and was squirming a little with embarrassment.

'They were involved, sometimes, sexually... Sophia and her sister had a weird relationship. Not sexually,' he added quickly. 'But Maria is very conservative. And they share – *shared* – a small flat. They'd alternate who had the bedroom and who had the couch, and Vicky would let Sophia meet guys at her flat if things were too busy at home.'

Erika sat back, surprised. Although she didn't know why she felt such surprise. Had she been projecting her own strait-laced Eastern European Catholic upbringing on Sophia, expecting her to behave in a certain way?

'How often did this happen? Vicky letting Sophia use her bed?' asked Peterson.

'I don't know. A few times. Vicky didn't exactly sit down and tell me. I just found out about them being close.'

'How did you find out? I don't follow?' asked Erika.

Shawn shifted uncomfortably again in his seat.

'It wasn't that Vicky *told me* as such. I, we, both ended up having sex with Sophia. One time. It was one evening after we finished working on her podcast recording, and we opened a bottle of wine. Sophia came over. She'd had another fight with Maria over something silly, and she wanted company. We had a few drinks...One thing led to another... We all ended up in bed together.' His voice trailed off, and he looked up at Erika. 'Am I in trouble?'

'For having consensual sex? No. Was it consensual between the three of you?'

'Yes! Yes, of course.'

'When was this?'

'It happened a while back, at the end of August, I can't remember the exact date.'

'So, what happened on Monday? Why did you go to Vicky's flat? If you were there to see Sophia?' asked Peterson.

'I texted Sophia in the morning. Just asking her what she was up to, and she said that she had the day off and she was due to go to work for a night shift. She asked if I wanted to come over...'

'To come over for sex?' finished Erika.

'Yeah.'

'And where were you planning to have sex? In Sophia's flat or Vicky's?'

'At her flat. But when I got there, Sophia wasn't answering her door, so I thought she must be at Vicky's flat. I crossed the hall and knocked on Vicky's door, but there was no answer either. I still have a key for Vicky's flat so I let myself in.'

'Why did you just let yourself in?' asked Erika.

'I thought Sophia might have fallen asleep. We'd just been texting to say that we would meet. And Vicky did let Sophia use her bed,' said Shawn, the distress showing on his face.

'And what was inside?' asked Erika. Shawn's bottom lip began to tremble.

'She was lying on the bed... She looked broken. There was so much blood.'

'You knew it was Sophia, didn't you?'

'Yes.'

'That's why you were surprised when we came to talk to you

at your flat and told you it was Vicky's body that had been found.'

'They do look alike, I thought I'd made a mistake, it was all a blur. I stood there for a few minutes and then, I panicked and left.'

'Did you touch anything?' asked Peterson.

'No. I closed the door and left.'

'What time was this?'

Shawn ran his hands through his hair.

'I can't remember exactly.'

'That's not good enough,' said Erika. 'We're establishing a timeline of who went in and out of Honeycomb Court on Monday afternoon, and if you can't account for your exact movements...'

'I have text messages between me and Sophia!' he blurted out, fumbling in the trousers of his jeans. He took out his phone and with trembling hands unlocked the screen and scrolled through. He slid it across the desk to Erika and Peterson.

They peered at the text message chain:

09.31 SHAWN M:
Morning, what u up 2? X

09.33 SOPHIA (Vick's mate)
Not much, U? x

09.34 SHAWN M:
In bed, twiddling my...

09.34 SHAWN M:
thumbs... 😂😂

09.55 SOPHIA (Vick's mate)
You know how to use them 😊 What u doing this afternoon?

09.56 SHAWN M:
Free to twiddle my thumbs and anything else 😊 but I have to be back at work by 6, I could do around 2.30pm?

10.58 SOPHIA (Vick's mate)
See u then

10.59 SHAWN M: 👍🤍

14.42 SHAWN M: Train has stopped outside station. Almost there. Delays zzzzzz. Don't want to twiddle my thumbs. Saving it for u.

14.50 SHAWN M:
Did u get my message???

14.55 SHAWN M:
We're moving. Almost there, sorry not my fault. TRAINS!

15.00 SHAWN M:
Just got off at Blackheath, see you in a sec.

'You can see that we were texting back and forth and she asked me to come over,' he said.

Erika scanned the text message chain.

'You didn't hear from her again after she answered your message at 10.58am?' she asked.

'Yeah, that was Sophia, she always liked to be aloof,' said Shawn.

'You arrived at Blackheath station at 3pm. What happened next?'

'I went to the flats. Well, no, I went to the co-op quickly first...'

'Why?' asked Peterson.

Shawn shifted and looked at Erika. 'To buy, er, johnnies. I mean, condoms,' he said.

'Do you have the receipt?' asked Erika.

'I dunno, I might do somewhere. I never used them cos I went to the flats and that's when I found Sophia.'

'How did you get in through the main front door?' asked Peterson.

'I had my key from Vick, which has an entry fob for the main front doors,' he said.

'So what time do you think that was, when you found Sophia's body in Vicky's flat?' asked Erika.

'I dunno, around quarter past three...You can see that I was late and texting her from the train... Please, I didn't do it!'

'We have a problem, though. You say that you arrived at Honeycomb Court around ten past, quarter past three. We can check train station CCTV to confirm this, and if you have that receipt for the co-op?'

'I do. I can find it, and yes, CCTV. I'll be on the train station CCTV!'

'Where did you go between the time you found Sophia's body at quarter past three, until you were captured on the Morrison Road bus stop CCTV at 4:25pm?'

'I...' His voice tailed off and he stared ahead, his eyes slightly out of focus. 'I was freaked out, so I went for a walk on the heath.'

'Did you see Vicky?'

'No.'

'Because we have Vicky caught on the CCTV at the same bus stop almost twenty minutes before you. You were both in the area.'

'I didn't see her. I was on the heath... Can't you check my mobile phone records?'

'Did you call anyone? Did you call Vicky after you found Sophia's body?'

'No. I was in shock and terrified that I was going to be blamed. I just walked about trying to work out what to do.'

'Did anyone see you?'

'I don't know, it was quiet and empty.'

There was a knock and McGorry poked his head around the door.

'Sorry. Boss, a word,' he said. 'It's important.'

25

'This better be good,' said Erika to McGorry when they were outside in the corridor. Peterson followed her out. He nodded, with an excited gleam in his eyes.

'It is. After Vicky was caught on the CCTV camera on the Morrison Road bus stop, she went to Blackheath railway station, and took a train to London Victoria. She then walked to Victoria coach station, and boarded a coach northbound. It was an overnight service to Glasgow...' He handed her a series of print-outs showing Vicky at Blackheath train station, the vast concourse at Victoria train station and then the smaller, more cramped and murky thoroughfare at Victoria bus station. In all of the photos she kept her head down, but they were able to follow her by the black Adidas cap.

'If she hadn't looked up at the bus stop on her road, we wouldn't know it's her. Good work,' said Erika.

'We had a timescale that we were able to use to request specific footage from TfL,' said McGorry. 'There's more. The bus she boarded going north from Victoria stopped three times in the night. On the third stop, Cairn Lodge motorway services, at two thirty on Tuesday morning, she got off the bus and made a phone call from the phone box.' He handed them another fuzzy photo of Vicky using a payphone in the motorway services forecourt.

'Can you put in a request for a call trace, if you have the time stamp and exact location?' asked Erika, excited to see that they were closing in on Vicky.

'This is where I utilised the McGorry charm, again. I called Cairn Lodge services, flirted with the old dear on the end of the phone, and she was very helpful. Their payphone is rarely used, and calls on it get routed through their main IT system. They were able to give me the number Vicky called, a woman called Cilla Stone, who lives in Whithorn in Dumfries and Galloway in Scotland. It's a pretty isolated address, about two and half hours from Glasgow.'

'Hooray for the McGorry charm. Shame it never works on me,' said Erika.

He grinned.

'Do we know who this Cilla Stone is?' asked Peterson.

'Not yet, but the team are on it in the incident room. I just thought you might find out from Shawn.'

'Okay. Good thinking,' said Erika. 'Where did Vicky go after the Cairn Services?'

'She got back on the coach and went on to Glasgow. We've got CCTV of her getting off in Glasgow's main station, and there the trail goes cold.'

'Good work. I need you to review the CCTV footage from Blackheath station and the Morrison Road bus stop around 3pm, that's when Shawn Macavity tells us he arrived on the train and then went to Honeycomb Court,' said Erika.

'Okay. On it,' said McGorry.

Erika and Peterson went back into the interview room, and Erika could see that the moment had broken with Shawn, and he'd composed himself. This was the risk when you brought someone in voluntarily, she thought. *In the short time we left the room, he's seen the cold light of day and doesn't want to say anything else.*

'Thank you for your patience and help here, Shawn,' Erika said as they sat down opposite him at the table.

'I think I should get a solicitor,' said Shawn, uncomfortable. 'I found Sophia's body, and I panicked. But I didn't do anything. I didn't touch anything. And I'm sorry.'

Erika looked over at Peterson. There was the unaccounted for hour and ten minutes between him finding Sophia's body and then being caught on the bus stop CCTV, and this was troubling. If they did push Shawn and get any kind of confession out of him, it could be challenged in court if they did it without a solicitor present. They'd gleaned a lot from him already, and the breakthrough on Vicky being in Scotland was big. Peterson looked as if he was thinking the same thing. He nodded in agreement.

'Okay. We'd like you to come back and talk to us with a solicitor present. How would tomorrow morning at 9am work for you?'

Shawn looked surprised that they were going to let him leave. He mulled over the question.

'Really? You're letting me go?'

'Yes, but we expect you to return tomorrow to speak to us again, with a solicitor. And we'd like to ask if you would consent to having a sample of your DNA taken.'

Shawn hesitated.

'Yes, okay,' he said.

'Great. We can do that tomorrow when you have a solicitor present. We have a list on the front desk of approved solicitors,' said Erika, getting up. 'Do you need a car to take you home?'

'Er, yes.'

Peterson got up from his chair.

'I can organise that for you,' he said. 'And we'll get someone to show you the list.'

'Oh, Shawn. Just before we let you go and get on with your day, can I ask if you know a woman called Cilla Stone?' said Erika.

'Yeah. She was our teacher at Goldsmith's Drama Academy,' he said. 'She's retired, I think. Why?'

'Do you know where she lives?'

'Somewhere up in Scotland. Vicky kept in contact with her more than me,' he said. 'Do you think she's there?'

'Thank you, that's very helpful. We'll see you tomorrow bright and early,' said Erika. They got up and escorted Shawn out to the corridor where an officer was waiting. 'Can you see Mr Macavity out?'

They watched Shawn until he got in the lift at the end of the corridor.

'He's such a greasy little rat, and he got two good-looking women to have a threesome with him,' said Peterson, shaking his head.

'Trust you to think of that. More importantly, do you think he's a murderer?'

'What would be his motive?'

'Drugs? Rage? Jealousy. Do you think he looked a bit wired during the interview?' asked Erika.

Peterson shrugged.

'He looked more scared than anything else. Are we taking a risk letting him go?'

'Yes, but if we bring him in and charge him, I need stronger evidence, and I want to do it properly,' said Erika.

When they got back to the incident room, McGorry was waiting for Erika, holding a piece of paper.

'I'm really working my magic today.' He grinned. 'Cilla

Stone, or *Priscilla* Stone, lives in Whithorn in Dumfries and Galloway in Scotland. She's the only "Cilla" registered in the area.'

Crane looked up from his computer.

'The only Cilla registered in the area!' he said. 'Just be thankful that Vicky didn't call a Liverpool number from that payphone. McGorry would be sending a squad car round to Cilla Black's house to bring her in for questioning!'

Erika and Peterson laughed.

'Only kidding, buddy,' added Crane to McGorry. 'Good work.'

'I've found the house on Google Maps,' said McGorry. He had the image on his screen with a satellite view of a vast peninsula by the sea. 'She owns a house on the coast with six acres of land.'

'A good place to hide,' said Erika, rubbing her tired eyes. This whole case was getting so complicated. She looked at her watch. It was coming up to 1pm, and she was hungry again for another sandwich. 'Okay, let's ask for the local police to drop by Cilla's house ASAP, and see what's going on.'

26

Time seemed to jump forward. One moment Vicky was standing on the beach, and staring out to sea, and the next, she was looking down at plastic bottles littered on the sand along a tall fence with razor wire spooled on top.

The wind was whistling through the wire, and her hands and face were numb with cold. On the other side of the fence was a block of sand and a long low building in the far distance, and there were signs with MINISTRY OF DEFENCE PROPERTY – NO ACCESS printed on them.

She heard Nutmeg bark, and she turned to see him running in the other direction. He twisted his head back to look at her and barked again. How long had they been walking? She'd gone quite a few miles up the beach, and she couldn't see Cilla's house anymore. There was just a line of mist where they'd come from.

Nutmeg barked again. Vicky looked at her hands. Her fingernails were blue. She thrust her hands into her pockets and headed back with Nutmeg.

It took an hour to get back, and it seemed such a slow trudge now that she was cold and hungry. Slowly, Cilla's house appeared again through the fog.

The silence was haunting Vicky. It should have been an oasis here on the coast surrounded by the breathtaking beauty of the landscape, but the silence only amplified her fears and the voices in her head. It allowed the nightmares and terrible images to encroach on her brain.

She knew now that she was in a perilous place, fleeing a crime. She was afraid to do anything, but the longer she hid, the worse things would get for her. She'd started to have crazy thoughts. She could implicate herself. If she was accused of killing Sophia, she'd be arrested and placed on remand. He couldn't get to her in prison. She'd be safe in a prison cell.

She was grateful that Cilla hadn't asked many questions of her, beyond the fact she knew Vicky was in some kind of trouble, but what would her reaction be when she heard there was a dead girl?

Cilla didn't have a TV, but she had a laptop. Vicky purposefully hadn't checked the news.

The house appeared on the horizon, and Nutmeg had run far ahead. He was probably hungry and tired. The walk back seemed to take an age and by the time she was at the base of the steps leading up to the house, she was exhausted. At the top of the stone steps, and next to the house, there was a small patch of gravel where a smart black BMW was parked.

Vicky took a deep breath, and went in through the back door into the kitchen.

Colin and Ray were sitting at the long wooden kitchen table, and Cilla was opening what looked like a second bottle of wine.

'Vicky! Darling! I was about to send out the search party for you,' she said. 'You remember Colin and Ray.'

'Hi,' she said. Nutmeg went running to his bowl of water and started to drink noisily.

'Victoria Clarke, I remember those expressive eyes,' said Colin, standing up and offering his hand. He was a handsome, tall thin man with a full head of dark hair, despite his age, which Vicky knew to be late fifties. He wore a blue woollen three-piece suit with a wine coloured Cravat. His hands were very soft and he carried with him a delicious scent of aftershave. Vicky took his hand. 'My word, you're frozen.'

Ray was the opposite of Colin. Short and balding with a grey goatee. He had been the dance teacher at school. He wore baggy jeans and a blue Adidas sports top. He smiled with a set of crooked teeth, and somehow still managed to have a sexual magnetism about him. Vicky wasn't sure if it made her feel entirely comfortable.

'Hello. We don't know each other quite as well, but I remember you,' said Ray.

'I didn't take many dance classes,' said Vicky.

He tutted and smiled again.

'Shame on you,' he said with a wink.

'We've started early,' said Cilla, holding up the freshly opened bottle of wine. 'How about a glass to warm you up, Victoria?'

'I don't want to intrude.'

'Nonsense. Here we are,' said Cilla, pouring her a hefty measure in a tumbler. There was a faint sound of a car engine and it grew louder.

'You expecting anyone else? Planning on making this a five-way?' said Ray, winking at Vicky again.

'Raymond, you need to behave yourself,' said Cilla, admonishing him with a twinkle in her eye. From outside came the sound of a car pulling up into the driveway. Colin took a sip of his wine and kept his eyes on Vicky, watching her. Doors slammed and Cilla went to the window.

'Good lord, it's two police officers,' she said. The doorbell rang and Cilla pulled her long cardigan around her.

'I wonder what they want,' she said, leaving the room. An image came to Vicky, of being chased, out of breath, across the flat wet sand to the water's edge until she was tackled by two police officers. The image felt so real. She could feel the sweat on her brow with the cold wind, and the feeling of her lungs burning with the effort of running.

Colin and Ray were watching her closely. It was like they could smell her fear. Colin took another sip of his wine, and Ray lit up a cigarette, sitting back as he exhaled.

That's the problem when you run to the end of the earth, there's nowhere else to run, but over the edge, thought Vicky, as she heard the police coming into the hallway with Cilla, and her name being mentioned.

Later that afternoon, Erika heard that local police in Whithorn had found Vicky at Cilla's house, and they put in place a plan to fly Vicky back to London later that afternoon. Erika decided to give Tess an update of events in person, and heard from the Family Liaison officer that Tess and Jasper were at their restaurant, so she drove over later that afternoon.

Goose restaurant was a converted townhouse at the end of the high street in Blackheath. It looked very quiet when Erika pulled up in her car. There was plenty of space to park on the road outside, and she locked her car and went inside.

The restaurant was light and airy. Beautifully decorated, rustic style with wooden tables and benches – much classier than she'd imagined – but it was empty, and she'd expected to see the tail end of the lunch crowd. Erika showed her warrant card to a young man who was standing behind the bar looking at his phone, and he directed her through a door towards the kitchens at the back.

Erika hesitated at the double doors when she heard raised voices.

'Six is a pathetic amount!' Jasper was shouting. 'We need to do eighteen covers at lunchtime, just to break even.'

'My sister is missing! I came here to see you, and you throw this crap at me!' cried Tess.

'I'm not throwing crap at you, but I need you to join me and acknowledge that we have a big problem. We're in deep shit with money, sister or no sister.'

There was a long silence. Erika took a deep breath, pushed open the doors and went into the kitchen. It was a long, thin galley of stainless-steel work surfaces, and jars of herbs lined the windowsill, injecting a splash of colour. Jasper was wearing spotlessly clean Chef's whites and leaning against one of the burner hobs with his arms folded. Tess was standing a few feet from him and looked like she was about to leave. She was wearing a scruffy ensemble of baggy jeans and another fluffy fleece and her hair was standing up in messy tufts.

'Who let you in?' said Jasper, noticing Erika at the door. 'Are you here to tell me about my knives?'

'Hello, sorry to intrude,' said Erika. At the mention of knives, she noticed a long magnetic strip above the steel benches where groups of metal spoons and forks were attached and interspersed with big gaps. Erika remembered that her forensics team had taken away all the knives in the restaurant for testing. They still didn't have a murder weapon.

'Do you have news about Vicky?' asked Tess, her tearstained face hopeful.

'Yes, we've found her, safe and sound. She went to stay with a teacher from drama school in Scotland.'

'Oh! She's really okay?' Erika nodded. 'When can I see her?'

'We're flying her back to London this afternoon. I want to

talk to her at the station, but we can have her back with you tonight.'

'Oh. Thank you. That's good. That's good, isn't it, Jasper?' she asked, turning to him. She hesitated and then gave him a hug. He nodded and look relieved.

'Yes, that's very good news. Thank you, officer...' He looked around the kitchen as Tess held onto him. She buried her head in his chest.

'If there's anything more you need, any questions, you can call Fiona and I'll make sure she keeps you up to date with Vicky's journey back,' said Erika. She went to leave them in peace, and noticed the magnetic knife rack again. 'I don't know when we can get your knives back. I will ask though, I understand that they're important for your business.'

'It's fine,' said Jasper, sounding defeated. 'Thank you.' He kissed Tess on the top of her head. Erika left the kitchen. The barman had left, and it was quiet in the empty dining area, so quiet that she could hear the fridges humming. When she left the restaurant and came out onto the street, she could see the other bars and restaurants were busy with people.

Her phone buzzed with a text message, and she saw that the police escort had just arrived with Vicky at Glasgow airport, ready for her flight back to London.

27

Erika looked down at the cigarette between her fingers, the tip glowing red in the darkness. She took a drag and exhaled the smoke into the pale orange sky. It was now dark, and she was standing on the steps in front of the police station, waiting for the squad car which had gone to collect Vicky from London City Airport. Moss came out of the front entrance, and joined her on the steps.

'Jeez. You're back on the smokes?' she said, crossing her arms over her chest and huddling down against the cold.

'Don't. I'm annoyed with myself. It's this case,' said Erika. 'And they say that moving house is just as stressful as a death in the family.'

'Try saying that to Maria Ivanova... It was awful at the morgue. She was so *angry* when she had to identify her sister's body. I've never seen anything like it. She actually shouted.'

'She shouted at you?'

'No. At Sophia's body.'

'What did she shout?'

'I don't know. It was in Bulgarian, maybe it was a stream of consciousness. There was one word she kept saying. *Putka*. And then all at once, the rage seemed to drain from her body and she leant over, cried and stroked her sister's hair...'

'*Putka* is the "c" word in Bulgarian,' said Erika.

'I thought I was used to things in this job, doing it for so long, but then something gets to you,' said Moss. She wiped a tear from her eye. Erika put out a hand, and gripped Moss's arm for a moment. She wiped her eyes. 'I'm being silly. Give me one of those cigarettes.'

'Are you sure?'

Moss nodded. Erika offered the packet and she took one, then she flicked her lighter and held out the flame.

'Lower. I'm not a giantess like you,' said Moss. Erika smiled and lowered her arm. Moss leant in and the tip of her cigarette burst into a glow. She inhaled and coughed. 'What time did Vicky's plane land?'

Erika checked her watch, and she saw it was almost 8pm.

'An hour ago. City Airport isn't far. They said they were going to blue light her over...' Erika's phone rang and she took it out of her pocket. It was a number she didn't recognise. 'Okay. This could be them... Hello?' There was a pause and then a man with a Slovak accent spoke.

'I'm just outside your house. Is twenty-seven the one with the red door?' he asked.

'What?'

'Argos delivery... You should have had a text alert.'

Erika held out her phone to check. She couldn't see a text message.

'No, I didn't get a message,' she said, putting her phone back to her ear.

'You booked delivery for 8pm. I'm outside your house,' he said. Erika's heart sank, she'd completely forgotten about the bed and the washing machine being delivered.

'I'm sorry. I'm not there.'

'Why did you book a delivery, if you're not going to be here?' said the man, sounding angry. Her phone beeped and she saw that there was a text message from the police officer escorting Vicky. They were one minute away from the station. Erika put the phone against her coat.

'Vicky's gonna be here in a sec,' she said to Moss. When she put the phone back to her ear, she could hear the man was now annoyed.

'Hello? Are you there?'

'Yes, hello. I'm sorry I'm not going to be there tonight. Can I reschedule the delivery?'

'I'm outside your door with a full van... *Do pici...*' he added with a mutter.

'Hey! I'm Slovak. I know what that means. What's your name?'

'I'll get someone to rearrange delivery,' said the man, and he hung up.

Erika didn't get the chance to reply, because she saw a police car turn off the main road and stop at the barrier. Just as it flipped up, Erika heard loud voices coming from the inside of the station reception behind her. They turned and saw Melanie coming out into the reception area with Assistant Commissioner Julian Wakefield and Charles Wakefield.

'What the hell?' said Erika under her breath. The Assistant Commissioner was wearing his dress uniform, carrying his cap under his arm, and Charles was dressed in an ill-fitting suit with his black trench coat and trilby hat. Erika thought of the CCTV footage of Charles, with his face hidden under the brim of the hat. The way he moved looked the same as it had on the CCTV footage, with his slightly rounded shoulders. There was also a man with them who had a professional-looking camera slung around his neck. She turned back and saw the car pull up in front of the station steps with Vicky in the back seat next to a plain-clothes female officer.

The man with the camera had hung back in the reception of the station. Julian and Charles were now shaking hands with Melanie by the reception desk, and then they came through the main entrance, just as the car doors opened.

Time seemed to slow down for Vicky when she stepped out of the car. The car park was bright and very cold, and there was a smell of smog in the air. The police station was a low, squat concrete building and there were two women standing at the bottom of the entrance steps, one tall and thin with blonde hair, and one short and stocky with red hair. The journey back to London had been too fast. The two hours in the car to Glasgow Airport seemed to fly by, where they were whisked through and onto a plane which took off as soon as they found their seats. And now she was here and had to face the music. The police officer who'd accompanied her on the plane was a no-nonsense young Scotswoman, difficult to read and inept at small talk.

As Vicky got out of the car, she froze. Coming down the steps behind the two women were Charles Wakefield and his brother, the senior police officer all dressed up in smart suits.

They both acknowledged the two women on the stairs.

'Evening,' said Julian as he slipped his cap back on.

'Evening, sir,' they both replied. Vicky could see tension in their faces. The blonde one looked panicked, and the short one's brow furrowed with concern. *They must have different fathers*, she thought. *They don't look alike as brothers.* Charles had often bragged to her about his brother being a senior detective, one of the most senior in the Met police. For a long time she didn't know if Charles had been flirting in his own cack-handed way, trying to impress her with his police connection, but now she realised he was warning her; don't mess with me. I *know* people. It was the latter, she knew that now.

They seemed to approach her in slow motion. And then Julian fixed Vicky with his brown eyes, and his interest lingered on her for a moment... And then Charles turned to face her as he passed. He took off his black trilby, and the light from the car headlights shone off his bald shiny head. And he looked at her with real menace. His eyes boring into hers, with just the faintest of smirks. A mere hint, meant just for her to see. He reminded her of that character in *Indiana Jones and the Raiders of the Lost Ark*. The bald Nazi with the rubbery lips. Charles seemed to hold himself in the same way, like a henchman with an evil streak. And then the brothers were gone, walking away to a car parked in the shadows at the back of the car park.

It was then that Vicky remembered she should breathe, and she took a deep inhale of the cold, dirty air.

Erika watched the moment where Vicky and Charles crossed paths. It was blink and you'll miss it, and Charles had his back to her, but the look on Vicky's face told it all. She was terrified of him. Terrified of Charles.

It was the oddest moment. Erika realised afterwards that she should have said something, but she hadn't expected to see Charles with Julian Wakefield at Lewisham Row the same moment Vicky arrived.

Vicky seemed ill-dressed for the late autumn weather in London, let alone the north of Scotland. She was wearing tennis shoes, a short tartan skirt, thick black tights, and a blue woollen roll neck jumper. Her dark hair was long and slightly messy and she carried a small hiking backpack. In the light spilling out from the station reception, her face was ashen, and Erika could see she was shaking as she watched Charles and Julian Wakefield get into a large black Range Rover. Erika could see the resemblance between her and Sophia. The shape of the face and the long hair.

'Hello, I'm DCI McGroarty,' said the plain-clothes officer coming around the car. She looked slightly older than Vicky. 'Can I leave her with you?'

There was something about the way she said it that implied she'd been dog sitting, rather than escorting a vulnerable young witness back to London.

'Hi, Vicky. I'm Erika and this is Kate,' said Erika, putting out her hand. Vicky took the hand warily. Her own hand was freezing cold, and she was shaking. 'We're investigating the murder of Sophia Ivanova. And I just want to say that you are not in trouble in any way, and you can leave at any point... We'll have a car take you home. But we really need to talk to you about what happened. Is that alright?'

Vicky nodded. She looked like she was going into shock.

'Let's go inside into the warm, and have a hot drink,' said Moss.

'Does my sister know I'm okay?' said Vicky, talking for the first time.

'Yes, she does,' said Erika. 'We're going to have a car take you home to her very soon.'

'And she's not angry with me?'

'No.'

Vicky nodded and followed them up the steps into the station.

28

'Let's go to the canteen,' said Erika to Vicky as they walked down the long empty corridor running through the centre of the police station. They came to a door and Erika pushed it open, flicking on the lights. She motioned to a small sofa with easy chairs in the corner.

'You want to talk to me here?' said Vicky, looking around at the vast empty canteen as the strip lights flickered on.

'Would you prefer somewhere else?'

'No. I thought we'd be going to an interview room.'

'As I said, Vicky, this is just an informal chat. You're not under arrest. And you're free to go at any time, but we need your help with this,' said Erika. She indicated the sofa, and Vicky sat down cautiously. Moss came into the canteen with a tray of steaming mugs and some biscuits on a plate. She handed them a mug each. Vicky cradled hers in her hands.

'Okay. Let's start at the beginning,' said Erika. 'Did you find Sophia Ivanova's body in your flat?'

Vicky gulped and put her hand to her mouth.

'Yes,' she said. A tear formed in the corner of her left eye and ran down her cheek.

'What time did you find her?'

'Just before four o'clock, on Monday afternoon. I let myself in the door... and I didn't know what it was at first. The sofa bed was rolled up, half-closed, but it looked like something...' She took a deep breath and closed her eyes.

'Take your time.'

'It looked like something was... stuffed, inside the rolled up bed, and then I saw all the blood, soaked through the mattress in patches... I opened the bed, and she was lying there, like a broken doll.'

'Did you touch Sophia's body?'

'No.'

'You were due to work at your sister's restaurant that afternoon. Why didn't you go?' asked Moss.

Vicky hunched down in her chair and closed her eyes.

'In the morning I went into the West End... To sell a microphone. Pawn a microphone.'

'What time?'

'I left around ten thirty.'

Erika looked at Moss.

'Why would you sell your microphone? You have a podcast,' said Erika.

Vicky hesitated, keeping her eyes on the floor.

'It was *a* microphone, not the only one. I figured I could get a hundred quid for it. It was worth a lot more, but I had to pay my rent to Tess... Selling an unwanted mic was better than a day shift at Goose.'

'You don't like working there?' asked Moss.

'No.'

'Why?'

'My brother-in-law, Jasper, isn't a fan of mine. I have the job out of pity. Tess makes him employ me.'

'I hated waitressing,' said Moss.

'It's worse when your family owns the restaurant, and they're having money worries of their own. The restaurant isn't doing well,' said Vicky, shifting uncomfortably in her seat.

'Did you sell the microphone?' asked Erika.

'Yes. I got eighty quid.'

'When you got home and found Sophia, what did you do next?' asked Erika.

'I just stood there for I don't know how long, and then I ran.'

'Why did you run? Why not call the police?'

Vicky shook her head, staring ahead. Then she shrugged.

'What did you take with you?'

'A bag. This bag, with a few bits,' she said, indicating the rucksack on the floor beside her. 'The cash I got from the pawn shop.'

'Did you plan to go to Scotland?'

'I didn't plan anything. I just ran.'

'Cilla Stone is a close friend of yours?' said Erika.

'Yes.' Her face had lit up for the first time at the mention of Cilla.

'Are you closer to her than you are to your sister, or Shawn, or your other friends?'

'Cilla is... She's a completely different type of person. A free spirit. A wonderful positive person. Without judgement. She always makes me feel I could do anything, be anything. She encouraged me to build my own studio, and pursue the podcast. What's that phrase, ride or die. She's my ride or die,' said Vicky.

'Cilla was your teacher at drama school, and she's in her early sixties. That's quite an age gap,' said Erika.

'What does that have to do with anything?'

'Is she married?'

'No.'

'Does she have children?'

Vicky hesitated, like she had to think about it.

'Yes, she has a son who lives in America.'

'And who is his father? If Cilla isn't married?'

'I don't know.'

'Is the son married? Does he have children?'

Vicky sighed impatiently.

'I think so... He has a couple of children. Yes, two girls.'

'What are their names?'

There was a long pause. Vicky was starting to get flustered.

'I don't know,' she said. 'What does this have to do with anything?'

'Vicky, I'm trying to work this out. Cilla is someone who you feel closest to. Your ride or die. You ran away to her house far up in Scotland. And, yet you don't seem to *really* know her,' said Erika.

'I do know her!' said Vicky, raising her voice. 'And I don't have to justify my friendship with her to *you*. Maybe it's because we're so different that we can be friends. I feel like I can breathe when I'm around her. She doesn't care about class, or money, or what other people think, and my fucking sister and my fucking life seems to be all about those things!' she said, sitting back and shaking with anger.

'Is that why you were drawn to Sophia? Because she thought differently?' asked Erika.

'Yes. She also had an overbearing sister, who expected things of her...' Vicky broke down again and her head tipped forward as her shoulders shook. Moss leant closer and gave her a tissue. The canteen door opened with a creak, and Erika saw Melanie put her head around the door.

'Sorry, I didn't know you were in here,' she said and she went to leave again. Erika looked back at Vicky and saw she had now melted into tears and sobbing. Moss moved closer and put out her hand to Vicky's shoulder. She nodded to Erika.

'Melanie. Can I just have a word?' asked Erika, getting up and hurrying over to the door.

Erika came out into the narrow corridor with Melanie, and closed the canteen door on Vicky's soft sobbing.

'Why was Charles Wakefield here?' she asked.

Melanie folded her arms. 'He was here to present a cheque to the Met police benevolent fund,' she said. Erika noted she was dressed smarter than her usual attire, in a sleek back Chanel trouser suit.

'At 8pm on a Wednesday night?'

Melanie cocked her head and looked up at Erika with a frown. She flashed a disarming smile.

'Yes. It was a large donation, so it came with a photo opportunity. Six thirty pm was the only time that the Assistant Commissioner could be present with Charles and the photographer,' she said.

'Charles Wakefield donated the money?' asked Erika, thinking of his strange little flat and the paucity of his possessions inside.

'No. He's on the board of the Boulderstone Trust, a local charity who give generously to the police benevolent fund.'

'Henrietta Boulderstone,' said Erika, sighing. Charles Wakefield had some powerful people in his corner. 'How big was the donation?'

'Hundred K.'

Erika raised her eyebrows.

'Melanie. The timing of this...'

'Yes,' she said, with a tone of warning in her voice.

'Did Charles Wakefield, or his brother, know that Vicky Clarke was coming to this station tonight, to talk about the murder of Sophia Ivanova?'

'No, Erika. And I didn't know. I had to find out from one of your team.'

'Yes, well, things have moved very fast today.'

'Which is good. But, I'll ask that you keep me updated.'

Erika could see that Melanie was angry, but she felt angry too, like she was being kept in the dark and her investigation was playing second fiddle to politics and faux diplomacy.

'How long has this been planned, the whole charity presentation, if you don't mind me asking?'

'Yesterday, I was told yesterday.'

'Does it seem strange to you? There is still a huge question mark over Charles Wakefield. He could be a suspect.'

'I thought you have CCTV to support his alibi?'

'We have CCTV of someone who we think is Charles Wakefield to support his alibi, but his hat is obscuring his face. And during this uncertainty, all of a sudden, a photo op with you here is being arranged, where he's handing over a whopping great cheque to a Met charity. And Julian Wakefield tags along.'

'Erika, the cheque, the charity and Charles's presence on the board are all legitimate. Is the timing tricky? Yes. Am I telling you how to do your job? No.'

'Vicky Clarke freaked out when she saw him,' said Erika.

'And that's proof of what?' said Melanie.

'She discovered a brutal murder in her flat, and the flat next door to hers, happens to belong to Charles. And she was so scared, for reasons I'm trying to discover, that she fled the scene. It's very fishy.'

'Well, Erika. I need you to find out more than just "fishy". You answer to me, but don't forget we all answer to the Assistant Commissioner. Now, I'll leave you to get back to your interview.'

Melanie started back up the corridor and Erika watched her for a moment. She was usually so calm and collected. Something had rattled her.

29

When Erika came back into the canteen, Moss had Vicky talking again.

'I used to let Sophia use my flat to meet guys,' she was saying in a small voice. Erika tiptoed back in and sat down. The fridge hummed in the background. They let the silence extend around Vicky, so she would feel compelled to elaborate. 'Sophia wasn't happy.'

'Why wasn't she happy?' asked Moss.

'Both her and Maria were pushed, to be the best at school, and to study hard. Their parents wanted them to be doctors, and to have medical training in English. Maria is more conservative. She wants to graduate and then her dream is to meet a nice doctor who she can marry, have his children, and be looked after. Sophia wanted to have fun. She wanted to break loose of the bonds that she'd been wrapped up in. I'm quoting her own words.'

'How well did you know the sisters?' asked Erika.

'I knew Sophia a lot better. She was more open, as a person.

I'm home a lot, so I took in parcels for them. I'd go over to the flat to have a glass of wine with her, when Maria was on her shift.'

'I still don't get how you made the leap to offering up your bed for her to use?' asked Moss. Vicky hunched over her mug of tea and looked between Moss and Erika and then at the floor.

'It wasn't just boyfriends she had sex with,' she said in a small voice.

'Did you have a sexual relationship with Sophia?'

Vicky sighed and nodded.

'It happened a few times, the first was on a quiet week night. She came to collect a parcel, stayed for coffee and then, wine. We got quite drunk. One thing led to another... I'd never, before, been with a girl...'

'Were you and Sophia in a relationship?' asked Erika.

'No. It was just something silly that happened a few times, and then, one evening Sophia came to collect a parcel, and there was a guy with her who worked at the hospital... Maria was at work. I invited them in for a drink. I knew what was going to happen. The three of us ended up in bed together.'

'What's his name, this guy from the hospital?'

Vicky put down her tea and rubbed her eyes.

'Dexter. I don't know his second name... That's how I made the leap to offering her my bed. Actually, it only happened twice. And she was very respectful, changed the sheets afterwards. She left me gifts of wine and nice chocolate. She was a good friend.' Vicky let out a long exhale and put the cup down on the table. Her hands were shaking.

'When was the last time Sophia used your bed?'

'Couple of weeks ago. She had a copy of my door key. The first time she gave it back to me, but this last time, afterwards, I didn't hassle her to have it back. I trusted her.'

'Did you know she was going to use your bed on Monday?'

'No.'

Erika knew she should tell Vicky that Sophia was due to meet Shawn on Monday afternoon, but she didn't want to distract her from the bigger picture.

'Let's go back. You arrived home on Monday, just before four. You opened the door and saw something was wrong. Sophia was rolled up in your sofa bed, lying dead. I can understand that you were very scared, but what made you run away?'

Vicky shook her head and wiped tears forming under her eyes.

Erika went on, 'Why run? Sophia had a key to your place, and you have an alibi. You were out all afternoon. You would have been recorded on hundreds of CCTV cameras in Central London, and we can confirm this. You have scores of true crime books in your flat. You do extensive research for your podcast. Statistically, you must know that only a tiny, tiny percentage of women commit violent crimes. You wouldn't be our first suspect. I don't think you being scared is enough of an explanation for why you ran away.'

Erika sat back and realised she'd changed gear quickly. Was she pushing too hard?

Vicky opened her mouth and closed it again.

'Have you ever found a friend brutally murdered in your bed?' she said, looking up at Erika and Moss with a hardness in her eyes. They both said they hadn't.

'Then you have *no concept* of what I was feeling, how I am feeling and how terrified I was!'

She sat back and crossed her arms with a sense of finality. Erika could see Vicky was shutting down and becoming angry, so she decided to take a risk and lean into this.

'Do you know who killed Sophia?' she asked.

'*No!* No, I don't. I really don't.'

'Are you aware that your sister found Sophia's body, and she wrongly identified her as you?' said Moss.

'What?' said Vicky, her head snapping up to stare at them.

'Tess thought she'd found your body, panicked, and for the first twenty-four hours we incorrectly identified Sophia's body as you.'

Vicky continued to stare at them with her mouth open, and then shook her head.

'I don't know what else to say,' she said.

'Do you want to ask us any questions?'

'No.'

Erika was disturbed by her lack of curiosity. Something was seriously off. She had a real interest in crime with her podcast, but she wasn't asking anything about the crime scene, or if they had any suspects. She'd been so scared of being blamed for killing Sophia. And then she was adamant she didn't know who killed her. It didn't make sense.

'Do you know any of the men who Sophia brought to your flat?' asked Erika.

'I know of Dexter.'

'What about Shawn?' asked Moss.

'What about him?'

'He told us that the three of you have sex together.'

Vicky looked coldly at her.

'You know, I don't have to be here. I can leave at any time.'

Erika could see that despite her bluster, her hands were still shaking.

'Is it possible that Sophia knew you were out and brought a man over without asking permission?'

'It's possible.'

'What did your neighbours think about this? You live in quite a small block of flats, and everyone must see people coming and going.'

'I don't care what they think.'

'And what about Charles Wakefield, your next door neighbour? You just saw him, and you didn't ask us why he was here?'

Moss glanced across at Erika. Vicky's face was difficult to read. She seemed to be cycling through several emotions: fear, disgust, impatience at being asked. She opened her mouth to say something and then closed it.

'What? Vicky? Do you think he killed Sophia? Is that what you're scared of? Please. We can only help you if you talk to us.'

'*No!*' she said, pushing her chair back and getting up. Such was the force of her reaction to the question, her feet hit the table and it upset her half-full mug of tea. Erika and Moss sat in the silence for a moment as they heard the tea splatter onto the stone floor. 'No... No. It's late. I'm so tired. No. I want to leave. You said that I can leave at any time. So I want to leave. Now! Please... officers... I haven't slept properly. I need to sleep. I can go and you need to let me go *now!*'

Erika looked at her watch. It was gone half past eleven. She felt like they'd barely scratched the surface of what had happened, and so much was disturbing in this situation. But she'd have to be patient. They needed to coax the information out of Vicky and to win her trust.

'Okay. Thank you, Vicky. We'll arrange for you to go to your sister's house.'

'Yes. Thank you.'

'You have to understand that you won't be able to go back to your flat for a while.'

'I don't ever want to go back,' said Vicky. 'Now, please. I need to go.'

30

Erika drove Vicky back to Blackheath from Lewisham Row, and it was midnight when they pulled up outside Tess and Jasper's house.

'Vicky. I know that you don't want to talk any more tonight—'

'I don't!' she said with gritted teeth. She went to undo her seatbelt.

'Then can I ask you to listen for just one minute? It might make you feel better.'

Vicky sat back and gave a long sigh, which made her seem younger than her twenty-seven years. Like a teenager being disciplined.

'If you know the person who did this, I promise you, *promise* you that you can tell me who they are and be safe. I will keep you safe... I have spent my whole career as a police officer going up against corrupt bastards, and many times they have been corrupt bastards in the police force. Officers who have a higher rank than I do...'

Vicky stared back at Erika in the darkness.

'How would you protect me?' she said in a small voice.

'I can call on resources to have police officers protect you, if you want to tell me anything.'

'And how can you be sure that you're not sending the corrupt ones to protect me?'

Erika realised she shouldn't have brought up the subject of corrupt police officers. Vicky hesitated, and Erika thought she was going to say something, and then she unclipped her seatbelt.

'Please. I want to sleep. I want to see my sister.'

'Will you come back first thing tomorrow and talk to me again? Informally, of course.'

'Yes.'

'Can I pick you up here, at, say, half past nine?'

'Okay.'

They got out of the car and went to the front door. There were no lights on inside the house when Erika rang the front doorbell. A moment later a light sprang on in the window above and then Tess opened the front door. She wore a thick woollen cardigan over a frumpy flowery nightdress.

'Oh God. Vicky. Why didn't you call me?' said Tess, grabbing her and pulling her into a hug. Vicky's voice was muffled for a moment, as she sobbed into her sister's chest.

Erika could see Jasper in the kitchen, standing at the hob.

'I'll come back at nine tomorrow morning,' said Erika. Vicky pulled away from her sister, her face red and blotchy, and nodded.

'Good night,' said Tess crisply, and slammed the door. Erika hung around for a moment, but couldn't hear anything through the door so she went back to her car.

Erika was frustrated. She knew very little, and this was a delicate situation. Technically, Vicky had fled the scene of a murder, and that was a crime, but she didn't want to go down that road yet. She hoped that Vicky would start to talk of her own accord.

Erika started the engine and drove the short journey home.

'I thought you were dead!' cried Tess, staring at Vicky with a mixture of anger and relief. The small living room felt hot, and Vicky stared back at her sister's accusing face.

'Why didn't you phone?' said Jasper, remaining behind the kitchen counter. It was like a barrier, keeping him distant.

'You wouldn't have understood,' said Vicky. Tess moved forward and Vicky thought for a moment that her sister was going to strike her. She flinched, but Tess pulled her into an embrace. She was taller, and Vicky felt her face being pushed into the material of Tess's fleece, and she felt her sister's arms encircling her grow tighter.

'Don't you ever do anything like that again, you hear me? You're all I have,' said Tess. She squeezed tighter and Vicky's face was pressed harder into the material. She could feel Tess's ribcage beneath her neck.

'Ow! You're smothering me,' she said, fighting to pull away. Tess held on for a moment longer and then let go. 'What are you doing? Trying to squeeze me to death?'

'What am I doing? Hugging you. I'm going mad with grief and worry!' shouted Tess, raising a finger and pointing it at her face. 'I thought you were dead! Do you know how that feels? Loss? I spent a day and a night thinking you were dead and that we were going to have to bury you! And now we hear you ran away! Jesus Christ, Vicky! I thought you'd pulled a few stunts in the past, but this!'

Vicky felt a sudden rage at her sister.

'Is that all you can say, you selfish bitch? Sophia is dead and all you can do is shout at me!'

Tess lashed out, and the slap was hard and unexpected. Vicky stood back in shock, holding her stinging cheek.

'How dare you speak to me like that in my house!' cried Tess.

'It's not your house. The bank owns it, like everything else!' shouted Vicky and she launched herself at her sister, nails out, wanting dearly to scratch her eyes out. Tess ducked out of the way, but not before Vicky gouged a corner of her cheek with a nail. Tess fought back and landed another hard slap on the side of Vicky's head. Her ear rang as she staggered back into the fireplace, hitting her back on the stone mantle and knocking a picture frame onto the carpet.

'*Enough!*' shouted Jasper. He slammed a frying pan down on the counter with a loud clang. 'Enough, the both of you!' He came around and stood between them. Vicky was leaning against the wall by the fireplace, clutching the side of her head. Tess was dabbing at a long scratch on the side of her cheek, which had started to bleed.

Vicky was surprised that Jasper seemed so hostile to them both. He didn't go to help Tess, or offer her a tissue to stop the bleeding.

'I'm glad you're okay, Vicky. But there's things we need to talk about, tomorrow,' he said. He looked at Tess again, and then went to the coat stand by the front door, grabbed his coat and left the house.

They were silent for a long minute after the front door slammed. Vicky picked up the photos; one was of Tess's wedding. She looked down and thought how happy they'd been. Tess beaming, radiant in her beautiful dress, as she signed the register with Jasper standing over her, sexy as hell in his dark suit. She smoothed her hand over the frame, and shook the inappropriate thought away guiltily. Relieved that the glass hadn't cracked in the fall, she placed it back on the mantelpiece. She looked back at

Tess, who was standing in the same spot, hand on her bleeding cheek, staring at the carpet.

'I'm sorry,' said Vicky. There was another long pause.

'Why didn't you come to me?' said Tess, in a small voice. 'Why did you go to Cilla?'

'It's complicated.'

'No, it's not,' said Tess, looking up at her with hostility in her eyes. 'You just don't want to tell me. What does Cilla have that I don't?'

'She doesn't judge me.'

'You think that's what I would have done? Judge you? Do you know who killed her? Sophia?'

Vicky kept eye contact with her sister, but didn't answer.

'What was she doing in your flat?'

'I just want to sleep,' said Vicky, feeling the weight of her exhaustion pressing down on her.

'So, that's it. Conversation closed? You cause this huge drama and that's it. Vicky's tired, she wants to go to bed. Vicky does as she pleases. Vicky gets what Vicky wants.'

'You have no idea what I've been through, Tess,' said Vicky.

'No, I don't... You'll have to sleep on the sofa,' said Tess, wiping at her chin with the back of her hand. She moved to the kitchen and grabbed some paper towels.

'Why can't I sleep in the spare room?'

'Because Jasper is sleeping in the spare room,' said Tess. She looked up at Vicky defiantly.

'Oh.'

'We've decided to take a break.'

'A break from what?'

Tess looked at her.

'Don't be fucking stupid. You know what that means.'

'Is this because of me?' Vicky started to say.

'No! Not everything is about *you!*' Tess exploded, seeming to surge with rage again. 'You are not the centre of the world! Whilst you were off living the life you wanted to live and doing whatever the hell you like, I've been here, trying to make money and keep hold of everything...' She dabbed the tissue on her chin. 'I'm going to put some antiseptic on this. God knows what's under your fingernails. I'm going to bed. There are blankets and pillows in the hall cupboard.'

Vicky watched her sister climb the stairs, and felt so alone in the empty front room.

31

When Erika arrived home, George the cat was waiting for her in the hallway, and purred and turned through her legs when she came through the front door. The house felt arctic. There was a small postcard on the floor in the hallway with *Argos Delivery* printed on one side. Typed on the other side was: *To change your delivery call this number*. Someone, presumably the delivery driver, had underlined the phone number in blue biro and added *because you weren't in!!!* She noted the three exclamation marks.

'Look at that, George, my first piece of post, from an angry delivery driver,' said Erika, leaning down and showing him the postcard. George sniffed at it, and then looked up at her with his emerald green eyes and a loud miaow. 'Are you agreeing with me?'

He miaowed again.

'Or is that, *feed me*?'

Miaow.

'I must learn how to speak cat. I wonder if Rosetta Stone do a cassette tape?' said Erika, walking through to the kitchen and flicking on the light. 'Oh bloody hell,' she said, seeing the mess of bare floorboards and boxes.

On her way back from dropping off Vicky, Erika had stopped at the petrol station and bought some food and two bags of wood and firelighters. The thought of another night on the floorboards was filling her with dread. She placed these in the corner of the kitchen. She opened another tin of her precious Májka pâté for George, made some toast, and heated up some baked beans in the microwave. She watched as George gobbled it down, and she hoped that he would stay and sleep on the end of her duvet. She looked up at the clock. It was long past midnight and she was eating her supper. Erika loved her job, but she longed to have at least one foot in the real world. She knew that having a man to come home to, was now most likely never going to happen, but she would settle for a cosy bed and an ordered house. She longed to have a bath and warmth and *carpets*.

Erika ate and then searched through her boxes until she found a stack of blankets. She was glad when George came with her. She lit a fire in the tiny grate of the back bedroom, and piled the blankets on top of the duvet. George walked onto the freshly made bed and turned in circles before settling down. He lay contentedly watching her.

Erika looked around the tiny warm room and realised how lucky she was. And then she thought of Vicky. The girl was burdened with secrets. And she thought back to the encounter with Charles Wakefield and the Assistant Commissioner, and how they didn't have a proper ID on Charles Wakefield's CCTV image.

Erika checked the time. It was now very late. She took a deep breath and dialled Marsh's mobile number, but it went straight to voicemail. She thought back to him jabbing his finger in the air in Melanie's office, demanding that he be updated on anything, however small. Erika dialled his landline number and pressed the 'call' button.

'Hello?' answered a woman's voice, thick with sleep. It was Marcie, Marsh's wife.

'Sorry to call so late. It's Erika,' she said.

There was a pause.

'Bloody hell, Erika. It's not late, it's early in the morning.'

'Yes, but it's urgent. Is Paul there?'

'He's asleep!'

'Can you wake him up?'

Marcie sighed heavily, muttered more expletives, and dropped the receiver with a clatter. There was a sound of bedsprings creaking and Erika listened as a door opened, and it sounded like Marcie went through to the hall and knocked on a door. Were Marsh and Marcie sleeping in different beds? A door opened.

'What is it?' said Marsh, sounding groggy.

'It's Erika on the landline,' said Marcie.

Erika felt uncomfortable overhearing the secrets of Marsh's dysfunctional marriage. A moment later, Marsh picked up the phone.

'What is it, Erika?' he said.

She quickly outlined what had happened when Vicky had seen Charles Wakefield at the station, and explained the problem with the CCTV footage.

'Jesus. You wake me up for this?'

'Paul, I can't verify Charles Wakefield's alibi for when Sophia was killed.'

'Sophia?'

'Yes, it was Sophia Ivanova who was killed, her body was wrongly identified as Vicky Clarke!' she snapped.

'Alright, don't bite my head off, you have just woken me up,' said Marsh.

'I need to prove Charles Wakefield is telling the truth and that he went into London, which gives him an alibi for when Sophia was murdered.'

'Come on, Erika, use your head. Go to that train station and get the staff member in the ticket office to verify it was him.'

'What if they can't? I need to bring him in for questioning, but Melanie is subtly warning me away, and the Assistant Commissioner pulled that charity stunt this evening, which sent a very clear message, even if everyone is insisting it was just a coincidence!'

Marsh sighed.

'Don't you have Charles Wakefield's DNA from his arrest?'

'Yes.'

'If you get a match with DNA at the crime scene, then you're free to arrest him, but until then, you need to tread carefully. I don't know what else you want me to say?'

Erika suddenly realised this phone call could have waited until morning. She'd allowed her anger and frustration to spill over.

'I dunno, maybe I just want someone to tell me that I'm not imagining things. That my instinct is right.'

'I was never an instinct copper,' said Marsh, in a rare moment of self-deprecation. 'I'm far better at brown-nosing in boardrooms.'

Erika laughed.

'Sorry to call so late.'

'Have you got any other suspects?'

'The boyfriend, Shawn Macavity. We have an hour or so of his time unaccounted for after he found Sophia's body. Again, we're waiting on getting a DNA sample from him. And, I dunno, I don't think he did it.'

'That isn't enough.'

'I know, it's my instinct though, and it's rarely wrong.'

'Watch that instinct, it'll get you into trouble.'

'Oh, it has, many times already,' said Erika.

'Good night, and good luck. I'm sure you'll have this sewn up in no time,' said Marsh. 'And feel free to call at a more sociable time if you need anything.'

When Erika came off the phone, she knew he was talking rubbish and trying to boost her confidence, but she appreciated the gesture nonetheless.

32

A short distance away from Erika's house, Vicky lay in the darkness of her sister's living room. The ceilings were low, like a country cottage's, and the house was very old, so it gave off strange creaks and groans. The front room and living room had been knocked into one, creating a long room with a double aspect view. The front window looked out from the living room half to the road out front, and the kitchen windows at the back looked out over a small yard with a huge ancient oak tree. A train rushed past on the tracks at the bottom of the garden, and as the ceiling creaked again, Vicky shivered and tried to get comfy under her blankets on the small sofa.

The fight with Tess had been terrible, but could she blame her? *How would I feel if the shoe was on the other foot, and she'd gone missing?* thought Vicky. And on top of all this Tess had other problems to deal with. She knew that the restaurant hadn't been doing well. Their rent was sky-high, and this coupled with the mortgage for the renovations on their house meant they were having money worries. And Jasper. How did he feel about her coming back from the dead? Not much, from the look of him.

She'd never quite understood the dynamic of her sister's marriage. Jasper was the one who came from money, but seemed to have no concept of it. It was always down to Tess to manage things. If the subject ever came up, Jasper would always make Tess feel common and low for 'talking about money', something he'd inherited from his background.

Vicky closed her eyes and shivered again. She was still dressed, and covered in three blankets and a duvet, but she couldn't get warm. She knew in her mind that she was skirting around the big issue – Sophia.

A car went puttering past on the road outside, and then all the sound seemed to fall away and an eerie quiet settled over the living room. She heard the rustle of dry leaves in the courtyard out back, and then, there was a soft knocking. She held her breath. *No. That was one of the old house noises. A wooden floorboard, or beam, settling.* The knock came again, slightly louder, from the back door.

Vicky sat up, pulling the blanket around her. The curtains were closed on both the front windows and the back, and just a thin strip of light from the street lamps on the road lit up the room with a soft orange glow.

The knock came again on the back door. *Tap tap tap.* And her heart leapt as a shadow crossed the curtain on the kitchen window.

'*Vicky, are you in there?*' came a voice. It was a man. Jasper. He'd stormed off and forgotten his keys. She got up and tiptoed across the room to the kitchen window, and parted the curtains. All she could see through the glass was the dark yard and the huge branches of the oak tree, lit up by the light pollution from the surrounding sky.

'*Vicky, are you there?*' came the voice again. It was Jasper, she thought. The knock came for a third time, soft and inoffensive, and she went to the door, slid the deadbolt across and turned the lock. It opened with a judder. It wasn't Jasper, it was a familiar, unexpected face. He smiled.

'Hello,' he said.

'Hello,' replied Vicky, thrown as to why he was here, at her sister's back door. 'What are you doing here?' she asked, feeling more confused than anything else.

' 'I know this seems odd, but can I come in for a moment?' he asked. 'Just out of the cold. We need to have a word. Talk and clear things up.' Vicky took a step back and pulled the blanket around her shoulders. She went to switch on the light but he put his hand up to her arm.

'No. Don't switch it on.'

'Why not?' she replied, now feeling unease creeping up amongst the confusion. He stepped forward and put his hand on her shoulder.

Vicky pulled away from him. She wanted to put the light on and see his face properly. She reached out for the switch again and he grabbed her hand, gripping it tightly.

'*No*,' he said. He suddenly pulled her towards him and she resisted. His body felt warm against hers, and his grip was strong. She went to shout but his hand closed over her mouth. He seemed to shift on his feet very quickly, propelling them both deeper into the kitchen, and then she felt a hollow thump on her back, between her shoulder blades. She felt his left arm tighten around her, pulling her close. His hand was still over her mouth, but she couldn't catch her breath. And then a sharp pain began to radiate out from her left shoulder, and something hard was pressing against her skin.

'Shh, *shush*, it'll be over soon,' he said, his voice soothing and his breath hot against her ear. Vicky gasped and heard her chest rattle and gurgle. He took his hand away from her mouth, but the only sound she could make was a muffled wheeze. The pain was dulling and spreading out from her shoulder. He pulled her closer and she could feel he was aroused. A wetness was spreading out at the base of her back, and she felt it on the tops of her legs. As she moved her arm up to feel behind her, pain shot through her shoulder joint. All this time he stared down at her, in a strange kind of matinee idol pose. To the unaware observer, it was as if he'd taken her in his arms. Her hand closed around the cold plastic hilt of a knife. Terror shot through her, and she tried to break free.

'Don't fight!' he hissed, his lips brushing her ear. He gripped her closer with his free arm and with his other hand he grabbed the hilt of the knife and twisted the blade, which she now knew was buried up to the hilt in her back. He was now rock hard against her, pushing himself against her body, pulling her deeper into him. Squeezing. Vicky could see the stairs, so tantalisingly close. Tess was sleeping upstairs. As she opened her mouth to try and call out, blood, hot and wet, began to bubble up her throat, and spilled out over her chin. It hit the stone floor with a nasty spatter.

'That's it, just another minute, it will all be over,' cooed his voice, still soft and syrupy in her ear. As he squeezed, she felt her heart pulsing as blood spilled out from her body, dripping down her legs, soaking the blanket still half draped around her shoulder. As the world began to fade out, she felt him tilt her body and lay her down on the cold tiled floor.

'*I got it wrong, it was you,*' she tried to say but it came out as just a rattle of blood.

She heard the clink as the hilt of the knife connected with the stone floor, and there was another explosion of pain, as her body weight pressed the blade deeper.

The last thing she saw were his eyes, burning deep into her, enjoying the final moments as the life left her body.

33

Erika rang Tess's front doorbell at 9am and there was no answer. She went to the front window. The curtains were closed, and so were the curtains in the rooms upstairs. She went back and rang the bell again. She was feeling groggy after dragging herself out of her nest of blankets, and having to take a cold shower. A minute passed, and then another. She rang the bell a third time, leaning on it slightly to lengthen it out. Finally, she heard bolts being drawn back, and when Tess opened the door, she appeared wild-haired and dishevelled.

'Morning... I told Vicky that I'd be back at nine, to talk to her,' said Erika.

'Sorry,' Tess said, rubbing at her eyes. She gave a big yawn. 'I think we had a power cut. My alarm didn't go off... I think Vicky's still asleep.'

Erika saw through the gap that the living room was in gloom behind her. Tess stayed in the doorway.

'Could you please wake her up? It's important I talk to her.'

Tess sighed, stepped back, and opened the door for Erika to come inside. The room was close and musty and there was a coppery tang to the air which put Erika on alert. Tess moved to the front window and opened the curtains. Light filled the room, and Erika saw that there were a couple of pillows and a discarded blanket on the sofa.

'She must have gone up to the bathroom,' said Tess.

'Okay. I can wait,' said Erika, peering into the gloom on the kitchen side of the room.

Tess crossed to open the kitchen curtains, and then she was quiet. Erika saw she was standing, very still, frozen to the spot, staring at the floor. The clock ticked in the silence, and a car engine idled on the road outside. The coppery smell suddenly seemed to come to the fore and Erika looked down to see a pair of feet sticking out from behind the large kitchen island.

Tess screamed and Erika rushed over. In the bright morning light, Vicky lay on her back on the kitchen floor with her eyes wide open, staring up at the ceiling. There was a large pool of blood underneath her.

Erika felt the floor drop. Tess was staring down with her eyes wide and her mouth was open now in a silent scream. Erika stepped forward and leant down to feel for a pulse but she knew that Vicky was dead. The pool of blood was wide, covering the pale stone floor, and she could see Vicky had been dead for some time. The blood was dark and shone like a mirror. There was blood over her face and down the front of her blue pyjamas, but Erika couldn't see any marks or wounds. There was a knock at the front door, making them both jump.

'No, no, no, no, no...' Tess was saying, shaking her head.

'Who is it?' shouted Erika, taking Tess gently by the hand and steering her away from the body to the sofa.

'It's Peterson!' he shouted from outside.

'The door's open,' said Erika. He came into the room and he saw Erika with Tess on the sofa. Erika tilted her head over towards the kitchen. Peterson walked over and stopped at Vicky's feet.

'Can you please call it in? ' said Erika in a low voice, keeping her eye on Tess, who was looking around the room frantically, not knowing what to do. Peterson reached for his phone, keeping his eyes on Vicky's body.

'Tess. Where is Jasper?' asked Erika gently. Tess frowned and stared at Peterson, standing over the body and talking into his phone.

'We had an argument. The last thing I said to her was that she had to sleep down here, on the sofa... I knew it would be cold. I was so angry at her.'

'Tess, where is Jasper, is he asleep?'

'What? Why are you asking me that? I don't know.'

'We need to wake him up and we need to leave the house.'

'Jasper? He isn't here,' replied Tess, hearing the question for the first time. Peterson was by the fireplace, talking on the phone to Lewisham Row control centre, asking for backup and forensics.

'Is he at the restaurant?' asked Erika.

'No... I don't know. I don't know where he is. He didn't come back last night.'

The room felt close and sticky. And the smell of blood and sweat seemed to be permeating Erika's nose and mouth.

'Tess, I need you to go upstairs and get dressed. Can you do that for me?'

'Why?'

'We need to leave the house so my team can take care of Vicky.'

'Vicky. She's dead, isn't she?'

'Yes. I'm sorry. Please, Tess can you get ready?'

Tess looked as if she was going to lose it, her bottom lip trembled, and then she nodded. Erika helped her up and over to the stairs.

Peterson came off the phone and a dark silence seemed to descend over the room, punctuated by small creaks and thuds as they heard Tess moving around above. Erika looked around at the room – had any evidence been compromised? There was a bloody shoe print by the back door. She moved closer and saw that it was from a heavy boot.

Vicky lay on her back, staring up at the ceiling with her eyes open. Her lips were slightly parted, and her long dark hair was splayed out, the back soaked with congealing blood. Erika pulled on a pair of latex gloves. Peterson did the same.

'Watch the blood,' he said, as Erika moved around to Vicky's head. She gently took one of her shoulders and lifted the body slightly. Peterson knelt down and peered under.

'Was she shot or stabbed? There's no sign of a murder weapon,' he said. Erika looked underneath.

'Looks like she was stabbed.' She gently replaced the body, got up and went to the back door, examining it.

'There's no sign that someone broke in. The door is intact.'

'So is the window,' said Peterson, skirting around the mirror of blood on the floor and peering out through the window to the yard out back.

'I should have put her in a safe house. I should have got the Family Liaison to stay with them,' said Erika, the horror of what had happened washing over her again. 'I thought staying with her family was a safe option.'

'There's no point going down that road, Erika,' said Peterson, reaching out to touch her arm. 'You were doing your job. You did a risk assessment. You can't predict what's going to happen.'

His phone rang and he answered it. Erika looked around at

the kitchen. There was the empty packaging from a ready meal and a dirty plate in the sink.

'It's number eight on the end of the short terrace. Yeah, top of the street,' Peterson was saying. He hung up the phone. 'Uniform will be here in a minute.'

'Doesn't it seem quiet to you upstairs?' said Erika, noticing that the creaking of Tess moving around had stopped.

She turned away from the body and hurried upstairs. There were two small bedrooms and a bathroom leading off the landing. She found Tess in the bedroom with a window facing the back garden. The bed was unmade, and she was crouching on the carpet in front of the open wardrobe doors. Erika could see inside that there was a small, built-in metal safe, like the type you see in hotels.

Tess was still in her dressing gown, and she turned to Erika with a bleak, dead-eyed stare.

'It's all gone,' she said.

'What's gone?' asked Erika, moving around the bed to join her. There was a pool of dirty dishes and mugs on the grubby blue carpet next to the bed, and the wardrobe above the safe was a mess of packed-in clothes on hangers.

'Money. We had cash in here. Three thousand pounds, and Jasper had some gold jewellery. I opened the safe to take some cash with me, and it's all gone...' Erika heard the sound of a police siren and a car pulling up outside. 'He's taken it. It must be him. Jasper is the only one who knows the combination for the safe.'

Erika was confused. Tess had just discovered her sister's dead body, and now she was worrying about what was in her safe.

'Tess, we need to leave the house, this is now a crime scene,' she said as gently as possible. She moved to a chair in the corner piled high with clothes; she couldn't determine if they were clean or dirty. There was a handbag on the arm. 'Is this your bag?'

Tess was still crouching in front of the empty safe.

'Yes.'

Erika saw a mobile phone by the bed on a charger and she picked it up and put it in the bag. 'Please, Tess. I know this is awful for you, but you need to put some clothes on. We need to leave.'

34

Two police officers arrived as Erika and Peterson came out of the house with Tess, who was now dressed, but still dazed and in shock. They were standing out on the pavement when a silver Ford Focus came around the corner, and slowed as it drew close. Erika saw that Jasper was driving. When he noticed them standing outside the house with the police car, he put his foot down and shot past.

'What's he doing? He must have seen what's happening here,' said Erika. They watched as the car came to a screeching halt at the end of the road, and then with a roar reversed back to the junction leading to the main road. He turned into it with another screech of rubber, and the car vanished. Peterson looked at Erika.

'I don't like this,' he said.

'Neither do I, come on,' said Erika. After quickly handing off Tess to be looked after by one of the uniforms, they jumped in to Erika's car.

'He's heading towards the South Circular,' said Peterson as Erika started the engine and put the car in gear. They set off towards the junction in pursuit of Jasper, and Peterson gripped the door as Erika floored the accelerator and switched on the blue lights and sirens. She took the left turn with a scream of rubber, and up ahead she saw Blackheath Common, the grass a dirty brown colour.

'There,' said Peterson. Jasper's Ford Focus was already halfway across the Common, waiting at a set of traffic lights.

'What's he doing? Why is he running away?' Erika kept repeating, almost under her breath.

An old lady was about to cross the road in front of them, laden down with shopping bags, but Erika honked the horn and she stepped back, falling into a thick hedgerow.

Peterson looked back at the old lady who was half-standing, half-lying in the hedge, her bags of shopping pooled around her, and oranges rolling into the road. The traffic lights turned green and Jasper sped off, opening out the gap between them. Erika grabbed the radio off the dashboard.

'This is DCI Erika Foster 34568, in pursuit of a silver Ford Focus by Blackheath Common. We're heading south towards the A20. Suspect driving is a Jasper Clark, no "e" white male mid-thirties...'

They crossed the junction and sped onward towards another set of traffic lights. Jasper's car shot over the junction just as the lights turned red. On either side of the road was the common, but it was built up in places and the grass was uneven.

Erika wasn't going to wait for backup to take over. She slammed the steering wheel to the right and the car bumped and the engine screamed as she drove past the line of traffic between the tarmac and the common, and rejoined the road with a bump. A lorry driving perpendicular over the crossroad screeched to a halt, and they narrowly missed another car coming from the other direction as they shot over the junction and continued in pursuit of Jasper, who was now close to a third set of traffic lights which were green.

'We have a squad car in Greenwich, on its way over,' said the voice at control.

'If you were trying to escape arrest, where would you go?' asked Erika. The lights up ahead turned amber. She saw Peterson glance at the needle on the speedometer as it hit a hundred mph as she pushed the car over the junction. When they reached the other side, the tarmac was uneven and dipped down. The wheels left the road for a moment and Erika felt her stomach lurch. Peterson pressed his feet to the floor and arms against the door as they landed back down with a bump. They were gaining on Jasper; his car was now twenty metres away.

'I'd head for the M20, and down to the south coast. Do you think he has a plan?' said Peterson, who looked a little spooked by Erika's driving. The radio crackled on the dashboard. Peterson grabbed it.

'This is control to 34568. Do you have a number plate on the silver Ford Focus?'

'No, it's covered in dirt. I can only make out the first two letters, B for Bravo D for David...' he said.

They were still hurtling along the road with the needle close to a hundred, and there was something in her face, the grim set of her jaw, that made Peterson think she'd do anything to catch this car.

'He's slowing down, look out!' cried Peterson. The back of the Ford seemed to be hurtling towards them and Erika slammed on the brakes. Jasper turned left into a thin alleyway, and they overshot it. A parade of shops was on their right, and another elderly lady was stepping off the pavement, and jumped back as Erika came screeching to a halt. Their sirens were blaring and pedestrians on the pavement were staring back as Erika put the car in reverse. They lurched back, and turned down into the thin alleyway running between two rows of houses backing onto each other.

Erika could see the Ford was now far down the alley. She ground the gears, swore and they started after it. The high walls either side sped past in a blur.

'Steady, easy,' said Peterson, pressing his hands flat against the window and his chair. Erika felt sweat between her shoulder blades. Car chases were much more fun to watch in the comfort of your living room, but she was determined not to lose sight of Jasper.

Why is he running? What's he done? Erika thought as the wing mirror on Peterson's side clipped a wheelie bin sitting nestled in an open gate, and as she swerved away the wing mirror on her side broke away with a loud bang and a spray of sparks as it hit the brick wall.

They burst out of the alleyway and were on a wide pedestrian footpath between blocks of council flats.

Peterson picked up the radio and updated control on their position, which was moving through the Forbes Housing Estate. Jasper's Ford was at the end of the path, where it looked like the land banked down and below was a kids' play park. Beyond it was the main road with a dual carriageway.

For the first time, Erika got a good close-up look at Jasper Clark when he stuck his head out of the car window. It wasn't until they drew close that she knew why he'd opened his window to look out. At the end of the pedestrian footpath, there was a set of steep steps leading down to the play park where the path continued, running alongside the grass and the swings, to the dual carriageway on the other side.

Jasper's face was flushed, with a hunted look about it; eyes wide with fear and his teeth bared. When he saw how close behind him they were, his head disappeared back inside the car.

'No, he's not going to...' Peterson started to say as they

came within ten metres of the Ford, before it pulled away and off the edge of the steps. Erika thought for a moment that Jasper was going to make it, as the car tipped forward and set off down the steep steps at a slow speed, but as he reached the bottom, the incline must have been too great, because the car hit the path below and flipped over with a roar of its engine. It rolled over twice on the grass, coming to a stop at the edge of the play park.

'No!' cried Peterson, grabbing the door as they reached the edge of the steps. Erika braked abruptly and could see how steep the drop was fifteen steps below.

'I wasn't going to drive down after him!' cried Erika, yanking up the handbrake and unclipping her seatbelt.

'I did wonder for a minute,' said Peterson. She opened the door and ran down the steps. He undid his seatbelt and followed.

Jasper's car lay on its roof with the back wheels still spinning and black smoke pouring from the exhaust. There was a row of thin trees lining the footpath by the play park and he'd hit one of them. The tree was bent over, but hadn't snapped, and was holding up the front of the car.

As they ran towards the upturned car, Erika could see people coming out onto their balconies from the blocks of flats. She heard Peterson behind her calling in to control with an update on the pursuit. And then she saw Jasper, bleeding from his forehead as he wriggled out of the driver's window. He started to limp away, picking up speed, but Erika reached him and grabbed hold of his shirt. He slithered out of it, and carried on running towards the play park. She stumbled with his shirt in her hand and for a moment she thought that, somehow, Jasper was going to get away. As he wound his way through the swings his arm caught on one of the chains and he went down onto the ground. Erika was on him a moment later, and Peterson was at her side with a pair of handcuffs.

'No! You can't do this!' Jasper cried. There was blood pouring from the gash on his head and running into his right eye.

'What are you doing? Why are you running?' said Erika, trying to catch her breath.

'I just wanted to go. I just... Want to leave this place, and everything in it.'

'Do you even know why we were at your house?'

He stopped fighting and sank back on the grass.

'Tess is okay, I saw her standing with you on the pavement...'

'We found Vicky's body this morning, in your house.'

He gasped, trying to catch his breath.

'What?'

Erika looked at Peterson.

'Where were you last night? Tess said you left and took cash and valuables with you.'

'I was at the restaurant. I slept at the restaurant,' he said. 'Oh, Jesus. Vicky's dead?'

'Yes,' said Erika. 'She's dead.'

35

The upturned car was drawing a crowd outside the block of flats, and people were watching and taking photos from their balconies above.

An ambulance had arrived swiftly on the scene, and Jasper had been taken to hospital to be checked out for concussion and have the cut on his head stitched up. A police car was parked beside Erika's car at the top of the steps, and three uniformed officers had cordoned off Jasper's car with a circle of police tape and were now standing guard and scowling up at the people watching from their balconies. Erika wasn't sure if this was causing more problems than it was worth. This was a rough block of flats on a dodgy estate, and the presence of the police was bringing out the usual clowns.

'Hey, Luther,' said a voice from above. Erika and Peterson looked up. A young lad with acne and a ratty fuzz of stubble on his face was looking down at them from a balcony on the third floor above. At his knee, poking his head through the railings, was a tiny elf-like boy in a fluffy blue dressing gown. They ignored him, and Erika looked back at the car. She didn't want to wait for the tow truck to arrive. The hatchback boot had been filled with bags of groceries, and during the crash, they'd discharged themselves over the inside of the car, littering it with oranges, apples, tins of beans and fruit and rice from a burst bag. Amongst the food, there were three large rucksacks on the back seat. Erika heard a whistle from above and something came raining down, splattering on the grass. Peterson jumped out of the way.

'Sorry, I spilled my tea,' said the young lad on the balcony above. The little boy with him cackled and shrieked with laughter.

'Do you want to spend the night in a cell?' shouted Peterson, looking up at them.

'Easy, Luther... I'd say that wouldn't be the best use of police resources, I only spilt a bit of cold tea,' shouted the lad.

'Can you please go back inside your flat,' Erika shouted, moving over to join Peterson.

'Is that your girlfriend, Luther?' shouted the lad.

'Are you British?' asked the little boy. 'You sound Polish?'

Erika looked at Peterson and rolled her eyes.

'Oi, that's a valid question. We haven't seen your ID,' said the lad, patting the little boy on the head. 'What's your name, blondie? You look a bit like Brigitte Nielsen, if she 'ad a tape worm.'

There were a couple of laughs from other residents on their balconies above and below.

'How do you know who Brigitte Nielsen is?' shouted a woman's voice.

'My granddad likes 'er,' shouted the lad. 'Last time I went up to see him, I caught him jerking off to *Red Sonja*.' Someone else whistled and a lit cigarette butt came floating down towards them. Erika had to duck out of its way.

'If one more thing gets thrown, I call for back-up and this

place will be swarming with coppers,' shouted Erika up at the balconies above.

'Hey, don't give 'em shit. Luther and Brigitte are only doin' their jobs,' said the lad, leaning out over the edge to look up at the flats above. He turned his head back. 'You see that, Brigitte, I'm looking out for you... I think the police do a good job,' he added with sarcasm.

'Let's get the stuff out of Jasper's car and get out of here,' said Peterson. 'Uniform can wait for the tow truck.' They ignored the shouts and catcalls from above, and pulled on a pair of latex gloves each. Erika and Peterson managed to get the rear passenger door open, which was harder than it looked when the car was upside down and balanced on a small tree trunk. The back of the car was at an angle, and Erika stepped into the interior of the roof and retrieved the three rucksacks.

They went to leave and heard a voice shout.

'What's Jasper done now?'

Erika's turned to where the voice had come from. The lad with the ratty beard was now standing across the grass at the main entrance of the flats. She put down the rucksack and pulled off her latex gloves. They ducked under the police tape and went over to him. He looked older close-up, and she could see he was in his late thirties, pale and bloated.

'Was that you yelling about Jasper?' said Erika. Close-up there was a horrible smell of stale booze on his breath. He wore a faded Man United football shirt with a thin jacket. Poking out of the breast pocket was a pack of cigarettes and a lighter.

'Do you still give narks cash for info?' he said.

'Are you a nark?' asked Peterson.

'I could be, Luther,' he said, lowering his voice and glancing up at the balcony above them. 'I was only kidding, what I said about you looking like Brigitte Nielsen with a tape worm. You look pretty good close up.'

'It looks like you could do with a tape worm,' replied Erika. She thought she might have taken the banter too far, but he grinned with yellowing teeth.

'Touché turtle,' he said, spitting on the floor. He looked between Erika and Peterson and took the cigarettes out of his top pocket. His nails were stained yellow from nicotine. 'I did time back in 2004. Belmarsh.'

Belmarsh was a Category A prison, which housed high-profile serious offenders.

'What do you know about Jasper?' she asked. The man lit his cigarette and exhaled, picking a piece of tobacco from the tip of his furry tongue.

'He was in for rape. *Jaspaaar. Jaspaaar Claaaark*, no "e",' he said, affecting a posh voice for Jasper's name. 'He was like a nasty posh boy, trapped in the body of a chav. He did eight years in all. His sentence was five, but he got extra for dealing inside. He had quite the operation going on. Bringing in mobile phones, heroin, cocaine. The screws didn't know how he was doing it. Nor did we.'

'How was he doing it?' asked Erika. She felt a little surge of interest and dismay that they were finding this out about Jasper from some random chav on the Forbes Housing Estate, if it was true, that is. The lad grinned and leaned in closer.

'He'd managed to run a zip line from the building opposite the nick. Thin, clear fishing line. No one could see it. He had someone working on the outside.'

'Who did he have working on the outside?'

'I dunno. When they busted him he got the extra time added to his sentence.'

'And you recognised him from five floors up?' said Peterson.

'Course I recognised him. I went to his restaurant a few months back. He wasn't pleased to see his old mate from inside. Had me chucked out when I tried to order a pint. What's he done now, with all this?' he said, indicating the upturned car with his lit cigarette and swirling smoke around in the process.

'We can't tell you,' said Erika. 'What's your name, in case I want to ask you anything else?'

'Call me Johnny. And that'll be twenty quid,' he said, holding his hand out. Erika rummaged around in her pocket and pulled out her wallet. She gave him a twenty. He pocketed it.

'Lovely doing business with you, Bridge, and you, Luther. I love your show. When are you doing a new series?'

'Come on, let's go,' said Peterson. They started back across the grass towards Erika's car. 'I can't believe that you gave him money.'

'He might be useful, you never know,' said Erika, looking back. Johnny was squinting at them, and lighting another cigarette.

'*Jaspaaar. Jaspaaar Claaaark*, no "e",' he shouted after them.

'Check if Jasper has a record,' said Erika. 'And we need to find out if he has an alibi for last night.'

36

When Erika and Peterson arrived back at Tess's house, the police had closed off the road, and there was now a forensics van and a police support van parked outside. They were about to ask to talk to Tess about Jasper's alibi, when Moss met them at the kerb, carrying a large clear plastic evidence bag.

'I need a word, I found something interesting in Vicky's backpack,' she said, holding it up.

'Let's get some privacy,' said Erika, indicating the police support van. They climbed in and sat at the small table inside.

'Vicky left London with just this bag,' said Moss, holding it up. 'It was inside Tess's house, in the living room. When I first looked through it, I didn't find anything, just some clothes, a bit of cash, toiletries and make-up. It was only when I was scrunching it up to put it into this smaller plastic evidence bag that I felt this tiny USB key wedged in the lining of one of the pockets.' Moss took out a small evidence bag from her pocket and slid it across the table to Erika and Peterson. The USB key was less than a centimetre square. When Erika saw it, she felt a buzz of excitement.

'Did it look like it had been hidden there? Concealed in the pocket?'

'It's a tiny pocket, and it was lodged in the lining, so it could have been hidden, or it could have been forgotten about,' said Moss.

'Have you looked what's on it?'

'No. We need a secure laptop.' Peterson got up and looked in the cupboards on the tech side of the support van, where they had access to multiple phone lines, fax machines and the HOLMES police database. He dug out a laptop which was secure for looking at digital evidence and placed it on the table between them.

Erika booted it up, and then inserted the USB key. They waited for an agonising moment, and then a file popped up on the desktop, named ROUGH CUTS. When Erika clicked on it, there were five audio files inside, which were simply named 1 to 5.

'God, I hope this is podcast stuff, and not Shawn's music – he writes music apparently. What if this is a demo for some angsty home studio EP?' said Moss.

Peterson rolled his eyes. 'Just click on the first file,' he said.

Erika clicked on the file marked "1", and adjusted the volume.

There was a crackle and some interference, and then they heard Vicky's voice. It sounded like she was in a busy bar or café. Indecipherable voices and the sounds of cutlery and plates hummed away in the background.

'Okay. This is for episode eighteen,' said Vicky. 'Wild track background for the interview I've already done with...' There was the sound of her flicking pages in a notebook. 'Becky Wayland. I'm here at Henry's in Covent Garden to do the recording. Any excuse to put this coffee and croissant on business expenses,' she added with a laugh. 'Okay. I'll shut up now.' There was more interference and then the digital recorder ran for a couple of minutes with the ambient sounds of humming and chatter. A loud laugh punctuated it at one point.

Erika paused the playback.

'She just referenced a notebook in the recording. Where are all of her notebooks? We didn't find anything at her flat.'

The second sound file started with more interference and background chatter.

'This is my interview with Becky Wayland,' said Vicky. 'Okay, Becky. So just ignore my phone. I'm recording everything. I'll edit stuff down, so feel free to just talk. Okay?'

'Okay, right,' said Becky. She spoke softly with a thick Norfolk accent.

'When did you first come to London and why?'

Becky sighed.

'It was back in 2012, and I'd applied to a few London drama schools, five drama schools in total, and I got an interview with GDA and RADA.'

'That's Goldsmith's Drama Academy? And the Royal Academy of Dramatic Art?' asked Vicky.

'Yeah. I had two interviews on the same day, the first was at RADA in Central London in the morning, and the second was GDA, a workshop for the whole afternoon until six. My mum wasn't keen on me going up to London by myself and coming home so late, but then GDA sent through details of accommodation in their student halls. So I arranged to stay, then get the train home early the next morning.'

'Can you remember the road the student halls were on?'

'It was Jubilee Road.'

'Okay. Thank you. Tell me what happened.'

'There were three other girls who auditioned with me at GDS, staying overnight. The student halls on Jubilee Road was a big old terraced house near New Cross Gate station. It had three floors and a shared bathroom on each floor. We found a chippy round the corner, and stopped up for a bit in the kitchen, talking. I went to my room around ten thirty. It was on the ground floor. It was a bit basic but clean. It was February, but the room was like a sauna. The old radiator in the room had the knob missing, which wouldn't turn down, but there were bars on the window, so I felt safe opening the small window at the top. The other thing that was weird was that the bulbs were missing in the main light and bedside lamp. There was a bit of light coming in from opposite. I had a torch on my phone, and it was late and I couldn't be bothered to do anything about it. I crashed out sleeping almost right away. And then I woke up at one thirty, cos I heard a noise outside my window...'

'What kind of noise?' asked Vicky.

'Feet scuffing on concrete. The window in my room looked out on a courtyard behind the building. The curtains were very thin, and didn't close properly. That's when I saw a shadow of a person outside move across the gap.'

'What did you do?'

'I thought it was another student out in the courtyard having a cigarette. I'd heard a couple of the other girls who were staying there say that's where people smoke... Then I saw a flicker of light, and smelt cigarette smoke, so I relaxed and fell back to sleep... I woke up again, later, and this time it was very cold in the room. The heating must have gone off. I heard this high-pitched sound. *Eek, eek, eek...*'

'What was it?'

'There was a pair of hands reaching through the small open window, working with a screwdriver, unscrewing the bars on the window.'

'The bars were attached to the inside of the window?'

'Yes. I didn't think that was weird until I saw someone reaching in and unscrewing them. It all happened so fast. He reached the top half of his body through, lifted the set of bars off the wall and lowered them onto the floor.'

'How did he reach down to undo the screws at the bottom of the bars?'

'They can't have been screwed in at the bottom,' she said, her voice quavering. 'With the bars off, he climbed inside, so his shoulders and torso were now through the narrow top window. I thought I was dreaming. He was so brazen and confident as I watched him.'

'Did he know you could see him?'

'I don't know. It was all in shadow. I didn't see his face... He slithered his way through that high window at the top, and down into the room, head first, putting his hands on the windowsill like in a head stand. He hit the floor with a thud and then he slowly stood up. His shadow seemed to grow and elongate at the bottom of my bed. It was terrifying. That's when I tried to run for it... He got to the door before me.' On the audio recording they heard her voice was thick with emotion. 'And he pushed me back onto the bed.'

'It's okay. Take your time,' said Vicky.

'I lay there as he stood over me. I should have screamed. I should have fought, but I just lay there. The room seemed so small and he seemed to fill it. He went to the door and checked that it was locked, and then he came back over.'

'Could you see his face?'

'No. It was very dark. The light bulbs were gone, and in the middle of the night there wasn't much light coming in from outside...'

There was a heavy silence, and they heard a rustle of something, maybe tissues.

'Take your time,' said Vicky.

'He pushed himself on top of me. I just remember the smell of him, he had a really horrible strong aftershave on. Like it was too much, and mixed in with this he had horrible breath... He said, "*Keep your mouth shut, bitch, and I won't hurt you...*" He grabbed my arms and pinned me down... put his knee between my legs... He kept saying "*shush, shush, shush*" like I was a little kid who'd woken from a bad dream. As he loomed over me with his breath, he started to drool. It was disgusting. He was drooling like a dog and I felt it on my neck and my cheek... And he was... he was hard. I could feel it... Then, *thank God*, I heard someone in the corridor outside, one of the other girls had gone to use the bathroom at the end of the corridor. The toilet flushing distracted him for a moment. I suddenly thought that this is not how my life was going to end. I managed to get my hand free. I'd been to this self-defence class where they showed us this move, where you hit someone with the flat of your hand up and under their nose... I don't know how I got the courage, but I hit him hard... And I must have got the bullseye, cos he screamed, and I screamed, and then he ran for it. He got the door open, and he was gone. The corridor was dark outside... I lay there for a second in shock with the door wide open. And then I freaked out and closed and locked it and put a chair up against it...'

'What did you do next?' asked Vicky.

'I closed the window. It was around 3am, and I was terrified he was going to come back... And I stayed there until it got light.'

'Did you report it?'

'I wasn't going to. I waited until six, when it started to get light and I just wanted to leave there and run for it and get the train... I saw one of the girls as I was leaving. And she saw me and asked if everything was okay, and I told her... She was the one who persuaded me to go to the police. And I reported it.'

'What happened after you reported it?'

'Nothing,' she said. 'I never heard from the police, or from anyone at GDA again. I didn't get a place at the drama school. I didn't want to go back. It was as if it never happened.'

37

'Vicky was due to upload episode eighteen of her podcast last week, but she didn't,' said Erika when the recording had finished.

'If it was an episode about a sex attacker, would we know about it? There could be something in the system, if this Becky Wayland reported it,' said Peterson.

'But we don't have an exact date of when it happened,' said Moss.

'But we have an address. We need to find out how many houses GDA operates as student accommodation,' said Erika. 'Again, we need to find out where Vicky kept her notes.'

'There are three more files,' said Moss. She clicked on the third one. They heard Vicky clear her throat, and she spoke with a heightened dramatic intensity.

'This is take one, introduction to act two of episode eighteen... With bulb lamp sound effect...' She cleared her throat, and then affected a more serious tone of voice. 'The three students I've spoken to all tell a similar tale. Whilst staying in ground floor rooms at student halls in and around New Cross Gate, they reported the radiator being broken and a sweltering room...'

There was a squeaking sound, of metal on metal, rhythmic. 'The old-fashioned screw-in bulbs were missing from the lights...' The squeaking sound continued. 'Had someone deliberately staged these rooms? Unscrewing the bulbs and setting the heating on high? I spoke to another woman...' There was a pause and then they heard the flicking of pages in a notebook, and her voice went back to her normal tone. 'Oh shit, what's her name?'

Here, the recording ended abruptly. Moss clicked on sound file number four. This was a second 'take' of the same and when they reached the same point where Vicky had cut off, she had the woman's name as Kathleen Barber.

'Kathleen managed to scare the man off before he could do anything... Another woman, Grace Leith, reported a man in her room, but he was scared off by Grace's boyfriend coming back from the bathroom.' At the end of the track there was a pop and a smash as the bulb broke. The sound file ended.

'Three names,' said Erika as Moss clicked on the final sound file. It was a recording of a phone call. The phone was ringing, slightly tinny, through the speakerphone. The phone was answered by a woman who announced that she worked for the GDA Student Welfare office. Vicky told the woman that her name was Becky Wayland, and that she was following up on an incident of attempted assault in their Jubilee Road student accommodation, which she had reported back in February 2012. There was a long silence on the end of the phone.

'Sorry. Why are you calling?' asked the woman, whose voice now seemed guarded.

'You see, I reported this to the police, and the Student Welfare office at GDA, and this was six years ago. I heard nothing back...' There was another long pause.

'Do you have a crime number?' the woman said finally.

'No. I don't, but I would hope that as this was a serious incident there would be something you could tell me.'

'This would be a matter for the police, surely?'

'Yes, but I was staying in the Jubilee Road building when someone broke into my room. There must be a record of this, and a police follow-up? I've got the other two names here. Kathleen Barber had a similar experience in the same building, a month before me, in January 2012, and Grace Leith in February 2014 in another student halls building in Hartwood Road near New Cross Gate station. Have you any other reports of incidents?'

The woman on the end of the phone now sounded very flustered.

'I'm afraid I'll have to get someone to call you back, and if you have a crime number I'd be better placed to direct your call...' Vicky gave her numbers and the woman hung up.

'Better placed to direct your call,' said Vicky after it ended. 'What am I? Someone who's phoning up about the curtains she's ordered?!'

The sound file ended abruptly.

'We have dates,' said Erika. 'And two addresses of student halls.'

'The light bulb thing is making me shudder,' said Moss. 'Imagine being somewhere where you can't turn on the light.'

'And in January and February it gets dark very early,' said Peterson.

'We need to run all of these through the system and see what happened to Becky Wayland's police report,' said Erika. 'And see if there are any similar incidents logged – did Kathleen or Grace report what happened?'

38

Later that afternoon, Jasper was released from hospital and agreed to be interviewed at Lewisham Row station.

Erika sat across from him in an interview room, flanked by Peterson and Jasper's solicitor. Jasper had a bandage on his forehead and a ripening bruise on the side of his head.

'Why did you run from us?' asked Erika.

He sat staring at the table, then took a deep breath. 'I was trying to clock out,' he said.

'What does that mean?'

'Leave. I want to leave. I'm clinging on. And I can't do it anymore. We're not going to make rent next month on the restaurant. We'll miss our fifth mortgage payment for the house. I didn't know about Vicky when I drove away...' He shook his head and looked genuinely horrified. 'Tess found her body?'

'Yes.'

'They had their rivalries, as sisters, but *Jesus*. This will destroy Tess.' He shook his head and looked down at the table.

'Do you still want to leave?' asked Erika.

'I can't now, can I?'

'Where were you between midnight last night when I dropped Vicky off, and this morning when we saw you drive past in the car?'

'I slept at the restaurant. There's a room upstairs where I sleep sometimes.'

'Can anyone corroborate this?'

'No, but I have CCTV at Goose. I can give you tapes which show me arrive and leave. And it's on the main high street.'

Erika looked at Peterson. Just because he had CCTV didn't mean he was there the whole time. She leafed through a file she had on the desk, and reached the page she was looking for.

'We know you have a criminal record, Jasper.'

'Who told you?'

Erika didn't want to tell him that they had to find out from some scally on the Forbes Estate.

'We have it all in our database. You served eight years in prison for stalking and harassing one woman, and raping another. And you were running a drugs ring inside which put extra time on your sentence.'

'Have you told Tess?' said Jasper, his voice hoarse. He was now turning red and shaking.

'Tess doesn't know you were in prison?' asked Erika, sitting back in surprise.

'She knows I was inside, just not, why, exactly.'

'Why did she think you were inside?' asked Peterson.

'Tax fraud,' he said, after a beat.

Jesus, thought Erika. *Tess had no idea who she was married to, and I put Vicky in that house.*

'No. We haven't told her,' said Erika. Jasper sat back and seemed to sag in his chair.

'Very good. We are now all aware of my client's previous offences,' said the solicitor. There was a tone to his voice that indicated he wanted to move on from this. Erika turned to the pinstripe suit, the upper-class accent, and saw the obvious disdain he had for the police.

'What's your name again?' she asked him.

'Martin Semple,' he said.

Erika opened the file in front of her.

'Mr Semple. On the 14th August 2004 the first woman, eighteen-year-old Kelly Chalk, was walking home from a night out in Brixton. Your client followed her home, and into the communal hallway where she lived. He pushed her into her flat, where he raped her. The second woman, Tina Rogers, was luckier. Your client broke in through the open window of her ground floor flat and found his way to her bedroom, but then her flatmate scared him off.'

The solicitor blustered a little and fiddled with his pen, looking down at the table.

'As I said, we are all aware.'

'Do you have a daughter, Mr Semple?'

'I really don't think this is appropriate... Detective Inspector.'

'It's Detective *Chief* Inspector,' said Erika. 'And I am bringing this up for a reason.'

He tilted his head in acknowledgement, but didn't correct himself.

'Addressing me personally is unprofessional and at worst distasteful. And I will remind you that my client is here *voluntarily*.'

'Distasteful,' repeated Erika. 'You might want to check what side of the table you're sitting on.'

'Is that what this is? *A game of sides?*'

Jasper was now looking between Erika and his solicitor with a morbid fascination.

'Erika. Can I have a word. Outside?' asked Peterson. She saw the look of concern on his face. She nodded.

'What are you doing?' he asked when they were out in the corridor. Erika leant against the wall, and folded her arms.

'Have you read the case file?'

'Not all of it. It's been a very busy day,' said Peterson, on the defensive.

'Okay, well, Kelly Chalk, the young woman he raped, was just eighteen. A student. She'd only left home three weeks before... The second woman, Tina Rogers, had grown up in care. She had no family there to support her at the time or afterwards. *Jasper* was educated at a very good fee-paying school, he has a family, people who care about him. His psych report mentions that he had – has – sadistic tendencies. James, I brought Vicky back to London to answer questions, I promised she would be safe, and then I go and stick her in a house with a fucking convicted rapist!'

'You didn't know he was a convicted rapist. And he's telling us that he didn't stay at the house.'

'Come on, James! That's pending the results of some crappy CCTV cameras at Goose. I should have checked the family out sooner. What if Vicky was close to finding out who this serial attacker was in the student halls, or she found out it was Jasper?'

'That's a big leap without any other evidence.'

'But it's a question we should ask.'

'Yes, but he's also one question away from walking out. Erika, he's here voluntarily with a fancy-schmancy solicitor,' said Peterson. He put his hand on her arm. 'I hope I'm not talking out of turn here.'

Erika put her face in her hands and rubbed her eyes.

'No, of course not. You're right, I need more evidence. It just burns that his solicitor thought I didn't have the right to bring up Jasper's past convictions for violence against women!'

'It's relevant, but Jasper's done his time for that,' said Peterson. He put his hands up in the air. 'I'm not making excuses, I'm just saying, he didn't get away with it.'

'He got six years! That's nothing in a seventy-five-year life expectancy. It's taken me longer to save up for a bloody deposit to buy my house,' said Erika.

'And what's your point?'

'Surely saving up for a mortgage deposit shouldn't take longer than a prison sentence for rape.'

Peterson shook his head and smiled.

'I think we should file that last comment under "white privilege".' Erika looked up at him, and felt mortified. 'I'm kidding,' he added with a smile. 'There should always be room for a bit of black humour, otherwise we'd go crazy.'

Erika shook her head. 'You can't joke about that,' she said, with a small smile.

'I can. And we're friends now, aren't we?'

Erika sighed and looked at him. Is that what they were now? Friends. She hoped so. The thought of him not being in her life in some way filled her with dread. She had a fleeting image of him with Fran, lying in their new bed. She shook it away.

'Of course,' replied Erika. 'Thanks for pulling me back.'

'As my mate Leon always says, sometimes, you've gotta check yourself before you wreck yourself,' he said with a grin.

'You don't have a mate called Leon.'

'I could. And if I did, I'd remember those wise words.'

There was a moment of silence between them.

'Seriously, James, I just don't like the similarities between that podcast episode Vicky was working on and what he went down for. Vicky was scared of someone... And Jasper says he's broke, and he was going to skip the country, but he's rocked up here with a very expensive solicitor. It's all very fishy.'

'Let's get back inside and work on him, before he gets fed up and leaves,' said Peterson. 'Softly softly.'

39

'Could we please talk about your relationship with Vicky?' said Erika. They were back in the interview room, and Erika felt she'd regained control of her emotions. Jasper was sitting hunched over, with the flat of his palm on the side of his head, just below the bandage now spotting with blood. He still seemed in shock from the morning's events.

'She was my sister-in-law,' he said.

'And she was your tenant. You own the flat at Honeycomb Court with your wife?'

'Yeah.'

'Have you always worked in the restaurant business?'

'I've always been a *restaurateur*. I owned three in the past, around the West End.'

'Why don't you own them anymore?' asked Erika.

'One went under and I sold the other two when I was convicted and sent down. I used the proceeds to start Goose, back in 2013.'

'When did you buy the flat in Honeycomb Court?'

'Around the same time. The owner is an old acquaintance of my family.'

'Henrietta Boulderstone?'

'Yes. She's owned the building for years, and one of the apartments came up for sale. Tess persuaded me to have Vicky as our tenant. She'd just left drama school and needed her own place in London.'

Erika paused. The connection to Henrietta Boulderstone had thrown her a little; everyone involved in this case seemed so closely intertwined.

'Was Vicky aware of your financial troubles?'

'I didn't have financial troubles until two years ago.... But to answer your question, yes, I'm sure Tess told her.'

'Why have you been having money worries?' asked Peterson.

Jasper sighed and looked to his solicitor.

'I really don't understand how any of this is relevant to the sudden and devastating loss of my client's sister-in-law?' said Mr Semple.

'We're just trying to build a picture of the family,' said Erika.

The solicitor nodded and sat back in his chair.

Jasper cleared his throat. 'Two years ago, I decided to expand Goose. I remortgaged our house to buy the shop next door. We planned to close for eight months. The first set of builders screwed us around, and then quit. By the time we found another, the reopening was delayed by six months, which kill... which affected our income.'

'How many months out of the last year has Vicky paid rent on the flat?'

'I'd say, three or four,' said Jasper.

'Is that rent she owes you still outstanding?' asked Peterson.

'Yeah.'

'Did you know that Vicky was making a podcast?' asked Peterson.

Jasper sat back, surprised at the change in direction of questioning. 'Yeah. I knew she was trying to get into voice-over work. She'd got a few acting jobs, but then the work dried up. We gave her a load of egg boxes to line her bedroom and make it into a studio.'

'Did you ever listen to her podcast?'

'No.'

'Did she ever leave any of her work at the restaurant? Notebooks with things she was working on? USB keys or CDs with recordings on them?'

Jasper raised an eyebrow.

'No. Why?'

'She was recently working on an episode about a serial attacker. He was harassing young women, and young students at Goldsmith's Drama Academy. Did Vicky know about your conviction?'

'No,' he said, shaking his head. His face was becoming angry again.

'No to the podcast episode she was working on, or no to Vicky knowing about your conviction for rape?'

'No to both. I told them, Tess and Vicky, that I got done by the taxman for fiddling the cash in one of my restaurants, laundering money, you know?' he said.

'You served eight years in Belmarsh. That's a harsh prison.'

Jasper tilted his head up and winced at the pain in his head.

'See? That's how harsh it was,' he said, tracing his finger over a long, thin, white scar which was tucked under the length of his jawbone. 'This nearly killed me. I needed twenty-six stitches and six pints of blood transfusions. The doctor said that if the knife had sliced me an inch lower, it would have hit a major artery and I'd have bled to death.'

Erika was tempted to say that his attacker had a problem with accuracy, but she resisted the urge.

'Why were you attacked?'

'Drugs. I owed money to someone on the outside. They got someone on the inside to deal with it. Happens a lot.'

'I thought you were selling drugs inside?'

He nodded.

'I did. I got sick of being the monkey, I decided to be the organ grinder.'

'Do you still take drugs?' asked Erika.

The solicitor leant forward and went to object, but Jasper put up his hand. 'It's okay. No. I don't do that shit anymore.'

'How well do you know Vicky's boyfriend, Shawn?' Erika asked.

Jasper blew out his cheeks, having to think about that question. 'I know him well enough to have a pint with, but I don't think him and Vicky were close anymore.'

'What about Vicky's neighbour, Sophia?'

Jasper shook his head.

'No, I really didn't know her. Vicky had mentioned her once or twice in passing, along with the other sister, but that was it. Apart from vaguely knowing Henrietta, I didn't know any of them. I never really went there, to be honest.'

'What about Vicky's neighbour, Charles Wakefield?' asked Erika. She looked closely at Jasper. He sat back and rubbed his hands together. Erika noticed for the first time how stringy and wiry his arms were. He wasn't muscular, but he looked to have real body strength.

'Who? I said, I don't know anyone there,' he said, narrowing his eyes.

'He works as the unofficial caretaker at Honeycomb Court. He's a close associate of Henrietta.'

'Oh, the caretaker. Yeah, I know of him. I had to deal with him, ages ago, to let the boiler man in when we bought the flat.

He's a bit odd. I've always thought he's a bit of a fag – that he's gay.'

'What makes you think that?' asked Peterson.

Jasper shrugged. 'The way he dresses. When I gave him the key he was wearing a fucking trilby and mincing around.' He put a hand gingerly to his bandage and then examined his palm for any signs of blood. 'What does he have to do with all of this?' he asked. Erika could see he was growing tired and restless.

'Vicky ran from the crime scene to stay with her lecturer from drama school. Cilla Stone. Do you know her?' she asked.

'No. I've heard enough about her though. Cilla this, Cilla that. Vicky was a big fan of hers.'

'Did you or Tess think to contact Cilla? Check she was there?'

'No. We thought Vicky was dead, then she wasn't dead, and now...' For the first time Erika could see what seemed like genuine distress from Jasper. 'Jesus. I just don't know how Tess is going to cope. It's bad enough that she thought Vicky was dead once and now after finding her, she's gone again.' He sat back and rubbed at his forehead. 'Do you have any other questions you want to ask me, officers? I'm here voluntarily, but now, I'd like to leave and go and comfort my wife.'

'We need that CCTV from the restaurant, if you can arrange that to be sent over as soon as possible,' said Erika.

40

'Do you think he's a flight risk?' Erika asked Peterson as they watched Jasper from the window as he climbed into his solicitor's Jaguar in the car park.

'He wanted to leave to escape his debts. He might still try, but would he leave Tess?'

'He's hardly Mr Morals...'

'I just don't have reasonable grounds to seize his passport right now,' said Erika.

'What about surveillance?'

Erika looked at Peterson.

'What's his motive for killing Vicky? She was in rent arrears? We don't have DNA evidence back yet for the scene of Sophia's murder. I can't yet prove he even knew Sophia... And we can't yet prove if there is a link between the two murders.' The Jaguar outside drove away, and Erika wondered again where Jasper was getting the money from for his fancy solicitor if he was broke. She made a decision. 'Screw it. Let's put a car on him, twenty-four-hour surveillance. I'll deal with Melanie's wrath.'

'Good call,' said Peterson. 'What do you want to do next?'

Erika had to think for a moment.

'I want to pay Goldsmith's Drama Academy a visit, and see if we can track down someone who knows something about the reports of assault on those sound files. We now have the three names of those women Vicky interviewed, and we should also get a list of the student accommodations. We could try and find out if Vicky was talking to anyone else there when she did her research for the podcast.'

It was a fifteen-minute drive from Lewisham Row over to New Cross. Peterson drove, so Erika could use the phone. She called in to the incident room and asked Crane to see if there was any record of assaults and break-ins reported by Kathleen Barber in January 2012, Becky Wayland in February 2012 at Jubilee Road, or Grace Leith at Hartwood Road in February 2014.

She waited and heard Crane typing in the background.

'Jubilee Road is coming up,' he said, finally. 'Number eighty-four Jubilee Road... There's a report dated 24th January 2012, about an intruder who tried to break in during the night. There's very little information, it just says that the young woman, Kathleen Barber, was unable to identify the intruder and the person was scared off. The police visited the premises, dusted for prints... But there wasn't anything to go on... Ah, yes, and there's also a report for a Becky Wayland. She reported an intruder on the 18th February 2012, again eighty-four Jubilee Road. The police came and, again, dusted for prints but there was no sign of a break-in.'

'No sign of a break-in? Do the reports mention anything about bars on the window of the room where Becky or Kathleen were staying being removed? Or missing light bulbs?' asked Erika.

'No,' said Crane after a pause.

'And there's nothing in the system for a Grace Leith in February 2014? If the address doesn't come up, the report could mention Goldsmith's Drama Academy,' said Erika. There was a pause as Crane typed.

'Nope,' said Crane. 'Nothing.'

'Okay, thank you,' said Erika to Crane. 'Can you send all that to my email?' She then made a call to Melanie to request twenty-four-hour surveillance on Jasper Clark, which Melanie approved without much pushback.

'I thought that was going to be tougher than it was,' said Erika when she got off the phone.

'She probably wouldn't have been as keen to approve surveillance on Charles Wakefield,' said Peterson. Erika gave a dry laugh. Melanie had sounded relieved, and she must have assumed their focus had shifted. 'What I don't understand is how Vicky tracked down that information about the break-ins,' continued Peterson. 'How did she find Kathleen Barber, Becky Wayland and Grace Leith? Did she know a police officer, or did GDA have records she got hold of?'

'I don't know,' said Erika. She flipped down the mirror in front of the passenger seat to check her reflection. She looked at her ragged tired face. 'Bloody hell. I need some sleep.'

They pulled up at a set of traffic lights next to Forest Hill station, close to where Erika had her first flat when she moved down to London. That had been four years ago. She'd had an intruder break in when she was there, and it had been terrifying. She thought of the women, who had all been young teenagers when this person broke into the student halls. It had been their first time away from home. Alone in London for the first time. It must have been horrific.

'Did you get a bed in the end?' asked Peterson, breaking her out of her thoughts.

'What? No. Not from Bed World, that's when I got called away by Isaac to the morgue. Did you?'

'Yeah. We had it delivered last night.'

'How is it? For sleeping?' said Erika. She wasn't crazy to hear about Peterson and Fran's domestic arrangements.

'Good. It's a nice big bed, so Kyle, of course, wants to sleep with us.'

'Is he still having the night terrors?'

'Yeah. It's a bad habit to get into, letting kids sleep in the same bed with you, but Fran doesn't want him to be scared at night if he wakes up from them.'

'Letting your kids share a bed is a bad habit?' asked Erika.

'According to my mother it is,' said Peterson. 'She keeps getting on at Fran about it. It's causing a bit of tension...' Erika nodded and looked out of the window. His mother could be quite a fearsome presence, and she'd made it very clear to Erika, when she and Peterson had been briefly together, that she wasn't suitable girlfriend material for her son, being older and career-obsessed. It gave Erika a little guilty pleasure that Fran wasn't getting an easy ride from the great Mrs Peterson.

'So, if you don't have a bed, you're still on the Lilo?' Peterson said.

'It's a burst Lilo. I'm on a pile of blankets... That reminds me...'

'What?' asked Peterson, as the lights changed and they moved off.

'I have to rearrange delivery.' Erika looked up and saw they had a few minutes until they'd be in New Cross. She rang the delivery helpline, and was surprised not to have to wait. The only spot they had for the next few days was for that evening at six thirty.

'I don't know if I can do six thirty,' said Erika, checking her watch. It was coming up to three thirty, and they had to go to

GDA, and then she wanted to show her face back at the station incident room.

'I can do what you need to do tonight,' said Peterson, overhearing the conversation. 'You need a bed.'

Erika covered the phone.

'I have to go back to the incident room and check on the surveillance team.'

'I can do that. Take the delivery slot. You need sleep to function. We all need you,' said Peterson. Erika felt a real warmth and affection for him offering to help, and she took the delivery slot.

As she hung up her phone they were driving past New Cross Gate station, passing the large campus of Goldsmiths University. Goldsmith's Drama Academy was half a mile past this, made up of a row of six terraced houses that had been knocked together.

They pulled into the front entrance just as a group of young men and women emerged from the front entrance, wearing leggings and dance gear. And two of them had on neon yellow headbands. They were chatting and shrieking with laughter, and didn't seem to mind the cold. The kids passed the car, and moved along to one of the other doors in the row of terraces.

Just as Erika and Peterson pulled into a parking spot, a bright yellow VW Beetle pulled up in the space opposite, and Cilla Stone got out. She was dressed in gaudy primary colours: lime-green tights with red Dr. Martens boots, and a strange tartan cape in blue and red, which came down past her waist.

'What the hell is she wearing?' said Peterson as they watched a more soberly dressed man in a smart blue suit lock the car and follow her up to the main entrance.

'Every colour she can. That's Cilla Stone,' said Erika.

'The Cilla Stone who Vicky stayed with in Scotland?'

'Yes. I recognise her photo from the university website.'

'And who is that with her?'

'I don't know.'

Cilla walked up the steps, and said something to the man, leaning in conspiratorially, almost flirting. She laughed and the man grinned down at her. Peterson went to get out of the car, but Erika put out her hand.

'Wait, let's hang back. I don't want to have to tell her about Vicky in the car park.'

41

They watched as the man pressed a bell on the door. It opened and he stood to one side to let her in.

'She's retired from GDA?' said Peterson.

'Yes. Vicky said that Cilla lives in Scotland now. What's she doing back here in London?'

They got out, walked up to the main entrance and rang the bell. A moment passed and then a pinched-sounding woman's voice came through the tinny speaker, asking who they were. Erika held up her warrant card to the camera and said they wanted to speak to the Student Welfare Officer. There was another long pause.

'What's this regarding?' she said.

'It's regarding two police officers who need to talk to you,' said Erika. There was a beat and then the door buzzed and popped open a couple of inches.

They stepped into the hallway, which looked like an institutionalised terraced house, with bright strip lights and a scuffed wooden floor. There was a long corridor, and by the main door was a noticeboard and rows of pigeonholes with names on them.

At the end of the corridor they could see a young woman in dance gear standing at a stable door, split in two. The top half was open. The young woman had red frizzy hair hanging down her back and heavy black eyeliner.

'I emailed my essay on time,' she was saying. 'Look.' She rummaged in a pink knitted backpack and took out a piece of paper. 'This is the time stamp when I emailed it, five minutes before the deadline.'

When they drew close, they could see inside the door to an open-plan office. A small, thin, suspicious-looking woman, with close-cropped grey hair and wearing a rather grubby blue roll-neck jumper and small half-moon glasses was regarding the young woman coldly with her arms folded. Three women were working at desks behind her, glancing up and pretending not to listen in.

'How do I know you haven't forged this?' said the woman, taking the piece of paper.

'I've never missed an essay deadline, and the computer system is saying that I missed it by *one second!*'

'It is students' responsibility to email essays over leaving enough time,' the woman said, handing it back. They went back and forth for another minute, and the older woman refused to budge.

'I'm going to talk to my tutor,' said the young woman.

'You do that.'

The young woman stalked past them in tears.

'Hello. We're looking to speak to the Student Welfare Officer?' said Erika, moving to the door.

'That's me,' the woman said, with the same hostility she had for the young girl.

'And what's your name?'

'Mrs Sheila Wright.'

She didn't open the door for them.

'We're investigating historical assaults on female students that happened in GDA's student accommodations. We'd like to talk to you about it, somewhere a little more private,' said Erika. She held out her warrant card again, and introduced herself and Peterson. Sheila leant over and looked at their cards, and then unbolted the door for them to come inside. The three other women looked up at them with interest.

'Please. Follow me,' she said. They moved through to another corridor with doors leading off it. Her office was at the end of the corridor and looked out over a small garden with a central courtyard, trees and empty flowerbeds.

'I hadn't been told you were coming today,' she said.

'We need to know if you have records of an intruder who broke into your Jubilee Road and Hartwood Road student accommodation and threatened and assaulted young women.' Sheila's eyes grew wide at this information. 'The names are: Kathleen Barber, the incident happened in January 2012 in Jubilee Road, Grace Leith and the incident happened in February 2014 at Hartwood Road, and Becky Wayland, who was assaulted at Jubilee Road in February 2012.'

Sheila looked between Erika and Peterson for a moment, then sat down and swivelled her computer screen around to face her. 'Wouldn't you already have this information, being the police?'

'Not all incidents are reported to us,' said Erika.

'And these young women were students here?'

'They auditioned for places here on the Drama course.'

'If they weren't accepted, then they never became full-time students. We don't keep records for temporary stays, or non-students,' said Sheila.

'But if a prospective student staying just for one night was assaulted, or their room was broken into, wouldn't you have some record of this? As a landlord the school must have an insurance policy,' said Peterson. Sheila's fingers moved in a blur as she touch typed.

'I have no record of these women in our alumni database. We only keep records of students.'

'What if a window is broken? Or an accommodation is broken into more than once? Do you have a record for the Jubilee Road building?' asked Erika.

'Yes. We keep some records on the student accommodations. If there are repairs or incidents...' Erika noted Sheila's touch was heavy-handed on the keyboard, as if she was taking out her annoyance on the keys. 'But I can't see anything here. Do you know if there was any serious damage when the person gained access? Was a window broken, or a door kicked in?'

Gained access, thought Erika. It was an odd way to describe a break-in.

'We don't know if there was any damage,' said Erika. 'So you're telling us that if you have an intruder in student accommodation, nothing is done about it?'

Sheila sat back and folded her arms.

'No, I'm not saying that. Pastoral care for students is a high priority, officers. We have strong security measures in place. Since 2017, all of our student halls entrances have a video camera. And back since 2000, we've had a card key entry system on all entrances and exits into halls. And the windows have bars on them,' she said.

'This person who broke in unscrewed the bars,' said Erika.

'I'm unaware of this.'

'How does the card key entry system work?' asked Peterson.

'Each student has a magnetic card key, and they use it to open the door. No one can get in without a card key.'

'Someone could borrow or steal a card key, though?' said Erika.

'Technically, yes. But we're very careful about security, and we upgraded the security to include a camera system in 2017.'

'Only last year?' asked Erika.

'Yes.'

'Why did you wait until only last year?'

'Officer, I don't make policy. I am merely the administrator for student welfare. I don't control budgets.'

'Were you the administrator for student welfare back in 2012?'

'Yes.'

'Would you be able to give us all records that you have of break-ins and assaults in student accommodation?' asked Erika.

'I told you. I don't have anything for the dates you specify,' said Sheila. She seemed defensive now.

'But you do keep records about students. We can come back with a warrant, and make a big old fuss, and say that Sheila the welfare officer is obstructing a police officer,' said Erika.

'I'm not obstructing you.'

Erika was now deeply annoyed with this jobsworth.

'Good. So you will comply with my request as a police officer, and hand over all of your files.'

'I would need to look through quite a lot of data. I don't even know if we would have this information.'

Erika rummaged in her pocket and took out her card.

'This is my number. When the files are ready, contact me, and we will arrange for a secure transfer. I will expect you to call promptly.'

'Yes,' said Sheila, chastised.

'Were you contacted by a former student about these assaults? A woman called Vicky Clarke.'

Sheila seemed to think about this for a moment.

'No, not that I remember.'

'Okay, thank you. Just before we came into the building, we saw a man enter with Cilla Stone. Who was that?'

Sheila went back to her computer, and Erika saw that she'd pulled up the CCTV images from the front door.

'That's Colin McCabe.'

'Does he have an office here?'

'His office is up on the top floor. Fourth floor.'

'What does he do here?'

'He's a senior lecturer in Classical Drama, and he's on the school board. If you follow me I'll buzz you through,' she said.

When she let them through the door, Erika and Peterson started up a poky staircase. On each floor was a fire door with clear safety glass leading onto a corridor.

'You looked like you wanted to give her a slap,' said Peterson, stopping at the second landing to catch his breath.

Erika stopped with him. 'You see how she spoke to that young student whose essay was handed in a second past the dead-line? Do you think she knew anything, or it was just her general demeanour to be obstructive?'

'I dunno. Jobsworths don't tend to care about the substance of what they do. They just tend to get a kick out of denying you information.'

42

Colin McCabe's office was at the end of a long corridor with windows looking out onto the busy main road. They heard a murmur of voices coming from inside. Erika knocked on the door. The voices stopped and then Colin opened the door. He had the slightest stubble on his face, and carried with him a strong scent of aftershave. Something woody and expensive. They could see through into the office, where Cilla was perched on his desk. Her long thin legs encased in lime-green tights poking out from under the tartan cape made Erika think of those episodes of *The Muppets*, when Kermit the frog sat on a wall to play a guitar and sing a song.

'Good afternoon, can I help you?' he asked, smiling broadly at Erika and Peterson. They introduced themselves and held up their warrant cards.

'We're here about a former student, Vicky Clarke,' said Erika.

'Ah, yes,' said Cilla, getting up off the desk. Her face was now gravely serious. 'I was going to make myself available to you. As you know, Vicky came to stay with me.'

Colin opened the door wider.

'Please, officers, do come in.' They stepped into the office. It was a large room lined with bookcases. There was a dusty, worn herringbone wood floor, and a huge battered green leather sofa in front of an iron fireplace. A bay window next to the desk looked down on the garden.

'Please, sit down,' said Colin, indicating the large leather sofa. Erika saw on a cork board up on one of the walls, there were scores of Polaroid photos of the students, all of them staring dead-on at the camera, with an intense confidence. Their names were written underneath. She fleetingly wondered if any of the students visited this leather couch in the office.

'I was expecting to have to contact you in Scotland,' said Erika.

Cilla hesitated. 'Yes... I wanted to come back down to London. To see if I could be a support to Vicky,' she said, clutching one hand to her chest as she spoke, as if to emphasise just how much she cared. 'And, as I said, to make myself available to the police.'

'When did you arrive in London?' asked Erika.

'Late last night. We took a flight, shortly after Vicky.'

'We?'

'I was staying with Cilla, along with another colleague of ours, Ray,' said Colin.

'Where is Ray?'

'He stayed in Scotland to look after my dog,' said Cilla. 'He teaches dance classes at Pineapple Studios in Central London.'

'You said you came back to London to make yourself available to the police, but we haven't heard from you,' said Peterson.

'I hope there's no problem?' said Colin. 'Cilla, as far as she's told me, was unaware that Vicky had run away from a crime scene. She could have stayed in Scotland, but chose to come back. That's not illegal.'

'Good heavens, I hope not!' said Cilla. 'If I'd known about

Vicky, and what had happened, I'd have told her to go straight back to London. I thought she was escaping some disastrous love affair.' She toyed nervously with a heavy silver pendant around her neck. Colin, in comparison, was very relaxed, standing with his arms uncrossed and hands on his hips.

'Do you know why Vicky chose to travel all the way up to Scotland to your house?' asked Erika.

'No... And yes, we're close,' said Cilla, still fiddling nervously with the pendant. 'We've always kept in contact.'

'Close friends?'

'Yes. I don't get close to many students, but Vicky is very special to me. I only recently moved up to Scotland, in the past year. I've asked her up to see me, or rather, I'd told her she was welcome at any time.'

'Have you socialised regularly with Vicky since she graduated from GDA six years ago?'

'Yes. We've seen each other at least once a month for dinner. I had a flat in Sydenham which I sold recently to buy my new place up in Scotland.' She stopped fiddling with the pendant and looked up at Erika. There was an awkward pause. Cilla looked between them. Colin's brow furrowed.

'What is it, officers?' he asked.

'I'm very sorry to tell you that Vicky was murdered last night,' said Erika.

Cilla stared at them for a long moment. Then she put her fingers to her temples, seemed to totter for a moment, and then she slowly slid off the desk and landed in a heap on the floor. Colin rushed over to her.

'Cilla!' he said. 'Cilla! Can you hear me?' He slapped her around the face, rather briskly. He shook her shoulders and her head lolled back. He slapped her again.

'Okay, okay, enough,' said Peterson, moving in. 'Let's put her in the recovery position.'

'She didn't have much to eat this morning,' Colin said, moving back to let Peterson help. He gently rolled Cilla onto her side and tilted her head back.

'Is she breathing? Is there a pulse?' asked Colin, his fruity baritone voice rising with emotion. Erika could see from where she was standing that Cilla was breathing. Her chest was rising and falling under the tartan cape and her skinny legs were poking out in their lime-green tights.

'Her pulse is strong,' said Peterson, feeling her neck as he knelt beside her. They stood for a moment, watching, and then Cilla's eyes fluttered theatrically, her lips parted, and her head shook from side to side. She opened her eyes.

'Where am I?' she croaked, squinting myopically up at them. Despite the seriousness of the situation, Erika had a sudden urge to laugh, and had to bite her lip.

'My darling!' Colin cried, elbowing Peterson out of the way to kneel beside her. 'You had a funny turn,' he said, in a soft voice at odds with the hard slaps he'd administered to her face.

'Vicky. *Murdered?*' she said, squinting at them both and then up at Colin.

'Yes,' said Erika.

'But I was, she was, in my house... What? How?'

Cilla groped at the air with her arms and Colin helped her to sit up and smoothed her cape down to preserve her modesty. She put her fingers to her cheek where a red hand mark was showing, and Erika thought she saw a brief flicker of annoyance cross her face. Colin helped her over to sit on the sofa.

'Would you like some water?' asked Peterson, crossing to a water cooler in the corner of the room.

'I think I need something stronger,' said Cilla. Colin nodded, and went to one of the shelves, where he took out a couple of leather-bound books. He retrieved a bottle of Glenlivet whisky from behind the row of books.

'I presume you are both on duty,' he said.

'We are,' said Erika. Colin filled a couple of the plastic cups from the water cooler with whisky, and came back over. He handed one to Cilla, and she took it with trembling hands. Erika noticed that Colin was trembling a little too. They both took a sip.

'How did it happen?' asked Cilla in a small voice.

Erika briefly explained the circumstances.

'Tess found her, in her own kitchen? Oh my God, that's awful. And she was stabbed! Oh, Vicky. Who would do that?' said Cilla. Her bottom lip started to tremble and Colin took out a folded white handkerchief from his top pocket and gave it to her. Cilla started to sob. Erika glanced at Peterson, and he raised an eyebrow.

'Do you have any idea who did it? Any suspects?' asked Colin, speaking over the top of Cilla's head as she buried herself in his jacket, pressing the hanky to her face. There was now a vivid red hand print on Cilla's cheek.

'No, we don't,' said Erika. 'Cilla, would you be happy to answer a few questions, if you feel up to it?'

'Now?' said Cilla, dabbing her eyes. 'You've just told me about the loss of a dear friend.'

'Please. It could help.'

She took a deep breath and appeared to centre herself. Colin stayed beside her.

'This may seem like an odd subject to start with, but what did you know about Vicky's podcast?'

'Her podcast? I know that it was very good,' said Cilla. 'We both listen to it, don't we?' She looked up at Colin and he nodded.

'What made her start doing a true crime podcast?' Cilla pulled a confused face. 'Please, understand, I'm going somewhere with this.'

'Vicky really struggled with getting work when she graduated,' said Cilla, looking down at her plastic cup. 'She got an agent, but he wasn't a particularly good one. She has... *had* a very good broadcast voice, so I suggested she try and get into voice-overs. That's all I did.'

'Did anyone else at GDA help Vicky?'

'I think Vince, who runs the technical team for the theatre here at GDA, gave her some advice on sound equipment.'

'And, of course, we were happy, at GDA, to come on board and help with casting,' said Colin.

'Oh, yes, casting,' said Cilla.

'What do you mean, *casting*?' asked Erika, thinking she'd misheard.

'For the characters. Have you had a listen? Every episode has additional characters,' said Colin.

Erika and Peterson looked at each other, unable to disguise their shock.

'Darlings, didn't you know that Vicky's podcast was fictionalised?' said Cilla.

43

Erika could feel them suddenly on the back foot. If the podcast was part-fiction, then what was Vicky working on before she was murdered? An investigation, or a story?

'We know that Vicky worked on the script herself,' said Colin.

'She did, and it was very good writing,' said Cilla, still dabbing at her eyes with the hanky. 'But she needed voice actors for all of the additional characters, and we helped with that.'

'Hang on. We've listened to the episode about the Croydon Cat Killer,' said Erika. 'That is a real case, and we know because the police have been dealing with it for several years.'

'Of course, her podcast is based on real crimes,' said Cilla. 'But she was taking what was in the public domain and *dramatising* it. It's a legitimate technique used by documentary makers, and some podcast creators.'

There was a long silence in the office.

'Officers, you suddenly look a bit green,' said Colin. 'Are you sure I can't tempt you to a drink? I won't tell if you don't.'

Erika needed a moment. She moved around to stand in front of the fireplace.

'We believe that Vicky was working on a new podcast episode, and she potentially uncovered something about a series of crimes that have taken place in student accommodation here at GDA,' she said.

'What?' asked Cilla, looking up at Colin. His eyebrows shot up into his hairline and he shook his head.

'Crimes, here, at GDA? I'm not aware of any crimes. What are these crimes, officers?' he asked.

'A series of break-ins at your student accommodations near New Cross. Three young women were threatened, and in one case that we know of, the attacker assaulted her.'

Cilla and Colin were both shocked into silence. Erika watched them carefully. Their shock seemed very genuine.

'Do you have proof of this?' asked Colin.

'Yes. Vicky interviewed these young women and the police records match what they told her,' said Erika.

'How do you know this? Did Vicky tell you?' asked Cilla.

'We can't go into much more detail at this stage,' said Erika.

'Because she said nothing about this to me when she came to stay. Did she say anything to you, Colin?'

'No. Nothing. When was this? When did these assaults happen?' asked Colin.

'In early 2012 and 2014,' said Peterson.

'I wasn't aware of this,' said Colin. 'Which is surprising. Students here like to talk. This would have been a big subject.'

'These women weren't students. They auditioned unsuccessfully to GDA, and only stayed for one night in student accommodation,' said Erika.

'Then we might not have heard about it,' said Cilla. 'I've been present at auditions every year. We only meet the auditionees for half a day, and most we never see again.'

Colin frowned.

'Do you have the names of these young women? In case we remember them? Or can help?'

'Yes, but as I said, we can't share that information with you,' said Erika.

'Have you spoken to Sheila, our student office administrator?' he asked, now sounding wary.

'No, but I'll make sure we do. I presume the school keeps its own records of incidents of assault at student halls?'

'Yes, but let me just say, we have a zero tolerance procedure here at GDA, isn't that right, Cilla?' said Colin.

'Yes,' she said.

'In all my years here, I've known the students to be fun-loving and kind, and as for the female students being assaulted, it's unheard of,' said Colin.

'Yes. So many of the male students are gay,' finished Cilla. There was an awkward pause.

'Can I ask where you are staying, and how long you are planning to be in London?' said Erika.

'I'm staying with Colin, just up the road at his house on Telegraph Hill,' said Cilla.

'What time did you land last night?' asked Peterson.

'Eight o'clock, eight thirty,' said Cilla. 'We flew Glasgow to Heathrow. And we can't have got back to yours until well after ten.'

Colin nodded.

'And you both stayed the night at your house in Telegraph Hill?' asked Erika.

'Are you asking us for an alibi?' said Cilla, suddenly with a flash of anger.

'We're just trying to establish all of the details,' said Peterson firmly.

She put her plastic cup down on the desk. 'I'll have you know that I don't appreciate this line of questioning. I have just heard that a very dear, dear, *dear* friend is dead. I am in shock, and you come in here and ask me these ridiculous questions and have the cheek to imply—'

'Cilla, darling. They're just doing their job,' said Colin, taking her hand in his. She pulled her hand free. He looked up at Erika and Peterson. 'Yes, we both stayed at my house. I think we got back from the airport around ten thirty and it was off to bed shortly after this. We rose late, and took a little time to get sorted this morning; we only left the house to come here a couple of hours ago. Cilla was very tired. Flying takes it out of her, however short the flight.'

'Why did you come here today?' asked Erika. 'I presume that your plans were to stay in Scotland with Cilla?'

'I'm head of the drama department, I always have work to do, papers to sign,' he said.

Cilla was still breathing heavily, and trying to get her anger under control.

'Is that all the questions you have, officers?' she said finally.

'Yes, I think so,' said Erika.

'Well, if you can excuse us there are things I have to do. I have to call Tess... I need time to process what you've just told me. I don't want to be here. I want to go home, back to your house, Colin,' she said.

He nodded. 'Yes, darling. Whatever you need.'

'Thank you for your time,' said Erika.

It was almost dark and pouring torrentially with rain when Erika and Peterson came outside, and they stood for a moment on the steps under the main entrance, debating whether to make a dash for the car or wait for the rain to subside.

'I still can't work out where Vicky's sources came from,' said Erika. 'And now Cilla and Colin tell us she was hiring actors and writing scripts!'

'It doesn't mean her whole podcast was fiction.'

'I need to find those women,' said Erika, wishing again that they had something to go on from Vicky's flat; notebooks or computer files. 'How did she find them, or find out about the break-ins? People who come here to audition don't stick around, they come for the afternoon, and then they stay a night in the student accommodation and they're gone.'

'Vicky graduated six years ago,' said Peterson. 'She might have known them, or heard about them. Her last year of study here would have been 2012, and in January and February of that year, Kathleen Barber and Becky Wayland reported the break-ins at Jubilee Road.'

'But if Vicky's podcast is a work of fiction, then that could scupper our theory that she was close to outing the attacker of these women,' said Erika. 'What if that's not the motive for her murder?'

'Why didn't Tess say anything?'

'Tess didn't take much interest in the podcast.'

'What about Shawn? He said that Vicky did all the work on the podcast herself, and he only contributed music...'

Erika rubbed her face. 'And don't you think it's weird that Cilla came back to London so fast? She must have had to buy a flight almost as soon as Vicky left.'

'And Colin and this other teacher, Ray, had only just arrived to stay at her place. They're both giving me the shivers, Cilla and Colin. That whole fainting performance,' said Peterson.

'Yeah, it was a bit theatrical. But who can tell? We meet a lot of weirdos in this job.' Erika checked her watch; it had just gone five thirty.

'You should get a wriggle on if you want to catch your delivery,' said Peterson.

'I'd forgotten all about it.' Erika looked at her phone and saw that she had emails from Crane and the team at Lewisham Row. 'I should cancel it. I need to check in with the surveillance team on Jasper Clark. And there's been two messages left by Maria Ivanova... She's asking when we're going to release her sister's body. She wants to have it flown back to Bulgaria so they can plan a funeral. And we need to follow up with Sheila in the admin department to see if Goldsmith's Drama Academy have any records on these assaults.'

'I can do those things.'

Erika carried on scrolling through, and saw more in her inbox.

'And I've had another message from one of Sophia's colleagues at the hospital, a student doctor called Olivia Moreno. She's willing to talk to us about her – she's available tomorrow morning.'

'Erika. Let me do those,' said Peterson. 'I don't mean to be horrible, but you look like crap. You haven't slept properly in days. Go home, get that bed delivered. Have a proper meal and a good night's sleep.'

Erika went to protest, but she felt ragged and exhausted. She looked up at Peterson's soft brown eyes, grateful that she could rely on him. She almost told him how much he still meant to her... But she bit her lip and held back. She looked at the emails again. She couldn't think straight, and a decent night's sleep on a proper bed was integral to her doing her job well.

'Okay. Thanks. I'll forward these to you now,' she said.

'And if you get anything else tonight that I can deal with—'

'—I'll forward them too,' she finished.

'Just don't ask me to help you put together flat pack furniture,' he said. 'Rapists and murderers I can deal with, but the thought of flat pack furniture instructions terrifies me.'

Erika laughed.

'I'll probably crash out on my new mattress and leave the bed frame for another night,' she said. The rain eased up, and they made a dash for Erika's car.

44

The break in the rain only held for a few minutes, and as Erika drew close to home it started again, pounding down on the car roof. Her phone rang with an unknown number. She picked up and heard a man with a Slovak accent.

'Courier. I have your washing machine,' he said. 'Are you there this time?'

Erika rolled her eyes. It was the same guy she'd had the argument with before. As she turned into her road she saw a large white delivery van sitting outside her house, its lights glowing through the rain.

'I'm just here,' she said. 'In the car behind you.'

Erika pulled in behind the van just as a tall muscular guy in a baseball cap stepped out into the rain. He looked to be in his late thirties, and wore jeans and a Corgoň beer-branded T-shirt, despite the cold weather. Erika got out of her car and ran over to him as he slid up the door at the back of the van. She hunched down and pulled up the collar of her jacket as the rain seemed to intensify.

'Do you want me to take it all through the front or the back?'

he shouted, jumping up inside the van, which was filled with boxes piled high. Erika had to think for a second. She had a back yard, but which route was the best to get there? She hadn't checked how wide the gate was.

'The front door is fine,' she said, hoping that the hallway was wide enough. She put her collar up. 'It's the red door, here.'

There was a whirr as a hydraulic ramp popped out, and he tilted the washing machine in its box onto a small trolley. Erika ran up the path and unlocked the door. When she stepped inside, she felt the cold and smelt the damp. George the cat was waiting for her in the hall, and he ran to her mewling and rubbing himself up against her ankles. She gave him a quick pat and was about to check where she would put the washing machine when the delivery man appeared at the doorstep with the huge box balanced on the trolley.

'Come through,' she said. He just managed to squeeze the box on the trolley through the front door. George gave an indignant little miaow and ran off down the hall to the kitchen. The man had a badge on his jacket which said Igor. This, coupled with the Corgoň beer T-shirt with the Slovak branding made it obvious he was a fellow countryman. For some reason this made her embarrassed about the state of her home.

'Where do you want it?' he asked.

'The kitchen, at the back.' George was mewling and weaving around her feet, so she picked him up as the trolley clanked and rattled over the bare floorboards following her through to the kitchen. He put the box down.

'I ordered a bed, too,' said Erika.

'Yes there is,' he said. He took the empty trolley back out and returned a few minutes later with a plastic-wrapped mattress and a long thin box on a bigger trolley.

'Upstairs,' said Erika. Still carrying George in her arms, she hurried up the stairs and tried to work out which room she would sleep in. She settled on the middle room, which was smaller but had a beautiful fireplace and a view out over the garden.

Igor carried the mattress into the room, and then the long box. There was also another big plastic bag containing bedding, which he left on the floor. They went back down to the kitchen where he'd left the paperwork. Erika saw that he was soaking wet. She'd bought a clean pile of tea towels and she handed him one.

'Thanks,' he said, taking it and wiping his face.

'Where are you from?' she asked, switching to speaking Slovak.

'Nitra,' he said. 'Well, just outside. In the village, Lehota.'

'I'm from Nitra, too,' she said. He took off his hat and wiped his forehead. Erika stared at him.

'How old are you?' she asked.

'Forty-four.'

He looked familiar, and then it all fell into place.

'Igor Mak?'

'Yes,' he said.

They stared at each other for a long moment.

'Erika Boledišova?' he said.

'Yes!' And Erika suddenly saw him as he'd looked twenty-six years ago. He'd been rail-thin back then – now he was stocky and solid, and looked like he lifted weights. She remembered him, skinny and lithe, in his school graduation suit, which had been brown, with a thick kipper tie. Sexy and a bit goofy. He'd been her first boyfriend, not serious, but still. He'd been a big part of her life and then they'd lost touch when she moved to the UK, aged eighteen.

'Jesus, *Erika*,' he grinned.

'I was so rude to you before. I'm sorry,' she said.

He waved it away. 'That's okay, we all have bad days.'

They smiled at each other for a moment and then he looked

down at himself. His T-shirt was drenched, and he was dripping on the wooden floor. He mopped at it with the tea towel. Erika didn't know what else to say. He picked up the clipboard from the top of the washing machine box. The paper was soggy. 'Did you order this plumbed in?'

'No.'

'Okay, I just need a signature,' he said, rooting around in his pocket and pulling out a pen.

'How much would it cost to have it plumbed in?' asked Erika. The thought of having to find and then hire a plumber was too much, and there was something wonderful about seeing him after all these years.

'You need to book it when you buy the machine. It's eighty pounds,' he said.

'What if I give you eighty pounds cash? Do you have time, now?'

He seemed to weigh it up for a second.

'Sure. This was my last delivery.'

'Are you hungry? It's late. I could order some takeaway, if that's not too weird? I just feel horrible for being so rude and it's so great to see you.'

Erika wondered for a moment if she was being too forward. He probably hadn't thought about her in years.

'Chinese?' he said.

'Chinese it is, I got a menu through the door the other day.'

For the first time in ages, Erika felt a little flutter of excitement in her chest, and she forgot all about work.

45

Igor unboxed and plumbed in Erika's washing machine, and then, unasked, he set to work putting together her bed frame. Just as he finished, the Chinese takeaway arrived. They ended up eating in the living room, sitting on each end of the plastic-covered mattress, drinking beer, and catching up with what had happened to them over the past twenty-six years.

'I remember that day you came to say goodbye to me at the coach station, when I was coming to England,' said Erika. Igor nodded, picking at the label on his beer bottle. 'It was the most frightening and exhilarating thing, like leaping off a cliff into the unknown. I knew about six words of English.'

Igor smiled.

'We wrote to each other, didn't we?' he said.

'We did,' said Erika, picking at her beer label.

'I'm trying to remember why we stopped?'

Erika hesitated, feeling awkward. A sudden rush of memories and emotions came back to her.

'We stopped because of me. I met someone else,' she said.

'Yeah. A British guy. *Mike*?'

'Mark.'

When she said it, his name hung ominously in the air. She realised that she didn't say it out loud that often.

'You were working in Manchester as an au pair for that professor of forensics, weren't you?'

'Professor Portnoy. It was a very weird, grand old house. Thick carpets. Ominous silences. Ticking clocks. It wasn't the happiest place.'

They listened to the rain on the roof for a few minutes.

'What happened to Mark? Where is he? I'd like to have strong words with him for stealing you away from me,' he said with a grin. Then he saw Erika's face. 'Oh. I've just put my foot in it.'

Erika rubbed at her temples. The stress of having to explain her widowhood never seemed to leave.

'The short version is, we got married. We both trained to be police officers, and then he was killed on duty. Shot by a drug dealer. That was almost five years ago.'

'I'm sorry. I didn't know.'

'Why would you know?'

'Did they ever catch the guy who did it?'

'No.'

'*No?* Do you know who it was?'

Erika hesitated.

'Yes. We had him under surveillance for... for a long time. He vanished into the woodwork...' She shrugged. 'I still check sometimes, to see if he's resurfaced somewhere in police records. He's vanished somewhere abroad, we think. What about you?' she said, changing the subject. She could feel the memory of what happened to Mark dragging her down. It was a feeling she didn't want to have in her new home.

'I studied English literature in Bratislava. I came to London in 1999 as a translator for a finance company. Married Denise, we had a little boy. I lost my job in 2009. We divorced in 2012. The last six years have been...' He shrugged. 'About trying to keep my head above water. Renting. Paying child support.'

'How old is your son?'

'Twelve.' He put down his beer bottle, sat up on the mattress and retrieved his wallet from his back pocket. He pulled out a small photo and handed it to Erika. It was of a brown-haired toddler, sitting on Igor's shoulders. They were both wearing sunglasses, and grinning at the camera. The sun was shining in the background, reflecting off the lens, bathing Igor and his son in a corona of yellow and white.

'He's cute,' said Erika, and she was glad to say she meant it.

'Thomas.'

'*Th-omas*. Not *Tomaš*?' she said. Igor shook his head and smiled. Erika handed back the photo.

'Don't get me started. I had so many arguments with Denise about his name. I wanted Tomaš, but she thinks "Mak" is a weird enough surname for a British kid to have.'

Erika laughed. Mak translated into English was 'poppy seed'. He looked at the picture again, and she saw his smile was tinged with sadness as he tucked it back into his wallet.

'Tommy Poppy-Seed. Sounds like a very cute little rapper,' she said. Igor laughed. 'No one could ever pronounce *Boledišova*. Foster is much easier.'

He took another sip of beer.

'What kind of police officer are you?'

'I'm a bit of a bitch, but I'm always fair.'

He laughed.

'No. Your rank?'

'Detective Chief Inspector,' said Erika. She got up and found her warrant card in her coat hanging over one of the deckchairs and handed it to him, feeling a pride she didn't acknowledge often.

'Wow. Congratulations,' he said, studying her photo ID.

'I don't have any kids, no pictures of kids... to show you.'

There was a long silence. They listened to the rain clinking on the roof. Igor handed back her warrant card. George yawned and stretched out between them on the mattress, making the plastic crackle.

'That fireplace, does it work?' he said, pointing to it.

'No. I've got five fireplaces, and only one works. And no heating.'

'If you wanted your fireplaces unblocked and cleaned, I could do it for you. I got all my qualifications. I did it for a few years, when I moved out. I was self-employed and... Anyway, I'd just need to hire the equipment for a few hours...'

'I hadn't thought about the fireplaces. Look at the rest of the house. So much needs doing.'

'I just thought I'd ask,' he said amiably, without pressuring her. Igor was easy-going. Calming to be around. She'd forgotten that about him. Mark had been so calm and easy-going. The thought of Mark flared up in her mind, and she quickly extinguished it. They sipped their beer and stared at each other across the mattress. Erika wondered how much he'd changed in the past twenty-six years. And she thought how much she'd changed.

'I'm this close to quitting London and going back to Slovakia,' he said, breaking the comfortable silence. 'This delivery job is awful, the hours and the pay. And what with Brexit, and the cost of living, I dunno. But then there's my son...'

Erika's phone rang, and she saw it was Isaac.

'Hi, is everything okay?' she asked.

'I'm just on my way round to your house, if that's okay? I thought you might want someone to help with housewarming, and I have some news about Vicky Clarke,' he said.

'You have the post-mortem results?'

'Yes. I'll be there in a couple of minutes,' said Isaac and he hung up.

'Is that a friend?' asked Igor.

'Yes, and no. Well, he's a colleague.'

'I should get going,' said Igor, getting up. He downed the rest of his beer. 'Thank you for the food.'

He went to the electric heater where his T-shirt was drying. He stripped off the dry T-shirt he'd borrowed from Erika and pulled it on. She caught a glimpse of his beautiful torso. *He really looks after himself*, she thought. She didn't know many forty-year-old Slovak men who still had a six-pack.

'Listen. I've got your number. I'll give you a call about the chimneys, when I'm sorted out here,' she said, still not sure if she meant it.

'That would be great.'

'And thanks for helping with the bed and washing machine.'

They walked out into the hallway, and Erika saw Isaac through the frosted glass in the front door, coming up the front path. He rang the bell and Erika suddenly felt odd at having Igor and him meet. When she opened the door, Isaac was holding a bottle of wine and a small plant in cellophane.

'Hello,' said Isaac, looking at Igor appreciatively. 'Sorry, I didn't know you had company.'

'I'm just leaving. I'm Igor,' he said, offering a hand. Isaac juggled the plant for a moment, and handed Erika the bottle of champagne.

'I'm Isaac Strong. Erika's friend... GBF,' he said, laughing nervously.

'GBF?' repeated Erika, surprised. She'd never heard Isaac use this phrase before.

'You know, Gay Best Friend,' said Isaac, blushing. Erika stared at him, and was surprised to see Isaac's usual cool demeanour disrupted.

'Oh, right,' said Igor, smiling uncertainly. He put a hand to his head. 'I left my hat in your kitchen.'

'I'll get it,' said Erika, starting up the hallway.

'And it's eighty quid, for the plumbing in,' added Igor, calling after her. Erika grabbed her purse and his cap off the kitchen table. When she returned, Isaac and Igor were standing in awkward silence. She handed Igor his hat, and gave him four twenty-pound notes, and an extra ten.

'Oh. Thanks,' he said. 'So, you'll call me?'

'Yes. I will. About the chimneys being swept,' said Erika. Igor leant over to kiss Erika on the cheek, European style. But she moved the wrong way and he ended up kissing her on the lips.

'Sorry!' she said.

'My fault. Anyway, good to see you and good to meet you, Isaac.'

When he was gone, Erika closed the door, and turned to Isaac.

'He was delivering my washing machine and bed and he offered to plumb it in. It turns out he's my old boyfriend from home. A very odd coincidence.'

'Interesting. He's handsome,' said Isaac with a smile. 'Happy housewarming,' he said, handing her the plant. 'And here's something to water it with.' He held up the bottle of champagne.

'Thank you. Come in. It's just a mattress on the floor in the living room or a deck chair,' she said. 'Do you want a glass of this?'

'Yes... I also have the results of Vicky Clarke's post-mortem. If you're happy to talk shop.'

'You do? That was fast,' said Erika, intrigued and glad to have the conversation back on safer ground. 'Come through.'

46

'Vicky Clarke died of a single stab to the heart,' said Isaac when they were settled in the living room. 'There were no drugs or alcohol in her system.'

'Were there any other signs of violence?' asked Erika.

'None. The heart itself is hard to stab because it lies behind the sternum,' said Isaac, putting down his glass and sitting up to indicate the hard bone between his pectoral muscles. 'The sternum is partially covered by the ribs, and the heart has its own fibrous layer covering the pericardium – that's the thick protective sac that surrounds your heart.'

'The person would have to use a very sharp, very long knife? And have a good aim.'

'Yes. Striking the heart with a knife itself is very difficult. The person doing the stabbing would need higher than normal upper body strength. And the person had confidence. There was a single stab wound. It was a very different crime scene to Sophia Ivanova. That was a crazed attack with little control. I've seen a lot over my years in forensics medicine, and a stab wound to the heart is very, very rare. With a crime of passion or rage, it's easier and surer to go for the neck, the hepatic artery close to the liver, the aorta in the torso, the kidneys from behind, or the femoral arteries of each upper leg.'

'So you don't think the two murders are linked?' asked Erika. 'I've been struggling to find a link beyond our assumption that the killer mistook Sophia for Vicky and killed her, and then when Vicky was found, he returned to finish the job.'

'I can't answer that. I can tell you that the murder weapons used for Sophia and Vicky are very different. The knife that killed Sophia Ivanova was wide and around twenty centimetres long, like an average kitchen knife. For Vicky, the killer used a long, narrow blade, which was essential to hit the heart in the way it did.'

Isaac held up his right hand.

'Make a fist,' he said. Erika put down her glass and made a fist with her right hand. 'Imagine you have a knife in that hand and try a stabbing motion.'

They both stabbed in the air, and Erika saw she could exert a lot of force in this way. She stabbed at the plastic-covered mattress which was filled with extra air, and the pressure made the plastic break with a soft popping sound.

'Okay, I'm stabbing. What's your point?' asked Erika.

'Do you have an actual kitchen knife so I can demonstrate?'

'Hang on.' She got up, went through to the kitchen and found the box marked CUTLERY. 'Here we go,' she said, coming back into the living room. She put down the cardboard box, which contained eight knives of various sizes.

'What do you use this for?' he said, holding up a huge silver meat cleaver.

'They were all Mark's. He was the one who loved to cook.'

'Okay. Imagine you want to stab me in the heart, and you pick that normal-looking kitchen knife,' he said.

Erika picked up a kitchen knife which had a thick blade and a serrated edge. She held it, feeling its weight.

'The average kitchen knife is not designed for stabbing,' said Isaac. 'They're made for slicing, applying pressure down on the length of the blade. *And* if you wanted to stab me through the ribs, you'd have to turn the blade horizontal, to fit between them, *and* it would make the knife less easy to control. This knife would be more for the purpose.' He picked up the long, serrated bread knife. It was older, with a smooth wooden handle which was worn away. It had belonged to Mark's grandfather, who had been a stickler for his thinly sliced bread. Isaac handed it to her.

'Imagine trying to stab me with this.' He turned around so his back was facing her. She looked at his shoulders and then took the knife in her hand, feeling how well the smooth wooden handle sat in her palm. She raised the knife above her head. It was very long, and even though she and Isaac were the same height, she could see how high she would have to raise the knife to get the speed and heft to penetrate the thick muscle on his back.

'It would be a challenge to aim, having to lift the knife so high.'

'And your arm would naturally give the stabbing movement an arc,' said Isaac, turning as she moved the knife down slowly so the point came close to the material of his sweater.

'A shorter knife would be easier to control,' said Erika, putting the bread knife down and selecting a small paring knife with a mother of pearl handle. It was fiercely sharp and had belonged to Mark's mother. She'd bought it on a holiday to Thailand, back in the 1970s, when souvenir knives could be brought back on the plane.

'A sharp paring knife like this would penetrate easily,' said Isaac, taking it from her, 'but it would be too short to actually reach the heart. I'm saying that a special kind of long thin knife or dagger was used to kill Vicky. And the person who did it used great precision and had upper body strength.'

'Would the person have needed the same attributes to kill Sophia?' asked Erika, putting the mother of pearl knife back in the box.

'Not necessarily, but as I say, I'm not providing a hypothesis. I'm just giving you the facts...'

'But it could be two different people who killed Sophia and Vicky,' said Erika, sinking back down on the mattress. She picked up her glass and took a glug of the champagne.

'There is something else,' said Isaac.

'What?' said Erika wearily.

'There was very little DNA found at the scene. We found Jasper and Tess Clarke's DNA, which is to be expected at their house, and some other benign samples that we've run through the database. These could have been delivery people, friends of the couple, etcetera. We also were able to lift a latent saliva sample from Vicky's left shoulder,' he said.

'How much saliva?'

'It wasn't a droplet. It was considerably more. When her body was found, she was wearing pyjamas and a sleeveless top, and this person's mouth could have made contact with her shoulder. There was one millilitre of dried saliva swabbed from the surface of her skin.'

'What's that in layman's terms?' asked Erika.

'A good bit of drool,' said Isaac.

'Do you have a DNA match on the saliva?' she asked. Erika could feel her heart lift.

'No. We ran it against all of the samples we were given, and the National DNA Database. We also took DNA samples from Tess, to eliminate her DNA from the crime scene. And it doesn't belong to Jasper. Nor is it Vicky's own saliva, which is something

I wanted to rule out. Whoever it is doesn't have a record. They've never given a sample.'

'And it counts out Charles Wakefield, too, because his DNA was taken when he was arrested on Monday. And Shawn. He gave us a voluntary DNA sample. What else can you tell from the sample?'

'It's from a Caucasian male,' said Isaac.

'Of course, there could have been someone else at the house that evening, before Vicky was killed,' said Erika. 'Do you think the same person killed Sophia who killed Vicky?'

'It's impossible to tell,' said Isaac. 'The methods of both murders are so different. A crazed violent outburst from the person who killed Sophia, versus a calculated controlled way of killing Vicky.'

47

Early the next morning, Erika and Peterson met with Olivia Moreno, a student doctor who had trained with Sophia Ivanova. It seemed to be a quiet morning at Lewisham hospital, and they found a spot in the corner of the empty cafeteria.

'I can't think of anyone who would want to hurt Sophia,' said Olivia. She was a striking woman and she made Erika think of a slightly bookish Penélope Cruz. 'She was very popular.'

'Did you socialise outside work with Sophia?' asked Erika.

'Not a lot. She didn't come to the pub that often. I think she saw drinking alcohol as something bad. She liked to have coffee, and we had coffee sometimes, but studying was important to her.'

'Did she ever talk about friends she had outside work?'

'No. She talked about her sister... Well, *moaned* about her sister *a lot*. She didn't enjoy their living arrangements, both of them trying to study in a one bedroom flat.'

'Did she ever mention a friend called Vicky Clarke?' asked Erika.

Olivia thought about it for a moment. 'No. Sorry.'

'What about boyfriends?' asked Peterson.

Olivia sat back for a moment.

'I've only known her for a year and a half. She'd been having – had – a thing with one of the guys who works here since we've been on our placements here, which I was quite surprised about.'

'Why?'

'He works as a porter.'

'Why is that surprising?'

Olivia hesitated and then smiled.

'The dynamics of a hospital. It's all very segregated. Doctors don't really socialise with nurses, and nurses don't socialise with porters or admin staff. And the NHS managers are hated by everyone, so for Sophia to start a thing with a porter was...'

'Odd?'

'Yes. He's quite sexy in a bad boy sort of way, but that kind of mixing is unusual.'

'What's his name?' asked Peterson.

'Reece. Reece Robinson. He works in the basement.'

'And were they dating?' asked Erika.

'They were screwing, with the odd cup of coffee thrown in.'

After they left Olivia in the cafeteria, Erika and Peterson went to find Reece. They got into a huge industrial-sized lift and pressed the button for the basement. The journey down seemed to take ages. They heard far-off clanks, creaks, and groans and then they came to a stop. The doors opened out into a long windowless corridor which was poorly lit. Up ahead there was a square of light glowing on the cracked linoleum. They followed a scuffed sign on the wall which read INCIN-ERATOR. Their shoes clacked loudly on the floor as they moved towards echoing crashing sounds. At the end of the corridor a metal double door was propped open. They felt the heat from the furnace, and it opened out into a huge round space made of concrete. There were a few dim lights set into the ceiling and at one end of the vast room was a huge metal furnace. A man wearing overalls opened the furnace door to toss in a couple of waste bags. They caught a glimpse of the white-hot glow of the furnace interior, before he slammed the door shut again.

He noticed them, took off his thick gloves, and came over. He was very tall and thin. Erika and Peterson both stood at over six foot, but he was a few inches taller than them both. His face had a blue five o'clock shadow, and dark, penetrating eyes which were almost black. He had a strong nose and prominent lips. There was an intensity about him that Erika acknowledged could be attractive.

'Can I help you?' he said. He had a strong cockney accent.

'Hello, are you Reece Robinson?'

'Yeah. Who's asking?'

Erika and Peterson introduced themselves and flashed their warrant cards. 'We'd like to ask you a few questions about Sophia Ivanova,' said Erika. She could feel the heat from where they were standing, and a warm smell of decay floated over. 'Can we talk to you more outside?'

'Yeah,' he said. 'I was going to go outside for a cigarette.' He led them to a fire escape and opened it. Light from outside flooded in and they stepped out into the cool cleaner air of the car park. Reece indicated a bench and they sat down. He lit up a cigarette and squinted in the morning light.

'I heard about Sophia. Terrible,' he said, exhaling smoke and picking a stray fleck of tobacco off his lip. Erika could see he had a silver bar piercing in his tongue.

'You and Sophia were in a relationship?' asked Peterson.

'I'd say we were more casual than that, if you know what I

mean,' he said. There was a little boast in his voice that Erika found distasteful.

'We're just asking everyone who knew her a few questions. Can you tell us where you were last Monday, 22nd October between 4pm and 8pm?' asked Peterson.

'Let me think...' He took a drag of his cigarette.

'It's a simple question,' said Erika.

'Yeah. I get that. I work shifts and my times are all over the place. Monday... Monday 22nd I met this girl late afternoon in the city, and then we went to her place and then we had sex.'

'What was her name?'

'I'll have to check that out,' he said.

'Can you check for us now?'

'I forgot my phone. I was late for work, and I have all my text messages in there,' he said, picking another piece of tobacco off his tongue.

'Did you ever visit Sophia at her flat?' asked Erika.

'Yeah. When her sister was out.'

'When was the last time you visited?'

He blew his cheeks out.

'Two weeks ago, I think. I'd have to check.'

'Keep a diary, do you?' asked Peterson.

Reece exhaled and spat on the floor. 'No. It'll be in my phone.'

'Did you ever meet Sophia's neighbour, Vicky?' asked Erika.

There was a flicker of something in his eyes.

'Has she got dark hair?'

'She did have dark hair,' said Erika.

'What? Did she dye it?'

'No. She died. Her body was found yesterday morning...' Reece sat up and went pale. 'Did you have sexual intercourse with Vicky?'

'Listen. I didn't know about this, Vicky...'

'Did you have sexual intercourse with Vicky?' repeated Erika.

'Yeah. And Sophia. At the same time. But it was consensual and...'

'When?'

'Again, I'd need to check my phone, and I can show you my text messages, but I'd say it was a couple of months ago.' The attitude he had was now gone, and he looked agitated.

'Would you be willing to provide us with a DNA swab?' asked Erika.

Reece hesitated. 'Do I have to?'

'No. But we will view your refusal as suspicious and we can obtain a warrant.'

'Okay. I'll give you the sample,' said Reece.

'Thanks for your time. Here is my card,' she said, taking one out and giving it to him. 'If you could send me the name and details of your date last Monday, and arrange for us to take a DNA swab.'

'What do you think?' said Peterson, when they were back in the car. They could still see Reece sitting on the bench, staring ahead in shock.

'He's not ringing any alarm bells, but I'll feel happier when we have his DNA swab,' said Erika, buckling up and starting the engine. 'And I'm not looking forward to asking Maria Ivanova about this.'

48

When they arrived at the huge glass entrance doors of Honeycomb Court, they saw Maria was taking delivery of a large cardboard box from a courier. Her face was bloodless, and she was dressed in black trousers and a shapeless black top. They passed the courier on the way in.

'Do you need a hand with that?' asked Peterson as he saw her trying to heave the squat square box through her front door. Maria let go of the box and straightened up. She'd tucked the silver crucifix under her top and she pulled it out again and smoothed down her hair.

'Have you caught the man who killed Sophia?' she said. 'I hear that Vicky was killed. Is that what you are here to tell me?' She was shaking with anger.

'Could we please talk to you inside?' asked Erika.

'I can help you with this box, too,' said Peterson. Maria hesitated and then nodded. The living room looked the same as when Erika visited the first time. Painfully neat and plain. Maria shifted the coffee table out of the way so that Peterson could bring in the box. He placed it down on the floor.

'It's heavy,' said Peterson.

'Thank you,' said Maria. 'It's a folding bed... My parents are arriving tomorrow. It will be the first time they've come to this country... They want to take Sophia's body back to Bulgaria, so we can give her a proper burial. I keep asking Fiona, the Family Liaison Officer, when you are going to release my sister's body?'

'I can check on that,' said Erika.

'*Check on that*,' repeated Maria with a snort. 'I'm not asking you to check if my burger is cooked. This is my sister's body!'

Erika cringed at her use of words.

'I'm sorry. I assure you that I will make enquiries.'

Maria took a deep breath and composed herself.

'My parents run a restaurant. They can't take long from work, we want to know when we can arrange for her body to be repatriated.'

'I promise you I can check on this with the coroner's office and make sure that they know about your circumstances,' said Erika. She didn't know if they would release the body any time soon due to the complexity of the case. 'Maria, we need to talk to you about a few things. Can we please sit down?'

Maria nodded and perched on the end of the small sofa. Peterson sat on the other end and Erika leant against the kitchen counter. She told Maria about Vicky's death, and what had happened. Maria closed her eyes and bowed her head, shaking it from side to side.

'Do you think it's the same person who killed Sophia?'

'We don't know yet. We're still waiting for the results of some forensic evidence to come through. Can I ask you some more questions?' asked Erika.

'What else do you want to know? I have told you and your colleagues everything that I know, over and over. I have things I have to do,' she said. Erika noticed that there were ingredients for baking out on the kitchen counter and an ancient recipe book was open to a picture of a plaited bread.

'This is very important.'

Maria put her hands up in the air and then gave a resigned nod.

'What did you know about Sophia's friendships here in London?'

'We know the same people from our medical course, but we don't socialise. We study.'

'We understand that you've both been working at different hospitals. Did Sophia mention anyone else that she'd met? New friends...' Erika watched her carefully before adding, 'A boyfriend, perhaps?'

Maria's head snapped up at the mention of this.

'Sophia had no time for that. We are here in London on a grant. We have very little money for anything other than food and travel.'

Peterson looked at Erika and gave an imperceptible shake of his head. Erika changed tack.

'Did you know what Vicky Clarke did for a job?'

'She was an actress, no?'

'Yes. And she also had a podcast, like a radio show.'

'I know what a podcast is,' said Maria with a withering look.

'Do you know if Sophia took part in this podcast?'

'Took part. How?'

'Vicky sometimes hired actors to play people on the recording. Did Sophia ever talk about doing a recording for her?'

Maria shook her head.

'No. She was a trainee medical student. She wasn't an actress.'

'Vicky told us that she knew both you and Sophia.'

'We knew her as a neighbour, yes.'

'Did you ever go over and socialise with her?'

266

'I didn't. No.'

Erika took a deep breath.

'Maria. When we spoke to Vicky, she told us that she and Sophia had grown very close as friends... And on a couple of occasions their relationship became... sexual.'

Maria stared at her. 'What? You come to my flat and say that about my sister, who isn't here to defend herself? No. No. I've seen how you people work. You try to say shocking things to provoke a reaction from me!'

'No, Maria, I'm not saying this to provoke a reaction. Vicky was very upset at Sophia's death, and she told us this information because she thought it would help find the person who did this—'

'What did Vicky know about Sophia being killed? She ran away and left my sister's body!'

'And we need to know why Sophia was in Vicky's flat. She told us that she let Sophia use the bed in her flat, for when she met a man she wanted to sleep with.'

'That's *enough!*' shouted Maria, standing up. Her fists were clenched and she had fury in her bird-like eyes.

'Maria, please. We need to ask you these questions,' said Erika, shocked at Maria's reaction to her sister having a sex life. 'There is a man at the hospital who works as an orderly and he was having a sexual relationship with Sophia. His name is Reece Robinson.'

'*Enough! I know she was a whore!*' yelled Maria. She lunged at Erika and landed a hard slap on her face. Peterson jumped up and restrained Maria, pinning her arms behind her back. It was a hard slap and for a moment Erika saw stars. She watched as Maria fought against Peterson's grip, and gave a blood-curdling scream. '*Fuck you! Let me go!*' It made Erika ask, was this grief or rage coming from Maria? The two were often connected, but calling Sophia a whore and hitting a police officer was an extreme reaction, especially from someone who was about to take an oath to do no harm.

'I'll let you go but you need to calm down,' said Peterson, having to raise his voice against Maria's screams. He released his grip, and then she broke down, turning into his chest, and leaning on him.

'She was good! I don't know why she threw herself away to these men! I promise you she was good!' she said through heaving sobs.

Peterson helped Maria to sit back down on the sofa. Erika was still reeling from where she'd been struck. There was a knock at the front door. Erika went to open it. The chain was on and it only opened a crack. Henrietta Boulderstone's face peered through the gap.

'What's going on in there?' she said sharply. Erika closed the door, unhooked the chained, and opened it again.

'We're asking Maria some questions,' she said.

'It sounded to me like you were harassing her!' said Henrietta. She pushed her way past Erika into the flat, and noticed Peterson, who was now sitting with Maria. 'Maria dear, are you alright? Do you want these police officers here?' Maria looked up at Henrietta and shook her head. 'Okay. Now, seeing as you don't have a warrant, I suggest you hotfoot it out of here!'

Erika wasn't in the mood for armchair law and order. She heard the beep of the front door, and saw through Maria's open front door into the hallway where Tess was coming into the building.

'Maria, we'll be in touch about releasing Sophia's body,' said Erika. They left her with Henrietta and moved outside to talk to Tess.

49

'Tess, can we have a word?' said Erika. Tess looked drawn, with huge bags under her eyes. Carrying a large backpack, she came through the glass front doors and stopped in front of Erika and Peterson.

'Officers. I've answered all of your questions.'

'I'm afraid you haven't,' said Erika. 'Can we talk inside the flat?'

Tess gave them both a look.

'What happened to your face?' she asked. Erika caught sight of her face in the small mirror in the hallway. There was an angry red hand print on the right side of her cheek.

'Nothing, can we please come in?'

Tess went to the door and put the key in the lock.

'Don't let them hassle you, dear,' said a voice from behind Erika. They turned and saw Henrietta Boulderstone emerging from Maria's flat. She closed the door behind her and came over to Tess, taking her hand. 'I am so sorry to hear about Vicky.'

'Thank you,' said Tess.

'It's just awful...' She looked back at Erika and Peterson. 'You police. When I was a young girl, the police were to be respected. Now, all I read about is how you harass people for posting nonsense on social media, and now under your noses, two, *two* young women have been killed, from this building. You should be ashamed!' She turned back to Tess. 'Can I do anything?'

'I just have to go in and clean up,' said Tess, indicating the flat.

'Oh, yes. I know Charles is well stocked up with cleaning products. If you need anything at all, he can help,' said Henrietta, tucking her walking stick under her arm and patting Tess's hand.

'Thank you.'

'Do you know when the funeral is?' Henrietta went on, lowering her voice out of respect. Tess shook her head. 'I suspect it's too early to know. Please, as soon as you have a date, let us know. We will all attend. This was Victoria's home and it is a devastating loss for all of us.'

Erika thought she was laying it on a bit thick, talking to Tess as if she were the Queen on a visit to Honeycomb Court.

'Tess. Could we please just talk to you in private?' asked Peterson. He indicated they should go inside the flat.

'You don't have to let them in, you know. They don't have a warrant!' parroted Henrietta.

For God's sake, fuck off, you old bag, Erika wanted to say, but she just kept her face neutral. Luckily Tess seemed to warm to Peterson a little more and she nodded.

Tess, Erika and Peterson went into Vicky's flat and Erika closed the door on Henrietta's withering stare.

Tess stopped in the middle of the room and put the backpack down on the floor. The flat was still a crime scene, with dried blood spatter on the carpet under the sofa-bed frame. Tess crouched down and unhooked the backpack, taking out a roll of industrial-sized black plastic bags and various cleaning products and cloths.

'Can we please just talk to you before you start doing that?' said Erika.

'What? What can you possibly want to tell me? That my husband has a criminal record for rape? That he's lied to me all these years? That he was planning to leave me on the morning my sister was murdered?' she said, standing up and moving closer to Erika. 'Jasper has given his solicitor a CCTV tape which shows that he went to Goose shortly after Vicky arrived at our house, and he stayed inside the building until ten past nine the next morning. The CCTV covers both entrances.' Peterson looked at Erika. If the CCTV images checked out, then that was one less potential suspect.

'If those CCTV images check out, then that will give you comfort, I'm sure,' said Erika. Tess closed her eyes, and opened them again.

'Comfort? My sister is dead. My house is still crawling with forensics officers, I've just told my husband I want a divorce, and I'm left as the only one holding everything together,' she said, speaking through gritted teeth. 'Our restaurant and our home are in danger of being repossessed, and this flat, *if* I can rent it out, might just keep the bank off our backs, but until I clean up the fucking blood and gore, nobody is going to rent it!' Her voice rose to a crescendo at the end.

'I'm very sorry, Tess,' said Erika. 'We just have a couple of quick questions which could really help our investigations.'

'Go on.'

'We asked Jasper about this—'

'I don't want to talk about his conviction for rape.'

'It's not about that. Did Vicky ever leave any notebooks, data drives or USB keys at your house or Goose? And by that I mean in relation to the work she did on her podcast? The reason I ask this is we think that she had been researching a podcast episode, and she'd uncovered the identity of a man who was assaulting students at her former drama school.'

Tess stood there for a moment, thinking.

'No. She never left things at work. And I always used to come and visit her here, she rarely came to our house...' Tess frowned. 'When you talk about these assaults, do you think that Jasper was the person who did them?' Her voice was small and defeated.

'Two of the assaults that we have on police record happened in January and February 2012. Jasper wasn't released from his jail sentence until May 2012. He couldn't have done it,' said Erika. Tess breathed out, relieved.

'Vicky never talked about her podcast, or she probably knew that I wasn't interested.'

'Did she ever borrow money from you, saying that she needed to pay actors?'

'Pay them for what?'

'To work on her podcast.'

'No... Sorry.' Tess's emotions seemed to have turned one-eighty and she now sounded meek and beaten down. 'She did so many random acting jobs, I tuned out in the end.'

When Erika and Peterson left Vicky's flat, Charles Wakefield was in the foyer, opening his box with a key. He eyed them over his shoulder and took out a pile of letters.

'Good morning,' said Erika. He nodded, closed the box and locked it again. 'I haven't had the chance to talk to you about the other evening.'

'And what happened the other evening?' he said, turning. His jowly face seemed to turn a millisecond after the rest of his body.

'When I saw you at Lewisham Row police station—'

'I was there to give a charitable donation with my brother, whom I'm sure you are aware is—'

'Yes we know who he is,' said Erika. 'Vicky Clarke had a very odd reaction to seeing you there. Do you know why?'

'No, I don't. I understand that she'd had a very stressful experience, and then she was hauled back to the police station late at night. I think I would have had a similar reaction...'

Erika nodded. The feeling was starting to come back into the side of her face after being slapped, and it was aching. She felt a sudden wave of hopelessness about the case. Both women were dead, and everyone they spoke to seemed to know nothing, or were very skilled at holding back information.

'I've just heard the news that the poor girl was killed yesterday morning,' Charles added. 'And before you ask, I have an alibi for Thursday night. I stayed at my brother's house. After the presentation at Lewisham Row, we dined at the Ivy late, and then I went back to stay at his house in Central London, and left the following morning. He has a house in Grosvenor Square. I'm sure he'd be happy to confirm this.'

Of course he would, thought Erika.

'Now if that will be all, officers,' he said. He started off to his front door and flicked through his letters. He gave a little yelp, an odd noise which made Erika and Peterson turn back to him.

'Is everything okay?' asked Peterson. They saw that Charles was gripping an envelope in his shaking hand. He turned and held the pile of letters to his chest.

'Yes,' he said, his face breaking into a hasty smile. 'Yes, I'm fine. Just surprised to get a letter from an old friend.'

They watched him as he went to his door and let himself inside, and then Erika and Peterson made their way back to Lewisham Row station.

50

A week passed, and then another. The case seemed to slow down, and with a dwindling list of suspects and their seeming inability to connect the two murders, it became more of a slog. The bodies of both Sophia Ivanova and Vicky Clarke were released from the pathologist, and Maria Ivanova had Sophia's body repatriated, and flew back to Bulgaria.

A DNA swab was taken from Reece Robinson at Lewisham Hospital, and there was no match to either crime scene, and his one-night stand confirmed that he'd been with her on the afternoon of Sophia's murder in North London. Shawn Macavity's DNA swab was taken, and some residual DNA was found in the recording studio in Vicky's flat, but this would have been expected if he'd helped her work on her podcast. It still troubled Erika that there was an hour of his time unaccounted for after he found Sophia's body, and there were no witnesses to prove he did or didn't spend that hour walking on the heath.

Sheila, the administrator from Goldsmith's Drama Academy, sent through the details of reported sexual assaults within the alumni. But it was threadbare and only applied to students who had studied at GDA. Very little in the way of records had been kept, which just made Erika and the team all the more suspicious. Kathleen Barber, Becky Wayland and Grace Leith were also proving difficult to track down. They were no longer known at the addresses on their police files. There was still a big puzzle: how had Vicky found them? They had only ever auditioned for GDA, and never been part of the faculty.

Late in the second week, Erika scored a small breakthrough. Looking through a Facebook page for former students of GDA she found a follower called Becky Church-Wayland. There was no profile photo and little information. Erika sent a message to the account, explaining who she was, and that she needed to talk to her in connection with Vicky Clarke's podcast. She heard nothing for a week, then an email arrived late on a Monday night.

It was Becky Wayland, now Becky Church-Wayland, confirming that she would be attending Vicky's funeral the next day in Worthing. She didn't include a phone number, but Erika replied with hers, saying that she would be attending the funeral with Moss.

The next morning, Tuesday 13th November, Erika and Moss drove down to Worthing in Sussex. It had been Vicky's wish to have her funeral in her home town. It was a two-hour drive from London, so they set off at seven thirty in the morning for the 11am funeral.

It felt strange for Erika and Moss to come back to Worthing. They had an odd connection to the town. It was where they had done surveillance two years previously, and tracked down the killer in the Night Stalker case.

As they drove into the town and took the road along the seafront, the sky was a beautiful gold and blue against a low bank of slivery cloud. The sea was completely still and flat, and reflecting the sky. The beach was clean and empty. It looked almost idyllic. Both their heads turned to the row of Victorian terraces.

'It was that one, number thirty-four,' said Moss, pointing out the green front door to the bedsit as it whizzed past. This was where Erika had confronted the Night Stalker killer, whilst Moss and Peterson sat two doors down, oblivious to what was unfolding.

'Let's hope Worthing weaves its magic again for us,' she said.

'Magic? What do you mean?' Moss grinned. 'You almost died in number thirty-four!'

'But I found the killer.'

'If we do have a breakthrough, let's hope it's a less dramatic one,' said Moss. They carried on past the seafront, and Worthing Theatre sitting on the end of the pier like a huge high-sprung pram.

The church was set back from the promenade, a small butter-coloured brick building with a copper roof and spire which had long ago weathered to a soft teal colour. They found a parking spot three roads away, and then doubled back. The air was crisp and clear and Erika could smell the tang of the sea in her nostrils. The town seemed very sleepy for a Tuesday morning, until they drew closer to the church where they found a big group of smartly dressed young men and women who looked to be in their mid-twenties. Shawn was with the group, dressed in a black suit and polished shoes. His long hair was scraped back into a ponytail.

Erika and Moss slowed a little to let the group into the church, and then went in through the main entrance. The pews in the church were filled almost to the back. There must have been a hundred people, thought Erika. Shawn was giving out the order of service with another young guy on the other side of the aisle. He stiffly said hello to Moss and Erika as they came in. They took an order of service each and found two seats on the end of row of pews at the back.

At the front of the church a polished oak coffin with brass handles was set to the right side of the altar. There was a small bunch of red roses on the lid, and Erika noted that the family had opted for the American style of funeral; there was a large framed photo of Vicky on a stand behind the coffin. *Had it been barely three weeks since she'd talked to Vicky in the canteen at Lewisham Row station?* thought Erika. *Could she have done any more to save her?* She should have put a police car outside Tess's house that night. Erika shook the thought away. Whoever did this, didn't break in, Vicky had let them in, and it burned Erika that after three weeks, they were still no closer to finding out who.

It also frustrated Erika that she didn't have a photo of Becky Church-Wayland. She stood up and scanned the mourners. There seemed to be so many young women in their twenties and thirties in the congregation.

Tess sat at the front on the left side, wearing a large black hat. She looked awful: thin and drawn, and like she hadn't slept in days. Cilla Stone was sitting on the front pew, on the opposite side of the church, and her outfit stood out amongst the sea of black. She wore a bright green trouser suit, with a yellow scarf and a green pillbox hat.

'What is she wearing?' whispered Moss, who was crouching up beside her. 'She looks like a cross between Willy Wonka and an Oompa-Loompa.' Cilla was flanked by Colin on her right and another gentleman to her left. Both men had opted for smart black suits.

'Who's the other guy with her and Colin?' asked Moss, mirroring her thoughts.

'I don't know, maybe that's Ray,' whispered Erika. The man looked to be a similar age to Colin, early fifties, but he was thinner, with a ragged swarthiness about him. His head was shaved and he wore a silver stud in his ear. The three of them were deep in conversation with their heads together. Cilla was nodding along and looked captivated by what they were saying. She put her hand on Colin's arm as Erika continued watching them, sliding it under the cuff of his suit jacket. The other man draped his arm over Cilla's shoulders and rubbed the nape of Colin's neck with his fingers. There was something about their body language which said they were all very close. 'The three of them look like a *throople*,' she added.

'What do you mean?' asked Moss.

'*Throople*, when three people are in a relationship together.'

'Don't you mean *thruple?*' said Moss. 'The word should rhyme with *couple*.'

Erika rolled her eyes and then noticed, two rows behind them sat Charles Wakefield with Henrietta Boulderstone. Charles wore a smart suit but it was ill fitting and seemed baggy on him. Henrietta wore a smart black trilby with a black band and had a long black coat around her shoulders hanging off her like a cape. Charles seemed to sense them staring at him, because he turned and looked at them both, and prompted by his gaze, Henrietta turned too. They both gave Erika and Moss a hard stare and then they were distracted by an elderly lady, who came hurrying into the church. She took an order of service from Shawn and seemed out of breath and apologetic. The woman was small and craggy-faced, and wore a black trouser suit and patent leather court shoes. Her feet were swollen-looking and her skin spilled out over the bridge of the shoe. A man arrived just behind her. He was tall and lean with a weather-beaten face, and a very good suit. His cheeks were sunken and he had black eyes, like chips of coal. Erika could see that the man was weaving slightly as he took an order of service, and he had that glassy focused look in his eyes as if he were taking pains not to appear drunk.

'I'm sorry, Jasper,' they heard the woman say in a loud stage whisper when she reached the front of the church, 'Your dad couldn't find a parking spot.'

She pecked Tess on the cheek, and then she leaned in to Jasper and took his head in her hands and gave him a lingering kiss on his cheek, pressing her face against his for slightly longer than necessary. Jasper shrank away from her, and she brushed at the lapels of his suit.

'You look very smart. You all do,' she said to the row of people. 'Conrad, *Conrad!* We're over here,' she hissed, turning to the old man who had stopped at the coffin and was standing, head bowed, with his hand on the polished wood surface.

'Do you think it was more like they stopped in the pub?' murmured Moss to Erika as they watched Conrad stumble as he moved off towards the front row.

'Conrad. You're here next to me,' whispered the woman, as if they'd come to watch a show and the curtain was about to go up. Even through her stage whisper, they could hear her harsh cockney accent, which cut through the sombre atmosphere.

Erika saw Henrietta was watching the woman with a look of distaste; she leaned over to say something to Charles, and he nodded his head in agreement.

The organ, which had been playing a melancholy tune as people filed in, stopped and a hush seemed to descend over the church. Shawn left his post on the door, and walked down the aisle towards the front and joined his group of friends, who sat a few rows in front of Erika and Moss.

A moment later, a soft voice said, '*All rise,*' and in the hushed silence the priest stood at the lectern. He started to recite, '*Our father, who art in heaven...*'

51

The church service was strangely stilted. Erika had expected this. She knew from experience that a Catholic funeral was more of a commercial for the Catholic faith than a celebration of the person who had died. The priest had announced (looking like it left rather a bad taste in his mouth) that after the church service, there would be another ceremony at the crematorium later at 3pm. After the service Erika and Moss left the church first, and hung around to watch the mourners filing out. She kept checking her phone, hoping Becky might call.

They overheard one of the mourners say that there was an unofficial plan for some of them to go to the Brewer's Arms pub on the high street for a drink and something to eat in between. There were four black cabs waiting on the road at the edge of the courtyard. Erika watched as Tess and Jasper emerged from the church and made a beeline for them. An ancient-looking old man and woman followed behind at a much slower pace. The woman leant on crutches and the man had a walking frame. They were helped by another man and woman, who looked to be in their forties and had the passive detachment of carers.

'I don't think my mum and dad could cope with the pub,' Tess said to Jasper, looking back at their slow progress towards them. 'There's a quiet coffee shop up on the high street,' she said. Jasper's parents appeared behind them, and Conrad murmured something in Jasper's ear, his crinkled lips pursing as he spoke.

'Mum and Dad want to go for a drink,' said Jasper to Tess.

'The pub's too crowded,' she said.

'Jesus, Tess. We need a drink!' said Jasper. It was an interesting tableau. Tess's parents were staring blankly at the doors of the black cab as the breeze off the beach flapped at their wispy hair and smart clothes, waiting to be told what to do next. Jasper and his parents were standing a few feet away in a huddle, and Tess was slap bang between them, alone in no-man's-land on a patch of pavement. She noticed Erika and Moss standing further away.

'Enjoying this, are you?' she shouted. 'Who invited you?'

'We're very sorry for your loss,' said Moss after a moment. 'We just wanted to pay our respects.'

Jasper's parents seemed emboldened by Tess calling out to Erika and Moss. They came over to them, and both seemed to switch from contemplation to fury.

'Our Jasper had nothing to do with this!' said his mother, pointing a rolled-up copy of the order of service close to Erika's face. Her cockney accent was harsh and shrill. 'Nothing! He loved Vicky like a sister!'

Conrad walked up and got very close to Erika and Moss, and they both took a step back. Erika felt alarmed by his aggressive behaviour. He smelt of alcohol and cigarettes. He was very tall, towering over Moss, and even Erika had to look up slightly to see into his eyes.

'The police don't need to be here. I think it would be best if you made yourselves scarce,' he said. His black eyes burned with a real hatred. Anger flared up in Erika, but she resisted the urge to show him her warrant card and remind him why they were there.

'Are you Conrad, sir? What's your wife's name?' asked Moss, looking up at him and keeping her cool. Erika noticed that Henrietta and Charles were standing watching, along with Shawn and his group of friends.

'*Fuck off* is my only answer today,' he said.

'Conrad, come away,' said Jasper's mother. He abruptly turned on his heel and started to walk away from the church.

'Can't you leave us alone? We're mourning,' she said. She turned away from Jasper, adjusted the collar of her coat against the stiff breeze coming off the beach, and hurried after Conrad who was now weaving his way down the seafront, the wind fluttering at the thin grey hair on top of his head.

When Erika looked back at the taxi, Tess and Jasper were climbing in with Tess's parents. Jasper glowered at them as they drove away.

'His parents know we had Jasper under surveillance for the best part of a week,' said Moss.

'And wasn't that an expensive week,' said Erika. Jasper and Tess had spent the first week after Vicky's murder staying with Jasper's parents in their house in Catford, and on the sixth day, Conrad had walked up to the police car and been abusive towards McGorry and Amir, telling them that the only thing they were trying to do was mourn, and having a police car skulking on the street was upsetting his wife.

Henrietta and Charles got into one of the cars, and Erika saw that Shawn and his friends were already halfway along the promenade, and the courtyard was almost empty.

'This Becky is a no-show,' said Moss, barely able to disguise the irritation in her voice. Erika checked her phone again, and her Facebook messenger. There was nothing.

'Let's go to that pub, just on the off-chance,' she said.

Erika and Moss walked the short journey to the Brewer's Arms. When they arrived, it was just past midday, and only a quarter full, and that quarter was mainly mourners. It was a huge saloon-style pub with two big bay windows looking out over the beach. A storm was brewing on the horizon, and the Pavilion Theatre looked like it was hunkering down over the water at the end of the pier, where a huge flock of seagulls were huddled, perching on the vast curved roof. The mourners had spread out over the space, and the radio was playing music softly in the background. A couple of lads in their twenties were playing pool in the corner, and an elderly gent was pushing coins into a fruit machine. His pint rested on the top of the machine, and plastic bags of shopping were pooled at his feet.

They went up to the bar, and Moss ordered them two cokes. Erika scanned the pub. Cilla was sitting with Colin and the other gentleman in armchairs by the bay window around a big table. The light was reflecting off her red hair. There was a group of four other students, two young men and two young women, who were sitting at the table chatting to Colin and the other man. Cilla and the other man got up and came over to the bar.

'Hello, officers,' she said. 'This is my colleague, Ray. He teaches dance at GDA.'

'Hiya, you all right?' he said with a thick cockney accent. Cilla leant forward and ordered two vodka and cokes and a half of Guinness from the barmaid.

'What kind of dance do you choreograph?' asked Moss.

'All sorts,' he said, looking them both up and down. He had a sexuality about him that Erika couldn't pin down. Did he like men, or women, or both?

'Were you a dancer?' asked Erika.

'Back in the day.' He grinned. He had a rather imposing set

of tombstone teeth, and a missing right incisor, which wasn't unattractive, but when he smiled it changed his face from sinister to a little goofy. The barman handed Moss their two cokes and she turned to pay.

'Did you know Vicky Clarke well?'

He pursed his lips and shook his head.

'She never did dance classes at GDA. I knew her through Cil and Col,' he said, scratching above his eye as he spoke. Erika saw he wore several silver bracelets on his right wrist.

Cilla paid for the drinks and then handed Ray the half of Guinness. She went back to the table carrying the remaining drinks, and Ray turned to leave.

'Could I just ask you a couple more questions?'

He took a sip of his drink and licked the foam off his upper lip.

'This is a wake, officer.'

Erika wanted to reply that it wasn't quite yet the wake, but she forced a smile on her face.

'Just quickly. Did you come back down to London with Colin and Cilla, on the 24th October?' asked Erika.

'You should know the answer to that. I spoke to one of your officers on the phone a couple of weeks ago.'

'We know you stayed up in Scotland.'

He took another sip of his drink and nodded.

'Why?'

'Dog sitting. Cil has a dog, Nutmeg, I looked after him for a week until Cil's neighbour got back from holiday. Do you have any more penetrating questions?' He smiled.

'That's all, thank you,' said Erika.

He gave her a mocking little salute, his bracelets jangling, and walked back to the table.

'Here's your coke,' said Moss, handing her a glass and taking a sip.

'Thanks,' said Erika, taking a long pull and savouring the lovely cold, sweet fizziness.

'He was a bit cocky.'

'Yes, but he has an alibi for Vicky's murder. And no motive that we know of to kill Sophia,' said Erika in a low voice. The main door into the bar was partitioned off with a screen of coloured glass, and the door squealed and light filled the room as Henrietta and Charles arrived, looking a little windswept. Charles now had on a black trilby which matched Henrietta's, and they looked a little like secret agents on an over-sixties holiday, thought Erika.

'What do you want to do?' asked Moss, scanning the room. 'It's like the who's who of our case in here.'

In the opposite corner, Erika noticed two young women that she hadn't seen in the church. They were both small and slender with long dark hair. They were standing next to a juke box, with their coats over their arms, and cradling bottles of Budweiser. The group of students around Colin and Cilla was growing, and they were getting quite rowdy and drawing the oxygen out of the room. The girls exchanged a look and the one whose hair was tied back pulled out her mobile phone and made a call.

Erika's phone rang and she saw it was an unknown number. She answered.

'Hi. Are you the police officers working on Vicky Clarke's case?' asked the woman. She had a quiet voice and seemed painfully shy.

'Yes,' said Erika, feeling a soaring triumph as she spoke into the phone. She smiled at the young woman.

'I'm Kathleen Barber, and this is Becky,' she said, indicating the other woman. 'We're willing to talk to you about Vicky's podcast.'

52

There was a small table in the corner of the bar that was still unoccupied, and Moss made a beeline for it. Kathleen and Becky arrived at the table at the same time. Kathleen's long hair was poker-straight, and she had a blunt fringe and a nervous tic where she kept flicking the hair out of her eyes. Erika and Moss introduced themselves and they all sat down.

'We weren't sure about coming,' said Becky.

'We didn't know if you'd received my Facebook messages,' said Erika.

'I did, and I told Kathleen,' said Becky.

Kathleen nodded and glanced around nervously. The group around Cilla, Colin and Ray were taking raucously, and Henrietta and Charles were adjacent to them, talking intensely.

'How did you find out about Vicky?' asked Erika.

'She was going to send us a final version of the podcast before she uploaded it,' said Kathleen. 'Just to check that we were still sure we wanted to be included.'

'When was this?' asked Erika, taking out her notebook.

'She said she'd send it by the twelfth of October. Then we

would have a few days to listen before she needed to upload it on the seventeenth,' said Becky.

'We didn't hear anything by the twelfth, and then on the eighteenth, when it was supposed to be uploaded I was really annoyed, so I phoned her, but her phone was switched off. Vicky had given me Becky's number. She said she hadn't heard anything either,' said Kathleen.

'When did you find out that Vicky was dead?' asked Erika.

'Last week. We saw a small piece on the *Daily Mail* website, where they wrote the story about an actress being found dead, and there was her photo,' said Kathleen. 'I phoned Becky and I told you, didn't I?' she asked with another flick of her fringe. Becky nodded. They both looked terrified, with their heads down and looking at the table, as if this was taking a huge effort to talk about.

'All of Vicky's notes, and her computer hard drive and sound files, have been deleted. We got your names from sound files on a USB stick we found in Vicky's bag,' said Moss. 'How did Vicky even find you?'

'She said there was a guy who worked at the university who helped her with the sound on the podcast. They'd got to know each other a little, and when he started to listen to the podcasts she'd recorded about the true crimes, he told her about the Jubilee Road student halls and the break-ins and assaults he'd heard about,' said Kathleen.

'But how did she find you both? How did she get hold of your names?' asked Erika.

'Vicky told us she had to do a lot of digging,' said Becky. 'There's a public website, a police website, Police.uk? She said that if you have an area and a date you can look up the crimes that were reported in that area to the exact address. She said that this guy at the university knew of a vague date of when it happened to me and Kathleen. January and February 2012. So

Vicky said she looked up crime data for the Jubilee Road post-code, and she saw the break-ins and assaults that were reported for that time.'

'She said there were only two cases for eighty-four Jubilee Road,' added Becky.

'Then she said she phoned up GDA and concocted some story, saying she was from the British Arts Council, and that they'd selected the school for an article about audition technique, and she wanted to track down people who had auditioned for drama schools. Something hokey like that. Anyway, she got them to give her a list of people who'd auditioned on the day of the assaults, saying she wanted to interview them about auditioning and what it's like. There were only six guys and six girls on the list. That's how she tracked us down. We'd both moved house a couple of times, but our mobile phone numbers hadn't changed.' Kathleen finished and there was a long silence. Moss looked at Erika and raised an eyebrow. 'What? Is something wrong?'

'No. I'm a little bit in awe. That's good detective work,' said Erika. Moss nodded.

'Okay. So. Vicky contacted you, and explained what she was doing with the podcast. What happened next?'

'For me, she explained that this was the first podcast episode that she was doing where she was actively investigating some-thing,' said Becky. 'She told me that in the past, she'd made her true crime podcast episodes based on information that was in the public domain and she'd just dramatised it, but this was more real—'

'She'd already talked to me,' said Kathleen, 'and I think she'd also talked to the other girl, Grace Leith, and she'd been quite shocked that there was a serial predator—'

'Yeah, so by the time she found me, I was another piece of the puzzle. She asked if I would come down to London, or if she could come up and talk to me, record what I had to say. She offered to pay for train travel and lunch for the day. And I fancied a trip up to London, so I met her in Covent Garden.'

'Where?' asked Erika.

'A nice restaurant in the covered market,' said Becky. 'I don't know if that helps? She was very kind, and we spoke for a long time before we then went to a café, a Starbucks which was empty, and that's where we recorded my interview. There was an opera singer outside the restaurant where we ate and Vicky said that we couldn't have the singing in the background on the tape,' said Becky. 'She paid my train fare, bought me lunch, and she was so excited about the interview. She thought that this would really launch her podcast to the next level.'

'Where did she talk to you?' said Moss to Kathleen.

'I've got kids. I'm on my own. I live out in the sticks in Suffolk, near a place called Beccles,' she said. 'Vicky came to me. I got my mother to look after the kids for a couple of hours and we met in a café locally. I thought the same as Becky. She was lovely. Paid for lunch and my bus fare.'

'Do either of you know Grace Leith?' asked Erika.

'No, she asked us about her, but she'd auditioned at a different time, a couple of years after us,' said Becky.

They sat in silence for a moment, as Erika tried to absorb this information. The time was ticking, and she could see that some of the students were already getting up to leave the pub. Kathleen took a sip of her drink and twitched her fringe.

'Did Vicky send you any recording material? Did she send you any sound files? Emails with details of what she found out?' asked Moss.

Both the young women shook their heads.

'Did Vicky tell you anything else about her investigations?' asked Erika. There was another pause. Kathleen flicked her fringe and looked to Becky.

'What was that thing she said to you about the neighbour?' she asked.

'What neighbour?' said Erika.

'Vicky said she has this creepy neighbour, an older guy who lives next door, and when she started looking into the assaults at the student halls in Jubilee Road and Hartwood Road, she found out that he'd been the caretaker for those buildings, and a couple of others at Goldsmith's Drama Academy, between 2007 and 2012. The same dates as when we were assaulted... She said she'd been round his flat to ask him about his time as caretaker, you know, and he must have heard about the assaults and break-ins because he was in charge of those buildings... She said he went *mad* and told her that he had nothing to do with it, and he threatened to report her for harassment. He pulled her out of his flat, dragged her by the arm. She said his reaction was so weird that it made her even more suspicious,' said Becky.

Erika sat in shock for a moment. She looked over and saw that people were getting ready to leave. Henrietta and Charles had already gone, leaving two empty glasses and two empty packets of crisps at their table.

'Are you absolutely sure she said this man was her neighbour?' asked Erika.

'Yes,' said Becky. 'She called him Charlie, Charlie-Boy.'

Erika was suddenly struck with the image of Charles and Henrietta, entering the pub in their matching black trilbies.

'Shit. Charles Wakefield,' she said, looking at Moss.

53

'It's true. Charles Wakefield was caretaker between 2007 and 2012,' said Erika, coming off the phone with Sheila at the GDA admin office. Kathleen and Becky had gone on in Becky's car to the crematorium, but Erika and Moss had stayed at the pub.

'And no one we've spoken to thought to mention this?' said Moss.

Erika put in a call to Peterson at the incident room. His phone rang out. She tried a couple of other numbers, and finally Crane answered.

'What's going on there, are you all at lunch?' she said.

'Sorry, boss. We've had a bit of a development here,' said Crane.

'What kind of development?'

'We've been going back over all the paperwork and files for the case, and McGorry found something, *alarming* to say the least.'

'What?'

'When Charles Wakefield was arrested three weeks ago, a

DNA sample wasn't taken when he was booked into the custody suite at Lewisham Row.'

'What do you mean? He was arrested. Everyone who's arrested has their DNA taken in the custody suite.'

'Not in this case,' said Crane. 'There's no entry on the National DNA database for a Charles Wakefield. And the arrest report is incomplete.'

'Christ! How?'

'Yeah. I had the same reaction. We're just going back over everything that was logged up until now to try and trace back to who was working in the custody suite on the night he was arrested and brought in.'

'Have you told Melanie?' asked Erika.

'No. I was about to call you first.'

'So all the DNA we've been running through the database for the past two weeks hasn't included a check against Charles Wakefield?'

'Not directly.'

Erika went on to tell him about the revelation that Charles Wakefield was caretaker at GDA during the time the assaults occurred, and that Vicky had confronted him about this when she was making her podcast.

'There was also something else. Charles and Henrietta both showed up for the funeral in black trench coats and black trilby hats. They're both the same height. I'm just thinking back to this CCTV from Blackheath train station taken when Charles said he went into London on the day that Sophia was killed. That's his alibi, but because his face is obscured on the CCTV footage, it's *not* an alibi. And now I've seen them together today, I had the awful thought, what if the person on the CCTV going into central London is Henrietta? Did you manage to track down any other CCTV that shows Charles Wakefield going into central London that day?'

'No,' said Crane. 'And we spoke to the person who was working on the ticket desk. They didn't recall seeing Charles that day, but the person did add that it was crazy busy, and they sell a lot of tickets and speak to a lot of passengers every day.'

There was a long silence from Crane on the end of the phone. Moss looked at Erika and raised an eyebrow.

'Okay. Where are you now, boss?' asked Crane.

'I'm still here with Moss, in the pub in Worthing. Everyone has gone on to the crematorium, including Charles Wakefield. Give me a moment, Crane. I'll call you back.'

Erika was now sweating as she filled Moss in on what had happened.

'What if it's Charles who assaulted these women at GDA? And then he found out that Vicky was investigating the assaults, and he threatens her, but Vicky keeps going and tracks down Becky and Kathleen and interviews them. And then she talks to Charles again, saying she has these two women on record.'

'Hang on,' said Moss. 'That doesn't explain why Sophia was killed.'

'What if it was as we first thought, mistaken identity? Sophia was in Vicky's flat. They did look alike. Charles breaks in, in a frenzy, thinking that it's Vicky. He beats her, rolls her up in the sofa bed mattress and stabs her... His focus would have been on clearing out and destroying the evidence that Vicky had accumulated on the case: all her notebooks, and USB sticks, the hard drive for her computer.'

'Again. Hang on, though,' said Moss. 'You saw what his flat was like when we looked round. He's a luddite. The only electronics he had were an old record player and a VHS.'

'Does that mean he's innocent? He might have learned how to use a computer at work,' said Erika.

'Okay, so Charles gets into Vicky's flat, kills who he thinks is Vicky, but it's actually Sophia... He cleans up and then resumes the cocktail hour with Henrietta. Then that would explain him being so wired when we arrive on the scene, and we arrest him with the frozen dead cats, which is unrelated. His brother happens to be the Assistant Commissioner... His DNA isn't taken on arrest. What about Henrietta? Is she involved?'

Erika rubbed at her temples.

'I don't know. I don't know. Would Julian Wakefield risk his career for his brother? And what does Julian Wakefield have to do with it, if anything?'

Moss put up her hands.

'Let's move on from that for a moment. So, back to the first murder... Tess *also* mistakenly identifies Sophia as Vicky. They look alike and in her beaten-up state—'

'I arrived on the scene almost as soon as Tess saw the body, which meant that the misidentification stuck with us. We didn't discover it wasn't Vicky until twenty-four hours later,' said Erika.

'Fast forward twenty-four hours. We find Vicky, she then comes back from Scotland and Charles Wakefield sees her that night as he's coming out of Lewisham Row station,' said Moss. 'Did he look shocked to see her?'

Erika thought back and tried to remember. Her focus had been more on Vicky's reaction.

'I don't know if I would call it shocked, but there was a very strange moment between them,' said Erika.

'So when he sees Vicky, Charles Wakefield now knows that he didn't kill her and she's about to talk to us... Does he hope she's scared enough that she won't spill the beans right away? He waits until she goes back to Tess's house. Then he knocks on the door late at night, and he's ready with a knife and stabs her in the back,' said Moss.

Erika thought it through.

'Bollocks. Would it stand up in court? I don't know, but it could have happened. Charles doesn't have an alibi for the night

Vicky was murdered. Well, his alibi is Julian Wakefield. With this inconclusive train station CCTV, he certainly doesn't have an alibi for when Sophia was killed, either. And now we find out he was the caretaker of GDA at a time when Vicky was investigating the assaults on students...'

'And we've just found out from Becky and Kathleen that Vicky was quite a serious operator, and a damn good investigator. What else could she have known, and what if she confronted Charles with something serious?' asked Moss.

Erika sat back and looked around at the empty bar.

'And without Charles's DNA, the saliva forensics found on Vicky's shoulder is back in play. We thought we'd already matched that against Charles Wakefield's DNA, but we haven't.'

She drummed her fingers on the table. They needed a DNA sample from Charles, and they now had grounds to arrest him and take a DNA swab. The only problem was the cremation – could they justify rocking up and making an arrest during such a sensitive time for the rest of the family?

'Are you thinking what I'm thinking?' asked Moss.

Erika nodded. 'What if Charles Wakefield recognised Becky and Kathleen when we were talking to them? He could make a run for it. We need to get him in custody, a DNA sample taken, and question him.'

'What about the fact he's—' started Moss.

'I couldn't give a damn if he was the King of England, let alone the brother of the Assistant Commissioner,' said Erika. 'He could be our man.'

Erika pulled out her phone and rang Crane back.

'Crane. I want to arrest Charles Wakefield and bring him in. I'm going to send you the address of the crematorium. We'll do it after the service, and try to do it quietly without disturbing the family. I need you to arrange backup from local police.'

'What about Melanie?' he asked.

'I'm the lead officer on this case. *I'll* worry about Melanie. Just get me two uniformed officers and a backup car,' said Erika.

54

Worthing crematorium was outside the town, and set amongst beautiful grounds. As they passed the tall trees and open fields down the long driveway, Erika saw that it might be difficult to make a quiet arrest. She'd hoped that the crematorium would be in a more built-up area.

'This used to be a stately home, before they demolished it and turned it into a crematorium,' said Moss. The sky was now clear and as the long driveway turned to the right, the trees parted and they saw the long, low crematorium building with a flat white roof. To their left and right were rows of tombstones, a lone mourner, and an older lady in a thick beige coat was placing a posy of flowers on a small square grave. A crow watched her from his perch, four stones across. It seemed so peaceful, and the idyllic scene was only marred by the sight of the long chimney rising up from the crematorium where the furnace was pumping a stream of dark smoke into the sky.

'I hate these places, the contrasts,' said Moss. 'I remember my gran's funeral. We all stood mingling in the lovely grounds after the service, chatting about her, but no one wanted to mention that the black pouring out the chimney and the burning smell was *her*.'

Erika looked across at Moss, surprised that she would mention something so negative. Moss was usually unflappable.

'Are you okay?'

'Me? Course,' said Moss, sitting up and taking a big breath.

As Erika turned the corner, they emerged into a gravel court-yard. There was already a police car parked up by the main entrance and two young uniformed officers were standing in front with their arms folded.

'No, no, no. I wanted plain clothes, subtle!' said Erika, guiding the car into a spot far away from the main entrance. The two guys had a stance about them, as if they were primed for action. 'These clowns are going to cause a commotion.'

'Heads up, everyone is coming out now,' said Moss, pointing to the main entrance, where Cilla, Colin and Ray were standing at the top of the steps. Cilla was between them, her hands hooked into their arms. She took a tissue from her pocket to dab her eyes. A moment later, more of the mourners started to file out behind them, filling the large wide set of stone steps down to the car park.

Erika could see the two policemen were the kind of belligerent male officers that rang alarm bells in her head. She was no stranger to belligerency herself, but these guys looked primed for a confrontation. The taller of the two pushed himself off the side of the car where he'd been leaning his hip, and straightened his hat. He checked his belt to see he had his cuffs and baton.

'We need to go and talk to them, now,' said Erika, slipping off her seatbelt. Moss did the same and they got out of the car and hurried across to the squad car. Erika fumbled to get out her warrant card as she saw Jasper and Tess emerge onto the steps with Shawn and a group of his friends.

'I'm DCI Erika Foster. This is DI Moss,' said Erika, keeping one eye on the mourners. Becky and Kathleen came out of the entrance, just in front of Jasper's father Conrad, gripping onto his wife's arm.

'I'm Constable John Fryatt,' said the dark-haired officer. 'This is Constable Murray Frazer.'

Murray put a hand to his hat in a casual kind of salute, which annoyed Erika.

'Is this the suspect?' said Murray, a red-head with a strong jaw and bright green eyes a little close together. He held up a print-out of Charles Wakefield. It was an unfortunate choice; it was the mugshot from his previous arrest, complete with wild eyes and a bloody bandage on his face.

'Listen. We need a quiet arrest. I want you to be prepared to wait until the mourners have dispersed, and then we'll approach Charles Wakefield.'

'He's accused of sexual assault? And murder?' asked Constable Fryatt.

'Yes...' Erika started to say. Then she saw both the men straighten up, like dogs about to charge. Constable Frazer held up the photo as Charles Wakefield emerged from the entrance last with Henrietta. They blinked up at the bright sky as Henrietta leant on her stick. Charles slipped on his trilby hat and then offered her his arm. Even though he was supporting Henrietta, there was something vulnerable about the way he held onto her, like a child about to be dropped off for its first day at nursery school.

Tess must have noticed them, it wasn't hard to, and she came stalking down the steps towards Erika and Moss with the two uniformed officers. Her eyes were puffy with tears.

'What's this? What's going on?' she said, her voice high with emotion.

'Nothing, please, we don't want to disturb you,' said Erika, feeling a flash of panic.

'You park a marked police car slap bang at the bottom of the main entrance during my sister's cremation?' she shouted. The mourners were all starting to look over at the police car. Jasper hung back with his parents, who looked concerned. When Charles and Henrietta reached the bottom of the steps they stopped and stared. Erika saw Henrietta nudge him.

'Please, we're going to move this car, I'm very sorry for this timing,' said Erika, keeping her eye on Charles and trying to placate Tess.

'I'm going to complain to your superior, Erika. This is harassment. You were *not* invited here today!'

Charles came down the steps to join Tess.

'Tess, my dear. Just come away, I've found this new breed of uniform officer to be very rude and to be honest, they don't have the first idea about policing...' Erika knew that Charles was speaking from the perspective of his brother being in the police, but for the two young police officers, this rudeness was like a red rag to a bull. What happened next was so fast that Erika stood in shock. Fryatt and Frazer lunged at Charles, who instinctively turned on his heel and started to run away across the car park with a surprising spurt of energy.

Henrietta gave a loud yell of 'Oh no!' which made everyone on the steps snap their heads over to watch as the two officers pursued Charles across the car park. They caught up with him at the edge of the gravel, where a line of bushes sat. There was grass on the other side, which banked down steeply and the grassy hill ended at the bottom where a small sign heralded it as *The Garden of Mourning*. Frazer grabbed Charles's jacket, but he slithered out of it, and then seemed to lose his footing and fall under the hedgerow, evading the two officers and rolling down the grassy bank.

'Get him!' shouted Frazer. 'Don't let him get away!'

By now, any hope of a quiet arrest had evaporated. Jasper had joined Tess on the crematorium steps and was shouting at Erika and Moss.

'What are you doing? He's an old man! You fucking thugs!'

Erika and Moss ran off across the gravel and as they reached the sparse row of hedges, and *The Garden of Mourning,* they could see through to the grassy bank on the other side where Frazer had Charles pinned down with his knee in his back. The other officer was kneeling over Charles's head, reading him his rights. And all the while Charles was making high-pitched squealing noises, like a piglet struggling to get free.

Erika turned to see the mourners all standing with their mouths open. The only person who didn't look surprised or particularly distressed was Jasper's father, Conrad, and his mother, who was standing neatly at the bottom of the steps with her handbag in the crook of her arm.

Erika and Moss hurried around the line of bushes, to where the police officers had Charles on the ground.

'Get off him!' Erika shouted. 'Now!' She was horrified at how this had all happened in such a short time.

Frazer took his knee off Charles's back and Fryatt sat back. They were both panting with the exertion. It was then that Erika saw that Charles had stopped squealing and he lay very still, face down on the grass. She hurried to his side and gently rolled him over. He was muttering and rolling his eyes.

'My arm! He broke my arm!' he cried with a ragged fury in his voice.

'Call an ambulance,' said Erika. She started to read Charles Wakefield his rights, but then his eyelids fluttered and his head lolled to the side. He was unconscious.

55

The police station was quiet, and a hush had descended over the corridors when Erika and Moss arrived back in Lewisham Row that evening.

'Do you want me to come upstairs with you? I'll tell them straight what happened,' said Moss.

'No. You get home to Celia and your kids. I'll deal with this,' said Erika. She was grateful to Moss for showing support, and she knew her colleague meant it, but Erika was the senior officer, and she'd made the call to arrest Charles Wakefield.

'Good luck. And let me know how it goes,' said Moss, squeezing Erika's arm.

She started to climb the stairs, feeling exhausted. She stopped at the top of the stairwell and looked out over the twinkling carpet of London stretching far away. It was a clear night, and she could see the coloured lights of the London Eye by the Thames.

'Sounds like you had quite a day?' said Melanie, when Erika sat in front of her desk. Her face didn't give anything away. She looked tired, thought Erika, and overwhelmed by reams of paperwork and files on her desk and in piles on the floor around her office.

'I had no choice but to arrest Charles Wakefield. The manner of his arrest was unfortunate,' said Erika. She then went on to explain what they'd learned from Becky and Kathleen. And that Crane had discovered no DNA swab had been taken on Charles Wakefield's first arrest.

'I will be conducting a full investigation as to why a swab wasn't taken. It *has* happened before,' said Melanie, her face creased with concern.

'But it's a funny coincidence, don't you think?' said Erika, raising an eyebrow. 'Do I need to repeat who his brother is?'

'Trust me when I say I'm not going to brush this under the carpet.'

'Has Marsh been in contact?'

'No. This is nothing to do with Commander Marsh. This is your investigation and this is my station,' said Melanie.

'Thank you,' said Erika, feeling relief. She couldn't deal with either of them right now.

'What is the medical status of Charles Wakefield tonight?' asked Melanie.

'I don't know if he feigned unconsciousness when we arrested him... He was read his rights, but the paramedic refused to let me take a DNA swab.'

'You can't get in the way of a paramedic.'

'I know, but what if he wriggles his way out of this again?' said Erika, rubbing her eyes. 'It was a real mess. And the two uniform police officers were louts. They escalated what should have been a simple situation.'

'In front of a whole congregation of mourners?'

'Yes,' said Erika. 'But Charles Wakefield is now my main suspect. If his DNA matches the saliva that forensics took from

Vicky Clarke's shoulder, it would put him in the room when she was murdered. We also took DNA from the Sophia Ivanova crime scene, and one of the samples hasn't been matched. I don't know when the hospital will discharge him.'

'Is he injured?'

'He claimed the officers broke his arm, but they did an x-ray, and it was just a sprain. The hospital want to keep him in overnight for observation, due to his age. Sussex police have been very vague, and I'm having to work across our jurisdictions.'

Erika sat back and suddenly felt exhausted.

Melanie tapped her pen on her desk. 'Listen. I know the Chief Superintendent in Sussex. I'll get on the phone now and recommend we get the officer that's there tonight in A&E to remind Charles Wakefield of his rights, and he'll take a DNA swab in the presence of a nurse. That way we do things by the book.'

'Even if we do, we won't get a DNA result through for another forty-eight hours.'

Melanie sat back and regarded her.

'Erika, don't be impatient. Do you really think the brother of a senior police officer will abscond? And there will be a point where Julian Wakefield has to accept what is happening, even if it is his brother.'

'I don't put anything past anyone,' said Erika.

'Listen, it's late. Go home. Keep your phone on, I will do as much as I can tonight.'

'Thank you,' said Erika.

When she came back out into the car park, it was gone 9pm. The revelations today had pushed the case forward, but she felt deeply uneasy that Charles Wakefield was going to slip through their fingers again. Her phone rang, and she was surprised to see it was Igor's number.

'*Ahoj*,' she said, answering in Slovak.

'*Ciao*. I hope you don't mind me ringing you?'

'Not at all. I said you should ring, but I haven't had time to think about the chimney stuff. The last two weeks have been crazy with the case I'm working on.'

She heard him hesitate on the end of the phone.

'Listen, forget about that... What would you say if I told you that...' He gave a nervous laugh. 'That I can't stop thinking about you?'

'I'd tell you that's one of the cheesiest lines in the book,' she joked.

He was silent.

'I'm being serious.'

Erika opened her mouth and closed it again. She had thought about him too, albeit not all the time, but she had been having lots of memories about their past, and how great it had been to re-connect.

'What are you doing now?' she said.

'Right now? I'm parked outside your house.'

'Okay. You're a stalker with cheesy chat-up lines?'

He laughed.

'No. My last delivery was in your area... because I made sure it was.'

'I tell you what. There is a fantastic fish and chip shop two roads up from my house. Go and get us dinner, cod and chips for me, and I'll meet you back at my house in half an hour. What do you think?'

'Sounds good,' he said, and she could hear the excitement in his voice.

Erika hung up the phone. It felt odd and totally unexpected to have a date with someone she knew fall into her lap. She almost felt guilty. But the world wouldn't come crashing down if she had a late dinner with an old friend, and she would get rid of him after they ate, so she could work.

It wasn't a date, she told herself, *he was just a friend*.

56

Erika woke with a start. The digital clock on her new bedside table was glowing 3am. She looked over and saw Igor, sleeping soundly beside her.

What am I doing? she thought. They'd eaten their takeaway fish and chips, and drunk a couple of beers, and despite everything going on with the case, Erika had forgotten things for a couple of hours and had so much fun. Igor made her laugh, and it was nice to talk to someone in her own language. And then, one thing led to another and they ended up in bed together *and* she let him stay the night.

Erika sat up and felt around on the end of the duvet. George was gone. He always seemed to leave at some point in the night. Erika lay back, and then she heard the noise. A rustle and a thud. She stiffened. There was silence for a moment, and then it came again.

Erika got up and moved softly across the floor. She was in thick pyjamas and barefoot. When she reached the landing and the top of the stairs, the streetlight on the road out front was shining through the glass front door and casting a sludgy orange glow through the landing and the hallway. There was another soft rustle in the kitchen downstairs, and the squeaking noise came again. As Erika moved down the stairs they creaked slightly, and she heard the noise in the kitchen stop.

George, she thought. *It was George.* Erika reached the bottom of the steps and hesitated, stepping down into the hallway. She skirted around the rectangle of orange light on the bare floorboards. She eased herself around the curved edge of the bannister, until she could see down the short piece of the hallway into the kitchen.

The soft padding sound came again, and in the dim light she saw something small flex and leap down from the kitchen counter, and land on the floorboards with a soft thud. The light shining in through the hall caught George's eyes with a glint of green in the darkness.

Erika felt relief that it wasn't an intruder and she smiled.

'What are you doing, you little shit? It's three in the morning,' she whispered.

George gave a loud miaow, and then batted at the floor with his paws before leaping back up onto the counter. Erika heard a squeak and a rustle and then there was a loud crash and a tinkle of glass. *It was a mouse, that little monkey had brought in a mouse*, she thought. She loved George, but the thought of a half-dead mouse, or a very much alive mouse, vanishing into the floorboards gave her the shivers.

She hurried down the hall towards the kitchen and was about to switch on the light when she felt the broken glass under her feet. It was too late to stop and she blundered into the pile of broken shards, feeling an agonising pain as a piece of glass sank into the bottom of her right foot.

Erika cried out and stepped back, but stood on another piece. She found the light and switched it on. George was on the counter in a goose-stepping frenzy, clubbing at a mouse with his paws, sending more of the takeaway chip papers and a mug clattering to the floor. There was a creaking sound from upstairs and then Igor's footsteps thudded across the floor above.

'Erika!' he shouted. 'Are you okay?'

George leapt on the mouse, disembowelling it with his claw, and at the same time flinging it up in the air. Blood spattered over the window and Erika, uncharacteristically for her, screamed. Igor came crashing downstairs, and emerged around the bannister running stark naked towards her. He had his phone torch lit.

'What is it? Are you okay?' he said.

'Stop! Careful! There's a broken beer bottle on the floor!' said Erika, trying to limp out of the pool of green shards. George had now finished with the dead mouse and he jumped down and looked up at them both, giving a miaow, as if to say, *what are you both looking at?*

Igor shone his torch down on the floor, and Erika saw the blood, a rather large amount of it, amongst the shards of glass and pooling under her foot. He put out his hand.

'Come on, let's get you out of this, I'll clean up the glass,' he said.

Erika turned and hopped out from the shards of broken green glass with her cut foot off the ground. 'Watch out for George, he could cut his paws,' she said, leaning on Igor's arm and looking back.

'He's okay. He's a smart pussy,' said Igor, as George leapt clean over the glass and padded along the hallway after them. The pain in Erika's foot was searing, but she laughed.

'What?' said Igor.

'Sorry. I'm being immature.'

'Are you laughing because I said *pussy*?'

'I don't know anyone who calls a cat that, apart from an old lady,' she said as he helped her hop down the hallway.

'I'm glad you find me funny,' he said with a smile.

'And you, running with no clothes on,' said Erika, laughing even more. She limped to the stairs and Igor helped her to sit on the bottom step. He stared at her, looking at her dissolving into hysterics with a curious look on his face, which made her laugh even more.

'It's tough when a woman laughs at you when you're naked,' he said.

'I'm not laughing at you... It's just a funny situation.'

George and Igor waited patiently as she laughed some more, and then she saw her foot. There was a nasty curved slash on the bottom of her instep, about four inches in length, which gaped wetly with blood. Now she could see it, she stopped laughing and the pain was even worse. She gripped his arm.

'That's a nasty cut,' he said, crouching down and examining it. 'You should really go to hospital.'

'No. Please, no hospital. It's fine. I'll bandage it up.'

'Erika. It's the bottom of your foot. There are big arteries there, and it's a deep cut. We should get it checked out. I'll take you. I should just put some clothes on first.'

Erika looked down at the yawning cut on the underside of her foot. The pool of blood was growing on the floor. Igor reappeared a moment later, dressed and carrying her clothes.

'You really want to take me to the hospital?' she asked.

'Of course,' he said. As he helped Erika on with her trousers, she felt so comfortable with him, like suddenly she wasn't alone in the world anymore.

It was a scary thought to have, but the throbbing pain in her foot pushed it out of her mind.

57

Peterson arrived, bleary-eyed, at Lewisham Row the next morning. It was very cold, and even at 8am the day seemed to be struggling to get light, a blue twilight hue hung in the foggy air.

He hadn't slept well, and as he grabbed his bag and the hot sausage rolls he'd bought from Greggs on his way in to work, he wanted nothing more than to go back to his comfy new bed with Fran. As he hurried across the car park towards the main entrance, a huge Argos delivery lorry pulled up to the barrier, and then came rumbling through. Next to the Argos logo on the side of the lorry was a huge garish photo of a smiling Father Christmas with his thumbs up.

It came to a stop at the main entrance, and a fit-looking young bloke with a beard climbed down from the cab and ran around to the passenger side. He opened the door, and Peterson was surprised to see Erika sitting in the passenger seat. The man half lifted her down, and she stepped gingerly onto the tarmac. Her right foot was bandaged, inside an ill-fitting flip-flop. The guy reached up into the cab and took out a pair of metal crutches, handing them to Erika.

Peterson stared, and the bloke nodded at him in acknowledgement. He could see Erika was embarrassed.

'Morning,' said Peterson. 'Is everything okay?'

The guy said something to Erika that he couldn't understand, and Peterson realised they were speaking Slovak. Erika muttered something back to him which looked like she was saying thank you.

'This is Igor, Igor this is James,' she said. There was a honk from behind the delivery van, and Peterson saw Moss had just driven through the barrier and was trying to get into the car park but the Argos lorry was blocking her.

'I have to go, can you help her inside?' said Igor in English to Peterson.

'Sure.'

'Bye. You call me, and take those painkillers,' said Igor to Erika.

'Yes,' said Erika.

'And if you have a shower, put a bag over your foot,' he said and he leant over to kiss her on the cheek. Peterson noticed that Erika didn't look too happy about the kiss but she didn't shrink away from it either.

'Bye, have a good day and thanks again,' she said to Igor.

Erika limped over to Peterson, leaning on the crutches, as Igor got back into the lorry, slowly backed it out of the car park, and then drove off with a wave. Moss pulled into the car park and came to a stop beside them, rolling down her window.

'What's happened to you, boss?' she said, looking at Erika on her crutches. 'And why were you being delivered to work in an Argos lorry?' she added. Peterson looked at Erika; he could see that she didn't want to explain the Argos delivery man.

'I stood on a broken bottle at home,' she said. 'A stupid accident. The cat broke the bottle.'

'Shouldn't you be resting?' asked Moss, peering out of the window down at Erika's bandaged foot.

'I'm fine. They stitched it up, and I have strong painkillers... I'll see you in the incident room.'

She limped off on her crutches, and Moss raised an eyebrow at Peterson.

'Do you know who the bloke was?' she asked quietly. Peterson shook his head. 'Never mind. I've got an Argos catalogue in the glove compartment. I'll see if I can find him in there,' she added with a smile. 'And since when has she had a cat?'

'No idea.'

'Good on her,' said Moss. And she drove off to park her car. Peterson saw that Erika was struggling to get up the front steps to the main entrance and he ran to help her.

Erika was cringing from the encounter she'd just had outside, but when she got into the reception area and up to the front desk, she soon forgot her discomfort. The officer on duty told her that Charles Wakefield had been discharged from hospital, and he'd been placed in a cell in the custody suite. Moss and Peterson came through the door into the reception area and joined Erika at the desk.

'What about his solicitor?' asked Erika.

'We've just called him. He should be here in an hour,' said the desk sergeant.

'Thanks,' said Erika. She took out her car keys. 'And could you arrange someone to bring my car from outside my house to the station.'

'Yes, Ma'am,' said the desk sergeant.

'Whose solicitor?' asked Moss.

'Charles Wakefield is downstairs in a cell.'

'Bloody hell. Good work. When do you want to have a crack at him?'

'As soon as his solicitor gets here,' said Erika.

Moss moved to the door and buzzed them inside the station. Erika limped in after her, with Peterson shadowing her.

'Are you sure you're okay, boss?' asked Moss. 'You look a bit green around the gills.'

'I'm fine,' snapped Erika, hating how people treated you differently if you were injured. 'Sorry. You go on, you go ahead,' she added. They both nodded and went off along the corridor towards the incident room while Erika limped along after them.

She'd had to wait for three hours in A&E with Igor before her foot was stitched up, and she'd been glad of his company during the wait. It had made her feel like someone cared. When they reached the incident room, Moss and Peterson looked back and she waved that she was okay.

'Do you want coffee?' called Moss down the corridor.

'Please, a strong one you can stand your spoon up in,' said Erika. She saw she was next to the toilets and she hobbled inside. She stopped at the row of sinks and looked at herself in the mirror. She didn't look too bad, but her night with Igor and then their adventure in hospital had taken her head out of the case. She hadn't expected to be questioning suspects today, let alone Charles Wakefield, and she didn't feel ready.

She balanced her metal crutches on the edge of the sink and leant over to splash her face with cold water. Just shifting her weight forward onto the front of her foot unleashed a new explosion of pain in her stitches. She'd been given a week's prescription of co-codamol, a strong painkiller, but she could already feel the tablet she'd taken four hours ago wearing off. Her next dose shouldn't be for another two hours, but she knew she needed to be on top of her game for Charles Wakefield. Erika pulled the packet out of her pocket, and took another of the tablets with a mouthful of water from the tap. She then smoothed down her hair with a little water and dug in her bag for the small amount of make-up she kept in there. With a bit of base and a subtle lipstick she looked more in control. She licked her finger and rubbed at a small chocolate stain on the sleeve of her black jacket. Satisfied that it would do, she grabbed her metal crutches and made her way slowly to the incident room, looking forward to a shot of caffeine to supplement the super-strength painkillers.

58

'Are you ready, boss?' asked Moss an hour later, when they were about to go into the interview room. Erika took a deep breath. She suddenly wished she could wind back the clock and still smoke in the police station. She remembered all those long-gone overflowing ashtrays in interview rooms.

She smoothed down her hair and nodded.

Charles Wakefield was sitting in the same suit he'd worn for the funeral. His hands were neatly folded in his lap, and he was staring at the wall. His solicitor was a swarthy-looking man in a suit that was a size too small, with a thick circle of hair surrounding a shiny bald spot.

'Ah, detectives, there you are,' said Charles calmly, sounding as if he'd been saving their seats at the opera, and the show was about to start. 'Oh, deary me...' he added when he saw Erika leaning on the metal crutches. 'What did we do to ourselves?'

Erika ignored him and took a seat next to Moss opposite him.

'Mr Wakefield, good morning.'

'Good morning to you too,' he said, peering at their ID badges. 'Just memorising your names and numbers.' He flashed them a nasty smile, and Erika noticed he had a couple of black teeth towards the back of his mouth. He also had terrible breath.

'Were you the caretaker for Goldsmith's Drama Academy between 2007 and 2012?' asked Erika.

'Yes, I was,' he said.

'We found it rather difficult to get this information from GDA. It seems their records are rather patchy.'

'Oh, are they? That's unfortunate. But yes, I can confirm that I was caretaker.'

'Can I ask why you left?'

'Of course. I retired.'

'What were your duties as caretaker?'

'I mainly oversaw maintenance.'

'Painting? Fixing things, light bulbs?' asked Erika.

Charles pulled a face. 'It was more about me arranging the tradespeople, but yes.'

'You don't own a passport. You haven't owned a passport since 2012, when your last one expired,' said Erika, looking at her file.

'Yes.'

'We can assume you've been in the UK all this time, since your last passport expired.'

'I certainly was in the UK,' he said. The solicitor pursed his lips and looked across at Charles.

'Why don't you have a passport?' asked Erika.

'Inspector, how is this relevant?' asked the solicitor.

'Mr Wakefield?'

'I don't like going away,' he said. 'I prefer my own bed.'

'So, you rarely venture away from home? Leave London?'

'That's correct.'

'And you have a real paranoia with authority—'

'Detective, really!' said the solicitor.

'You don't have a passport or a driver's licence. Your phone is ex-directory. You don't have a mobile phone or an email address, no television licence. You don't even have a credit or debit card, and every bill, and the ownership of your flat, is in your brother's name. You don't even own a bank account. How do you pay for things?'

'That's private, and nothing to do with this,' said the solicitor.

'You aren't registered with a doctor or a dentist, Mr Wakefield? It's rather odd, don't you think?'

'I've always been blessed with good health.'

'In fact, you seemed to vanish off the face of the earth in 2012, as far as bureaucracy is concerned. Why is that?'

'No comment,' said Charles.

'Why no comment?'

'Because I am legally allowed to do whatever I like within the law. And there is no law to say that I have to have any of these things!' he snapped.

'We've been back through the records of your arrest for assaulting a police officer on Monday 22nd October. Your brother, the Assistant Commissioner, stepped in and ordered the custody sergeant not to take a DNA swab from you. Why would he do that?'

'He wasn't ordering them not to take a swab. I suffer from Odontarrupophobia... A phobia of toothbrushes and other objects being in my mouth.'

Erika could see Moss trying to suppress a smile.

'Don't you dare send me up!' said Charles, slamming the flat of his hand down on the table and making them all jump. 'It is a legitimate and debilitating phobia.'

Is that why your breath stinks like a dog's backside? Erika wanted to say.

'We would like a doctor to verify this, but as you don't have a GP or a dentist—'

'I do have a GP. A private doctor. And I do have a diagnosis. With regards to the DNA sample, I didn't want the swab, and that was my right. I was, however, willing to give a blood sample, but then things moved very fast the next morning...'

'And you were fast-tracked out of here,' finished Erika. 'However, we do now have your DNA sample, which we're checking against the DNA found at both crime scenes. It seems that the nurse in Worthing was able to take this.'

'Which was extremely distressing! Anyway. You'll find that my DNA doesn't match either crime scene, because I was never there,' he said.

He seems so bloody confident, thought Erika. She turned the pages in the folder of research Crane had compiled overnight and emailed to her.

'Did Vicky Clarke approach you to talk about her podcast?'

'No. Why would she?'

'Vicky was working on a podcast episode about an intruder who broke into the student halls at GDA, and assaulted three young women. When she heard that you had been the caretaker at GDA around this time, she wanted to talk to you.'

'You are mistaken. She didn't talk to me.'

'We have two people who say she did.'

'Bully for you. Did you find any actual evidence? Notes she left, or any recordings where she mentions this, that we spoke?'

'We have recovered some recordings,' said Erika.

'I would be interested to hear them,' he said with another sly smile.

'Your alibi for Monday 22nd October...'

'I have already given her these details,' said Charles, turning to his solicitor.

'We have a problem verifying this,' said Erika. 'You provided us with a receipt and a train ticket, and we checked the CCTV for the time that ticket was purchased. The person in the video is wearing a trilby and the brim obscures their face.'

'I own a trilby.'

'Owning a trilby is not an alibi.'

'Detective, we're going around in circles here.' The solicitor sounded bored. 'Have you exhausted all avenues? Does the ticket seller recall seeing my client? What about other CCTV?'

Erika looked back at the case notes.

'His face is obscured on all CCTV, and we haven't been able to find him on any other CCTV across the network. The person working in the ticket office at Blackheath train station that day doesn't recall seeing Mr Wakefield. How close are you to your neighbour, Henrietta Boulderstone?' she asked, addressing Charles again.

'She's a good friend.'

'She also owns a trilby and a long black trench coat. When I saw you at Vicky Clarke's funeral, I noted how you both have similar dress and height. This person on the CCTV image buying a train ticket could just as easily be Henrietta.'

Erika took out the CCTV photo from her file and slid it across the table.

'Detective, my client may not have an alibi that satisfies you, but this is just ridiculous and demonstrates that you are clutching at straws. You would need to link my client's lack of alibi to more than just circumstantial evidence. You have no murder weapon for either of these murders. There was no forensic evidence found in my client's flat when the police entered on Monday 22nd October. He didn't know either of the young women beyond a casual acquaintance. And now you think, what? That he sent his elderly neighbour off disguised as him to provide him with an alibi? Really.'

His rebuke stung. Erika gritted her teeth.

'Your client blocked us from taking a DNA sample on his

first arrest, which has severely hampered our investigations,' she said.

'No, he didn't. He had a valid medical reason for a swab test not being taken. And you have this sample now, no?'

'Yes, we do.'

'Do you have any more questions, or are you going to release my client? You certainly have no evidence to charge him.'

Erika stared at them both.

'We have up to ninety-six hours before we need to charge your client. I suggest we take a short break.'

Erika and Moss came out of the interview suite and went back to the incident room. Her head was feeling fuzzy, and after round one with Charles and the solicitor, Erika was worried she had already lost.

Crane and Peterson had been watching the interview on the monitors, and they came out into the corridor. They met McGorry coming back from the main entrance.

'Boss, we've just been back at Charles Wakefield's flat,' he said.

'Did you see his neighbour, Henrietta?' asked Erika.

'No. But listen, we found this hidden in a drawer in Charles's hallway,' he said, handing Erika a clear plastic evidence bag.

Inside was a white envelope and a small A5 letter. There was no date or signature, but written in black ink in the centre of the paper was:

TWO WORDS, 'LILY PARKES'. YOUR SILENCE
KEEPS YOU ALIVE

59

Back in the incident room, Erika had the letter in a clear plastic evidence bag, and held it up in front of everyone.

'I need us to divide into teams and work our way through this. It could be something and it could be nothing. Why was Charles sent this letter? Who is Lily Parkes and why is she relevant to his silence?' She checked her watch. 'And can someone chase up the DNA results we took from Charles Wakefield yesterday?'

The first answers came from Crane a little while later.

'The paper comes from Venice,' he said. 'It's not what I call rare, but it is specific to a certain small supplier in Italy.' He held the bag up to the light. 'It has a watermark with the name Benatku stamped in it.'

'So, not your average Basildon Bond?' said Erika.

'No, but I was able to find the shop where it came from easily on the internet. I'm sure many people go and visit Venice every year and come back with souvenirs like this... along with those carnival masks and aprons with the statue of the naked guy.'

'I've got one of those aprons,' said Moss.

Crane smiled. 'Course you have. Oh, and along with the paper, there's also a matching envelope from the same place.'

'Couldn't there be hundreds if not thousands of people living in London with this paper?' said Erika, going back to her desk.

'Yes. But very few people write letters,' he said. 'That makes this a rarity. There's something about getting a handwritten letter that's quite a shock. I can't remember the last time someone wrote to me. And then add to it that we have to presume, from the envelope, this was delivered by hand with no stamp,' he said, holding up the evidence bag again. 'There is just his name on the envelope. It would have freaked me out, and I'm a nice guy.' Crane grinned.

Erika rolled her eyes and smiled.

'You keep telling yourself that,' she said. She thought back to the last time they were at Honeycomb Court, on the morning that they had spoken to Maria and then Tess. Didn't they see Charles at his mailbox, acting a little weird? And thinking about his mailbox, what kind of post did he even get? He'd made sure there was very little about himself on record. If you don't exist on paper, then no one is going to write to you. Erika took the letter in the evidence bag and went over to where Moss and Peterson were working on Lily Parkes.

'There's a criminal record for two people called Lily Parkes,' said Moss. 'One is eighty and she's doing time at Wormwood Scrubs, and the other Lily Parkes was inside from 2009 to 2013 for stabbing her husband, in Scotland. Do you want me to do a deeper dive?'

'Yes.'

'What about social media?' said Erika to Peterson.

'There are seventy Lily Parkes on Facebook. Lots of anony-mous or non-photograph profile pictures,' said Peterson. 'There are a lot less on Instagram. I haven't started on the other social media sites.'

Erika got back in contact with Sheila at the admissions department at GDA and asked about a student they have, or had, called Lily Parkes. Sheila said they didn't have anyone on the course currently or any past students with that name on the system.

Of course not, thought Erika.

'We don't keep extensive records about our staff. This isn't the Gestapo, Detective Foster. You keep asking me for this bizarre information. We keep names, dates of births, and details about their singing ability. I can give you a list of all the baritones and sopranos, but I certainly can't tell you who is a deviant who likes raping and pillaging,' finished Sheila, sounding irritated on the phone.

'Okay, thank you,' said Erika, ending the call. The dull throbbing pain in her foot wasn't going away. If anything, it was increasing. She checked the time. It was two hours before she could take another co-codamol tablet.

Erika then put a call through to Kathleen and Becky to ask if they had any idea about the name, or if Vicky had mentioned it. She left messages for them both asking to call her back ASAP. She also left a message with Cilla, asking the same thing. Morning turned to afternoon, and Erika worked through lunch, sending one of the administrative staff out to get her a sandwich.

Igor called her just as she was finishing her sandwich, and she was about to answer when Charles Wakefield's solicitor called down to say that he had to leave in an hour, and if they wanted to question Charles after that they would have to wait for one of his colleagues.

For the second time that day, Erika went into the interview room feeling on the back foot. This time Peterson accompanied her and Moss sat with Crane and McGorry in the observation room.

'Who is Lily Parkes?' asked Erika, watching Charles carefully across the table. She saw him flinch, ever so slightly, and then he tried to cover it up by scratching at his nose. He had very long shiny fingernails which made Erika shudder.

'I have no idea what you mean,' he said. He looked to his solicitor, who shrugged. Erika took out the evidence bag with the handwritten note and placed it on the table.

'One of my officers just found this in your flat. It stands out, because it's handwritten to you, and you receive very little post.'

'How do you know what post I receive?' he said imperiously, almost offended by the notion no one ever wrote to him.

'You barely exist on paper, Charles. Your utility bills are in the name "Julian Wakefield". This letter was found hidden down the side of your armchair.' There was a long pause. Charles looked again at his solicitor, who remained blank-faced. Erika picked up the evidence bag. '"*Two words, 'Lily Parkes'. Your silence keeps you alive*",' she said, reading off it and watching him. He flinched again.

'It was *hand-delivered* to you,' said Peterson. 'Now, we can believe that you have no idea what the letter means, but you just lied by saying that you didn't know anything about the letter's existence.'

Charles blushed. The colour spread across his soft shiny cheeks.

'No, that is not what I said... I will not be called a liar! Did you hear what they called me?' he said, looking to his solicitor again.

'Mr Wakefield. Two women are dead, both of whom lived a few feet from your flat,' said Erika. 'Vicky Clarke was making a podcast about sexual assaults in the student halls where *you* worked as a caretaker. You would have had keys to every flat, and been able to access them at any time. Now, we need to start to make sense of this. Lily Parkes was not a student at GDA. We know that. You say you don't know her, but someone thinks you know her well enough to try and guarantee your silence, or worse still, threaten you with death.' Erika leant forward. 'Let me help you. And to do that you can start by acknowledging what is happening here. Your behaviour, your denial, is setting off all kinds of alarm bells.'

Charles was now shaking with anger, and he looked like he was trying to get it under control.

'Yes. I got the letter. Yes! But I just thought it had been delivered in error,' he said carefully, still shaking.

'Charles. It's got your name on the envelope,' said Erika, holding it up to his face. 'It was hand-delivered to your address. Whoever did deliver this would have to know how to get into Honeycomb Court. The front door has a card key entry.'

Charles shook his head and his shaking became worse; all colour had now drained from his puffy face.

'I just... I just... I just...'

'You just what?'

'I thought it was kids, mucking around.'

'Stop lying!' shouted Erika, slamming her hand on the table, feeling a rush of anger herself. 'This is more than kids mucking around!'

'I don't know!' he roared, crashing his fists down on the table. 'I don't fucking know, okay? If you *tortured* me, I still wouldn't know!'

'Who is Lily Parkes, Charles?'

'Stop saying her name.'

'What did you do to her?'

'Nothing!' he insisted.

'What did she do to you, Charles? She did something, didn't she?'

'She lied. Tricked me.'

'Tricked you into what?' asked Erika, leaning in, and feeling she was so close. 'What did she lie about?'

At this point, he really lost it and stood up, his face red, and screamed at Erika. He thumped his fists on the desk. '*No! Why can't you leave me alone! Leave me alone. Alone!*'

He stepped back and staggered over his chair, and then he leant forward and threw up all over the floor. His solicitor leapt up off his chair and stepped back in disgust, sweeping his papers away off the table.

Erika and Peterson sat back in shock. Charles stood there, staring at the carpet, retched and then spat. Then he wiped his mouth, and all the anger seemed to drain away from him and he sank down on his haunches, shaking and wailing.

'Oh dear... Dear me... I've made a mess. I'm very sorry about that,' he said.

'That's enough, we need a doctor in here, now!' said his solicitor.

60

'Blimey, we haven't had a puker in a while,' said Moss when she and Peterson came out of the interview room. Charles Wakefield had been led back down to the custody suite by one of the uniformed officers, and when he'd left the interview room, he'd snapped from being wild and crazed with anger to mute and withdrawn.

'Do you think we should get the doc down to have a look at him?' asked Peterson in a low voice. 'I think he could be on the edge, and maybe...'

'Put him on suicide watch?' finished Erika. Moss nodded in agreement with Peterson. 'Okay. Yes.'

Erika was deeply frustrated. She had come so close to getting it out of Charles, who Lily Parkes was, and what she'd done to him. They walked back to the incident room in silence, and her foot was now throbbing.

'Do we have anything on the DNA sample taken from Charles Wakefield?' she asked, for what seemed like the tenth time that day.

Crane looked up, and over at McGorry. 'We've just heard that it was sent to London, from Hove,' he said.

'What? They didn't process it in their lab?' she asked, dismayed.

'I think there was a mix-up and they thought it should be sent to London for the Met lab to process it,' said McGorry.

Erika felt a flash of anger. She took two more of her painkillers with some cold coffee. 'And how long is that going to take?'

'I've been promised the results in the next few hours.'

The rest of the afternoon moved slowly. A doctor was called for Charles Wakefield and until he'd been seen, he was off limits for any more interviews. Erika had a reply from Kathleen, who told her that she'd never heard of a girl called Lily Parkes. Erika then had a call from Cilla.

'I'm sorry I missed your call, detective. How can I help?'

Erika said she wanted to ask a few questions about past students.

'Listen, I'm just about to get on the Tube to go and teach a voice class. Would you like to come over to the house?'

'I'd like to talk to you today, it's urgent,' said Erika, checking her watch.

'You could come for dinner. I'm cooking for myself, Colin and Ray. Why don't you stop by and you can pick our brains.'

Erika could hear the rattle of the Tube train approaching in the background.

'I'd rather talk on the phone.'

'I'm very busy, detective. Come over and I can give you my full attention.'

'I'll come after you've eaten. How does 8pm sound?'

Cilla agreed and gave her the address of the house on Telegraph Hill. As the afternoon wore on, the rest of the team started to leave, and at 7pm Moss was the last to go.

'How's the foot?' she asked as she saw Erika shifting and grimacing.

'I have my last dose in a couple of hours,' she said, wondering how she was going to sleep if she couldn't take any more until the morning.

'Okay, be careful. Let me know how it goes with Colin, Cilla and Ray.'

Before she left, Erika checked in on the lab with the DNA results, and was told they were still pending.

'Time is ticking, I only have this guy in custody for a few more hours. If I don't have a DNA result, I'll have to release him. Pull your finger out and get that over to me!' she snapped, slamming down the receiver. She stared at the phone for a moment afterwards. That was probably a bad move, pissing them off, but it was done now. Erika got up. She had to talk to Charles again. She debated for a moment and then set off, down to the custody suite, taking the lift, annoyed that the journey took three times as long with her gammy foot.

'How is Charles Wakefield?' she asked the police officer on duty.

'I just checked on him, he's sleeping like a baby. They gave him a sedative,' she said. Erika nodded and looked around. The custody suite was empty.

'Can I look at him?'

'Look at him?' she repeated.

'Yes, I want to see him. Check he's all right.'

'His doctor has been here.'

'Yes, I just saw him,' Erika replied, hoping that the doctor was indeed a 'he'.

The duty officer debated for a moment and then nodded. She accompanied Erika down the long narrow corridor to Charles's cell. She slid open the hatch and Erika peered inside into the gloom. Charles was curled up in a ball on the small bare bench, snoring gently. He looked fast asleep.

'See what I said, like a baby,' whispered the duty officer. 'He's my only prisoner tonight, so I'm hoping for a quiet night with a good book.'

'Was the doctor concerned?' asked Erika. 'With his condition and all that?'

'The schizophrenia? Yes. He'd thrown up all of his meds, so the doctor had to get him to take them again. It was a battle.'

Schizophrenia, thought Erika, and she remembered the pill bottles they'd found in his medicine cabinet with all of the labels ripped off.

'Did the doctor confirm that he was non-violent?' asked Erika.

'Yes. He's not violent but can become very paranoid. He's also terrified of technology. The doctor said that during some of his more severe psychosis, he's ripped out his landline, and he won't even have a radio in his flat.'

'I just hope I can still talk to him tomorrow,' said Erika.

'The doctor is coming back in the morning, and you must know his brother is the Assistant Commissioner?'

'Yes.'

'Between you and me, he's been pushing the doctor to have him sectioned under the Mental Health Act.'

'Really,' said Erika. She looked back at Charles sleeping, and her heart sank. If he was sectioned, and he'd suffered a psychotic episode, then they couldn't interview him again. And anything he'd already told them in the interview room could be ruled inadmissible.

The duty officer gently slid the hatch back up, and Erika left the custody suite.

61

Erika was glad to see her car had been delivered to the car park, but as she limped across to it, she wondered if she would be able to drive. Her foot was sore, but the painkillers were taking the edge off, and she managed and set off for Telegraph Hill.

Telegraph Hill was very close to Goldsmith's Drama Academy. It was an affluent slice of London on top of a steep hill leading up from New Cross. There was a park and lots of red brick terraced houses. It reminded Erika of the plush area where Marsh lived. Colin's house sat at the very top of the steepest hill. It was a grand-looking detached house set back from the road on a large plot of land. A small tower with a stone spire rose up out of the brickwork, which seemed a little ostentatious for South London.

'Fancy,' muttered Erika, peering up at it. 'People in stone houses, act like kings,' she added. There were no spaces on the road, and she saw there was a decent-sized driveway outside which led to a wooden car port. There was a space next to two other cars, so she pulled in off the road and used the parking spot.

It was very secluded from the road behind the high row of bushes and tall trees lining the front wall. A security light flicked on as she limped her way to the front door. A bell jangled from deep inside, and she half expected a creepy butler to answer the door.

It was Cilla who answered, wearing a baggy smock-like dress in a bright green fabric with deep pockets on each side. She had on a towering pair of high heels in emerald green, with a crusting of silver glitter on the toes. Her hair had changed colour since the funeral. It was now pillar-box red.

'Good evening, you're just in time for coffee,' she said, greeting her with a theatrical enthusiasm. Erika stepped inside, wincing as she moved up the two steep steps, leaning on her crutches. 'My goodness, what have you done to your foot?' added Cilla when they were in the hallway.

'I stood on a broken bottle, smashed by my cat,' she said. Cilla helped Erika off with her coat, which she hung on a huge iron coat stand by the front door. Erika looked around at the large hallway. There was lots of wood panelling and a flagstone floor. A small stained-glass window faced the car port and it felt like she was inside a small castle, or a boutique with delusions of grandeur. A delicious smell of food wafted along the hallway, and Erika could hear men's voices coming from the first door, and then laughter. She wished she hadn't accepted this invitation to come over. It would have been easier to talk on the phone.

'Do come through,' said Cilla. Erika followed her into a large living room-cum-dining room. It was stuffed with white furniture and brass fittings, and there was a huge modern concrete fireplace where a fire was crackling in the grate.

'Ah! Detective, good evening! Can we offer you coffee?' asked Colin. His bonhomie was as forced as Cilla's welcome. He was next to Ray at the table, and the two men were sitting very close.

Ray shifted his chair, and Erika felt like her entry into the room had broken an intimate moment.

'Black. Thank you,' she said.

'Have you been in the wars?' asked Ray, tapping a packet of cigarettes on the table and pulling one out. He stared at her as he lit his cigarette.

'It was a silly accident, I stood on a chunk of broken glass,' she said.

'Please, sit down,' said Colin, indicating the chair opposite. Ray got up and moved around the table to pull it out for her to sit. Cilla came back into the room with a china cup of black coffee on a saucer.

'Fag?' asked Ray, holding out the packet.

'No thank you,' she said.

Ray went and sat back down with Colin.

Erika checked her watch. She took out her painkillers and popped two out. Colin was watching her.

'Sorry,' she said, swallowing them with a gulp of the hot coffee. 'That's better.'

Cilla sat down next to Erika. There were the remnants of a shepherd's pie in a dish, with smaller dishes of vegetables.

'Are you sure we can't tempt you?' asked Colin, indicating the food.

'No, thank you,' said Erika. Her stomach was grumbling, but she wanted to get on with this and then get home.

'I wanted to ask you all a few questions about GDA, past students and Charles Wakefield.'

They all looked at her a little imperiously. Erika went on.

'Can I ask why Charles Wakefield left the school as caretaker?'

'Who is he?' asked Ray, stubbing out his cigarette and lighting another.

'Charlie Wakefield was the caretaker for some of the student accommodation, he was in the post a few years back,' said Cilla.

'That's not really my department, darling. I teach the students to dance, I don't really get involved with their *accommodation*,' said Ray.

'But GDA is a small faculty—' Erika said.

'Oh, I hear that. Sometimes it's too small,' said Ray.

'Wouldn't you have heard gossip if the caretaker, Charles Wakefield, was accused of any inappropriate behaviour with a student?'

'I never had anything to do with him, what about you?' Ray said, turning to Colin and Cilla.

'I was aware that he was a bit of an oddball,' said Cilla. 'I did overhear a few comments about him, from some of the female students, that he was a little creepy. Hanging around... but of course nothing serious. I know that on the few occasions I heard something, the young girls were speaking in jest.'

'Can you be sure of that?'

'I think so.'

'Vicky was making an episode for her podcast about an intruder who broke into student halls. She didn't mention Charles Wakefield to any of you? Ask questions?' said Erika.

Colin and Ray shook their heads.

'No, I've already told you, Vicky said nothing,' replied Cilla. 'And if you don't mind me asking, what is happening with Charles Wakefield? There was such a commotion at the crematorium when those police officers took him away.'

'He's still in custody,' said Erika.

Cilla, Ray, and Colin exchanged glances.

'Do you suspect him of these murders, seriously suspect him?' asked Ray.

'He is of great interest to us,' said Erika. 'This brings me on to another question. Have any of you heard of a young woman called Lily Parkes?'

A look passed between them all. And the temperature in the room seemed to drop.

'Yes. She was a local girl who worked at GDA for a short time, she used to help out in the scene dock,' said Cilla. From her tone of voice, Erika got the impression that she didn't like Lily Parkes at all.

62

'The scene dock? What's that?' asked Erika. It had started to rain outside and it clattered on the roof in the silence. Ray sucked on the butt of his cigarette, squinting, and looking beadily between Cilla and Colin, almost drinking up the awkwardness.

'The scene dock is where they make all the scenery, and get it ready for plays and shows,' said Cilla. She looked between the two men, confused as to what was happening. 'She came to us from the DSS, or Job centre, as you now say.'

'Why isn't there any record of her employment with the school?' asked Erika.

'I would have thought that there was,' said Colin.

'When did she work at GDA?'

Cilla looked to Colin.

'When was it?' she asked.

'Back in 2009, I think. She was what you'd term *work experience*, we didn't pay her. She worked a few hours a week in return for her state benefits,' said Colin. 'We've had other people do this. She was by far the youngest and least experienced.'

Ray stubbed out his cigarette in the ash tray.

'Darlings, and Lady Detective, I didn't know of this Lily Parkes, but I'd love to meet her. It seems, even though she was languishing on benefits, she still had the ability to set the cat among the pigeons. I regretfully have to take my leave. I have a drinks invitation in the West End,' he said, getting up.

'Is there a problem?' asked Erika.

'No, darling, I *genuinely* must dash. Cilla can give you my number if you'd like to catch up further tomorrow,' he said. 'Colin. I need you to move your car, to get mine out.'

'Cilla, would you move my car?' asked Colin. She looked surprised at the request.

'I've had a lot of wine... And my heels.'

'Those shoes are not for driving,' said Ray. 'Well, they drive the point home that you look fabulous.' Cilla tilted her face up and Ray dipped down and pecked her on the cheek. Colin looked annoyed that she'd refused.

'Colin, if I take these heels off, then I won't get them back on.'

'Very well. If you could keep Erika company whilst I'm gone,' he said. Ray gave Erika a wave and they left. She had needed to pee since she arrived, so she asked Cilla where the bathroom was.

'At the end of the corridor, on the second floor,' said Cilla, pouring herself another glass of wine. Erika grabbed her crutches and started down the long corridor, past a large kitchen to the end. The rain was louder in this part of the house, and as she reached a staircase, she could see it was open, and the three flights of stairs led up the tower to a stained-glass skylight high above. The stairs were steep, but Erika's painkillers had kicked in. She made it up to the second floor and found the bathroom next to two large bedrooms. She poked her head around the door of both. One was decorated in a Moroccan style, with lots of gold lacquering on the furniture and bright colours. There was a giant photo of the great dancer Martha

Graham on one wall, and above the bed was a print of a topless male model. The second bedroom was decorated all in white, and there were bookshelves on every wall which added a splash of colour.

Who slept where? thought Erika. She needed to pee urgently, so she went into the bathroom and closed the door.

As she sat on the toilet, Erika looked around at the theatrical decor. The toilet, sink and bath were Art Deco style, and there was a vast mirror on the back of the door, which was beautiful, but she wondered why it was there. Why would you want to watch yourself sitting on the lav? There was something odd going on with the three of them downstairs. Was it a strange dynamic, or were they just very bohemian? Erika couldn't put her finger on it. As she was drying her hands, she heard a clatter of heels on the stairs outside.

Erika came out of the bathroom, and was about to go back downstairs, when she heard Cilla shouting from the floor above.

'Colin! Is that you? I'm trying to find the photo album for *West Side Story*... I'm in your office, where are they?'

There was no answer. Through a window opposite her on the landing outside the bathroom, Erika could see down to the driveway and the road out front where Colin was waving Ray off. She started up the stairs towards Cilla on the top floor. It was a steep drop to the ground three floors below.

Erika found Cilla in a large wood-panelled office, similar to Colin's office at GDA. There were rows of bookshelves and a busy, cluttered desk. Cilla heard Erika on the stairs and turned with a photo album in her hand, tottering on her high heels.

'Oh, I thought you were Colin,' she said. She seemed a little rattled and closed the album.

'What have you got there?' asked Erika.

'Well... I really wanted to ask Colin. These are his photos... I found a photo of a cast production of *West Side Story*.' She opened the album and hesitated for a moment. 'That's Lily Parkes,' she added.

Erika looked at the photo. It was a picture of the whole cast and crew standing on the stage of a theatre. There was a small, skinny girl with long, dirty blonde hair standing on the end next to Colin. She was the only person not looking at the camera, and instead she was looking up at Colin with an intense stare. He was looking ahead and grinning, with his arm around her waist. Erika peered closer. No. His hand was higher than her waist and seemed to be cupping just under her breast.

'I've never really seen this photo before. Or should I say, never really looked at it, maybe,' said Cilla, talking to herself.

Erika looked around at the rest of the office. There was a set of shelves on the other side of the desk with office supplies, and above it was a carnival mask. Erika heard Crane's voice – *'one of those ones the tourists buy from Venice'*. She moved closer to the shelf and saw there was a pile of paper and envelopes. She picked one of the sheets up and held it to the light. It had the same watermark with the name *Benatku*. She looked through the papers on the desk; there were bank statements and tables with figures and budgets for GDA. She wanted to find something with handwriting on it. She pulled open a drawer and under a pile of utility bills, she found an envelope with 'FOR RAY – FOR TICKETS'. Feeling a surge of excitement rising in her chest, Erika fumbled in her pocket and took out her phone. She scrolled through and found the photo of the note to Charles with ***TWO WORDS, 'LILY PARKES'. YOUR SILENCE KEEPS YOU ALIVE*** written on it. Comparing the two, she saw the handwriting was the same, particularly on the word 'TWO' written in capital letters.

'What are you doing?' asked Cilla, turning at the sound of Erika searching through the drawer. There was a creak of wooden floorboards, and she saw Colin standing in the doorway. He stared at Erika, holding the envelope with his handwriting and the photo on her phone.

'What is it?' asked Cilla, looking between Erika and Colin.

He came into the room and saw the album in her hand, and the picture with his arm around Lily's waist. Erika's phone rang, but she kept staring at Colin.

'Perhaps you should answer that,' said Colin.

Erika silenced the call. 'Does this belong to you?' she asked, holding up the envelope.

Colin smiled and shook his head.

'This is your office? And is this your handwriting?'

Colin started to chuckle, shaking his head. Cilla kept staring. She looked completely in the dark as to what was going on. Erika's phone chimed with a text message, and she glanced down, seeing it was from Crane. It was a CCTV photo of Charles Wakefield, walking along a tube station platform, wearing his long black coat and trilby. His head was angled up at the departures board, and his face was clear to see. The timestamp at the top of the photo read: 22.10.2018 16.58pm.

My contact at TfL just sent this, taken at Baker Street tube station the day of Vicky's murder. Charles was telling the truth. he did go into London, his alibi checks out!
CRANE

Colin moved swiftly over to Erika and grabbed at her phone. She was shocked at how fast he moved and twisted it out of her hand. She watched as he read the message and went pale.

'What is it? Colin, will you tell me what's going on?' said Cilla.

'He killed Sophia, thinking it was Vicky,' said Erika. 'And then when he realised his mistake, he came back and finished the job and killed Vicky.' She was watching Colin, who still held her phone. 'But Vicky hadn't found out it was you who was breaking into the student halls and assaulting those young women... She was close, though, wasn't she? She'd questioned Charles Wakefield. Did he know? He was the caretaker at the time. How did he find out?'

Colin's jaw was tense, and a vein was pulsing in his forehead.

Erika looked back at the photo in the album. 'What happened with Charles and Lily?' She watched Colin's face and looked at the photo again, of him and Lily, and she thought back to what Charles had said in the interview room, how Lily had lied, and tricked him. In the photo, the young woman was looking up to him with an intense look in her eyes. Lust and subservience. 'Lily slept with Charles, didn't she? Did she do it for you?'

Colin moved to stand between Erika and Cilla. Erika went on, 'Charles found out about you, breaking into those rooms late at night, and you had to get some dirt on him, to keep him quiet, so you seduced fifteen-year-old Lily, and then you made sure she seduced him...' Erika was thinking out loud, working it out, but she could see that Colin was panicking.

'Colin?' said Cilla. 'This can't be true? You told me nothing was going on with you and Lily. You knew she was underage.'

'And once Charles had been seduced by Lily, then you had him under your thumb. He was mentally very fragile, and he could have been charged with sleeping with a minor. His brother is a senior police officer. I'm sure you made it very clear to him that Lily would co-operate with the police, and how rough a prison sentence could be for a nonce who has a police officer in the family.'

'You shut up!' said Colin.

'Colin! This is ridiculous! You tell her it's not true right now!' said Cilla, her eyes wide with fear.

'And this big house you own, on top of the hill. You can see down the hill to the Drama Academy, and those student houses on Jubilee Road and Hartwood Road,' said Erika, indicating the window where the criss-cross of streets around New Cross Gate station could be clearly seen, lit up against the night sky. 'They're so close. Hardly any walk at all for you...You knew we were getting close to the truth, didn't you? So you wrote this letter to Charles, reminding him of the stakes,' said Erika. She tutted and shook her head. 'It's always the little details. I've seen it so many times, with psychopaths like you. You think you've got away with it and it gives you a false sense of confidence. That's when you slip up.'

She waved the envelope in the air, but she didn't see Colin's fist coming until it was too late. He punched her hard in the face, and Erika crumpled on the floor.

63

Erika lay on the floor of the office. The side of her face was numb, and she was dazed. She opened her eyes and saw Colin standing over Cilla, who was still holding the photo album. She was shaking and staring back at him. Suddenly he grabbed her by the back of her dress and dragged her across the room. She screamed and dropped the photo album. Even in her dazed state, Erika could hear the terror and confusion in Cilla's protests.

'Colin, no! What are you doing?' she cried as she wheeled around, her heels clattering on the wooden floor. She hit the bookcase as he dragged her out of the office, and when they were out on the landing he slammed the office door shut. There was a moment of quiet and then Erika heard Cilla's voice soft and pleading, and then she started to scream.

'No! What are you doing! *No, please!*' There was a scuffle, a crash and her long chilling scream seemed to expand in the hall-way, it echoed through the house, and then there was a sickening thud and silence. A minute passed and then in the silence, the sound of the rain took over.

Erika managed to sit up against the bookcase and tried to

focus, but the room was spinning. The metal crutches had toppled away, and they lay out of her reach. Colin still had her phone. She heard footsteps outside the door, the wooden floor creaked, and then Colin came back into the room and stopped in front of her. He crouched down and stared at her for a moment. Erika tried to pull herself up, but she was too dazed and dizzy. Colin reached up and grabbed the top of her head, gripping her hair, and slammed the back of her head into the back of the wooden bookshelf. Once, twice, a third time. Stars and pain exploded behind her eyes and she thought she was going to black out. He let go of her hair.

'Life is full of opportunities,' he said in a calm voice. She could feel his hot breath on her face, and there was a sour smell of garlic and wine. He reached forward and felt around in the right-hand pocket of her trousers and then the left, allowing his hands to linger on her thigh and between her legs. 'Ah, here we are.' He took out the packet of co-codamol painkillers, removed the foil sheet of pills and started to pop the tablets out into his cupped hand. '*Six.* Is that too many? Too few?' he said. 'No, one more for luck,' he said, popping out another tablet. He leant closer and Erika tried to shrink away. With one hand he clamped his fingers on her jaw and squeezed her mouth open. He shoved the pills into her mouth. He then put his hand over her lips and nose. She tried to fight, but he tilted her head back, the pills slid over her tongue, and as a reflex she swallowed. The pills stuck in her throat, and he tilted her head back and squeezed harder, making her swallow the rest.

'Now, let's have a look at your phone,' he said. He held the screen up to her face, and she saw her reflection in the phone camera; bloodshot eyes, a swollen lip and a bloody, bruised nose.

'I'm going to put you in prison,' she tried to say, but her voice was thick and distorted. He ignored her. The facial recognition camera registered her face and her phone unlocked. Colin stood up and started to scroll through.

'Who did you tell you were coming here? Is Crane a colleague?' he asked, holding up the phone. Erika could feel the room spinning, it was like she couldn't grip hold of the floor, and it was hard to focus on the screen. 'It doesn't matter. Even if you did tell everyone you were coming here, they are going to think you left here by yourself.'

Colin finished writing a text message and pressed send. Erika must have blacked out, because when she came to Colin had changed into casual clothes, and he was wiping down her phone on his shirt, removing his fingerprints. He slipped it back in her pocket, pressing his fingers between her legs again.

He sat back and regarded her for a moment, and checked his watch. 'How are those painkillers working out for you?' He placed his shoe on top of her injured foot and pressed down. Erika felt a dull, far-off ache. In the back of her mind she knew that it should be hurting like hell, and she should be fighting what he was doing, but she felt like she was floating and it was all very far away, like looking at things through the wrong end of a telescope.

Colin came close and reached out to her. He hooked his arms under hers, then everything turned upside down. The room swivelled and the floor and ceiling switched places. He'd picked her up and thrown her over his shoulder in a fireman's lift.

The wooden floor in the office bobbed and swayed, and then she was in the hallway, and there was a tinny thud as he moved down the stairs carrying her, swaying. The motion lulled her and she felt her grip on consciousness loosening.

And then they were at the bottom of the stairs, and there, lying in a crumpled heap was Cilla. One of those sparkly green shoes lay in the corner of the hallway, and one was still on her other foot. Her head was bent back at an angle, and she lay still.

'Poor Cilla, I always warned her about those silly shoes on the stairs,' said Colin.

Erika tried to focus on Cilla's body, willing herself to do something, but everything faded away for a moment.

She didn't know how much time had passed, but she was in the driver's seat of her car. They were underneath the car port. She was angled forward, leaning half out of the seat with her chest pressed against the steering wheel and her face close to the windscreen. Colin was leaning into the door and he was tucking her feet under the seat so she was kneeling. Her feet and ankles were bent back. She tried to move, but she couldn't. Her limbs were heavy and wouldn't move. Colin closed the driver's door and she watched as he walked around the car, and opened the door to the passenger side. He leaned in and took off the hand-brake. She could see he was now wearing leather gloves and a baseball cap. She watched as he stepped away and closed the door and walked out of the driveway to check the road, looking up and down.

He came back and opened the driver's door. She felt the steering wheel shift and move under her chest as he turned it. Gripping the steering wheel in one hand and the outside of the door, he pushed the car off and rolled it out of the driveway. The steering wheel moved under her to the left as he turned onto the road. He pulled up the handbrake and the car stopped with a jerk.

Erika could now see the steep hill through the windscreen. It was a dead straight hill, almost like a steep drop, all the way down to the main road far away at the bottom. She tried to lift her arms and move her legs, but they were trapped under the seat by her heavy shoes.

Colin looked up and down the road then swiftly leant over, twisting the steering wheel under her chest, so it locked in place. He leaned over her, undid the handbrake, and the car lurched forward. He pulled his body out and slammed the door. The car rapidly picked up speed. Erika saw him grow smaller in the rearview mirror as he ducked back into the driveway. When Erika looked back through the windscreen she could see the car was hurtling down the hill, rolling in neutral with the engine off. She couldn't move her legs, and when she lifted her hands to the steering wheel, it was locked into place with the wheels straight on.

Erika felt a deep detached calm, like she was watching this on a movie screen from far back in the cinema. But there was a small voice screaming in her head to *do something!* Even with the engine off, the speedometer was hitting forty mph. She was hurtling past the rows of parked cars lining the street on either side, and the houses set back from the road. The busy junction at the bottom of the hill was streaking fast towards her, where the cars were moving past in both directions.

Erika tried to sit up, but her knees were on the floor, and her feet were trapped painfully under the seat. The junction at the bottom of the hill was coming up fast, the traffic was roaring past in both directions and the cars and houses on either side were now a blur of colour.

Erika managed to flex the fingers in her right hand. At the angle her body was lying against the steering wheel, she could reach down towards the pedals.

The car reached the bottom of the hill and burst out across the junction. Where the gradient of the road changed, the car hit the tarmac and jolted her violently, her head hitting the roof. She narrowly missed being hit by a huge lorry whose driver honked as she crossed the first lane. A large grey SUV skidded to a halt with a screech of brakes, and as Erika sped across the second lane, she just managed to reach down and push against the brake pedal. The car slowed, but it was too late. With a bone-shattering shudder, it hit the kerb on the other side of the second lane, mounted the pavement and shot across a wide stretch of flowerbeds that separated the pavement from a supermarket car park.

Her car landed in the car park and slammed into the back of a small black Porsche. The last thought that went through her head before she lost consciousness was that people would think she had had a car crash on the way back from Colin's house, and that he would get away with it.

EPILOGUE

For a long time, Erika felt herself drifting in and out of consciousness, but always below the surface. There were beeping sounds, a hiss of air and a clank of metal, and the voices of people she recognised, and occasionally the feeling of a cold breeze on her bare skin. Apart from this, she seemed to drift on a warm sea of oblivion.

When she started to feel the pain, that's when reality returned. A couple of times, she'd woken in an empty room with a dull throbbing pain, but it was on the third or fourth time she opened her eyes that she saw it was day, and she was lying in a bed next to an array of machines beeping and pulsing with small lights.

Everything was a blur and a familiar face loomed over her, and then it all faded out.

When she woke again, the room was different. The high-backed chair in the corner was closer, and the familiar face was clear. It was her sister, Lenka.

'You're awake,' she said, smiling. Lenka was petite and short in comparison to Erika, and her long blonde hair was tied back.

'What's going on?' asked Erika. Her voice sounded distorted. She tried to lift her hand and saw her arm was crisscrossed in scabbed-over cuts, like she'd fought through a bramble bush. There were tubes in her wrist. Erika tried to sit up and a terrible pain shot through her chest, and her legs. She couldn't feel her legs.

'Don't try to get up,' said Lenka, sitting up and gently taking her arm.

'Am I paralysed?' she croaked.

'What did you say?' asked Lenka. 'Do you want some water? The doctor said I should try and get you to drink.' She picked up a cup with a straw and Erika took a sip. She could now feel something on her face and she couldn't breathe through her nose. She put up her hand, which set off a spark of twisting pains in her chest again. There was a huge rigid bandage on her nose.

'My legs, what's happened?' she said, trying to sit up so she could see her legs. The covers at the bottom of the bed gave nothing away. She couldn't make out the shape of her legs, or even if she still had legs. There was no feeling down there.

'It's okay. You broke both of your legs, below the knee. You've had pins put in and you're on a lot of painkillers... Don't you remember? I've told you this three times already,' said Lenka. She didn't seem annoyed, just concerned.

'My face?' sighed Erika. Even this short conversation was tiring her out.

'The airbag in the car broke your nose, and six of your ribs... They thought you'd fractured a cheek, but it's bad bruising.'

Erika put her head back against the pillow. She wanted to ask more but exhaustion rolled over her again and she closed her eyes and slept.

Erika didn't come back to full consciousness for another week. Her sister had been a constant presence at her bedside. Erika didn't know how much time had passed, but she noticed Lenka wore something different every time she opened her eyes. It was on this particular afternoon that she was awake when the doctor was doing his rounds, and she was pleased to hear that she was healing well, but it would be a long road to recovery.

'How long have you been here in England?' asked Erika.

'Two weeks. We're staying at your house. Marek is here too. The kids are with his mother back in Slovakia,' said Lenka.

'What's Marek doing?'

'He loves your cat, and he's been fixing things up a bit.'

Erika sighed and winced at the pain in her ribs.

'He better not be painting my walls green or orange,' she said.

'What's wrong with green and orange?' asked Lenka, defensively. 'Anyway. Igor is helping him.'

Erika sighed.

'You've met Igor?'

'Yes. I remember him from before, very handsome. His sister still lives in Nitra, I know her a little bit. Is it serious?'

'Lenka, this is serious,' said Erika, indicating the bed and the wires in her arms. 'What's happening with my case?'

'Your colleagues are coming later today. You never told me you worked with someone whose name was Kate Moss!'

Erika smiled; she wanted to see a familiar face from her life in London. Having her sister here was too surreal.

Later that afternoon, Moss and Peterson came to visit. The looks on both of their faces made Erika scared.

'Hello, Boss,' said Moss. She had with her a big bunch of flowers which Lenka put on the corner on a small table. 'You've got a private room. Fancy.'

'Hey Erika,' said Peterson. He leaned over and kissed her on the cheek, and she saw the concern on his face as he came close.

'I'm not dying,' she said.

'Of course not,' said Moss. 'We just, we're just...'

'Concerned,' finished Peterson. 'We saw the aftermath of the crash.'

'I didn't do it,' said Erika, as the memory of what happened came flooding back, and she suddenly felt deep distress and panic. 'I wasn't driving. He put me in the car. Made me take a load of painkillers. It's Colin! It was him!'

'It's okay,' said Moss. 'We got him. He's in custody. He's been charged with the murders of Sophia and Vicky, Cilla Stone... And the attempted... Attempting to kill you.'

Erika lay back and felt a small amount of relief.

'Was anyone else hurt in the crash?'

'No,' said Peterson. 'You should see the photos.' Moss shot him a look.

'Have you got them, the photos?' asked Erika.

'You don't need to see them,' said Moss.

'No. I want to.'

Peterson looked at Moss, got out his phone, scrolled through and held the screen up for her to see.

In the photo, Erika's car was a twisted wreck, smashed into the back of a small Porsche, which had come off even worse. Her windscreen had been obliterated, and there was glass everywhere. The photo had been taken facing the hill up to Colin's house, and you could see the path of carnage; on the road directly in front of the car park, a police officer was directing the traffic into a single clear lane. The second lane was blocked by a three-car accident, where a grey SUV had a blue Smart car buried in the back of it, and an ancient yellow Sierra had smashed into the back of the Smart car. Another ambulance was dealing with the three drivers, who looked dazed and bloody, but they were all standing by the road and staring open-mouthed at the ploughed-up flowerbeds.

'I can't believe I survived that,' said Erika in a small voice, the shock of seeing it hitting home.

Peterson scrolled through his phone. 'This one might make you feel better,' he said. It was a screenshot from the BBC News website with the headline:

SOUTH LONDON TEACHER ARRESTED FOR MURDER AND HISTORICAL SEX ASSAULTS ON STUDENTS

Underneath the headline was a photo of Colin being escorted out of his house by two police officers. His hands were cuffed in front of him.

'How did you get him?' Erika asked.

'Colin had been so confident of his plan to stage your car crash that he waited to call the emergency services until an hour after they took you to hospital. He'd told the operator that Cilla had an accident and fell down the stairs. The police who responded to the crash saw that the keys weren't in your car, which made them question Colin's version of events, that you drove away from his house after your visit. He'd pushed your car off in neutral with the engine switched off, but in his rush, the idiot forgot to put the keys in the ignition,' said Peterson.

'The police found your car keys on the floor in his office,' said Moss. 'When we searched the house, we found blood-stained clothes in a bin liner in his garage. The blood was Sophia's. We also found Vicky Clarke's notebooks and USB keys in his garage. They're a treasure trove of information. She was very close to finding out it was Colin who carried out the assaults in the student halls.'

'And since this has hit the headlines, more young women who auditioned at GDA have come forward to talk to the police,' said Peterson.

'Does this give the CPS enough to now take Colin to trial for the murder of Sophia and Vicky? And Cilla?' asked Erika, her heart lifting at this news.

'Yes. And he'll be tried for your attempted murder, we're making sure of that. Colin's legal team are trying to argue we can't prove a link between him and Sophia's murder, he says that the blood-stained clothes were planted in his garage, but they now have his DNA in Vicky's flat and the blood-stained clothes. They've just pulled another microscopic saliva sample off the bed frame of the sofa bed, and his DNA matches. And his DNA also matches the saliva on Vicky Clarke's shoulder.'

'What about the murder weapons? The knife from Vicky's flat that was used to kill Sophia?' asked Erika.

'No. We think he got rid of the murder weapons. And he's not telling us where,' said Peterson.

'Do we have any witnesses yet? Anyone who saw anything at Honeycomb Court? I have this horrible feeling he's going to worm his way out of it.'

'There has been another development,' said Moss. 'I told you we tracked down Lily Parkes. Well, we've interviewed her, and it turns out mathematics is not her strong suit.'

'How do you mean?'

'She went on record and told us she was coerced by Colin to sleep with Charles Wakefield aged fifteen, when she was still a minor. Anyway, the dates she gave us don't match and it transpires that she was sixteen years old, almost seventeen, when she slept with him, not fifteen, as they led Charles to believe. So, although it's still a rather disturbing concept, Charles wasn't sleeping with someone underage in the eyes of the law. We've told him this, and he's now willing to testify against Colin McCabe.

He's now saying that he caught Colin on a couple of occasions, attempting to break into the downstairs rooms of female students in Jubilee Road.'

'Why did he keep it a secret? Why didn't Charles report Colin when he found him?' asked Erika.

'Charles is mentally, very vulnerable.'

'Will Charles get prison time for concealing evidence?' asked Erika.

'The CPS is looking to cut a deal, which will protect him, and Julian Wakefield.'

'When do we think it will go to trial?' asked Erika.

'The CPS say they need six to eight months to build their case, so the autumn. Plenty of time for you to get back to full fitness,' said Moss.

Erika suddenly felt relief and tiredness flood through her.

'Maybe she needs to rest now,' said Lenka, who had been sitting patiently in the corner, and had seen how tired Erika had become.

'Do we know why Colin did it, why he stalked and attacked those women?' asked Erika. Moss gave her a long look and then shrugged.

'No. We think he did it, because he got off on it. It's as simple, and disturbing as that. Erika nodded, and pushed the *why* away. She couldn't dwell on why he did what he did. The most important thing was that they got him.

'Thanks for coming, guys,' she said, feeling pleased to see her colleagues. 'And for the flowers.'

'Everyone had signed the card,' said Moss, 'Isaac, and McGorry and Crane. They're all asking about coming to see you. But for now, you rest. Just know that we got Colin McCabe, and we're going to make sure he goes down for a long time.'

Five weeks later, on a cold, bright sunny December morning, Erika was discharged from hospital. It was the day before Christmas Eve, and Isaac came to pick her up. He had been a regular visitor during her stay, and she was recovering well, able to hobble small distances on her crutches. He helped her down to his car and drove her back to the new house. She was quiet on the journey and he asked her why she seemed sad.

'I'm not sad, I'm just nervous, going home to a house full of people, and not just people. My family,' said Erika. 'My sister, her husband Marek, and my nieces and nephews are staying – and they've decorated.'

'There's no need to worry about that,' said Isaac, putting up his hand and smiling. 'I've been very strict with Lenka. It's all nice, neutral and clean.'

'And she's invited Igor for Christmas.'

'Igor is cute,' said Isaac. 'He took his shirt off to paint your kitchen and I was impressed.'

Erika smiled.

'We only had two dates, and for the last few weeks he's been visiting me in hospital, seeing me like this,' she said, indicating her crutches. 'I'm most excited to see George.'

'He's very popular with the kids,' said Isaac. The car turned into Erika's road, and she saw her front door had been painted, and a Christmas tree sat in the front window.

Isaac looked over at her.

'Erika. You're alive. You just solved a huge case, and you have a house full of people waiting who love you. Please, give me a tiny bit of Christmas cheer.' They came to a stop outside the house. She noticed her upstairs windows now had curtains.

'And if you need a break from all the festivities, I'm only around the corner,' he said with a grin. He took her hand and she gripped it hard. 'Take a deep breath.'

'Okay, I'm ready,' she said. He helped her out of the car, and up the steps to the front door. Erika took another deep breath and opened the door.

'Hi, everyone,' she said. 'I'm home.'

A NOTE FROM ROBERT

Writing a book is a strange mix of solitude and teamwork. Thank you to my brilliant editors, Charlotte Herscher, Robin Seavill and Tom Felton. Thank you to the skilled translators from around the world who bring my work to life. Thank you to Henry Steadman for another excellent cover. Thank you also to Jan Cramer, who brings the Erika Foster audiobook editions so wonderfully to life in audio.

Thank you, as ever, to Team Bryndza - or as they are now known - Raven Street Publishing. Yes, we're now a publisher, too! Janko, Vierka, Riky, and Lola. I love you so much, and thank you for keeping me going with your love and support!

An enormous thank-you goes out to the most important people, my readers. Thank you for all of the heart-warming messages you send. When I started, you were there reading and championing my books, which is still the same today. Over the last few years, what has struck me most is just how much books bring us together. I receive messages from readers who don't do politics, and I get messages from readers who do. The thing that warms my heart in these divisive times is that the politics of my readers may vary wildly, but you all love to read the same books, and that makes me think that we aren't so different after all. I love reading because books open doors to a different world, and everyone is welcome.

And finally, I always write about word-of-mouth, but it is the most potent form of advertising. If you loved this book or any of my others, please tell your friends, family, colleagues, neighbours, etc.

As I always say, there are many more books to come. Next up, there will be another Kate Marshall, Erika Foster, and some other exciting things. I hope you stay with me for the ride!

ABOUT THE AUTHOR

Photo © 2022 Ján Bryndza

Robert Bryndza is best known for his page-turning crime and thriller novels, which have sold over five million copies.

His crime debut, *The Girl in the Ice* was released in February 2016, introducing Detective Chief Inspector Erika Foster. Within five months it sold one million copies, reaching number one in the Amazon UK, USA and Australian charts. To date, *The Girl in the Ice* has sold over 1.5 million copies in the English language and has been sold into translation in 29 countries. It was nominated for the Goodreads Choice Award for Mystery & Thriller (2016), the Grand prix des lectrices de Elle in France

(2018), and it won two reader voted awards, The Thrillzone Awards best debut thriller in The Netherlands (2018) and The Dead Good Papercut Award for best page turner at the Harrogate Crime Festival (2016).

Robert has released a further five novels in the Erika Foster series, *The Night Stalker, Dark Water, Last Breath, Cold Blood* and *Deadly Secrets*, all of which have been global bestsellers, and in 2017 *Last Breath* was a Goodreads Choice Award nominee for Mystery and Thriller.

Most recently, Robert created a new crime thriller series based around the central character Kate Marshall, a police officer turned private detective. The first book, *Nine Elms*, was an Amazon USA #1 bestseller and an Amazon UK top five bestseller, and the series has been sold into translation in 18 countries. The second book in the series is the global bestselling, *Shadow Sands* and the third book is *Darkness Falls*.

Robert was born in Lowestoft, on the east coast of England. He studied at Aberystwyth University, and the Guildford School of Acting, and was an actor for several years, but didn't find success until he took a play he'd written to the Edinburgh Festival. This led to the decision to change career and start writing. He self-published a bestselling series of romantic comedy novels, before switching to writing crime. Robert lives with his husband in Slovakia, and is lucky enough to write full-time. You can find out more about the author at www.robertbryndza.com

facebook.com/bryndzarobert

twitter.com/robertbryndza

instagram.com/robertbryndza

bookbub.com/authors/robert-bryndza

tiktok.com/@robertbryndza

Lightning Source UK Ltd.
Milton Keynes UK
UKHW011323100822
407118UK00004B/1191